Dream On, Ramona Riley

ASHLEY HERRING BLAKE

T0356695

Berkley Romance
New York

BERKLEY ROMANCE
Published by Berkley
An imprint of Penguin Random House LLC
1745 Broadway, New York, NY 10019
penguinrandomhouse.com

Book design by Alison Cnockaert

Library of Congress Cataloging-in-Publication Data

Names: Blake, Ashley Herring, author.
Title: Dream on, Ramona Riley / Ashley Herring Blake.
Description: First Edition. | New York : Berkley Romance, 2025.
Identifiers: LCCN 2024033920 (print) | LCCN 2024033921 (ebook) |
ISBN 9780593815991 (trade paperback) | ISBN 9780593816004 (ebook)
Subjects: LCGFT: Lesbian fiction. | Romance fiction. | Novels.
Classification: LCC PS3602.L3413 D74 2025 (print) | LCC PS3602.L3413 (ebook) |
DDC 813/.6—dc23/eng/20240724
LC record available at https://lccn.loc.gov/2024033920
LC ebook record available at https://lccn.loc.gov/2024033921

First Edition: May 2025

Printed in the United States of America
1st Printing

The authorized representative in the EU for product safety and compliance is
Penguin Random House Ireland, Morrison Chambers, 32 Nassau Street,
Dublin D02 YH68, Ireland, https://eu-contact.penguin.ie.

"The final installment in the Bright Falls series only further demonstrates why these books have been so beloved: because Blake is a master at her craft, creating carefully plotted stories around flawed, lovable characters that explode with chemistry and tension. . . . A thoroughly satisfying, heart-clutching conclusion."

—Anita Kelly, author of *Something Wild & Wonderful*

"A perfect conclusion to Ashley Herring Blake's sexy-cozy Bright Falls series. It's sweet, it's spicy, it's sapphic, it's satisfying—everything readers of Blake's work have come to love."

—Elissa Sussman, bestselling author of *Once More with Feeling*

"Blake continues to write compelling and lovable characters with engaging and empathetic storylines. Readers will love this foray back into Bright Falls."

—*Library Journal*

"Blake masterfully weaves a tale of growth where friendship, confidence, and passion ensue. A treat for fake-dating fans and happily-ever-after lovers alike."

—*Kirkus Reviews*

"Filled with steamy sex scenes while also tackling emotional issues, this book will delight fans of the previous books in the series and will appeal to other rom-com readers as well."

—*Booklist*

For everyone with dreams deferred.

It's never too late.

Author's Note

While *Dream On, Ramona Riley* is a joyful romance, please be aware that the story contains alcohol use, mentions of parental neglect, mentions of parental abandonment, mentions of past drug use, a scene of drunkenness, and discussions of sobriety. There are also consensual and explicit sex scenes. Please take care of yourself while reading this story, and always.

Dream On, Ramona Riley

Chapter One

RAMONA RILEY WASN'T prone to astrological panic.

She wasn't prone to any kind of panic, really. In her thirty-one years, she'd learned that everyone's life—including her own—ran a lot smoother when she kept both feet planted on the earth. So the fact that April—her best friend since fourth grade—was currently reading Libra's fate out loud for the second time in ten minutes with her eyebrows vaulted into her short crimson-streaked hair did very little to stir Ramona's sense of urgency.

"Did you hear that?" April asked, tapping at her phone from her perch on a desk in the backstage area of the Clover Lake Middle School auditorium.

"I heard it," Ramona said as she pinned a ribbon of teal lace onto a twelve-year-old's shoulder. "Camila heard it too."

"I did," Camila said, fiddling with the lace and smiling at herself in the mirror. Her long dark hair was hoisted into a high ponytail, and her all-black-and-teal costume—torn jeans, ornate lace, glittery teal lipstick and eyeshadow—had turned her into a perfect steam-punk Peter Pan, if Ramona did say so herself. "You're going to have a life-changing week."

"How exciting for me," Ramona said, winking at Camila and

moving on to securing the black belt covered in soda bottle caps with a seat belt buckle around her waist. It hung low, and with the girl's lanky frame and big stomping Doc Martens, she looked fucking badass.

Not that she'd ever say such words in front of one of her father's preteen students, but she could think it.

"Okay," April said, crisscrossing her own black-jean-clad legs on the desk and folding her heavily tattooed arms over her chest. "Clearly, neither one of you were actually listening. Madame Andromeda's uncanny insight into Libra this week does not involve anything life-changing."

"Life-affirming?" Ramona asked.

Camila giggled. "Life-giving."

"God, that sounds like I'm going to get preg—" Ramona froze, meeting Camila's precocious expression in the mirror. "You know what, let's go with life-affirming."

"It says," April said, tapping violently at her phone again, "and I quote, *This week, as Venus moves into Cancer, be prepared for challenges and opportunities that could shift your perspective and deepen your understanding of your life's purpose.*"

Camila shrugged. "Sounds life-changing to me."

"Of course it does!" April said, throwing up her arms and letting them flop back down onto her thighs. "Of course it's life-changing, but Madame Andromeda didn't *say* life-changing. She said *could.* And *could* is what you make of it, isn't it?"

And with that declaration, April let out a huffy breath and went back to scrolling through her phone.

"Is she okay?" Camila whispered.

Honestly, Ramona wasn't sure, but she didn't want to get into the intricacies of how her BFF thought Ramona was wasting her life in Clover Lake, New Hampshire, with a middle schooler, now or ever. She'd had plenty of experience with the age group, from her own sister Olive's tumultuous time at Clover Lake Middle to her father's position as an eighth-grade English teacher and drama club director, and Ramona had learned that this particular species of human didn't exactly do nuance.

"She's fine, love," Ramona said, then took Camila's hands and held them out. "And you, Peter Pan, look amazing."

Camila beamed, then skipped off to stage right to join her Lost Boys, a gaggle of students that Ramona had outfitted to look like degenerates from a posh private school with distressed plaid skirts, torn stockings, boots of all colors, seventies band tees—pretty much anything she could find for five bucks or less at Thayer's Sift-N-Thrift shop downtown.

"You're up, Tink!" she called to a kid named Bellamy. They bounded over, already wearing a fitted brown leather vest over an ivy-pattered green skirt that Ramona had made herself, and their brown arms were streaked with a bit of strategic glitter. All they needed now were the gossamer wings, thick belt full of gadgets—dull garden shears and a magnifying glass—and a pair of vintage leather goggles atop their head.

April observed Ramona coolly while Ramona fussed over Bellamy's final touches.

"What?" Ramona asked, smearing some glitter over Bellamy's cheeks.

"How many is this?" April asked.

"How many is what?" Ramona asked, even though she knew. And from the way April lifted a single eyebrow, she knew that Ramona knew.

Ramona sighed, gave Bellamy a fist bump, and sent them along to join the rest of the cast awaiting their Saturday afternoon matinee curtain call. Since Steven Riley, Ramona's dad, had taken over the drama club eight years ago, the group put on a spring play every May. The entirety of Clover Lake came out to at least one of the four shows over the course of the weekend, even those without any kids enrolled at the school or acting in the play.

Steven's productions were that good.

And Ramona's costumes were half the draw.

At least . . . that's what she'd heard.

"Nine," Ramona said.

"*Spring* plays," April said. "At the middle school. Don't get me started on the high school and how much free labor you give Jane Davenport every fall. Oh, and let's not forget Clover Lake's preeminent community theater. Priceless opportunities found in those Broadway-esque productions. Jesus, if they do a cabaret this summer, I'm going to fucking lose—"

"What is your point?" Ramona said, adjusting her utility belt around her soft hips that held her measuring tape, safety pins, Velcro, and anything else she might need during a show in case a costume went awry.

"My point?" April asked. "You don't already know it?"

"Apes, come on."

"It's May."

"This I know."

"Olive leaves for Nashville at the end of August."

Ramona looked away toward the stage, her cheeks immediately hot. She didn't automatically start crying anytime she thought of her little sister graduating from high school and leaving for Vanderbilt University at the end of the summer, but her body definitely reacted as though entering fight-or-flight mode.

"Honey," April said more softly. "She's going to do great."

Ramona nodded, didn't trust her voice yet. Except for the single year Ramona had spent at the Rhode Island School of Design, she had rarely been away from Olive since her birth when Ramona was thirteen. Their mother had been gone since Olive was six months old—apparently motherhood wasn't all she dreamed it would be, and Rebecca Riley took off for a better life god only knew where. So, near the end of Ramona's freshman year at RISD, when Ramona and Olive's single dad suffered a shattered leg in a car accident they were all lucky didn't kill him, there was nothing else for Ramona to do but come home, get a job at Clover Moon Café while her father learned how to walk again, and help raise six-year-old Olive.

That was twelve years ago.

Twelve years of Olive's scraped knees and softball games—including the three years she did travel ball in high school, which meant Ramona was constantly driving all over the state. Twelve years of Olive crying over mean girls into Ramona's lap, then Ramona's intense relief when she became friends with Marley Bristow in eighth grade and they both left the mean girls behind for pitching strategies and ornate braids for game days. Twelve years of Olive's myriad crushes on boys Ramona was convinced weren't good enough for her sister, walking in on Olive making out with Ethan Townes in her bedroom when she was sixteen, and a conversation about condoms, which ended with Ramona setting a box on Olive's nightstand while her sister fled into the shower.

Twelve years of laughter and tears and questions, and now all of that was coming to a close. Ramona no longer had to worry about her schedule at the café conflicting with one of Olive's away games. Soon, she wouldn't have to stay up until Olive got home from a party or take Olive to the gynecologist.

Olive was an adult.

Olive was leaving home.

And she wouldn't be coming back like Ramona did. Ramona would make damn sure of it.

Still, in all her excitement over Olive's future, she had to admit, facing an empty nest at the age of thirty-one was a bit overwhelming.

In April's opinion, Olive's departure was Ramona's golden ticket. April adored Olive, had helped Ramona and Steven raise her for god's sake, but April was passionate about passion. She'd studied at RISD too, then came home with a degree in illustration and immediately opened her own tattoo shop, a dream she'd had since she got her first tattoo at eighteen—a black-and-gray woman sporting a scorpion's tail on her inner forearm for her Scorpio sun, moon, and rising signs—and had been happily inking tourists and locals alike for nearly ten years.

"You at least need a list," April said when Ramona still hadn't responded.

"A list."

"A *list*," April said again. "A goal. A five-step action plan or some shit."

"What's this about an action plan?" Ramona's dad asked, walking over from where he'd been reviewing some cues with the school's art teacher, who was running the lights. Steven still had a bit of a limp in his left leg, and he always would. Still, he was tall, with a full head of salt-and-pepper hair, a real catch for the over-fifty set.

"You need one too, Mr. Riley," said April, who could never quite get used to calling him Steven. "Ever heard of Bumble?"

Steven frowned. "As in the bee?"

Ramona laughed. "It's a dating app, Dad."

"Oh," Steven said, cutting a hand through his hair, cheeks going a little pink. "Well, um, you know, that's—"

"Ridiculous," Ramona supplied for him. Her father did not need help dating. If he wanted to date, he would.

April tilted her head at them both with that potentially terrifying look in her eyes, the one that meant she was plotting.

"Anyway," Ramona said, tightening her belt even more. "It's showtime."

⁓

THE PLAY RAN for only an hour, and Ramona had a shift at the café starting at four. After helping the kids store their costumes on hangers instead of the dressing room's poured-cement floor, she and April walked toward downtown.

"Okay, hear me out," April said, turning around on the sidewalk to walk backward. The watery May sunshine sprinkled gold through the flowering trees, the clear blue sky making Clover Lake glitter like a sapphire in the distance. The lake was huge—not quite Winnipesaukee huge, but close—and the entire town wrapped around it like a crescent moon. Summer people were already starting to move in, lake houses shut up for the long winter airing out, shiny cars in once-empty driveways. Ramona loved summer in Clover Lake—she loved all the seasons, really, but summer held a certain magic to it, a freedom and possibility.

"Don't you have someone's body part to draw on?" Ramona asked, but she was smiling.

April grinned, the Nirvana tee she'd cut the neck out of dropping down her tree-inked shoulder. "Not until six, so you're stuck with me until then."

"Never *stuck*," Ramona said, looping her arm with April's. "Just . . . attached."

"Nice spin, but that's half the problem."

"What?"

"You're too fucking nice!"

Ramona sighed. "I *like* doing costumes."

"Yeah, I know. Costume design was your endgame. LA, New York, stages or films full of actors who've actually been through puberty. You know, dreams?"

"Hmm," Ramona said, tapping her chin. "Think I had one last

night where my hands had turned into crab claws. Wonder what that means . . ."

"We'll google it," April said, stepping around a turquoise bike leaning against a lamppost. "In the meantime, you need to do something that doesn't involve safety pins, prepubescents, or pouring bad chardonnay for tourists who don't realize all chardonnay is disgusting and tastes like butter. I'm thinking some dates."

Ramona nearly choked on the air. "Dates?"

"Yeah. Romance. Hot people. Sex?"

Ramona opened her mouth.

"And *not* Logan Adler," April said.

Ramona snapped her mouth shut. Logan was Ramona's on-again, off-again boyfriend of the last five years or so, a lifelong Cloverian just like Ramona. He was a nice guy—a hot guy—who ran his family's furniture shop in town, and with whom Ramona had very good sex and very little else, which was why they kept breaking up and then falling back into bed with each other.

Over and over again.

Needless to say, April did not approve, said that Ramona needed someone more emotionally stimulating than a celery stick in human form.

"Logan is a good guy," Ramona said.

April groaned and Ramona laughed. It wasn't like she hadn't dated anyone else in the last few years, she just hadn't dated much. As for sex, there had been hookups, which April knew, but yeah, the last one had been . . . last fall? No, last summer, that tourist named Andrea who came into the café twice a day because she thought Ramona was cute.

Okay, so it had been a year—with a little Logan sprinkled in here and there, maybe, probably—and Ramona was in a bit of a dry spell, but Olive's senior year had been busy. Landing a full softball scholarship to a top-tier private university was no small feat. But they'd done it. And now . . .

And now what?

Ramona felt a wave of nerves crest in her stomach.

"Dating people not named Logan is a baby step," April said. "Something to get you out of your comfort zone so you can get serious about getting out of the café and into an actual design job. It's easy."

Ramona laughed. "Oh, easy as pie, huh? I think you know better than that, April Evans." April hadn't dated anyone seriously in over a year, when her fiancée, Elena Watson, dumped her a month before their planned and paid for spring wedding. Not only that, but she did so for another woman, a twenty-two-year-old painting student named Daphne Love, and April had not reacted well. She'd met Elena three years before at a bar in Boston, then spent a magical night together—they walked the cobblestone streets hand-in-hand, took a ghost tour, shared their life stories, then went back to Elena's posh apartment and had, in April's words, *DNA-altering sex*. Even April's stoic parents—the Drs. Preston and Jacqueline Evans, who rarely understood anything April said or did—had adored Elena. The whole town had. Elena was beautiful and elegant, a curator at the Boston Museum of Fine Arts, and she had loved April's wilder, darker personality. She'd celebrated it, even, which was all April had really ever wanted.

Since the breakup, April had reverted to her pre-Elena ways, sticking to hook-ups and casual dates, rarely seeing anyone more than once. That was all well and good, but Elena was the only person April had ever truly fallen in love with, and Ramona worried April was simply too scared to try again.

"If I date, then *you* date," Ramona said softly. "And *not* fuck-bois like Leigh Reynolds."

April narrowed her eyes—Leigh was an old high school friend of April and Ramona's, and April's favorite hookup whenever Leigh swaggered back into town to see their mom.

"Don't knock it till you try it," April said, then shoved a single finger into the air. "Oh wait, you already have."

Ramona scoffed. "I haven't slept with Leigh!"

"I'm referring, of course, to the Golden Fuckboi of Clover Lake, Logan Adler."

Ramona fought to hold in a laugh. "My point stands."

"Fine," April said, shoulders drooping in defeat. "If not dating, then what? Trip to New York? LA? Re-enrolling in RISD? You can—"

"I am not going back to RISD," Ramona said firmly. She could think of nothing more humiliating. Plus, she could never afford it—or any school for that matter. She'd attended on a full scholarship before, something she was pretty sure RISD didn't hand out to thirty-one-year-olds in the food service industry.

"Fine," April said. "But have you even sent your portfolio to anyone? Agents? Talent scouts?"

Ramona pressed her eyes closed for a second, took a deep breath. She loved April, dearly and deeply, but Scorpios were all about transformation—at least, according to April—and Ramona was the kind of person who ate a turkey sandwich with avocado, spinach, and Havarti for lunch every single day of her life.

"I'm still perfecting it," she said to April, thinking about her digital portfolio sitting on her iPad, half-finished, half-dreamed. "Plus, the chances of—"

"What the hell is happening in this kooky town now?" April asked. She'd stopped on the sidewalk about a block away from Clover Moon Café, brows furrowed. Ramona looked around, shops with awnings in deep hunter green, navy, and gray lining both sides of Lake Street. It was a gorgeous Saturday afternoon, so there were a lot of people out, but nearly everyone was clustered in groups of two or three, hovering over their phones and gesticulating excitedly.

"God only knows," Ramona said, pulling April along, stopping in front of the café and checking her reflection in the window. Last week, she'd finished a dress rehearsal at the middle school and come into work with a fake eyelash stuck to her cheek and glitter in her hair. Honestly, she didn't trust April to point out any irregularity in her appearance—April loved a good laugh too much and thought Ramona took herself too seriously anyway.

Ramona pulled her wavy brown hair up into a high ponytail and fluffed her fringe. Her myriad freckles were glitter-free, her dark brown eyes clear of any mascara smears or extra lashes. She had on a high-necked black-and-white top, abstract patterns swirling over the fitted cotton. It was one of her own creations, designed years ago when she was still working on her portfolio on a daily basis. Also, she had such a hard time finding unique pieces to fit her plus-size figure—her boobs in particular—she designed most of her own clothes back then. Luckily, most of them still fit. She smoothed her hands down her jeans just as April smacked her on the butt.

"You look hot," April said. "In fact, let me get a shot for your dating profile—"

"Oh, what's that? Oops, can't hear you," Ramona singsonged, then swung open the café's door and let it fall closed in April's face. She winked at her best friend through the glass and received yet another middle finger.

Clover Moon Café was a diner, coffee shop, and bar all in one. The atmosphere was warm with an amber wood bar top and tables with mismatched chairs, and Mason jar lights hung down from the pine ceiling in various shades of blue and green. Ramona loved it here, and as she and April sat at the bar so Ramona could eat before her shift, she reminded herself of just how lucky she was.

She loved her town.

She loved her café, even if she didn't always love the work.

And she had a best friend who loved her enough to be a pain in the ass about, well, everything.

Ramona Riley was just fine, thanks very much.

"It's happening in here too," April said out one side of her mouth.

Ramona flicked the corner of the plastic menu she knew by heart, taking in how at least three-fourths of the diners were also staring at their phones and chattering a little louder than normal.

"Hey, dolls," Marion said from behind the bar, setting glasses of water down in front of them. "The usual?"

"Marion, what the hell is happening around here?" April asked.

Marion popped her gum, her eyes going wide. "You haven't heard?" She was in her fifties and had been working at Clover Moon since she was a teenager. Thus, she knew everything about everyone.

"Heard what?" Ramona asked.

Marion grinned. "You'll like this, Mona."

She took her phone out of her apron and clicked around, then handed it over to Ramona. April leaned in close to read one of Penny Hampton's daily posts on her blog about the goings-on in town, aptly named *Penny for Your Thoughts*. Clover Lake had a town newspaper, but if you wanted the gossip, the *true stories*, as Penny said, Clover Lake residents knew just where to find it.

"Holy shit," April said, always a speed-reader. Ramona had barely made it past the first couple of sentences.

For several months now, Clover Lake's mayor, Amira Gates, has been in secret—very tricky, Mayor Gates!—negotiations with Skylark Studios regarding the possibility of a feature film coming to Clover Lake's shores. Well, those negotiations are at an end, and Hollywood is indeed arriving in our beloved hamlet in three weeks' time.

That's right, Cloverians, the full cast and crew for
As If You Didn't Know, a romantic comedy based on the
bestselling book, will arrive at the beginning of June.
Prepare for celeb sightings and possible shutdowns
for a few of our small businesses and a more-clogged-
than-usual downtown. It might not be convenient, but
it sure is exciting! Sources close to the mayor say the
studio is paying handsomely for our cooperation, and
we all know money makes the world go round. So
buckle up for a summer like we've never had before!

"Is this for real?" Ramona asked. Penny didn't *lie* necessarily,
but she'd been known to stretch the truth for the sake of drama.
"This sounds—"

"Perfect," April said, already on her own phone and tapping
away.

"Oh, it's true," Marion said. "The movie is one of those 'love is
love' stories, so you two ought to like that."

Ramona and April—bisexual and pansexual, respectively—shared
a look, though Marion had a point. Plus, in a small town like Clover
Lake, where minds could be, admittedly, a wee bit small, a queer movie
taking over the streets for the summer was a pretty big deal.

"It's based on that book that famous book club picked a while
back that hit all the bestseller lists," Marion said. "Can't remember
the author's name, but—"

"Iris Kelly," April said, who had returned to typing furiously on
her phone. "Queer romance author, total Leo, love her."

Marion shrugged. "Anyway, Owen confirmed it when I came in
at noon. Apparently, one of the main characters is a waitress, so he's
getting paid the whole hog to close the café here and there for
filming."

"Really?" Ramona said, wondering just how much the studio

must be paying Clover Moon's owner. This place was Owen's whole life, had been in his family for three generations.

"Really," Marion said, taking a pen out from behind her ear and tapping it on her order pad.

"That'll be interesting," Ramona said.

"Sure will," Marion said, then sauntered away to put in Ramona's turkey sandwich order.

Ramona took a sip of water just as April grabbed her arm, nails digging into the soft flesh above her elbow.

"Ow," she said flatly, but April didn't budge, her eyes glued to her phone.

"Noelle" was all she said.

"As in . . . Christmas?" Ramona asked.

April finally looked up. "As in Yang."

Ramona felt her breath go still in her lungs. She blinked, but couldn't seem to get her mouth to close, her brain to properly compute. Noelle Yang was a costume designer. A legend. Had studied at RISD as well, decades ago, then moved to LA and famously camped out in front of Emmeline Roth's trailer on the set of *When Skies Collide* until the iconic designer agreed to speak with her. Noelle was even escorted off set in handcuffs a few times, though Emmeline never pressed charges. As the story went, Emmeline finally grew so fed up with seeing Noelle's face peering into her windows, she let the twenty-two-year-old present her portfolio just to get the girl out of her hair.

What Emmeline saw changed both of their lives. They started a mentorship that lasted five years until Noelle got the chance to lead a design team for *Better Off Dead* and promptly won an Oscar for the costume design. Since then, she'd dressed actors in rom-coms, science fiction adventures, indie films no one understood, and mythological fantasies. She *was* Hollywood costume design.

And Ramona's idol since she was nine and fell in love with the costumes in *Greatness*, a sexy romp of a movie about Catherine the Great that won Noelle her third Oscar.

Now, Ramona finally managed to swallow. "What about her?"

April couldn't keep the smile off her face. "You know what about her." She turned her phone so Ramona could see the *Variety* article she was reading about *As If You Didn't Know*, a paragraph that featured Noelle's name and the words *leading the design team for the queer rom-com* highlighted by April's cursor.

"This is it," April said, turning her phone back around and scrolling.

"This is what?" Ramona said.

"The *thing*," April said, waving a hand around. "The thing that's going to shift your perspective and deepen your understanding of your life's purpose."

"I thought that was supposed to happen this week," Ramona said. "Cast and crew don't show up for another three."

April stuck out her tongue.

Ramona chuckled, but inside, her stomach was in knots. Noelle Yang. In Clover Lake. In this café even, getting coffee to get through her day. Or maybe a croissant. Clover Lake's famous honey whiskey pie, which Ramona had recently perfected baking.

Ramona's mind flashed to her portfolio, the designs filling her sketchbook, the myriad files on her digital program, the fully realized garments she'd sewn herself, crowding the spare room in her father's house, no one to wear them, no one to flourish inside their seams.

Once upon a time, she dreamed about exactly this kind of opportunity. As a RISD student, walking the same halls as Noelle had years before, planning out her own destiny to get herself to LA, get herself noticed, refusing to take no for an answer. Dressing actors in ornate gowns, warrior garb, or even a simple pair of jeans and a cardigan—the clothes that made actors come alive, made stories feel *real*.

And then her dad got hurt, her family needed her, and all that just . . . faded.

And now it was too late.

Wasn't it?

"Who else is in the film?" she asked April, just to give herself something else to focus on.

April scrolled and paused, scrolled and paused. She smiled. "Aubrey Daniels. She's playing Mallory. God, I'm so excited this book is going to be a movie."

Ramona snapped in approval, as Aubrey was a vocal lesbian who'd recently started dating the singer Reneé Ramirez.

"Who's playing the other character? What's her name? Elise?"

"Eloise," April said.

Ramona nodded, vaguely remembering the name as she laid her napkin in her lap. She'd read *As If You Didn't Know* last year, just like everyone else in the world once it was picked up for the book club, but she'd been an Iris Kelly fan for a few years, both she and April devouring any queer romance they could get their hands on.

April's eyes narrowed, scanning her screen, then widened. "Oh, shit."

"What? Who is it?" Ramona picked up her water and took a sip.

April looked up, mouth hanging open slightly. "It's Dylan," she said softly. "Dylan Monroe."

And with that, Ramona not only spit her beverage all over her lap, but also dropped her drink, sending ice and water and shattered glass all over the pine floors of Clover Moon Café.

Chapter Two

DYLAN MONROE LOVED being miserable.

That was the only explanation for the way she was glued to her phone right now, eyes scanning the disaster that was her life. She sat on her turquoise couch in her cavernous house in Silver Lake, pausing her scrolling to stop on a picture of Jocelyn Gareth, her platinum-blond hair a blur next to her new girlfriend's shiny black waves.

The picture itself wasn't the problem. Nor was the new girlfriend, Ruby Chopra, an actual nice human Dylan had worked with when they were both in their midtwenties in Hollywood, acting as the BFFs of a main character in the teen sitcom *Girlish*, which had lasted only one season. The problem wasn't even Jocelyn, Dylan's ex, although Dylan's teeth clenched at the sight of her angelic smile and sparkling blue eyes.

No, the problem, as always, was the copy in this Page Six article, which wasn't even about Jocelyn and her new leading lady, but rather how Dylan would react to the new pairing. And not a single line of text hypothesized that Dylan would take the news with grace and charm and dignity.

While Dylan Monroe has been silent on the subject and her team declined to comment on Jocelyn's new love, it comes as no surprise that Dylan was recently spotted at Bacari Silverlake nursing several vodka tonics and cursing out anyone with a camera in their hands.

"I was at dinner with my aunt, you vultures," Dylan said to absolutely no one, her jaw clenched. "How dare I want to eat some fucking Bacari fries in peace."

She should put her phone down now. She knew she should, go eat something with protein, maybe take a swim and read through her script in the sun, soak up some vitamin D.

But she was never very good at *should*.

She kept reading, her temples aching from grinding her teeth.

But that's what we've come to expect from America's favorite party girl. The only child of nineties rock icons—Jack Monroe of Evenflow and Carrie Page of Halcyon—Dylan Monroe isn't known for grace. Always the bad girl on-screen, Dylan's life off-screen matches up pretty perfectly, filled with wild parties, public arguments with her mother, and drama-laced breakups.

The latest of which occurred just this past March at Jocelyn Gareth's thirtieth birthday party atop the Mondrian Los Angeles hotel. A private event with tight security, yet nothing stopped videos leaking featuring a rabidly angry Dylan Monroe throwing nearly twenty bottles of Veuve Clicquot into the pool, all while screaming about Jocelyn's alleged cheating. Cheating, mind you, that has never been confirmed. The affair took a dark turn when the police were called, and Dylan's people removed her from the scene via helicopter.

Yes, you read that right.

Hel-i-cop-ter.

"The elevator was malfunctioning!" Dylan yelled, collapsing back onto the cushions and releasing a grunt at the ceiling. She tossed her phone into the L-curve of the couch. Goddamn gossip columnists. Granted, the Clicquot . . . yeah, that had happened, as well as the screaming, but it wasn't about cheating. Jesus Christ, everyone in Hollywood thought every single romantic issue was about infidelity. But Jocelyn hadn't cheated on Dylan. Instead, she'd done something even worse, something Dylan couldn't even talk about without sounding petty and bratty and like an all-around bitch.

She huffed, got up, and grabbed her phone from the other side of the couch, this time flopping onto her stomach as she continued to read.

> Shockingly, Dylan is headed to a small town in New Hampshire in a few weeks to start filming a rom-com, her first ever, playing a simple darling pining after her first love opposite Oscar nominee Aubrey Daniels. As for us, we'll buy that sweet little story when we see it.
>
> Good luck, Nowhere, New Hampshire—trouble is on the way.

Dylan swiped out of the article, letting her head fall into her arms. She released a scream, her voice muffled against the couch cushions, making her little tantrum sound much milder than she felt. She stayed like that for a while, until her self-loathing really kicked into gear and she swiped over to Instagram, scrolling through the comments on Jocelyn's latest post about how she, Killin' Dylan Monroe, would be out for Ruby's blood.

"I don't like blood," she said loudly. "I *pass out* at the sight of blood."

"I always thought that was an interesting quality for a former vampire," Laurel's voice called from the entryway.

"I'm full of surprises," Dylan said, still scrolling as Laurel, her manager for the last four years, strolled into the room dressed in a hot-pink blazer, fitted lace blouse, and wide-legged black pants. "Plus, it's hard to get squeamish when you know it's just corn syrup and dish soap."

"Fair," Laurel said, setting a cocoa-brown box with a simple white-and-gold label on the quartz counters in the mammoth, mostly unused kitchen.

Dylan tilted her head at the box. "What the hell is that?"

Laurel only pursed her mouth. "I don't know what you mean."

Dylan crawled up to her knees, pointed an accusing finger at the box. "That's from Lark Cake Shop. You only ever bring me Lark Cake Shop—a chocolate tart, to be exact—when you have to deliver some awful news, and I swear to god, Laurel, I'm not in the mood."

Laurel was not swayed in the least, not that Dylan expected her to be. Her manager was one of the best in the business—as a Black trans woman who had started transitioning when she was only sixteen and living with her supportive widower father in south Georgia, she'd seen and dealt with more than her fair share of other people's bullshit. She knew exactly how to handle Dylan's drama, which was exactly why Dylan would never, ever fire her, even if she wanted to, which she certainly didn't.

Her manager's dark eyes flicked down to the phone in Dylan's hand, then she sighed. "Please tell me you're not—"

"I am. I *am*, Laurel, because they're lying their asses off. I don't give two shits about Jocelyn and Ruby, and I—"

"Of course they're lying their asses off, Dylan, it's *Hollywood*, or did you forget what you do for a living?" Laurel plucked Dylan's phone from her hand. "Who your parents are?"

Dylan's throat went thick, that decades-old feeling of helplessness cresting over her. As if she could ever forget who her parents were, the king and queen of nineties alternative rock, still adored and revered in all corners of the music world, despite their incredibly messy past—one divorce and another breakup from each other with a final reconciliation five years ago, the fug of drugs and sex and booze in which they attempted over and over to raise Dylan, and the still-constant mention of their names in the tabloids, usually alongside Dylan's as their fucked-up, wildling daughter, the collateral damage to a *legendary* life of rock and roll.

Since the day she threw her first toddler temper tantrum in Carrie's too-skinny arms on a busy Brooklyn street, the press had spun every single emotion she displayed even semi-publicly as a meltdown, so, yes, she knew full well who her parents were.

She just didn't like it.

And, granted, she had a lot of emotions. She never tried to pretend she didn't. She had a therapist, kept a list of breathing exercises in her head, and had an app on her phone that blasted green noise into her skull anytime she felt like she was going to lose her shit.

Which, lately, was often.

Ever since her breakup with Jocelyn, she'd felt even more trapped than normal. Sure, she'd had her fair share of breakups, some of them very public and very intense, but she'd been in her twenties then, still under her old agent Vance's thumb, still clueless about what the hell she was doing with her life, with her fame, with her parents.

She was only eleven when she'd been launched into acting, a cherubic face all her father's and her mother's ice-green eyes. She hadn't slowed down since, hadn't made a single choice of her own as she was thrown into role after role playing the troubled child, the troubled teen, the troubled and morally bankrupt vampire named Giselle in *Spellbound*, a supernatural show that ran for six seasons and that catapulted her into a fandom that felt all her own for the first time in her life.

Still, even with the Spellbinders, as they called themselves, she was the villain, the one they loved to hate, loved to lust after, a role that Vance pushed her into as a nineteen-year-old and spent six years trying to make fit. Sure, she had some good times on the show. A lot of them, but she also struggled to understand her character and fought constantly with other cast members.

Lonely.

That was the predominant emotion she took from her time on *Spellbound*. After the show ended, she did a brief run on *Girlish*, which some critics say tanked because she was thoroughly unconvincing as a science-nerd seventeen-year-old.

After that, she fought Vance for more roles she truly wanted to play—romance leads, heroes who caught the bad guy, introspective millennials in indie films—all of which Vance scoffed at and refused to even try for.

You're not that kind of actor, Dilly, Vance had said. *You're femme fatale. You're . . .*

She'd lifted her eyebrow at him, waiting for him to say something truly creepy, considering he'd been directing her life since she was a preteen.

He'd shut his mouth though. He never crossed those lines, which was the one decent thing Dylan could say about him. Still, he was a balding cishet white man who called her Dilly and treated her like she was forever one glass of wine away from a stint in rehab. But he was a famous LA agent—a true legend in the business—who'd approached a perpetually high Jack and Carrie after an Evenflow concert one sultry summer night with *a solid plan of success* for their young and precocious daughter. *Money* is what her parents heard, so they trusted him, gave their daughter to him, essentially, and Dylan spent the next fourteen years contorting herself into Vance's image of her, into Hollywood's image, her parents'.

Even her own image of herself, which was cloudy and unformed in her mind, never clear, never something she created herself.

So at twenty-five, she went behind Vance's back.

Cold auditioned for *Picture This*, a swoony romance where she would play a powerful advertising executive who falls for the down-on-his-luck owner of a bakery she's trying to rebrand. Dylan loved the idea of playing a badass woman, getting into her vulnerable side, tapping into emotions other than vengeance and anger and teen angst. Actually being one half of a love story.

The audition did not go well.

She barely made it to the end of the scene, as the casting director and director himself—Cale Richter, a popular creator of Hollywood rom-coms—pretty much laughed her out of the room. Oh, they let her read, but did so with amused expressions, lifted eyebrows, and chuckles when she got to an especially emotional part in the script.

Needless to say, she didn't get the role, and by the time she dragged herself home, Vance was already blowing up her phone with messages about how *unprofessional* and *immature* and *embarrassing* she was.

After that . . . well . . . Dylan had a tiny little quarter-life crisis. She fired Vance, fired her assistant, and spent the next six months locked up in her house eating delivery food and reading multiple novels a week, consuming anyone and everyone's story except her own, and feeling ridiculously sorry for herself.

"Come on," Laurel said now, bringing the cake box over to the couch and sitting down next to Dylan. "Eat it."

"What, this bribe disguised as a goddess-tier chocolate delicacy?"

"Yes, exactly," Laurel said, setting the box in her lap and Dylan's phone in her own pocket.

Dylan sighed, but opened the box, sugary heaven drifting into the air. She could never say no to Laurel—well, except for the times she *did*, but it was never about anything really important—because unlike Vance, she trusted Laurel with her life, with her career, with pretty much everything. She was infinitely grateful for Laurel and that her aunt, Hallie—her father's very normal sister who taught gender studies at the University of Georgia where Laurel had gone to undergrad, and who helped take care of Dylan through the years when Jack and Carrie fell off the planet—had sent her favorite former student Dylan's way four years ago.

Without Hallie and Laurel—along with Dylan's agent, Adriana, who was a badass in and of herself and worked closely with Laurel to keep Dylan's career on track—Dylan would most likely still be buried under a pile of paperback books and Cherry Garcia.

"Okay, so," Laurel said, propping one ankle on her knee and brushing a dark curl from her face. "You want the good news first, or the bad news?"

"Bad," Dylan said through a mouthful of chocolate. "Always bad."

Laurel nodded. She knew Dylan was a "rip off the Band-Aid" kind of person, which Laurel always did with a tough-love yank that often left Dylan gasping for breath. She braced herself.

"Aubrey is out," Laurel said.

Despite her preparedness, Dylan nearly inhaled a chunk of tart into her lungs. "Out?" She coughed, banged on her chest. "Out of what?"

"Out of the movie."

"*My* movie?"

Laurel nodded. "Skiing accident. Broke her leg. Surgery, rehab, the whole nine yards."

"Fuck," Dylan said. "Is she okay?"

"Will be," Laurel said, nodding. "After those whole nine yards I mentioned."

"Right." Dylan blinked, her mind whirring. She liked Aubrey Daniels. They'd never acted together, but had met at several events over the last few years, and they'd done well together during the film's read-through last month. Moreover, she was queer and kind and treated Dylan like she belonged exactly where she was. Never even mentioned Evenflow or Halcyon or what it was like to see pictures of herself as a two-year-old asleep on top of a half-eaten pepperoni pizza in a trashed hotel room.

She'd been looking forward to playing opposite Aubrey in *As If You Didn't Know*, her first rom-com—a *queer* rom-com at that, and with a plethora of studio money behind it. Dylan still couldn't believe Adriana had secured her the co-lead.

Finally.

The kind of role she wanted, dreamed about, with a costar she admired and respected and who seemed to respect her too.

"What the hell is the good news?" she asked Laurel.

"We're not quite done with the bad."

"Shit." Dread coiled into Dylan's belly. "Who's taking Aubrey's place?"

"Blair Emmanuel."

The name flitted through the space between them, a ghost.

Or, rather, a witch.

"Blair," Dylan deadpanned.

"Blair," Laurel deadpanned back.

Dylan felt half of the chocolate tart she'd already consumed threaten rebellion in her stomach. Blair Emmanuel was gorgeous and talented and bisexual just like Dylan, and she had played Cressida, a much-beloved witch hell-bent on Dylan's own vampiric character's destruction for six straight seasons of *Spellbound*. They hated each other on-screen because that was their job, but the vitriol bled into real life too. They were constantly bickering on set about everything from Dylan eating the last vegan doughnut when she wasn't even a vegan to a screaming match mid-scene over either Dylan's or Blair's tone, an eyebrow raised too dramatically or some such shit.

Dylan knew their enmity was petty and childish and didn't matter five years later, but she hadn't worked with Blair since, never wanted to, and now they were suddenly romantic costars.

As in *romance*.

Swooning and smiles and vulnerability and fear and kissing, all the things Dylan was excited to explore as an actor and now dreaded digging into with Blair, whose own reputation in Hollywood was that of an absolute class act.

She swallowed hard, glanced down at her half-eaten torte. "Is that it?"

"That's it," Laurel said, waving her hand through the air. "Can totally move on to the good news now."

"And what's that? My father's working on the movie's soundtrack?"

Laurel simply cleared her throat, ignoring Dylan's comment altogether. "The good news is *Spellbound* fans are going to go rabid over this pairing."

Oh, Dylan just bet they would. Spellbinders were drama thirsty, and they loved it when the gossip sites inevitably posted some article about how Dylan had dared to raise her voice in public while Blair was spotted demurely sipping cava by the sea.

"Great publicity for the movie," Laurel said. "And for you."

"For me?"

"You're not exactly America's sweetheart right now, Dylan."

Dylan huffed and set the dessert box on the tufted ottoman, her appetite for comfort chocolate completely sapped. "Thanks for putting it mildly."

"That's not what you pay me to do. And America loves Blair. They love *Spellbound*, and the producers think this could go a long way to smoothing over your image."

"My image."

Laurel sighed. "You're about to play a major role in a major *queer* film, and the studio needs it to do well. *Really* well. You're playing a hometown lesbian who serves coffee for a living, and this morning, there are pictures of you in TMZ making a very rude gesture while hanging out of a helicopter."

"God, those are surfacing again?"

"So, yes, Dylan, *your* image," Laurel said without missing a beat.

Dylan rested her elbows on her knees, dropped her head into her hands. "Why did they even cast me?"

Laurel was silent for long enough that Dylan looked up. "Laurel."

Laurel blinked, shook her head. "They cast you because you're right for the role. That, and Adriana is very good at her job."

Dylan exhaled heavily. "She really is."

"Now you just need to ensure they continue to see how perfect you are to play Eloise Tucker, small-town sweetheart."

Dylan nodded. Took a deep breath. A few deep breaths. She could do this. She *had* to do this. She wanted these kinds of roles, wanted to prove she was more than the villain, more than pools full of Clicquot and waggling her tongue through her fingers from a helicopter.

More than her parents.

More than that toddler asleep on a pizza, tomato sauce streaked over her little arms and legs.

She pressed her eyes closed—the memory she was too young to remember felt so real, full color in her brain, her blood. The longing, the mess, the fame, it was all there, pulsing just under her ribs.

And she wanted more than that.

"Okay," she said, straightening her shoulders, smoothing her hair. "This is fine."

"It is. It *will* be," Laurel said.

"Blair and I are more mature now," Dylan said. "Perfectly capable of being civil to each other. Professional."

"And if not, you fake it," Laurel said, a favorite tagline of hers. *Fake it, fake it, fake it. That's all Hollywood is anyway.*

"I'm shocked Rayna hasn't concocted some fake dating romance between Blair and me," Dylan said, laughing, but Laurel's expression sort of . . . froze. Dylan's eyes went wide. "What. Tell me you're kidding."

Laurel winced. "Rayna suggested it. Blair's people shut it down."

Dylan blinked, this news settling in slowly. Rayna was her publicist, brought in by Laurel, and was a heady mix of sweet tea and arsenic, a viper disguised as a debutante. Fake dating between two starlets was probably her wet dream.

"So, Blair didn't want to fake date me," Dylan said.

"She did not."

It shouldn't bother her—she didn't want to fake date Blair either, Jesus. But at the same time, why didn't Blair want to fake date her?

She shook her head, stood up. "Okay, whatever. This is fine."

"You said that already."

"Well, it is," she said, impressed by how calm she felt, how smooth her tone was. She was going to focus on what she could control, just like her therapist, Eli, reminded her to do every week.

Simple.

Easy.

"Did you make sure the diner is still ready to train me?" she asked, picking up the thick script for *As If You Didn't Know* from the ottoman and tucking it under her arm.

"All set. Three weeks and you'll be a bona fide waitress in Clover Lake, New Hampshire."

The town's name wrapped around her like a hug, a soft smile settling on her mouth as sweet memories warmed and loosened her tight chest. "You ever been there?"

"Clover Lake?" Laurel asked, standing up too. "No."

"It's lovely."

"You've been?"

Dylan nodded. "Hallie took me for a week during the summer I was thirteen. My parents were . . . well." She cleared her throat. "It was a good few days." Her memory drifted to a dark-eyed girl, a long fishtail braid, and a cherry-print T-shirt. The girl's face was blurry now, but the feeling was still there—comfort and hope and excitement, first kisses and laughter.

Just two girls being kids. Something Dylan never really got to be, not like other children. Not like that girl on Clover Lake's shore.

"Anyway," Dylan said, shaking off the dreamy memories. She returned to them too often, whenever she was stressed or overwhelmed, that singularly happy moment in her life. But she had work to do now. She had to focus, not dwell in a fairy tale that she sometimes had a hard time believing was even real. "It'll be a great location. Good to get out of LA, that's for sure."

Laurel dug Dylan's phone out of her pocket and held it out. "Can I trust you with this?"

Dylan flicked her eyes to the device, then picked up her cake box and turned away. "Probably not."

She headed out onto her back patio and into the perpetual LA sunshine to try her damnedest to become the best small-town queer gal the world had ever seen.

Chapter Three

"OLIVE!" RAMONA CALLED from the kitchen as she sipped her coffee and worked a mini-crossword on her phone. "Isn't Marley picking you up at eight?"

"I'm coming! Jesus!" a voice screeched from upstairs.

Ramona winced. Olive had graduated this past weekend—Ramona had made sure to wear waterproof mascara and took at least a hundred pictures—and this week marked a Clover Lake tradition where the graduates fluttered through town in different costumes as a symbol of their newly minted independence. During Grad Week, they went to movies and restaurants and the beach and got ice cream, all dressed up in the theme of the day. Despite all this frivolity, Olive seemed a bit on edge. Neither their dad nor Ramona could really put a finger on why—school was over, Olive had a full ride to Vanderbilt with her best friend, Marley, and she was only a few months from getting out of *this backassward shoebox of a town*, as Olive put it.

If anyone should be losing her shit a little, it was Ramona.

And she was.

Quietly, while she tried to think of a four-letter word for an unexpected blessing, her heart rate increasing the longer she listened to Olive stomp around upstairs.

"Good morning!" April trilled as she came in through the back door, just like she did most mornings. She lived on the next street over, bought her own house and everything like a real adult after college, a tiny sage-green bungalow with two feline roommates and walls covered in all manner of strange and beautiful art. Her parents still lived in the same house April had grown up in on the other side of town, still practiced medicine at Evans Family Medicine, but April, for all her love of Clover Lake, needed her own space.

She'd always needed more space than the Evanses knew how to give or create.

Her parents were one reason April loved astrology so vehemently—because Jacqueline and Preston Evans did *not*. They were people of science, doctors who moved their practice from San Francisco to Clover Lake for a quieter life for their only daughter. As April grew up, it became wildly clear that she was never going to be contained by their standards, their logic, their stoic and practical approach to life.

"Oh, thank god," April said, beelining for the glass carafe that held Steven's precious pour-over. He always made enough for both April and Ramona before he left for work during the regular school year, and for the past few years, he also taught summer school, which had just started up this week. April drained the last of the coffee into a mug with David Rose's face on it, along with the admonition to eat glass. April held the mug close, steam curling into her face, and inhaled deeply. "Bless."

Ramona laughed. "Just drink it already."

"I'm enjoying this masterpiece."

Ramona shook her head. She loved her dad's coffee, but she also had had to make peace with the burnt flavor of the diner's brew.

During a double shift, one couldn't be picky about their caffeine intake.

April cleared her throat after a sip. "Speaking of masterpieces—"

"I wasn't."

"Well, I was."

Ramona clicked out of her crossword. "Here we go."

"We need to get you on that movie set."

Ramona sighed, opened her mouth to protest, but then Olive bounded into the room, her long brown hair flying behind her in two pigtails, her face covered in white makeup with each of her eyes smudged and streaked with red and blue paint, respectively, lips red and smeared. She wore a red-and-white baseball tee that read *Daddy's Lil Monster* across the chest.

Ramona blinked at her. "What is happening right now?"

"Harley Quinn," April said, popping a grape in her mouth from the bowl on the counter. "Badass."

"Today's theme is superhero day," Olive said. "Marley is Puddin'. We're meeting people at the Pancake Corner in Concord."

"*Puddin'*?" Ramona asked.

"Harley's pet name for Joker," April said.

Ramona sighed. "I'm officially old."

"We knew that, puddin'," April said.

Ramona flipped her off but laughed.

"What's this about the movie set?" Olive asked as she took a sip of Ramona's coffee.

"Nothing," Ramona said.

"Everything," April said, then proceeded to explain about Noelle Yang and Ramona's dashed dreams. Olive narrowed her eyes as April waxed on, gaze flitting to her sister over and over.

Ramona's chest tightened. Everything April was saying was essentially true—she *did* have dashed dreams and she *had* deferred her career plans, all of which Olive knew about—but she never wanted Olive to feel as though she was second place or a backup plan or, even worse, had ruined Ramona's life.

Olive *was* Ramona's life. The best part about it.

"Okay, she gets it," Ramona said, cutting April off before her best friend's excitement let something slip about Dylan Monroe. Not that Dylan mattered all that much—she was a blip in Ramona's past, a firework in the sky lasting only seconds—but Ramona was already struggling against this tiny flicker of hope under her ribs ever since she'd learned about the movie and Noelle Yang coming to Clover Lake. And with Dylan Monroe soon to be strolling through town as well, she wasn't quite sure how to feel about any of it.

"But do *you*?" April said, frowning at Ramona. "Get it?"

"It's not your job to reignite my career, Apes. Give me some time to process."

"You've had twelve years of processing."

"That's a long time," Olive said softly, and Ramona reached out and squeezed her hand, relieved when Olive squeezed back.

"Plus, it's June—Pride Month!" April said. "All the queer deities are smiling down on you."

Ramona huffed a laugh, then stood and took her empty mug to the sink. "What do you expect me to do? Camp out in front of Noelle's trailer and most likely get arrested for harassment?"

"There are other ways to meet her," Olive said. "Isn't the café doing a lot with the movie? What about deliveries or catering or something?"

"Olive, you're a genius," April said, grabbing Olive's face and kissing the top of her head.

"I know that," Olive deadpanned, and god, Ramona loved her. Every choice she'd ever made for Olive was worth it . . . but she also couldn't deny that little flicker near her heart was growing, brightening the dark places where she'd tucked away her own plans and visions for her life.

A few nights ago, she couldn't sleep, that spark burning just enough to keep her awake. She'd taken her iPad and crept into the spare bedroom, the one with the daybed no one ever slept in, four different dress forms she had used for various genders and plus-size designs huddled in one corner, and the closet filled with Ramona's creations from high school, from RISD, and from the few years after she first came back home from Rhode Island. She'd flipped on the red swing arm lamp on the drawing table she hadn't used in years. Soft, warm light filled the room, and she sat on the edge of the bed, her iPad held tight to her chest. She eyed the closet, wary, like a monster lurked behind the honey-colored wooden doors.

It took her a good ten minutes, but she finally made herself stand and let that monster out.

And it was beautiful.

Sharp and hungry and eager for attention—smooth silks, colors in every shade, unique buttons and stitches, tartan and wool and chiffon, all lined up like scenes from Ramona's dreams. Her heart fluttered like a kid with a crush, her fingers reaching out to drift over the things she'd created.

She loved clothes.

Always had, really. She could remember being as young as four and tucking herself into her mother's closet, a walk-in filled with all manner of colors and fabrics and styles. She loved the textures under her fingertips, how her mother transformed depending on what she was wearing, everything from a simple pair of jeans and an old band tee to a sleek black suit to a floor-length dress the color of champagne. Clothes were art that one got to wear, got to present to the world and declare *This is me* without uttering a word.

After her mother left when Ramona was thirteen—taking a bit of Ramona's sense of security and understanding of love and family with her—Ramona fell even deeper into fashion, finding solace in the creation and work that was just for her, retreating to this room after school or on weekends while baby Olive napped. What started as a hobby turned into a passion, an obsession really, oxygen while her tender family of three struggled to breathe, to get up every morning and put one foot in front of the other.

Clothes became Ramona's mood ring, a way to express herself without saying anything out loud—she was never great with words, taking after her more reticent father. She wasn't sure there even *were* words to describe what it felt like to be left by your own mother at thirteen.

What it still felt like, a lot of the time.

She hadn't seen or heard from Rebecca Riley in eighteen years. And she didn't want to—she'd long let go of the idea of having a mother, accepted the fact that the problem was Rebecca, not Ramona, not Olive.

But.

Feelings and facts rarely coincided, and if she let herself think about it just a bit too long, a knot formed in her throat, even at thirty-one years old. Which was why she didn't think about it very much at all—what good would it do? She'd raised Olive. And Olive was incredible. She'd carried this family forward, she and her dad, and it no longer mattered what she'd had to give up to do it.

But as she'd stood in front of that closet, pulling out piece after piece of her heart and hanging them around the room, she felt like she was eighteen again, the whole world spread out before her.

Possibility.

It had been so long since she'd felt that word—really *felt* it—for herself. She felt it all the time for Olive, worked for it, sacrificed to make sure Olive had endless supplies of it.

And she'd succeeded.

And now . . . Ramona felt a hollowness inside her, a space Olive had carved out and nestled inside of for so many years, and she didn't know what she needed to fill it once Olive left home.

Or did she?

Now, as she stood at the kitchen sink and gazed out the window of her father's house at the cloudless June morning, she knew exactly what she needed. And what's more, she wanted it, foolhardy as it was, a thirty-one-year-old waitress trying to restart a whole career in costume design. A laugh escaped her throat, her chest hitching with a few tears at the same time.

It was just so . . . *unlikely.*

But so was a queer romantic comedy coming to Clover Lake, and here they were.

She took a breath and turned around, resting her palms on the counter behind her to steady her shaking hands. Olive and April both stared at her, expressions expectant.

"Okay," Ramona said. "Okay, let's do it."

And the battle cry April released could've woken the dead.

THANKFULLY, APRIL HAD several morning appointments and Marley arrived to pick up Olive, so no one had time to hunker down and create the twenty-point plan April wanted to draft to *restart Ramona's sad little life,* as she so eloquently put it. Ramona wasn't sure how much she wanted Olive involved in the process anyway, as April seemed hell-bent on, well, framing it as *restarting Ramona's sad little life.*

She walked to her shift at Clover Moon alone, glad for the fifteen minutes left to her own thoughts, but as soon as she turned off Birch and onto Lake Street, the world exploded. It was a gorgeous morning anyway—the trees green and lush and still hanging on to their spring blossoms as they got ready for summer, the sky a cerulean blue, the air sweet and fresh. There were even a few rainbow flags fluttering outside of businesses here and there, including the café. A perfect day, by all accounts, but the town itself was a riot of activity.

Chaos, Ramona would even say.

People crowded the sidewalks, their phones out and pointed toward the small green space in the center of the town square where white vans were parked with their back doors thrown open, all manner of film equipment smattering the area. People Ramona didn't recognize with iPads in their hands and headsets over their ears milled about, calling out orders and huddling around cameras, inspecting the screens and adjusting knobs and buttons.

Ramona froze, her own curiosity creating a flurry inside her chest. She couldn't help but look around for Noelle Yang's iconic salt-and-pepper hair, for a rack of clothes, anything to do with costumes, but she didn't spot anything of note.

At least not yet.

Just knowing Noelle Yang was somewhere in Clover Lake—or would be—was enough to make Ramona's heart race against her ribs.

Her eyes scanned for another face too . . . ice-green eyes, pale skin . . . she realized she had no idea what color Dylan's hair was right now as she had favored pastels here and there in the past. It was naturally brown, like chocolate or the bark of a maple tree in the rain, and—

Ramona pressed her lips together, tight enough to ache.

Dylan Monroe didn't matter—she was just an actor, a wild one at that, and Ramona had more important things to focus on. Plans. Aspirations. Goals. And Dylan had nothing to do with any of that.

Nothing at all.

She hurried down the sidewalk toward Clover Moon, squeezing through the rubberneckers and offering up hellos when townsfolk greeted her. Inside the café was just as busy, everyone who'd come out to see the film move into town settling in for a cup of coffee and a plate of Owen's whoopie pie crepes.

Ramona skirted around the tables, waving when she heard her

name, finally making it behind the counter to where Owen was frothing milk at the espresso machine.

"Can you believe this?" he said, but he was smiling.

Owen was approaching fifty and blissfully married to his high school sweetheart and sported a trimmed gray-and-brown beard. His pale head was bald as a cue ball, and he was covered in tattoos, several of which April inked on for him in the last few years. Ramona's favorite was the spray of wisteria curling down his right forearm to his wrist.

"I can't," Ramona said, tying on the apron embroidered with tiny sewing needles and spools of thread Olive had given her two Christmases ago. She clocked in at the register, then scanned the dining room for who might need what. "You want me to take section four?"

Owen topped off the drink he was working on with a foam heart and shook his head. "Not today, no."

Ramona frowned. "But I always take section four."

Owen set the mug on the bar, and the coffee was promptly whisked away by Beth, another server who'd started just a few months ago. Ramona smiled at her, then folded her arms at Owen.

"You're up to something," she said. "Did April talk to you?"

He laughed. "She talks *at* me all the time, but in this case, I'm not sure what you mean."

Ramona sighed. Owen was family to her, an uncle or much older brother, if you will, but he also liked to wax on about Ramona not living up to her full potential and had threatened to fire her on more than one occasion just to get her to leave the proverbial nest.

"Sorry," she said, pulling her hair back into a low ponytail. "There's just a lot going on."

He nodded. "Well, I hate to add to your load, but I've got something I need you to do for me."

She let her arms flop to her sides. "See? Up to something."

He presented his palms. "It's strictly business, I swear."

"Fine. What is it? You need me to find a new bread supplier again? I thought we were going to try to make it in-house?" She dug into her apron pocket and found her pen and order pad, popped off the pen cap, and scribbled on the first page to test the ink. "I told you a million times, I think fresh-baked—"

"It's not the bread," he said. "It's the movie."

She froze. "The movie."

"Yeah, they're going to be filming in the café here and there."

"Marion mentioned that . . ." Ramona said, but trailed off as details about the actual story of *As If You Didn't Know* flitted through her mind. She'd read the book, of course, and knew Dylan was playing Eloise, but other than a fake dating plot in a small town, she couldn't remember much else. But now . . .

"There's a character who's a waitress," Owen said.

Ramona stopped breathing.

"Eloise?" Owen said as he wiped down the stainless steel counter behind the espresso machine. "Is that her name?"

Ramona's mouth dropped open to answer, but she couldn't get out the word, the *yes*, and she was pretty sure her heart was slowing down or speeding up, she couldn't exactly tell, but something was happening in the center of her chest and—

"Anyway, in addition to some scenes shot here in the café, the actor who's playing the waitress wants some hands-on experience," Owen went on. "Jack Monroe's kid—god, I love Evenflow. You think he'll come by the set?" He had a dreamy look in his eyes. He actually sighed before shaking his head. "His daughter wants to do method acting or something, I don't know. But the studio is forking over enough money to hire that in-house baker you want so badly, and you're a great trainer, so—"

"No," Ramona said.

Owen's brows went up. "No?"

"I just . . . I'm sorry, Owen, I don't think I can—"

But right then, a swollen hush fell over the dining room as the bell over the door trilled, a harbinger of doom, and Ramona felt her blood freeze—surge, dry up, *something*—as she sensed everyone's eyes lock onto whoever just walked inside.

Ramona's back was to the door, but she swore to god, she could *feel* it—an energy she hadn't experienced in eighteen years, but that still seemed familiar, fresh and wild and free.

"Hi, everyone," a husky voice said. "Don't stop eating on my account. That looks delicious."

The diners laughed, then started talking again. Ramona saw a few patrons get up, phones at the ready for pictures, but Owen rushed to the door, asking everyone to give Dylan some room.

Dylan.

Give *Dylan* some room.

Ramona couldn't seem to make herself turn around. Not yet. Of course, she'd known for three weeks that Dylan Monroe was playing Eloise. And she knew that they were going to film some scenes in Clover Moon, but none of that really clicked until this moment. Ramona hadn't thought she'd even see Dylan—why would she? If filming was happening in the café, the studio would bring in trained extras for the patrons, for the other servers, wouldn't they? She had no clue how movies worked on that end, had only ever been interested in costuming, but Ramona never imagined she'd be here, at her place of work, about to help Dylan Monroe serve coffee and french fries.

"Ramona?" Owen said from behind her. "There's someone I'd like you to meet."

Ramona counted to three. Then she took a deep breath and turned around, eyes locking with the ice-green gaze of the first person she'd ever kissed.

For a second, the world slowed down, just a blip of a moment as she and Dylan looked at each other, a small smile settling on Dylan's lovely mouth, her head tilted just a little, those nearly transparent eyes narrowing as though she were trying to place Ramona.

Ramona, for her part, had completely stopped breathing, because goddammit, Dylan was gorgeous. Ramona had seen her only through screens for eighteen years, but she still recognized the girl she'd met at the lakeshore on that Fourth of July all those years ago. Her limbs weren't as gangly, of course, and she looked a little less haunted than she had as a thirteen-year-old, the hollows in her cheeks filled out, full of health and radiance now, but it was her. Those eyes . . . that perfect rosebud mouth. The mouth that had smiled and laughed and made Ramona smile and laugh when she hadn't thought she'd ever smile or laugh again. The mouth that had trembled just a little when Dylan had put her hands on Ramona's waist and leaned in, her breath catching just before she—

"Hi," Dylan said, sticking out her hand. "I'm Dylan."

Her tone was so professional, so staid and even rehearsed, Ramona couldn't help but blink in confusion.

"I know," she said, slipping her hand into Dylan's and waiting for the light of recognition to flare in Dylan's eyes.

And waited . . . and waited.

Dylan's brows creased, and she released a tiny laugh as the moment stretched on.

Owen cleared his throat, patted Ramona on the shoulder. "This is my best server, Ramona. Makes a pretty mean honey whiskey pie too."

"Is that so?" Dylan said politely. So, so politely. "I'll have to try that."

Ramona could only nod as it became apparent—embarrassingly, mortifyingly apparent—that Dylan had no memory of Ramona Riley.

Granted, they'd never shared their names. At the time, Dylan had thought it would be fun and mysterious to keep their names from each other. At least, their real names. She'd called Ramona "Cherry" for the night, because Ramona had worn a tee with a cherry pattern all over it, and Ramona had called Dylan "Lollipop," because Dylan had had a green apple sucker in her mouth when she'd first approached Ramona on the beach, her lips tinged bright green.

Moreover, Ramona was one of those people who looked nothing like her younger self. Her hair had thickened with puberty, loose curls forming in her once stick-straight tresses, and she'd been a wiry kid, growing too tall, too fast. Now, she was wavy-haired and fat—a word she didn't use negatively at all, just as a descriptor of her curvy body—and her face was covered in freckles that had also increased in number as she'd gotten older.

On top of all of that, she'd told a teenage Dylan that she too was a summer person, just visiting with her family. With her mom and dad and baby sister, a whole family. A normal family who vacationed by the lake every summer. She'd wanted to be someone different—not Ramona Riley of Clover Lake, whose own mother didn't even want her—but someone else entirely, someone carefree and normal, whose biggest worry was whether or not she and her best friend would be in the same homeroom class come fall.

So, no, maybe there was no reason Dylan should remember her at all. She was *Dylan Monroe*. Child of icons, Hollywood starlet, everyone's favorite villain, the wild girl on all the gossip sites, dater of gorgeous actors and musicians. The evening they had once shared a million years ago was like a nanosecond compared to all the things Dylan Monroe had done and seen and been.

"Right," Ramona said, more to herself than to Dylan and Owen. "Right, well . . ." She swallowed around the sudden knot in her throat, a bowling ball by the feel of it, and pulled her hand from Dylan's.

"How can I help you, Ms. Monroe?" she asked once she was sure her voice would come out steady.

"Oh, god, please call me Dylan," Dylan said, smiling and tucking her hands into the back pockets of her light-wash jeans. She wore a cream-colored muscle tee that read *Cool Banana* on the front, along with a pair of rugged brown boots, pants cuffed just above the laces. "I'm just excited to dive in." She waved at the dining room, eyes glittering with intrigue and a little trepidation.

"Have you ever worked in the service industry before?" Ramona asked, even though, of course, she knew the answer.

Dylan pressed her tongue to her top lip, then laughed. "Um, no, I can't say that I have." Her cheeks went a little red, as though the admission embarrassed her.

"Well, it's pretty simple," Ramona said, but then her phone buzzed in her back pocket. She didn't like to leave texts unanswered, as it could be Olive, which Owen knew full well. "Excuse me one second."

She fished out her phone, rolling her eyes when she saw the notification on the screen.

April: Dylan fucking Monroe is in your diner??????

She tucked her phone away again without answering, despite the perpetual buzzes against her ass. Damn small towns. News didn't just travel fast, it moved like light, zinging through the atmosphere quicker than a blink.

"Sorry," she said. "Where were we?"

"You were getting acquainted and then getting Dylan here an apron," Owen said. "I'll leave you to it." He shook Dylan's hand one more time, then whispered, "Don't let her spill hot coffee on any customers, I beg you," in Ramona's ear before meandering deeper into the dining room to talk with patrons.

Ramona huffed a breath. A lawsuit would serve him right, springing Dylan Monroe on her like this. Not to mention the fact she'd be losing tips from her very generous regulars in section four.

She glanced at Dylan, who was still watching her with an interested expression. Ramona squirmed a bit, fluffed her fringe and adjusted her pink short-sleeve blouse, tiny lipstick tubes printed on the cotton, buttoned all the way to her neck. Her hair was in a high ponytail today, her dark jeans high-waisted and cuffed over a pair of high-top white sneakers.

"Um," Ramona said. "So . . . first things first . . ."

But then, for the life of her, she couldn't think of what was first, what was second or third either. She had no plan, no strategy here. She felt like a fumbling teenager.

"An apron," Dylan said.

"Yes," Ramona said, snapping her fingers. "An apron."

She turned and headed toward the back, nodding for Dylan to follow her. In the employee break room—a large closet, really, with a few lockers and a mini-fridge filled with bottled water and Gatorade—Ramona plucked a plain sage-green apron from the wall hook, hoping it was clean, and handed it over to Dylan.

Dylan held it between her thumb and forefinger for a few seconds, long enough that Ramona wondered if she was going to have to teach her how to tie it on, but she finally slipped it over her head and, after a few struggles with the strings, tied it around her waist.

Ramona's phone buzzed against her butt again. And again.

She sighed, plucking it out of her pocket.

April: You're training her????

Ramona: Ok when did you plant cameras in the café and did you see when I picked my nose last week?

April: Can't believe you didn't wash your hands after

Ramona laughed, eyeing Dylan as she tried to figure out what to do with the long apron strings.

April: Seriously though, this is it

Ramona: What is it?

April: Your way in. To the movie. Noelle!!!

Ramona frowned, the realization of what April meant settling over her.

Noelle.

Dylan would be working with Noelle.

Dylan would be costumed, fitted, made up. She'd be on set. Obviously she'd be on set, but . . . *she'd be on set.*

Ramona's thoughts swirled. She wasn't a schemer like April. Should she simply ask Dylan for a favor? No, not now. Not yet.

They didn't even know each other . . .

"I'm ready," Dylan announced, then popped her hands on her hips. She'd pulled her long brown hair back into a ponytail as well, the apron tied tight around her slim frame. "How do I look?"

Adorable was the first word that popped into Ramona's head, but she banished it like a ghost in a haunted mansion.

"Good" is what Ramona settled for, focused on her actual task. "Okay, let's start with a tour, shall we?"

Dylan nodded vigorously, but Ramona caught a flash of nervousness behind her eyes, which was also adorable, which meant Ramona had to exorcise that word for the second time in thirty seconds. This did not bode well.

Her phone trilled again.

April: So how is she?? Does she remember you???? I mean, of course she does

Ramona's chest went tight, and she felt her mouth tremble a little, something settling over her bones that made her feel small and young.

"Hey," Dylan said, tapping her elbow. "You okay?"

Ramona tucked her phone away, shook her head to clear it. "Yeah!" Too bright, too loud. "Yeah," she said more calmly. "I'm perfectly fine."

Dylan smiled and they held each other's gaze for a split second before Ramona yanked hers away, then focused on training her first kiss who didn't remember her in the slightest how to effectively carry multiple plates of cheeseburgers and fries.

Chapter Four

DYLAN HAD NEVER worked so hard in her life.

After only an hour, her lower back was killing her, she'd broken two nails, and she was pretty sure she had a blister on her left heel. And on top of all that, she'd made a complete idiot of herself in front of a cute girl.

Several times.

"Oh, god, no, don't touch the glass part of the coffee carafe," Ramona said, snatching Dylan's hand away. "It's hot."

"Right," Dylan said, her cheeks burning red for the zillionth time in the last thirty minutes. The awful part was, she *wasn't* an idiot. Sure, she'd never worked in food service, but she did have common sense, for god's sake, and she knew not to touch the glass part of a fucking coffee carafe. She was just nervous—more nervous than she thought she'd be, more nervous than she'd ever been on *Spellbound*'s set—and her trainer's freckles and swaying hips and overall sweetness were not helping matters.

Dylan lifted the coffeepot by the handle and then faced the dining room, which was full of patrons, a great number of them looking at her, smiling, waving even.

She smiled back but couldn't get herself to show her teeth. She felt as though she was facing a pit of vipers. Not that the townsfolk had been anything but nice to her, but Dylan had underestimated the effect of *Dylan Monroe* waiting tables, and how everyone would be watching her, phones at the ready. Laurel had gone with her to the café this morning, but Dylan refused to let her manager walk her inside like a child on her first day of school. She'd wanted to be an everywoman, just plain ole Dylan showing up for a shift, but she was pretty sure pictures of plain ole Dylan were going to show up online tomorrow, frizzy haired and sweating with her apron covered in ketchup and mustard and coffee and honey and god only knew what else.

"Just walk slowly," Ramona said beside her. "Ask before you pour. 'Coffee?' That's all you have to say."

"Right," Dylan said, but she couldn't seem to coax her feet to move. This was a bad idea. Killin' Dylan was going to turn into Disaster Dylan, she just knew it.

"I'll walk with you," Ramona said.

Dylan shifted to look at her, eyes so dark brown, they seemed fathomless. And freckles. Ramona had so many freckles—Dylan never knew she liked freckles, but god, she did. And paired with Ramona's long lashes and pert little mouth, Dylan was having a hard time focusing.

Ramona wasn't her usual type, that was for sure. Jocelyn had been long and lithe, blond and elegant and cold. Before her, there was Jackson Muñez—apparently Dylan also had a thing for *J* names—who had been named *People*'s Sexiest Man Alive two years ago with his black hair, amber eyes, chiseled jaw, and impressive arm muscles she used to like to bite during sex.

God, Dylan was a cliché. A walking, talking advertisement for Hollywood dating drama. Everyone knew what to expect from Dylan Monroe, which was why she was here in this diner. To change all that. That was probably why she found Ramona so attractive in this moment—she was simply latching on to the unexpected. Not that Ramona wasn't empirically attractive—she certainly was. It was just that Dylan had never gone for a non-Hollywood kind of girl. Unfamous. Hell, Ramona probably wasn't even queer.

Were there queer people in New Hampshire?

Jesus, of course there were.

Dylan shook her head . . . god, even her thoughts were babbling right now. She had to focus. Had to pour coffee. That was it. That was her whole world right now. She could do that . . . couldn't she?

"Thanks," Dylan said to Ramona, rolling her shoulders back. "But I've got this. I'm okay."

"You sure?"

Dylan nodded, then circled the counter and drifted into the dining room. Eyes followed her, but she kept her smile in place.

This was a role.

Simple as that.

Eloise.

She was Eloise and she did this every day. She woke up every single morning, poured a bowl of hearty Cheerios, pined after a girl she'd met at camp forever ago, and showed up for the people in her life.

"Coffee?" she asked a cute little old lady with bluish hair.

"Oh, yes, dear," the lady said, pink painted nails resting on her green mug.

Pour. No spill. Success.

"Coffee?" Dylan asked a beefy man with a bright red beard.

"Yes, please!" he boomed. "I loved you in *Spellbound*."

"Thank you so much," she said, smiling as she tipped the carafe toward his mug. He wasn't exactly the normal demographic for that show, which Dylan found sort of endearing, and—

"What was it like hanging out of that helicopter?" he asked.

Her smile dipped, as did the carafe, spilling a puddle of coffee onto the floor. It landed with a splash, sprinkling the man's tan boots and jeans.

"Watch it, darling!" he said, scooting his chair back, the legs screeching against the wood floors.

"I'm so sorry," Dylan said, but stood frozen, no clue what to do. "I—"

"Coffee's on us today, Hal," Ramona said, appearing next to Dylan with a towel and bending to mop up the spill. She looked up at Hal, eyes dark and lovely. "Thanks for being patient with Dylan. She's training. You know how it is when you start a new job."

Hal frowned at the coffee splatters on his jeans, but then he nodded. "Sure do. Just started a new contracting job, myself. No worries at all."

"Thank you, Hal," Dylan said evenly, though her heart was galloping under her sternum, hands shaking.

"It's just coffee," Ramona said to her, taking her elbow and leading her away. "It's okay. It'll wash out, and Hal usually leaves here with bacon in his beard anyway."

Dylan managed a laugh, but her nerves were close to shot. It *was* just coffee, but it also felt like so much more. She couldn't even handle a simple question about one of the most infamous moments of her life; how was she ever going to remake herself? *Become* Eloise Tucker?

"Table five's order is ready," Ramona said. "Why don't you handle that? It's only two plates. Easy peasy."

Dylan smiled at Ramona. "Easy peasy?"

Ramona laughed. "Well, it is."

She bumped Dylan's shoulder then, lashes lowered against her freckled cheeks, like they really were in this together and Ramona wasn't being paid to be nice to her. For a second, Dylan felt like she'd known Ramona for much longer than two humid and stressful hours in a small-town diner. It felt . . .

She took a deep breath.

Didn't matter.

Ramona *was* being paid, just like everyone else in Dylan's life.

"Right," she said, to both herself and Ramona. "I got this." She headed toward the service window and lifted the plates, fingers strong under the edges just like Ramona told her. She turned, ready to whisk them to their table like a damn professional, when she saw her.

Blair Emmanuel.

Coming into the diner with her longtime manager, Brian Laveaux, looking gorgeous and relaxed in jeans and a white sleeveless blouse and not at all like a sweaty mess covered in condiments. Her brown arms were toned and glowing, her dark curls an angelic halo around her face.

And Dylan meant to stop moving.

She fully intended to stop walking with her hands full of hot food, thought she *did* stop, but somehow, her feet kept going while she watched Blair smile and tell the hostess they were a party of two before she locked gazes with Dylan.

And just as expected, Blair's smile dipped, then shifted into something like surprise, eyes drifting down Dylan's aproned body.

"Dylan. Hello," Blair said, but there was no warmth in her voice, just deadpan politeness.

Hi, Blair is what Dylan meant to say, what she'd opened her mouth to say, but somehow her body finally stopped moving right then, though not by her own choice. She hit something—some*one*— and it was like one of those slow-motion moments in a teen movie, when the already friendless kid is searching for a place to eat in the cafeteria and slips on a patch of coleslaw or a soggy hamburger bun or whatever the hell and goes down, food covering their shirt and pants, chocolate pudding in a very unfortunate spot, lettuce in their hair.

Yeah. It was exactly like that.

Because before Dylan could even register what was happening, she was on the ground, turkey and ham and blackberry jam in her lap, fries scattered all over the floor. Beth, another server, was also on the floor with what looked like Clover Moon's honey whiskey pie smeared all over her chest.

A shocked hush fell over the dining room.

One of the plates Dylan was carrying spun in a circle next to her before stilling with a *thunk*.

Dylan blinked, her arms held out in shock. She saw phones aimed at her, conversation starting up, surreptitious laughter and expressions of sympathy—*oh, that poor thing*—even as they snapped photos.

Dylan finally looked at Beth, who seemed just as shocked as she was but shifted into action much quicker, getting to her knees and starting to pick up the Monte Cristo detritus.

"Beth, I'm so sorry," Dylan managed to say, but then, dear god, a horrible thing started happening.

Her throat closed up, eyes swelling, cheeks aching with the effort to hold back the tears that were threatening to spill over.

No, no, no, she would not fucking cry in front of the whole town, in front of *Blair*, on top of everything else. She absolutely would not.

But tears rarely listened to reason, and one made a run for it down her cheek. She swiped it away fast, started picking up food and piling it onto the plates. She made quick work of it, then stood and headed for the kitchen without looking at anyone, camera clicks following her as she went.

She dumped the dishes into the bus bin, the cooking staff silent and watching her as she did so, then all but ran for the bathroom. It was a single room, gender neutral, and it was locked.

"Fuck," she pretty much yelled as she jiggled the handle, then heard a soft *oh* from a few feet away, a patron holding up a phone, eyes wide, catching her meltdown second by second.

She put up a hand but felt rage boil in her chest, more expletives lifting to the surface.

"Oh, that's really nice," she started, dropping her hand. "Good to know even cute small towns are made up of complete ass—"

"Hey, Violet, come on," a voice chided from behind the patron.

The person—a middle-aged white woman—winced and turned to face Ramona, who had her hands on her hips and a disapproving look on her face.

Which was sort of hot.

That is, if Dylan weren't on the precipice of a complete meltdown turned PR disaster.

Another one.

Jesus.

She took a deep breath, scrubbed a hand down her face.

"Sorry, Ramona," Violet said. "I guess I lost my mind a little there." She tucked the phone into her pleated jeans. "It's just so exciting! All this movie hubbub!" She turned toward Dylan again. "I'm a huge fan."

Dylan opened her mouth to tell Violet exactly where she could put her fandom, but Ramona hooked her arm through Violet's and led her quickly back toward the dining room.

"Thanks, Violet, go enjoy your pie now," Ramona said, then gave her customer a little shove. Violet went, thank god.

Ramona stood there for a split second, making sure Violet sat down, before she turned to face Dylan.

And that was it.

That was all she could take.

Dylan burst into tears—and not attractive movie tears either. Big gulping sobs that took them both by surprise. Ramona's eyes went wide, but she didn't waste a lot of time staring. She simply grabbed her bag out of the break room, then walked toward Dylan and put an arm around her heaving shoulders before leading her out the back door.

∽

THEY ENDED UP in the woods.

Dylan barely noticed where they were going when they left the restaurant at first. She simply followed Ramona, not toward the main street and the sidewalks, but through what seemed to be the backyards of a residential street behind the café, until they ended up inside a fortress of trees so thick, all Dylan could see was green.

She stopped for a second, once the forest closed around them, and lifted her face to the cool canopy above her.

Breathed.

There were so many shades of green Dylan had never really noticed before—lime and chartreuse, hunter and kelly and sage, a kaleidoscope of green. And it was so quiet, nothing but a breeze through the leaves, birds chirping, squirrels chittering. Even when at a park or on a trail in LA, the city was never so far away that she couldn't hear its hum underneath everything, like a buzzing in her blood.

But here, her blood just felt like blood. Flowing through her veins like everyone else. She couldn't remember the last time she'd felt so instantly at peace, so calm and relieved. She felt young again— but *good* young. *Safe* young, like that week she'd come here with Aunt Hallie all those summers ago, just a regular kid on a vacation. All the details of that week were blurry—the cabin they'd stayed in, the fireworks on the Fourth, the girl she'd met who was also visiting Clover Lake, cherry-print T-shirt and tears on her cheeks that she'd never explained were the only things Dylan really remembered— but the *feeling* was still there, and she'd been chasing that feeling since she arrived, the two of them playing hide-and-seek.

And it seemed like she might've finally found it.

She took a deep breath, filling her lungs with clean forest air, then glanced at Ramona.

"Thanks," she said. "For getting me out of there for a sec. I'm sorry that was such a shit show."

Ramona waved a hand. "It's fine. It was never going to be normal."

Something in Dylan's chest sank into her stomach, her shoulders literally drooping.

Ramona clocked the motion, her brows lifting. "You wanted it to be normal."

It wasn't a question.

Dylan opened her mouth. Closed it. Ramona nodded toward the trail, and they started walking, a slow amble through the woods.

"I wanted it to be not like *my* normal life," Dylan finally said. "You know, people only interested in me because of what I do, or don't do, or do in a dramatic way. Or they just want something from me."

"Does that happen a lot?" Ramona asked, her forehead crinkling. "People wanting things from you?"

"God, yeah. Usually just pictures or videos, but I've had perfect strangers come up to me on the street and thrust screenplays into my arms. Like a hit-and-run."

"Really?"

Dylan nodded. "Screenplays, demos to give to my parents, portfolios of stage design—I don't even do theater, but people see someone like me and think we're made of fairy dust, I guess. I don't know."

Ramona was quiet beside her, frowning at the ground.

"It's not just strangers either," Dylan said. "Every ex or friend I've ever had wanted something from me."

"That must be hard," Ramona said, eyes still on the pine needles under their feet.

"It can be." Dylan sighed. "Today, I just wanted to be . . . yeah, normal, I guess. Small-town Dylan." She laughed, but it wasn't a happy sound. "I wanted to do one thing right."

Ramona kept her hands in her pockets, apron slung over her shoulder. "So what's something you do right?"

Dylan laughed. "Lately? Not a lot. I get angry the wrong way. I break up the wrong way. I scroll through Instagram the wrong way—"

"Instagram?"

"My manager confiscates my phone on the regular. It's a whole thing."

Ramona nodded, didn't ask anything else about it, and Dylan sort of loved her for it.

"Anyway," Dylan said. "We start filming tomorrow and I can't even carry a plate of food twenty feet, so, yeah, my confidence is a little shot. Silly, I know."

"It's not silly," Ramona said, bending to inspect a patch of blue-green mushrooms that looked like tiny cups spreading over a log, then taking out her phone and snapping a picture. "It's natural to want to feel competent at things, no matter what it is."

She squatted now, squinting at the mushrooms and clicking another picture, this one closer up.

"What are those?" Dylan asked, squatting too. "I've never seen them before."

"Elf cups," Ramona said. "Aren't they gorgeous? If you've ever been walking along in the woods and see some bark that looks stained blue, it's probably because of these little beauties."

Dylan looked at Ramona, whose face was full of wonder. "You like mushrooms, huh?"

Ramona laughed and stood up, Dylan following. "Yeah, I guess I do."

"Explains the bag," Dylan said, nodding toward the bag criss-crossing Ramona's body, tiny red-and-white mushrooms dotting the dark gray canvas.

"Oh, yeah," Ramona said, hand swiping down the material as they started walking again. "My sister gave this to me. We got really into mushrooms when she was around four. We'd spend hours in the woods behind our house, foraging and searching, then we'd come home and look up everything we found, learn about them."

"I never really thought about it," Dylan said.

"They're just so amazing," Ramona said, talking fast and then tapping her foot on the ground. "Underneath us, there's a whole other world going on. Mushrooms talk to each other, help the trees talk to each other. They care for each other. It's incredible."

"What do they talk about, I wonder," Dylan asked.

Ramona laughed. "Olive—that's my sister—and I once wrote a really bad poem about that."

Dylan smiled. "I'd like to read it."

"Oh, no, you would not, trust me."

"Come on, don't be modest."

Ramona just smiled and shook her head.

The trail curved and the lake came into view, sparkling and blue under the late morning sun. The main beach area was visible, a plethora of people dotting the dark sand. Dylan hoped they weren't heading in that direction.

Because she loved this.

A simple walk.

With a simple girl who loved mushrooms.

She couldn't remember the last time she'd done something like this. When she and Jocelyn were together, everything was a show. They couldn't go out for sushi without ending up on Page Six or TMZ the next day, or on some random person's Instagram. And they never even tried to do things like this, quiet things, things where the two of them became Jo and Dylan, instead of Jocelyn Gareth and Dylan Monroe.

But right now, Dylan Monroe was fiction, a character, and Dylan . . . she was just Dylan.

She never wanted it to end.

"You and your sister are close?" she asked Ramona.

"Oh, yeah," Ramona said. "Our mom left the summer I was thirteen. Olive was only a baby, so I've pretty much helped raise her. Then my dad got injured my freshman year of college, so I came home to help out. Been here ever since."

Dylan slowed, tilted her head at Ramona, whose expression was pretty placid. "That sounds tough."

Ramona shrugged. "I wouldn't change it."

They were silent for a bit, angling around the lake through the trees. They didn't pass anyone, as though Ramona had made sure to take them on the less beaten path.

"What were you going to study in college?" Dylan asked.

Ramona faltered for a second, gazing out in front of her, a frown pushing her brows together.

"Design," she said finally.

"Really? What kind?"

Ramona looked down, fingered the hem of her pink shirt. "Apparel," she said quietly, as though she was embarrassed.

"I can see that," Dylan said.

Ramona met her gaze. "Really?"

"You have that air about you." Dylan waved her hand around Ramona's form. "Effortlessly cool."

Ramona laughed, her cheeks going a little pink. "Wow, I must really be on my game today."

"I think you are." Dylan grinned at her, her own face warming a bit, another phenomenon that hadn't happened to her in years—the flush that came with flirting.

Because they were definitely flirting.

Which absolutely could not happen. Dylan and a normie—no matter how much Dylan wanted to pretend she was a normie too at this moment—would be nothing short of disaster. She flung the idea out of her head, flattened the smile that had sneaked on her face, and focused on friends.

Friends.

She didn't have any of those. Throughout her entire life, anyone she spent time with fell into one of three categories—colleague, employee, or romantic partner. Laurel was the closest thing she had to a confidant, and Dylan paid her handsomely for it.

Friendship . . . Dylan wasn't even sure what that was. She had no idea how to just be *Dylan* with someone without the *Monroe* automatically attached. Didn't know how to parse the fact that Ramona hadn't asked about her parents or being famous or the helicopter or if she was really going to unleash Killin' Dylan on Jocelyn's new girlfriend. Ramona was simply walking with Dylan in the woods like . . . well, like a *friend*.

"Hey," Dylan said, stopping on the trail under a maple tree so green, it was nearly fluorescent.

"Everything okay?" Ramona asked, stopping too and facing her.

Dylan nodded, but her stomach roiled with nerves. She didn't want to rush a friendship, knew enough that one couldn't force it. But she was all fire and action, and didn't always give herself the time she needed to process. Luckily, she had no clue what *action* was required here, so she just asked a question.

"Can we do this again?" she asked.

Ramona tilted her head. "Do what?"

"Just . . ." Dylan waved her hand around at the scenery. "Normal stuff."

Ramona frowned. "Normal stuff."

Dylan laughed, shook her head. "I know, it sounds ridiculous—"

"It doesn't," Ramona said. "I just need more information."

Dylan nodded—self-deprecation was a favorite practice of hers, she knew, but she didn't expect Ramona, a stranger, to recognize it so quickly.

"Right," Dylan said. "I don't get to do this very often. Hikes. Be in nature. Go . . . I don't know. Bowling."

"Bowling."

"Or play Putt-Putt. I've never actually played Putt-Putt before."

Ramona's eyes widened, but sparkled with humor. "How is that even possible?"

"I know!" Dylan said, smiling. "That's my point. I need this. I think it's good for me to just . . . get in touch with *me*, you know? Not Dylan Monroe, but *me*. And other people, like you, who aren't out for the whole Dylan Monroe experience."

Ramona's expression went soft. "Okay," she said slowly.

Dylan took a deep breath. "So . . . I know you're doing a lot for me at the diner already, and you have your own life, but could we . . ."

"Play Putt-Putt?" Ramona said, brows lifted.

Dylan released a relieved laugh. "Yes. And other stuff. Stuff without the whole town snapping photos of me when I get mad and throw my golf club."

"Oh, god, you're an Aries, aren't you?"

Dylan mouth dropped open. "How did you know?"

"My best friend is obsessed with astrology. You'd probably love her."

"Okay, well, let's all go play Putt-Putt, then. And forage for mushrooms. And swim at a quiet spot in the lake. I bet you know all the secret places, don't you?"

Ramona shook her head, but smiled as she gazed off toward the lake. But then her smile dipped, her eyes going distant as though she was lost in a memory.

"Ramona?" Dylan asked. "If it's too much, I understand. I just thought maybe—"

"No, no, it's just . . ." Ramona trailed off, blinking at the lake.

Dylan's chest went tight. "It's fine, Ramona. Really."

Ramona looked at her, eyes searching hers for so long, Dylan was sure she was discovering every single secret, every pretense.

"No, let's do it," Ramona said. "I'll be your guide to all things normal and mundane."

"Yeah?" Dylan said. "You're sure?"

Ramona nodded, her motions fast as she started walking. "Starting with a little stop by my best friend's tattoo shop."

Dylan's smile was so big, her cheeks hurt as she rushed to keep up. "I've always wanted a tattoo."

Chapter Five

RAMONA WAS IN full-blown panic mode.

Granted, her panic mode took the form of serene smiles and calmly walking down a sidewalk with a very famous person next to her, all while her heart rammed against her ribs at what felt like two hundred beats per minute.

No, let's do it.

That's what's she'd said when Dylan was giving her a very clear, very kind way out.

Let's do it.

Why the hell had she said, *Let's do it*?

Of course she knew why—her demon best friend April's voice in the back of her head, whispering all sorts of nefarious plans.

Seriously though, this is it. Your way in.

And somehow, someway, in the last three hours since April had texted those fateful words, Ramona had truly considered them—Dylan *could* be her way in.

A connection.

That's all it was. Not like she'd be *using* Dylan, but it was just—

Let's do it.

Ramona wanted to smack herself in the head, a wash of guilt cresting through her stomach.

Okay, breathe, Ramona. She had to breathe.

"I really do love this town," Dylan said, jolting Ramona out of her guilt spiral.

They'd just turned onto the block where April's tattoo shop—Wonderlust Ink—was located, and Ramona couldn't get there fast enough. Unfortunately, the source of a lot of her stress was also the only person she wanted to talk to when she was melting down internally.

"Oh yeah?" Ramona asked, her voice way too high-pitched and obvious. "It's cute, I guess."

"Cute?" Dylan waved at the vintage lampposts, the navy and hunter green roofs lining the street, the cobbled sidewalks. "It's adorable. I actually came here once, years ago."

Ramona nearly tripped on her own feet.

"Did you?" she managed to squeak.

Dylan nodded, ambling along with her hands in her pockets. "With my aunt. We stayed in this cabin by the lake. It was over the Fourth holiday, and I met this—"

"Oh, wow, look, here we are," Ramona said quickly, because one thing she knew she could not do right now was hear her own story come out of Dylan's clueless mouth.

She swung open the glass door of Wonderlust, the sound of a buzzing tattoo gun drifting through the room. The place was small, but in a small town, a tattoo shop didn't need to be huge, and April did plenty of business. There were only two work areas—one for April and one for Mac, her apprentice turned full-time artist—but April made up for the lack of space with lots of flair. Art covered nearly every inch of the walls, but in a way that felt both sophisticated and cozy. Multicolored frames of all different sizes featured various illustrations, most of them April's from her time at RISD and beyond, everything from flowers and luna moths and queer identity flags, to Moira in her crow costume from *Schitt's Creek* and Dolly Parton's dimple-cheeked face. The fixtures were all antique bronze with amber lighting, the walls a moody teal. It was strange and beautiful and very, very April Evans. She'd redone a lot of it over the past year, as Elena's taste had bled into the shop when they were together. Needless to say, Ramona liked April's style much more.

"Hey," April said when she spotted Ramona. She was with a client—Molly Engle, a fortysomething mom who had nearly two full sleeves on her arms—and, by the looks of it, April had just finished inking a tendril of ivy around her left wrist. "I didn't know you were—" But she froze when Dylan came into view, her mouth falling open only a little before she smiled broadly. "Well, hello."

"Hi," Dylan said. "I'm—"

"Dylan Monroe, oh my god," Molly said. She was sitting in the workstation's chair, her brown eyes wide and her short red hair sleek and lovely.

"Hold it together, Molly," April said out of the corner of her mouth.

Molly nodded, cleared her throat. "Right, right, sure, yeah."

Dylan just laughed. "It's nice to meet you, Molly. And you, April. Very cool place."

Ramona smiled. Despite the mess back in the diner, Dylan was good with people. Or maybe, she was just better in smaller, more intimate settings, which made sense. A lone tattooed MILF was probably much easier than an entire room of excitable, small-town oglers.

"What brings you here?" April said, her eyes widening in Ramona's direction.

"Um, just thought Dylan would like to see your shop," Ramona said.

"It's beautiful," Dylan said.

"And, you know," Ramona said, "now that I think about it, I need to talk to you about that thing."

April's perfect brows lifted. "Thing."

"Yeah."

"Going to need some more information."

"That thing, you know. With Olive," Ramona said.

Liar, liar, pants on fire, but she needed to talk to her best friend and she needed it now.

"Ah," April said loudly. "That thing, yes, well. I need to wash up anyway and get a fresh wrap for Molly's new piece." She stood, snapped off her latex gloves, and nodded her head toward the back.

"You good?" Ramona asked Dylan.

"Oh, sure, I want to hear all about Molly's tats." She sat down in the chair April had just vacated, while Molly looked like she was about to internally combust right there.

"Great, be right back," Ramona said, then grabbed April's arm and all but dragged her to the office, a tiny space where April worked on designs and kept extra supplies.

"What is happening?" April said when Ramona closed the door and leaned against it, breathing hard as though she'd just escaped a serial killer.

"I'm a horrible person," she said, then jabbed a finger in April's direction. "And it's your fault. You've got me thinking thoughts and feeling feels."

"Oh, no, not thoughts," April deadpanned.

Ramona flipped her off, then explained about her walk through the woods and Dylan's request to *hang out* and how *let's do it* had just come out of her mouth because she was an ogre of a person who just wanted to thrust a screenplay into Dylan's hands.

"You don't write screenplays," April said, her voice maddeningly calm.

"It's a metaphor," Ramona whisper-yelled. "And Dylan is gorgeous and smart and kind, and I'm a lying liar who lies."

"You didn't lie about anything."

"I told her I studied apparel design."

April blinked at her. "You did."

"But I didn't tell her why!"

"Why would you?" April said.

Ramona released a grunt of frustration that lasted a whole five seconds.

"Okay, take a breath or ten, I beg you," April said, closing her hands around Ramona's arms. "This is not a crisis."

"It is."

"No, it's *good*."

Ramona just narrowed her eyes.

"Look," April said, releasing her and then leaning her butt against the desk. "You said this very bonny morning that you were in. You want to find a way to meet Noelle and shoot your shot. Yeah?"

Ramona swallowed hard. She did. Goddammit, she really did. She nodded.

"Okay, so, you can't just *want*, you have to *do*."

"I know that," Ramona said.

"Do you?"

Ramona sighed.

April sighed.

They'd been having this sigh-inducing conversation for Olive's entire senior year. And it wasn't that Ramona didn't understand that dreams needed action to become reality, it was just fucking scary. Plain and simple.

"She doesn't remember me," she said softly, sudden tears swelling into her eyes. She swiped them away fast, though April caught them. She always caught them.

April's eyes went gooey. "Honey."

"It's fine," Ramona said, waving a hand through the air. "It's better, actually."

April let that settle between them for a second. "You're not doing anything wrong or dishonest, Ray. You're hanging out with her, which is what *she* asked for. If you happen to get on set in the process, where's the harm in that? It's not like you'll ever see her again after this summer."

Ramona folded her arms. April was right. Dylan was *Dylan Monroe*. And Ramona was just . . . Cherry. A small-town girl whom Dylan once kissed. A forgettable kiss. Forgettable girl.

And Ramona, honestly, was sick and tired of being forgettable.

"Yeah," she said, forcing resolve into her voice. She rolled her shoulders back, straightened her posture. "You're right. We're just hanging out."

"Exactly. Like gal pals."

"That sounds gay."

"It is gay."

Ramona flapped her hands in the air. "Well, this can't be gay!"

"Everything is gay, Ray, we're queers."

Ramona laughed and dropped her head into her hands before popping back up again. "Acquaintances. Not gal pals. I'm helping her at the diner, and I'm helping her feel normal. Whatever that means."

April nodded vigorously. "Yes. Right. And in turn, she'll help you meet Noelle. Hell, I doubt she'll even mind after a few hangouts and she realizes how awesome you are."

"Yeah," Ramona said, a flurry of excitement and lingering guilt warring in her gut. "Yeah."

April grabbed Ramona's arm and yanked her into her arms, hugging her tight. "You deserve this," she whispered in her ear.

Ramona could only nod.

"Okay," April said, releasing her best friend and taking a deep breath. "The real question is . . . will Dylan Monroe allow me to tattoo her ass?"

"Oh my god, Apes," Ramona said, but she laughed. She felt better, as she knew she would. For all of April's persistence, she was also Ramona's fiercest champion, ever since the fourth grade when April and her parents moved to Clover Lake. On her first day of school, April had promptly shoved Caden Haskins to the mulched ground during recess for stealing Ramona's swing.

They'd been best friends ever since, through Olive's birth and April's struggles to relate to her stoic parents, through April's beloved grandmother's death when she was ten, through Rebecca's abandonment and Steven's accident and Olive's preteen moodiness.

April was Ramona's person, and she couldn't imagine ever being away from her.

And LA . . . well, it was far, far away.

She shook off the thought, shook off Olive leaving, the idea of her father being all alone, shook off anything but right here, right now.

"Seriously, though, I need a plan," she said. "In writing."

"You and your plans."

"I'm a *designer*."

April grinned. "You sure as shit are."

Ramona rolled her eyes, but took her iPad out of her bag and flipped open the folio, slipped her Apple Pencil out of its slot, tapped on her Notes app.

"Okay, Dylan wants to play Putt-Putt," she said, writing it down as number one.

"Putt-Putt?"

"Yes, Putt-Putt. But I think the new course will be too crowded, especially in the summer."

She met April's eye and they both grinned.

"Dickie's," they both said at the same time.

Dickie's was Clover Lake's first Putt-Putt course, just on the outside of town. It was run-down and featured creepy clowns on a lot of the holes, along with all manner of plastic animatronics covered in moss. Dickie, the owner, refused to close when the new course opened near downtown, and the result was a cult classic attraction that was mostly frequented by high teenagers.

"Dickie's is perfect," Ramona said, when a knock sounded on the door.

"Ramona?" Dylan called from the other side.

Ramona turned and flung open the door, her stomach swooping to her feet when she saw Dylan's face. Not only because she was a very famous person just, *right there*, but because god, she was pretty.

"Hey," Ramona said.

"Sorry to interrupt," Dylan said, then jutted her thumb toward the shop. "Molly needs to go."

"Oh, shitballs," April said, scrambling up from where she was leaning again on the desk and opening the small closet, grabbing a couple of packages of wrapping. "Thanks, Dyl." Then she was out the door, waxing apologetically to her customer.

Dylan's eyes followed her out, a smile on her face. "Already have a nickname. I like her."

Ramona laughed. "She loves her nicknames."

"What's yours?"

"What isn't my nickname?" Ramona said. "Ray is her go-to. Mona when she really wants to annoy me. Ona."

"Using all syllables, I see."

"She very resourceful. Nothing wasted."

Dylan's eyes sparkled. "What else?"

"Ra, Ram, Llama Face, Am—"

"Wait, wait, wait," Dylan said, holding up her hand. "Llama Face?"

Ramona fought a smile. "Pretend I didn't say that?"

"Oh, absolutely not."

Ramona dropped her chin to her chest, cursing how easy it was to talk to Dylan. "Then can I at least defer any questions until a later time?" she asked. She tapped her iPad screen. "I'm making us a plan."

Dylan narrowed her eyes. "I won't forget Llama Face."

"I would never expect you to."

Dylan folded her arms. "Fine, then. What's the plan?"

Ramona breathed a sigh of relief—no need to bring Llama Face into all this quite yet. She waved Dylan over to the bright green pleather love seat in the corner, and they both sat, the iPad balanced between them. "I've got a Putt-Putt option."

"Dickie's?" Dylan read from the screen. "That's bound to be incredible."

"It is," Ramona said. "Just wait."

"I trust you." Dylan nudged her shoulder, and Ramona fought against a flutter in her stomach.

"What else?" Dylan said.

Ramona wrote *Moon Lovers hike* on number two of her bulleted list.

"Moon Lovers?" Dylan asked.

"It's a great trail. Lesser traveled during the day because it doesn't go around the lake, so we shouldn't run into a ton of people."

No need to mention that Moon Lovers Trail was also a local legend, that any couple who walked its path under a full moon—which draped the trail in a silvery glow at its height—would fall in love and live happily ever after. His junior year of high school, Owen took the girl he had a crush on for a moonlit walk, and they've been married for twenty-six years.

"Sounds perfect," Dylan said.

"You mentioned bowling, but I wonder if that would be too complicated," Ramona said.

She explained that there was only one bowling alley in town, and it was constantly busy with professional leagues and families sending gutter balls down the lanes, especially during the summer.

"Hmm," Dylan said, tapping her chin. "I've never bowled before."

Ramona dropped her pencil against the screen. "We should make a list of things you *have* done."

Dylan laughed. "That's a long list too, only filled with scandalous shenanigans I would shield you from. Though you've probably read about them."

Ramona said nothing, because honestly, she probably had. She wrote *Bowling* with a question mark on number three. Her cursor blinked on number four, mind whirring for ideas, things Dylan had said she wanted to do.

Swim at a quiet spot in the lake. I bet you know all the secret places, don't you?

And just like that, all she could think about was Mirror Cove, where she and Dylan had first met. First laughed. First kissed. Well, their only kiss, she supposed. Their only anything.

"I think three is enough for now," she said, closing the folio over her iPad. "We can think of more later."

"I like that plan," Dylan said.

Ramona nodded, but she couldn't get rid of the knot in her throat. She needed a second, a few actually, and probably had to get back to the diner anyway. She was technically still on shift.

"Hey, Dyl," April said, appearing in the doorway. "Allow me to show you a cornucopia of options for a tattoo on your ass."

Dylan laughed, but immediately popped up and headed into the workspace. April winked at Ramona on her way out, and Ramona had never felt so thankful for her best friend in all her life. She collapsed back against the couch and let her mind wander through memories of a night she hardly ever let herself think about anymore.

Chapter Six

EIGHTEEN YEARS AGO

BABY OLIVE WAS still screaming when Ramona closed the door of her house behind her, the July night thick and sweet around her, but she hardly noticed it.

She just needed out.

Guilt tightened in her chest as Olive's cries crew fainter, Ramona's feet hurrying down the sidewalk in the dark, tears already starting to race down her cheeks. She'd held them in all day—well, for the last two weeks, really, except for at night when she was finally in her room alone and her dad wouldn't see her cry. Her dad, who'd been walking around like a ghost, wandering from room to room with Olive in his arms since Ramona's mom left, as though looking for something he'd misplaced.

Go, he'd told her tonight.

He'd taken the last thirteen days off work—vacation time to try to put his family back together—but he'd had to return today, as his landscaping business didn't make money unless he finished projects. Which meant Ramona had been with Olive all day, the normally docile six-month-old now inconsolable, a tiny, wailing litmus test measuring the stress in the house.

Go, Dad had said after they had dinner. Ramona had made boxed mac and cheese again and ate very little of it, as though her appetite had left with her mother. When Olive started crying in her highchair and slung her tiny bowl of mashed carrots onto the floor, splattering orange all over the hardwoods and nearby wall, Ramona had made a mistake—she'd shoved her hands into her own hair, fingers closing tightly and pulling at her scalp.

And her dad had seen it.

Go, he'd said.

Ramona had shaken her head. At thirteen, she didn't think she'd ever *go* anywhere ever again.

But her dad had reached across the table and taken her hand, his brown eyes red from lack of sleep. *Baby, go. Go find some fun.*

And so she had, though *fun* wasn't really on her agenda. She knew exactly where she was heading the moment she stepped out of her house. She knew her friends would be at the main beach, grilling hot dogs and getting ready for fireworks, but April was on a trip with her parents in Maine—they took one every July—and Ramona couldn't handle everyone else's sad glances and whispers.

Her mom just left.

Can you believe it?

Do you think they saw it coming?

No, Ramona was just fine being alone tonight. Quiet, that's what she really wanted. Space to cry, maybe even scream a little.

She speed walked down the sidewalk toward downtown, but right when the lights started to glow in front of her, she veered left, through the Abernathys' yard and into the woods. She used a tiny flashlight on her keys to guide her way, though she could've navigated Moon Lovers Trail with her eyes closed.

Soon, she headed off the trail and into an unmarked section of the woods, dodging bushes and fallen limbs, the earth sloping downward now until it spilled her out onto a tiny slice of beach.

A cove, surrounded by trees.

Mirror Cove, the locals called it, as the water here was usually very still and clear, reflecting the sky. Hardly anyone ever came here to swim or hang out, because the lake floor was rocky, and the beach wasn't the easiest to get to. Ramona wasn't surprised to find she was the only one here.

She tumbled onto the beach, her limbs immediately relieved of stress and purpose. She plopped onto the sand, tucked her knees to her chest, and waited for the tears to release. They took a while to come out of hiding, her body slow to realize it was safe. But they finally flowed, warm and salty, almost a comfort, as though her heart was setting down a burden.

After a few minutes of this, she reached into her back pocket and pulled out a piece of notebook paper, crudely torn from one of her school spirals. She'd been carrying it around for weeks now, so the paper was soft as a blanket, creased and wrinkled from how many times she'd folded and unfolded it, eyes scanning the few words inside for anything new.

Anything that made sense.

I'm sorry, Ramona. Take care of them for me.

That was it. That was all her own mother had written to her, set on her daughter's neatly made bed the day she'd left. She'd packed everything—her entire closet, her jewelry, even some kitchenware she liked, a few candles from the living room—then taken off during the day while Ramona was at school and Steven was at work. She'd asked their neighbor Sally Ryerson, who worked from home as an editor, to watch Olive.

She had an emergency, she'd said to Sally.

She'd left behind every single framed family photo.

More tears spilled over as Ramona remembered coming home

from school to an empty house, a few odd things missing, then finding this note on her bed. She'd rushed to her parents' bedroom, some part of her already knowing what she'd find when she flung open their closet door.

One side empty, nothing but swaying hangers where all her mother's beautiful clothes used to be, drifting like fashionable ghosts.

She folded up the letter now, put it back in her pocket, only to fish it out five minutes later, starting the whole process again. She wondered, not for the first time, if her dad had gotten a letter. If she'd left one for Olive. Ramona didn't dare ask him—she wasn't sure she wanted the answer either way.

She stuffed the letter into her pocket for the fourth time, hugged her knees tighter to her chest, and looked up at the sky. It was a clear night, the moon not quite full, the stars bright and hopeful. Fireworks would be starting soon, she knew, shot off from a boat near the main beach's shoreline. She'd have a good view here, not that she was really in the mood for—

"Oh wow, this place is pretty."

A voice.

Another person.

Ramona looked to the right, dread filling her chest, and spotted a shadow emerging from the path that circled the lake toward the main beach.

A girl.

Around her age, she thought, though she'd never seen her before. A summer person, then, the vacationers who all but took over the town from May to September every year.

"Hi," the girl said. She was skinny—too skinny even, like she hadn't eaten a decent meal in a while—and wore cutoff jean shorts and a black tank top with the word *Halcyon* printed on the front in turquoise text. She sucked on a lollipop, her lips shiny with sugar in the moonlight.

"Um. Hi," Ramona said as the girl came closer and then plopped down in the sand next to Ramona, as though they were old friends.

Ramona scowled.

The girl sucked on her lollipop and smiled.

"Are you lost?" Ramona asked.

The girl shrugged. "Maybe. Probably."

Ramona had no clue what to do with that.

"What's your name?" the girl asked, then grabbed Ramona's arm before she could answer. "Wait, don't tell me. Let's make up names for each other. You can be . . ." Her eyes roamed Ramona's face, then slid down to her shirt. "Cherry." She grinned.

Ramona stared at her for a few seconds, trying to figure out how to play this. She just wanted to be alone. Just wanted to cry and feel sorry for herself before she had to go back home and pretty much be a mom to her baby sister.

But as the girl smiled at her, Ramona caught sight of her eyes in the moonlight—the lightest green, like the pictures she'd seen of those icebergs in the Arctic. Her hair was short, cut to her shoulders, and a milk chocolate color.

Her eyes though . . . it wasn't just the color, but the look underneath them too.

Dark circles.

Her cheeks a bit hollowed out.

The girl looked haunted, her ghosts trailing behind her even, but she smiled and sucked on that lollipop—Ramona got a whiff of the sour apple flavor—and suddenly Ramona smiled too.

The first smile she'd managed in two weeks. The first real one, at least.

She even laughed, unbidden and surprising, the sound like a rusty gate opening for the first time in years.

"Okay," she said. "You can be Lollipop."

"Lolli," the girl said.

"Perfect."

The girl—Lolli—nudged her shoulder with her own, and Ramona felt a tiny swoop through her belly. She felt a lot of things all at once, actually—there was the smiling, of course, but there was also a sort of relief, because Lolli seemed just as hungry as Ramona. Not for food, but for . . . *something*.

Understanding, maybe.

Camaraderie.

Someone who *got* it.

And with that haunted look in Lolli's eyes, Ramona knew Lolli got it. She didn't have to explain it. She didn't have to tell her sob story about her mother, and she didn't need to hear Lolli's.

They just got to *be*, right here, right now, under the moon and the stars, with their fake names and laughter and that lollipop.

Ramona didn't realize how much she was craving that until this moment—just *being*. Since her mother left, even April, who could turn any situation into some sort of party, watched her with wary eyes, as though she was always waiting for Ramona to fall apart.

Lolli smiled at her, her shoulder still pressed to Ramona's, and Ramona felt another feeling right then too. She'd been thinking about it a lot before her mother left, for over a year maybe, but in the last two weeks, she hadn't had any room to process it, this . . . wondering.

About girls.

About how back in the fall, she couldn't stop thinking about Nala Young. They'd done an English project together on Emily Dickinson, and it was all fine and they'd gotten an A, but afterward, Ramona kept daydreaming about Nala's curly black hair and the little freckle above her top lip, the way her jeans fit on a certain day or the curve of her shoulder in a tank top.

It was exciting and confusing, because maybe Ramona wished her own thighs looked like that in a pair of jeans or that her hair had a little more curl to it . . . but the butterflies in her belly every time

Nala said hey or sat down between Ramona and April in the cafeteria said otherwise.

They said Ramona had a crush.

She knew the signs, had felt them for Wesley Branson in seventh grade, and Ashton Lee in sixth. Nala was the first girl though, and she wasn't quite sure what to do with all those feelings.

So she did nothing

Didn't even tell April.

Didn't tell her mom.

She just waited, letting herself think through it, feel through it, see if it passed.

Nala moved away this past spring, back to her mom's hometown in Georgia, and Ramona waited for the thoughts and wonderings to go away too.

But they didn't. She still *thought*. Still *wondered*.

And now, here was Lolli, a girl with ice-green eyes and a hungry heart, just like Ramona's, and those butterflies were suddenly in full flight again.

Ramona looked away from Lolli, out at the moon sprinkling silver over the lake. She tried to breathe through those silly butterflies, get them to go to sleep.

"You visiting here too?" Lolli asked.

Ramona opened her mouth to say the truth, but "yeah" came out instead. She wasn't sure why. Maybe she just didn't want to live in her real life tonight—she'd come here to cry, but found a kindred spirit instead, and she just wanted to be Cherry tonight.

Lolli nodded. "It's nice in this town. Wish I lived here all the time." She tucked her knees to her chest, rested her chin on top, looked out at the water too.

Ramona wanted to ask her why. Ask where she lived during the year, but she had a feeling Lolli didn't want to answer those questions any more than Ramona did.

They sat there in silence for a bit. It wasn't even awkward, their shoulders still touching, like they'd known each other for years and years.

"Do you ever wish you could be someone else?" Lolli asked.

"Like Lolli?" Ramona asked.

Lolli smiled, but there was a sadness in her eyes. "Yeah. Like Lolli. Or . . . I don't know. Molly. Polly." She started to laugh then.

"Holly," Ramona said.

"Dolly."

"*Hello, Dolly*," Ramona sang. The high school had just done the musical, and Ramona had designed a set of costumes for the show. Of course, no one knew about them—they were hidden away in her sketchbook.

"You sing pretty," Lolli said.

Ramona laughed. "I don't."

"You do!" Lolli said, then got to her feet, crunched her lollipop, and then stuck the bare stick into her pocket before taking Ramona's hands and pulling her up too. "Let's be someone else tonight."

"Aren't we already?" Ramona asked. Lolli's hands were warm in hers, but soft. Gentle.

Lolli nodded. "Anyone we want. Keep singing."

"What?" Ramona said, laughing.

"You're a singer tonight. A famous Broadway actor."

Ramona shook her head, but she couldn't stop smiling. She liked singing and could carry a tune, but nothing close to a future Broadway star. Still, Lolli's excitement was contagious, infecting her bones and blood and heart, and she loved it. She never wanted a remedy for this.

"What should I sing?"

"Keep singing what you were. That funny song."

Lolli spread their arms out, fingers still laced, then held them like that, staring at Ramona with those eyes until she started singing.

Ramona laughed again, her face ablaze, but she cleared her throat and sang the classic Louis Armstrong tune.

> *Hello, Dolly.*
> *Well, hello, Dolly.*
> *It's so nice to have you back where you belong.*

As Ramona sang, Lolli lit up. She grinned and danced, as though she were Dolly herself, swinging Ramona around in a circle on the sand as she moved, always holding on to at least one of her hands. When Ramona came around to *You're still glowin', you're still crowin'*, Lolli put one hand behind her head, prancing and really hamming it up to the point that Ramona could barely sing anymore she was laughing so hard.

"I think you really are Dolly," Ramona said.

"I think I might be," Lolli said, then grinned before slowing down to look at Ramona. "And who are you?"

"I'm Cherry," Ramona said, plucking at her shirt with her free hand.

"Who are you really, though?"

Ramona blinked, a myriad of words spilling into her brain. *Sister. Friend. Daughter. Artist.*

Motherless.

Queer...?

She'd heard the word before, of course had heard *gay* and *lesbian* and even *bisexual*, though she'd had to go hunting for that one on the internet.

"I don't think I really know yet," she finally said.

Lolli nodded. "Yeah. Me neither."

They looked at each other for a few seconds, interrupted only when a flurry of color erupted into the sky.

"Oh my god," Lolli said, her mouth dropping open at the sight.

She kept hold of Ramona's hand but turned to face the display. When she spoke, her voice was dreamy. "I've never seen these, you know."

"You've never seen fireworks?"

Lolli just shook her head, and Ramona could swear her eyes were a little watery.

Ramona squeezed her hand.

Lolli squeezed back.

Another explosion rocketed into the sky, this one silver and gold and sprinkling down like a willow tree.

"When my best friend and I see fireworks that look like that," Ramona said, pointing to the drizzling color against the black night, "we yell out, '*Willow!*'"

Lolli laughed. "Willow?"

"For the willow tree shape it makes."

Lolli turned back toward the show, watching as more colors lit the sky. When that willow tree silhouette appeared again, she glanced at Ramona.

Ramona smiled.

"Willow!" they both yelled, holding out the *ow* sound. They did this over and over again, just like Ramona and April always did, until they were dancing around in the sand, screaming, "*Willow!*" into the night like a battle cry. It was silly and perfect and it seemed to light Lolli up from the inside. Maybe Ramona imagined it, but she didn't look quite as lost as before.

And Ramona didn't feel quite as alone.

Soon, the finale burst into the air, one blast of color after another, the *pop-pop-pop* echoing in their ears. They stood side by side holding hands, and when it was done, Lolli laughed and turned toward Ramona.

"That was amazing," she said.

Ramona nodded. "It was."

They kept looking at each other, and Ramona felt it again—that swoop in her belly, a wave cresting. She would've looked away by now with anyone else, but with Lolli . . . there was a freedom with her. A rightness.

A *knowing*.

"You're . . . you're really pretty," Ramona said, her voice so quiet she barely heard herself.

But Lolli heard her. She smiled softly, lashes dropping to her cheeks for a second before lifting back, her eyes searching Ramona's.

"Really?" she asked.

Ramona nodded.

"You are too," Lolli said.

Ramona didn't know if that was actually true, but it felt true right then. She believed Lolli believed it, and it made her feel light and airy, a gauzy curtain blowing in a summer breeze.

The two of them moved closer, and Lolli put a hand on Ramona's waist . . . then another. Ramona's hands were drifting free then, but she wanted to touch Lolli's face—that too-thin, lovely face that had smiled so much tonight.

So she did.

Her hand shook as she moved it to Lolli's cheek, but she didn't stop, because Lolli smiled again and leaned into her palm. Ramona brought her other hand up, thumbs swiping gently at Lolli's cheekbones.

They were so close.

Then closer.

And then their lips touched.

Gentle and sweet, like a whisper.

Ramona felt her whole body light up, like glitter, like a firework, like happiness. They bumped noses, and laughed, and then kept kissing, figuring each other out, and it was weird and wonderful and awkward and perfect. When they finally pulled away, they laughed again, then kissed again, and it went like that for a few minutes, a dreamy cycle Ramona couldn't believe was really happening.

But it was.

And it was everything she'd dreamed her first kiss would be like. No, it was better. She knew not everyone got to say that. April's was with Jared Lassiter at the high school's homecoming football game this past fall, and he had pizza breath and tried to take out her eye with his tongue, in April's own words.

This was nothing like pizza breath and a tongue sword.

This was sour apple sugar and sparklers and summer.

"So that's what all the fuss is about," Lolli said, lacing her fingers with Ramona's and holding their hands out wide.

Ramona's breath caught for the millionth time that night. "That was your first time too?"

Lolli laughed. "I haven't even seen fireworks before. You think I just go around kissing cute girls all the time?"

Ramona laughed too, shrugged. "I don't know. You seem cool enough that you might've."

Lolli shook her head. "First time."

Ramona grinned. "First time."

"Dolly's still crowin', I guess," Lolli said as she pressed her finger into the single dimple on Ramona's left cheek.

Ramona smiled, then laughed so hard she knew her muscles would be sore tomorrow. Lolli laughed too and spun them around and around in a circle, the stars twirling above them, their giggles joining in with the gentle sound of the lake lapping at the shore, the cicadas in the woods behind them.

"Dylan?"

The word—the *name*—cut through the night, their dancing and laughter.

"Dylan, where are you?"

Lolli stopped spinning, her head turning toward the voice. A woman emerged from the trail. She was tall and curvy, had long brown hair down to her waist, and wore a sundress that hit at her knees.

"Good lord, there you are," she said, pressing her hand to her chest. She wore several gold chains of different lengths, and they shimmered in the moonlight. "Why did you disappear like that? Don't you know how dangerous that is?"

"Sorry, Aunt Hallie," Lolli said.

Aunt Hallie shook her head, took a deep breath. "It's okay. But, baby girl, there are rules with me. You know that."

"I know," Lolli said. She was still holding one of Ramona's hands, fingers all tangled up together.

"And who is this?" Aunt Hallie asked, walking a bit closer to get a better look at Ramona. Her eyes were careworn but gentle, her voice soft but firm.

Ramona opened her mouth, her name on the tip of her tongue because Aunt Hallie did not seem like an adult who would put up with any kind of fake name, but Lolli spoke first.

"That's Cherry," she said. "She's visiting Clover Lake too."

Aunt Hallie nodded, slid her eyes down to their joined hands. Ramona waited for Lolli to pull away, but she didn't. She even squeezed tighter.

And Aunt Hallie's gaze softened.

"I see," she said. "I'm glad you met a friend, honey, but we have to go. We're leaving tomorrow and we haven't even started packing. Your room's a disaster. And I'm sure Cherry needs to get back to her family too. It's late."

Family.

The word cut through Ramona's heart, fast like a flash of lightning.

She had no idea how long she'd even been out here. Her dad was probably wondering where she was, the fireworks long over.

But her mom wasn't. Her mom didn't care at all.

Her throat knotted up, tears threatening, but then Lolli turned back toward her, and she felt herself relax. It was short-lived though, because this was it. Lolli was leaving tomorrow, and Ramona didn't even know when she'd be back, where she lived, what her real name was.

Dylan.

That's what her aunt had said, but Ramona didn't dare use it. Lolli hadn't wanted her to know it.

They were Lolli and Cherry.

"Well," Lolli said. "I guess I've got to go."

Ramona nodded, looking down at their entwined hands. "Yeah."

"I'll let you two say goodbye," Aunt Hallie said. "I'll be right over here." She motioned toward the path back to the main beach, then disappeared into the shadows of the tree-thick trail.

"This was . . ." Lolli said, but trailed off, her voice wobbling right before she kissed Ramona one more time, her mouth hard and trembling.

Then, before Ramona could get a word out, kiss her back, or even hug her, Lolli pulled away and pressed her finger into Ramona's dimple again, then turned and ran toward the shadows, and was gone.

Chapter Seven

DYLAN SAT ON the cream-colored couch in the lake house Laurel had rented for her, going over the first scene they'd be filming today, when a hand jutted her phone into her face.

Jack flashed across the screen.

"Jesus, no," Dylan said.

"He's been calling since six a.m.," Laurel said. "And I'm going back to LA this afternoon, so you've got to handle your phone again."

"Can't you just get me a flip phone?"

"No. Put on your big-girl panties."

Dylan stuck out her tongue at her manager, and Laurel—already resplendent in a pair of white shorts and a sleeveless silk blouse—just smiled.

"Love you," she singsonged, then dropped the still-buzzing phone on top of the script in Dylan's lap and walked away.

Dylan closed her eyes, counted to three. In that time, the phone stopped ringing, only to start up again a second later.

"Goddammit," Dylan whispered, then slid her finger across the screen. "Dad, hi."

"Hey, Dill Pickle, how's my girl?" her father said.

Dylan opened her mouth to answer, but Jack Monroe barreled onward.

"I've got Mom here too," he said.

"You're on speaker!" Carrie Page trilled, her voice pleasantly raspy from spending the nineties sucking on a pack a day. "You ready for your first big scene? We sent you some flowers. Did you get them yet?"

Dylan sighed, already exhausted, then made her voice as cheery as possible. "No, not yet."

"Oh, that's disappointing," Carrie said. "I asked for them to get there by nine. You're starting at ten, yes?"

Dylan didn't even know how her parents had this information. She certainly hadn't told them. Though they were Jack Monroe and Carrie Page—they could pretty much find out whatever they wanted about anyone at any time. Jack's band, Evenflow, was one of the most popular bands of the nineties, grunge rock, as they called it then. Jack and his best friend, Aaron, started the group in Aaron's parents' garage in Marietta, Georgia, when they were seventeen, then soared to stardom after moving to Seattle when the rock scene was exploding in 1991. He met Carrie on tour—her angry-girl band, Halcyon, opened for Evenflow—and the rest was history.

A very wild, very fraught history.

By the time Dylan came along four years later, Jack and Carrie were only twenty-three and internationally famous, had no permanent home—just popped in and out of luxury hotels—and were only a few short years from their first joint stint in rehab, though Carrie had managed to stay clean while she was pregnant with Dylan.

Now, Dylan knew neither of her parents had touched a single drop of alcohol or drugs in ten years, and she was proud of them for that, but her childhood was filled with lines of coke on glass coffee tables and hotel suites packed with fans and fellow musicians until two a.m. Her aunt, Hallie, had taken her in a few times—when her parents were in rehab, or when Hallie had heard enough horror stories and took Dylan back to Georgia with her, but she never sued for custody. She'd always hoped her brother would get it together, always believed when he said he had.

By the time Dylan was twenty, her parents had already been through a divorce and another breakup, only to get married again when she was twenty-five. Now, they were living in Laurel Canyon and grew avocados, acted like eternal newlyweds, and seemed to be attempting to make up for their past shitty parenting. They called and texted Dylan all the time, asked about her life way too damn much, and made sure she knew they *believed in her* and thought she was *the most beautiful and talented girl on the planet.*

"Yes, ten o'clock," Dylan said now. "In fact, I should get going."

"Of course, sweetie," Carrie said. "Have you seen Blair yet?"

"How did you even know Blair was—" Dylan started but stopped herself. There was no point. "No, I haven't," she said instead, leaving out her run-in with her costar at the café.

"Well, it's going to be fine," Carrie said. "We believe in you."

"You're the most beautiful and talented girl on the planet," Jack said.

Dylan blew out a long breath. "Thanks. I've got to go."

"Good luck!" her parents chimed together. "We love—"

But Dylan hit the red button before they could finish their saccharine chorus, then flopped back onto the couch, blinking up at the bamboo ceiling fan as she took deep breaths.

In for four . . .

Hold . . .

Out for eight.

Just like her therapist, Eli, had told her to do whenever she felt like she wanted to scream and cuss and throw her phone against a wall.

Her parents often had that effect on her, a feeling that also brought a wave of guilt with it. Jack and Carrie loved her. She knew that. And she should be grateful. She just had a hard time reconciling her current parents with the parents of her past. Eli called it *repressed anger*, called it justified. They also called it something Dylan needed to deal with—*repressed* rarely meant anything healthy—but she had no idea how the hell to do that, not when every piece of her life had been shaped by Jack and Carrie's decisions and fame.

Or infamy, as the case may be.

Her phone buzzed in her lap. She groaned, knowing what she would see before she even looked—a text featuring a Bitmoji of both her parents shooting her a thumbs-up with the words *You got this* arcing over their cartoon heads in rainbow letters.

TWO HOURS LATER, Dylan's hair was in a messy fishtail braid, and she was wearing a pink sleeveless blouse tucked into high-waisted denim shorts, a yellow apron with curated grease stains tied around her hips. Her makeup was subtle and her shoes were sensible.

She was Eloise Tucker, small-town waitress who grew up in a tiny apartment on the outside of town with an unreliable mother and dreamed of opening her own flower shop. She was quiet and cerebral, knew the meanings of every single flower in creation, and was a terrible driver.

So, pretty much the complete opposite of Dylan. All except the *unreliable mother* part, an experience Dylan had zero clue how to tap into for theatrical fodder. Now, she stood in the grassy town square with its adorable white gazebo as Noelle Yang and her assistant debated whether or not her apron needed a smear of mustard.

"I think the more, the better," the assistant, Vee, said. They had pale skin, and their pixie-cut hair was such a light strawberry blond it was nearly pink. "It says she's exhausted."

Noelle, a designer famous for her attention to detail, tapped her red mouth. Her straight salt-and-pepper hair hit her shoulders, cut so bluntly Dylan thought the ends might slice a finger open if touched. She wore all black—simple jeans and a tee—and her entire air was elegance and style and just fucking *cool*. Dylan would be intimidated if Noelle weren't also extremely gentle and calm and snorted when she laughed.

"I think you're right," Noelle said. "You good with that, Dylan?"

"Oh, sure," Dylan said.

"Great," Noelle said, then tapped away on her iPad as Vee finger-painted a blob of yellow mustard near Dylan's hip. "Then we're a go. Yes, that means I'm finished."

It took Dylan a second to realize Noelle was speaking into her headset, which also meant it was time. Butterflies swelled into her stomach, an entire swarm. She smoothed her apron, but then came away with a bit of mustard on her fingers.

"Oh, that's okay, that's okay," Vee said, fluttering around her with a napkin. "Gives it a good smeared look."

Dylan nodded, smiled. She would not be the high-maintenance actress on this set, she would *not*, but god she hated mustard. The smell alone triggered her gag reflex.

"You good?" Laurel said, sidling up next to her, phone out. She eyed the mustard Vee was currently wiping away.

Dylan could only nod, the scent lingering on her fingers making her regret not having any breakfast.

"Just channel your inner small town," Laurel said. "You'll be fine."

Dylan said nothing, as Laurel knew full well Dylan had no inner small town. She'd been to this particular small town once in her life and barely remembered it because she couldn't stop worrying about her parents, who had been just about a month away from entering rehab. At the time, she only knew that something was very wrong with them, and she'd gone far too many days without an actual meal when Aunt Hallie came and picked her up. All she really had to pull from was an inner fucked-up kid of rock icons. Where was the rom-com for that character?

She sighed, pressed her hands to her stomach. She was an actor. She could *be* anything, anyone. That was her job.

All around her people buzzed and barked orders. She hadn't seen Gia Santos, the director, yet. Nor had she seen Blair, but they were filming a conversation between their characters that took place several scenes into the movie. At this point in the story, Mallory, Blair's character, had just arrived in town for the summer at her family's lake house and run into Eloise—the girl she'd loved for many summers as a teen, then lost touch with after she went to college—at the diner, and she'd already begged Eloise to pretend to be her girl-friend to satisfy Mallory's wealthy parents, who hesitated to trust her with the family's publishing business unless Mallory settled down and *got serious.*

Dylan would much prefer to start filming with the meet-cute—at least then she could build up the feelings and emotions alongside Eloise—but Gia wanted this scene first, where the two women meet at the town gazebo to go over plans for a boat party Mallory's family was throwing, their maiden voyage as a fake couple.

We want to establish chemistry straightaway is what Gia had written in the film itinerary.

So not only did Dylan have to figure out how to smile at Blair after so many years of, let's be real, *enmity*, she also had to flirt with her. Be shy and uncertain. Laugh with her eyes sparkling. Lower her lashes in that way that Ramona did when Dylan had made her laugh yesterday . . .

Dylan smiled, remembering those lashes. They were so long. And dark. She wondered if Ramona used mascara, or if—

"Dylan?"

She jolted from her thoughts as Laurel shook her arm. "They're ready for you. And I've got to go."

Dylan all but whined. "Do you have to?"

"I've got a partners' meeting I can't miss. I'll be back later this week."

"That's two days away."

"Big-girl panties."

Dylan sighed, then patted her hips. "Fine. I've got them on. Pulled all the way up."

"Careful, it's not a thong," Laurel said, and hugged Dylan tight before shoving her toward the gazebo, then took off through the grass in her three-inch heels, calling out, "Think small town!" as she went.

Dylan forced herself to keep moving, spotting Blair standing by the gazebo's stairs and laughing with Gia Santos, a tall woman with short black hair and thick, turquoise-rimmed glasses. Gia was a seasoned director and writer of rom-coms—she'd developed this script with the book's author—and was a lesbian married to cinematographer Zara Hollister, and was also famously demanding. She wanted what she wanted out of her actors, and exactly when she wanted it.

"Hi, there," Dylan said from a few feet away, and both women immediately stopped talking, aiming too-bright smiles in her direction.

Dylan caught a whiff of mustard, swallowed a gag.

"Dylan, hey, great, you're here," Gia said brusquely, shaking Dylan's hand with one soul-squeezing pump. "Let's get you both in the gazebo."

"Dylan," Blair said.

"Blair," Dylan said, hating the already-stilted tone to both of their voices. She rolled her shoulders back, tried to *think small town* and breathe normally as she settled on the white bench inside the gazebo next to Blair, but her stomach refused to un-clench.

Crew members swarmed, setting up the mics, getting the cameras adjusted to their positions. Vee came and blotted her face, then Blair's, then yanked some strands of hair out of Dylan's braid so they feathered around her face.

"Okay, thanks, Vee," Gia said.

Vee started to leave, but Dylan latched on to the assistant's wrist. "Stay," she whispered desperately. Vee's eyes widened and they fiddled with the strands of hair around Dylan's face a bit theatrically, but Dylan would take any delay she could get right now. So much for her big-girl panties.

"Vee, get out of there," Noelle said from where she was tapping on her iPad in the grass.

"Sorry," Vee whispered, then vanished.

Dylan's throat thickened, her heart galloping throughout her entire body.

"All right, I trust you're familiar with this scene," Gia said.

"Yes," Blair said.

Dylan could only nod.

"We need unsure and shy from you, Dylan," Gia said, adjusting her headset. "Blair, I know you missed the read-through, but I think you can handle it. Mallory is brash and full steam ahead. But with nuance. Be a *person*, not a character. Let's make our fellow queers proud, shall we?"

"Hell yes," Blair said, smiling and fist-bumping Gia.

Dylan just nodded again, like that fucking bobblehead version of herself she knew went for hundreds of dollars on eBay.

"Okay, let's do this," Gia said, then yelled, "Places!" as she jogged down the gazebo's steps, turning to face Dylan and Blair. Gia asked a few more questions of the camera crew, the sound, then Dylan heard the word "Action," and she completely forgot what she was doing.

What her name even was.

Blair said something—her line, Dylan presumed, but Dylan couldn't remember what it was or what she was supposed to say next.

"Cut," Gia said calmly, then simply stared at Dylan with her arms folded.

Dylan blinked, glanced at Blair, who also wore an annoyed expression.

"Sorry," Dylan said. "Just . . . warming up."

"*I don't know how this will work,*" Blair said.

"What?" Dylan asked.

"That's your first line," Blair said. She was dressed in white shorts that showed off her lovely brown legs, red Keds, and a silky blue-and-white polka-dotted tank top. Her hair was natural and curly and fanning out around her face. She was a perfectly posh Mallory.

Because of course she was.

"Right," Dylan said. "Yeah. Good. Thanks."

Blair sighed.

Dylan felt like an idiot.

She shook her head, trying not to flash back to all the scenes she'd filmed with Blair on *Spellbound* that always seemed to include Blair sighing and Dylan feeling like an idiot.

"Again," Gia said. "Action."

"*I can't tell you how much I appreciate this,*" Blair said as Mallory, crossing her legs and tilting them toward Dylan.

"*I . . . yeah, I . . . um . . . I don't know.*"

"Cut," Gia said on a sigh. "Stick to the script, Dylan. You've got to earn the right to improvise." She looked down, scrolled through her iPad. "Jesus, I can't believe I let them . . ."

But the sound of her voice trailed off as she shook her head, then continued to mutter under her breath.

Dylan swallowed, her mouth completely dry, confidence shrinking like a prune under a summer sun. "Sorry."

"Take a second to review your lines," Gia said, scratching her forehead.

Dylan's whole body washed hot, then cold. It was clear that Gia wasn't her biggest fan, which did not bode well on the first damn day.

"Haven't you known about this role for months?" Blair asked.

Dylan didn't answer, just did as Gia told her and closed her eyes, running through her lines.

"I've known for two weeks," Blair said. "I wasn't even their first choice."

"And you know all your lines and mine," Dylan said. "Am I right?"

"You're right," Blair said, flicking a tiny bug off her arm.

"I know my lines," Dylan said. "I'm just nervous."

Blair pursed her mouth, didn't look at Dylan. "You get handed the role on a silver platter and still can't even appreciate it. Typical Dylan Monroe."

"What do you mean I got *handed*—"

"Let's go again," Gia said. "Action."

Dylan's spine snapped straight, like her teacher just slapped a ruler on her desk, the back-and-forth and sudden shifts making her dizzy.

"*I can't tell you how much I appreciate this,*" Blair said again, a wry smile on her mouth, Mallory in complete control.

"*I don't know how this will work,*" Dylan said, then wanted to pump her fists in the air in triumph.

She did it.

She said the damn line.

"Cut," Gia said.

"Fuck," Dylan said under her breath.

"Can we get a little less robot, more person?" Gia asked. "You know, *acting*?"

Blair blew out a breath through puffed cheeks.

Dylan slumped back against the bench, her prune-like confidence nothing but a dried-out seed at this point. It was going to be a very, very long day.

Chapter Eight

"HEY, YOU," RAMONA said when she came out of the diner's kitchen to see her sister sitting at the bar.

At this time of day, it wasn't unusual to find Olive and her best friend, Marley, at Clover Moon hunting free pie. Today was Decades Day for Grad Week, and Olive wore a black flapper dress, complete with fringe and sparkles, beaded straps curving over her toned shoulders. Ramona had designed and made it herself, as well as the band of bedazzled silk tied around Olive's head. They'd pinned her long hair underneath to create a faux bob, and her bright red lipstick was still firmly in place.

"Hey," Olive said, her attention on her phone, thumbs flying.

"Hey, Ramona," Marley said. Her short, dark blond hair was styled high and dyed a dark blue at the tips, and she had on a muscle tee and acid-washed jeans, and huge clomping combat boots. Ramona wasn't sure what decade she was supposed to be from—she was a baby butch every day of the year, so she didn't really look all that different aside from the blue hair flair.

"Pie?" Ramona said, setting two waters in front of them.

"What do you have?" Marley asked. Meaning what was Owen going to toss when they closed because it was already a day old.

Ramona surveyed the pie case. "Looks like peach and strawberry rhubarb."

"No honey whiskey?" Olive asked, not glancing up from her phone.

"You know we run through that like water," Ramona said. She grabbed a slice of each flavor and two forks, knowing the girls would share anyway. "Who are you talking to so furiously?" she asked Olive.

Olive's fingers froze, and Marley became very interested in a slice of peach that had fallen out of the pie and onto her plate.

"No one," Olive said.

Which meant someone, as everyone who spent any time with teenagers knew, and a major someone.

"A boy, huh?" Ramona said, and grinned.

"No," Olive said, hiding her phone in her lap.

"As long as it's not Jameson Reece," Ramona said. "That guy has frat boy written all over him. Am I right, Marley?"

"What?" Marley asked, blinking at Ramona like a baby dear. "Oh. Yeah. Sure." She went back to staring at her pie.

"It's not Jameson," Olive said.

"Henry?" Ramona said, still watching Marley as she shoveled pie into her mouth.

"Which one?" Marion asked as she passed behind them with three plates in her hands.

"Henry G.," Ramona said, laughing. "Henry W. is dating Elizabeth Ng."

"How do you know all this?" Olive asked. "I didn't even know that."

Ramona waved her hands at the dining room. "Behold, the gossip hall."

"You need a life," Olive deadpanned. "Desperately. How's that whole thing going?" She dug into the strawberry rhubarb pie, and

Ramona decided to let her evade the possible boy conversation for the moment.

"What thing?" Ramona asked.

Olive gave her a look. "The whole 'get a life' thing. Movies? Costumes?"

"Oh, are you trying to design for the movie?" Marley asked, finally coming to life.

"No," Ramona said, which was the truth.

"She's trying to not be such a sad sack," Olive said.

Ramona frowned, a little stung. "I'm not a sad sack." Though she realized knowing the dating lives of teenagers before her teenage sister in a small town was a wee bit sad.

"What's the designer's name?" Olive asked. "Noelle?"

"Shh," Ramona said, flapping her hands at her sister. "Gossip hall, remember?"

"April said you found a way in," Olive said, chewing and completely unfazed by all the buzzing townsfolk around her. "What is it?"

Ramona opened her mouth. Closed it. She was going to tattoo April in her sleep. Something awful like Tweety Bird or Mr. Burns from *The Simpsons*, right on her ass. And it would be awful because Ramona had no idea how to wield a tattoo gun.

"I didn't find a way—"

But before she could finish her sentence, the door flew open, bells jingling, and *her way in* walked into Clover Moon looking like she'd just barely escaped a pack of wild dogs. The cacophony of the dining room dimmed—not completely vanishing, but the volume definitely went down, all eyes taking in the woman in the doorway.

Dylan Monroe looked around, her shoulders clinging to her ears, but they dropped as soon as she spotted Ramona.

Ramona's stomach flipped and flopped, and she pressed a hand to her diaphragm, as though the pressure could force it to calm down.

"Hey, good, you're here," Dylan said, approaching the counter. Her hair was in a messy fishtail braid, flyaways all over her face, and she wore a food-splattered apron Ramona would never have allowed into a dining room, along with a sweet pink top. Ramona assumed this was part of Dylan's costuming, and she had to admit, the star looked pretty cute all harried and, well, small town–ish.

"Hi," Ramona said. The conversation around them finally started up again, though Olive and Marley stared at Dylan unabashedly, their mouths hanging open. "How'd your first day go?"

Dylan groaned. "I need coffee. And chocolate. Preferably at the same time. Through an IV if you've got it."

Ramona laughed. "I can take care of the first two."

"That'll have to do, I guess," Dylan said, climbing onto a stool next to Olive, who was still gaping like a fish along with Marley.

Dylan turned her head slowly to look at them. "Hello. Nice costumes."

"Holy shit," Marley said.

Dylan pressed her lips together, suppressing a laugh. "Well . . . holy shit to you too."

Ramona grinned. "Olive, Marley, this is—"

"Dylan Monroe," Olive said.

Dylan pointed two finger guns at her, and Olive's cheeks bloomed red.

"Dylan, this is my sister, Olive, and her best friend, Marley."

Marley stuck out her hand. "I'm gay."

"Smooth," Ramona said.

But Dylan just laughed and shook Marley's hand. "Hi, gay, I'm bisexual."

"I've never been so disappointed to be straight," Olive said dreamily, shaking Dylan's hand too.

Dylan tilted her head. "That sentiment might be a sign you're not."

Olive's eyes went wide, and she glanced at Ramona, who just

winked at her as she dished up some pie for Dylan. While Clover Lake was small and packed with heteros, Olive's circle was overwhelmingly queer—Marley, Ramona, April, and her softball coach Jasmine and her wife, Sarah, who was also Olive's AP English teacher. Olive had never expressed much interest in any gender other than boys, but this kind of stuff was fluid, Ramona knew full well. She just wanted Olive to be happy, to know herself and be proud of who she was, no matter who that turned out to be.

"Things to ponder," Marley said softly, nudging Olive's shoulder, her eyes cast down as she did so, cheeks a little pink.

"Hmm," Dylan said, looking between the two teens. "Indeed." Then she took a deep breath and dived into the thick slice of mocha silk pie Ramona had set in front of her. "Anyway, today sucked, and I'd like to forget my own name, thanks."

"Not much chance of that," Ramona said.

Dylan groaned again. "Maybe not, but oh my god, this pie."

"Right?" Marley said. "Owen makes the best pie."

"I made that one," Ramona said.

"Did you?" Dylan asked.

Ramona nodded, her cheeks warming, her own eyes locked on Dylan's. Looking at Dylan was like looking at art—those Pointillism paintings made up of a million tiny dots, so intricate, you could spend hours just staring, getting lost, trying to make sense of how it all came together so perfectly.

She shook her head. Looked away.

"Can you teach me?" Dylan asked.

Ramona looked back at her—dammit, it was hard not to look at someone when they were speaking to you. "Really?"

"I need all the small-town waitress help I can get."

Ramona felt something in her plummet. She knew Dylan didn't mean for it to sound so derogatory, but that's how it hit the center of Ramona's chest.

Just a waitress.

A sad sack.

"Yeah, sure," Ramona said, grabbing a towel and wiping down the counter for something to do. "I'll add it to our list."

"List?" Olive asked.

"Oh," Ramona said. "It's noth—"

"Your sister is helping me be a normal human being," Dylan said around a mouthful of pie.

Ramona pressed her eyes closed. The last thing she needed was Olive all tangled up in whatever she was doing with Dylan.

"Normal is overrated," Marley said.

"True," Dylan said, "but I'd still like to go bowling without attracting every paparazzo on the East Coast just waiting for me to, I don't know, throw my bowling ball into the vending machine or something."

Ramona just laughed, but Olive looked suddenly pensive, even tapping her fingers to her lips like she did when she was thinking hard.

Then her eyes went wide.

"No," Ramona said.

"What?" Olive said. "I didn't even speak yet."

"I know that look. Whatever it is, no."

"It's a good idea," Olive said.

"You've been hanging around April too much," Ramona said.

"Two words. Costume. Bowling," Olive said, flourishing her hand down her 1920s garb, then sat back and folded her arms triumphantly.

"Yes," Marley said, clapping once. "I'm in."

"Olive," Ramona said.

"You have a ton of costumes," Olive said, then waved her hand at Dylan. "Dress her up. Change her name like she wants!"

"Oh, I'm intrigued," Dylan said, then tilted her head at Ramona. "Costumes?"

"Clothes," Ramona said quickly, that guilty prick in her chest jabbing at her again. Still, they *were* clothes. "From when I was at RISD."

"Oh, yeah, apparel design," Dylan said, nodding.

Olive lifted her brow at Ramona but said nothing.

"What kinds of clothes?" Dylan asked. "The kind where I could go by, I don't know, *Dolly*, and have platinum blonde hair?"

Ramona's mouth dropped open, adrenaline flooding her system like someone just popped up from behind the counter and yelled *boo*. *Dolly*.

That night flashed back to her for the millionth time in the last thirty-six hours, the two of them young and hungry and dancing under the stars.

She got her breath back, watched Dylan for a second for any sign of recognition, but Dylan just smiled at her, eyebrows raised, waiting for Ramona to say something.

And she realized Dylan would never find Cherry in Ramona's face or voice or eyes. She wouldn't recognize anything about her, because Dylan probably didn't remember Dolly or Lolli or Cherry anyway, and Ramona had known that from the second Dylan walked through the door yesterday morning.

Why would she?

Why *should* she?

And now, eighteen years later, why shouldn't present-day Ramona take this opportunity in front of her? Grab it with both hands, fingers curled tight, and run with it all the way to Noelle Yang.

There *was* no reason. April was right. Dylan was *Dylan Monroe*, and she was a celebrity, child of icons, the topic of conversation wherever she went. At the end of the summer, she'd leave, never come back, and forget Ramona all over again.

But Ramona . . . Ramona would still be here, waiting tables at Clover Moon. And as much as she loved Clover Lake, she wanted more. Or different. She wanted both—her home and her dream. She wanted both so damn much. Hadn't realized how much until this very second, everything suddenly so clear—Olive leaving her soon, her father with his own life.

She needed her own life too. No matter how terrifying it was, no matter what she had to do to get it. Noelle fucking Yang was in her town. Here. In Clover Lake. Probably no more than a mile or two away at this very moment.

"You know what?" she said, tossing her towel onto the counter and literally sticking out her chest a little. "Let's go costume bowling."

⌒〜

DYLAN MONROE WAS in Ramona's room.

It was strange, even more strange than walking with the famous child of rock icons through the woods or helping her brew coffee. This was Ramona's space, the place where she'd even dreamed about Dylan—well, of *Lolli*—too many times to count. Now, as the sun set behind the trees in Ramona's backyard, gold and pink filtering through the window, Dylan made the room she'd slept in all her life feel small, as though Dylan were a too-bright lamp switched on in a dark room.

She was also just . . . Dylan.

A person wandering around a bedroom and looking at photographs and prints hanging on the wall.

"Olive plays softball?" she asked, picking up a photo of Olive and Ramona at the state championship two years ago, Olive still in braces, her freckles pronounced after the season.

"Yeah," Ramona said as she arranged the costumes—*clothes*—she'd grabbed from her workroom on her bed. No way she could take Dylan in there, not with the illustrated prints of iconic movie costumes she'd gotten for Christmas her senior year of high school all over the walls. Single costumes on bright backgrounds, like Mary Poppins's coat and hat and umbrella, Dorothy's blue dress and ruby slippers, Vivian's red opera dress from *Pretty Woman*.

"She's going to Vanderbilt on a scholarship this fall," Ramona said.

"How queer of her," Dylan said.

Ramona laughed. "I think you definitely gave her something to think about today. Not that she didn't have enough to ponder already with me and April and Marley around."

Dylan glanced at her, lifted a brow. Set the photo back on Ramona's dresser slowly. "So . . . you're queer?"

Ramona swallowed, focused on the 1950s-esque dress she was holding, kelly green with different-colored hands printed all over it giving the middle finger, complete with a turquoise belt and a mint green tulle petticoat.

"Um," she said brilliantly. "Yeah. I'm bi." She said it fast, then immediately changed the subject. "I think this will fit you."

She held out the dress, the tulle rustling.

Dylan's eyes locked on hers for a split second before sliding down to the dress, then widened.

"Wow, that's . . . gorgeous." She came closer, hand reaching out to touch the material. Her fingers were gentle on the skirt, almost reverent. "Very . . . Donna Reed meets Miley Cyrus."

Ramona laughed. She'd made this her freshman year at RISD— her only year—for a unit called the Subversive Past in one of her foundation classes. "Is that a good thing?"

"It's a very good thing," Dylan said. "And that's for me?

Ramona grinned. "Well, it won't fit me, so yes." She looked back at the assortment of fabric and accessories on her bed, grabbed a Marilyn Monroe–style lace-front wig. "And platinum hair, as requested."

Dylan's smile was so big. "Oh my god."

"And," Ramona said, "while you'll have to change into bowling shoes, I've got some combat boots that will complete the look."

"Combat boots."

Ramona nodded, then held out the dress and wig.

Dylan took the clothes but then tilted her head. She had a way of doing that, this little inquisitive glance that made Ramona feel as though she could read all Ramona's secrets.

"What are you wearing?" Dylan asked. "You're dressing up too, right?"

Ramona just smiled. "You'll see."

Chapter Nine

DYLAN MONROE WASN'T Dylan Monroe anymore.

She was someone else entirely. She was Lennox. Or maybe Fallon. Or Delilah or Nova or Frankie or some other badass-sounding name. She twisted, viewing herself in Ramona's full-length mirror, marveling at how different she suddenly felt in a uniquely beautiful dress and a wavy blond bob.

Behind her, she heard the bedroom door open, Ramona coming back in from changing in the hall bathroom.

"I can't believe how much I love this dress," Dylan said, still surveying herself. "It's so—"

But she cut herself off when she spotted Ramona in the mirror. She blinked, trying to process what she was seeing, the Wild West come to life in New Hampshire. Ramona stood in the doorway in brown pants and matte leather chaps, and she wore a textured maroon button-up shirt with some sort of tie Dylan didn't have a name for. Over that, a tweed vest fully buttoned and formfitting, Ramona's . . . well . . . *chest* very much filling every fiber. A low-slung leather holster belt around her curvy hips and a dark brown hat completed the ensemble.

"Wow" was all Dylan could think to say.

"You think?" Ramona said, smoothing her hands down her full thighs . . . thighs that looked . . . very good in those chaps.

Dylan shook her head to clear it.

"No?" Ramona asked.

"No! I mean, yes! God," Dylan said. "Sorry. You just . . . had that on hand? It looks straight out of a cowboy movie. Or cowgirl, I guess."

Ramona's freckled cheeks went a little pink. "It was a project. For a class."

"Wait, you *made* that?"

"No, just designed it. Well, I did make the vest, but that's all."

"Oh, that's all," Dylan said, still flabbergasted. "It's really good."

"Thanks," Ramona said, then looked Dylan up and down. "You look perfect."

Now Dylan's face washed warm, and she knew she had to get her shit together. Of course—*of course*—she'd noticed yesterday that Ramona was cute. Beautiful. Sweet and gentle and altogether lovely, but with the knowledge that she was also queer—bi just like Dylan, even—Dylan felt the room tilt.

And it just kept tilting.

No.

Absolutely not.

Impossible, stupid, and completely unnecessary, especially as Ramona didn't deserve to have her entire world potentially—*probably*—ruined by any attachment to Dylan Monroe.

Friends.

That's what Dylan wanted. Nice, normal, everyday, never-end-up-in-a-tabloid friends.

Downstairs, a door slammed, startling them both out of their awkward-as-hell staring.

"Ra-Ra!" a voice yelled. "Let's move it! Oh, sorry, Mr. Riley."

Ramona laughed, rubbed her forehead. "That would be April."

"Right," Dylan said, glad for the mention of another person. "Let's go, then, Ra-Ra."

Ramona rolled her eyes, and the two of them headed downstairs, where a man with salt-and-pepper hair and khakis stood in the foyer talking to April, who was costumed as . . . well, Dylan didn't really know what.

"April, why does it appear you're being carried around by an extraterrestrial?" the man asked.

April laughed. It did, indeed, look like she was being carried around by an extraterrestrial—her head was visible atop a small human body filled with air from a motor in the back of the costume, while behind that, a bright green alien held on to her with three-fingered arms as though taking her back to its planet.

"It's just for fun, Mr. Riley," she said. "Costume bowling. Miraculously, not my idea."

"That is miraculous," he said, then glanced at Ramona as she and Dylan hit the bottom of the stairs. "Well, look at you two." He met Dylan's eyes and held out his hand. "Hi there, I'm Steven Riley."

"Hi, I'm D—"

But her mind froze, blank. She wasn't Dylan. Didn't want to be, but she had no idea who the hell she was, all names flying right out of her head, addled by Ramona and chaps and freckles, so now she just stood there gaping like an idiot with her hand in this man's while he frowned at her.

"Dolly," Ramona said. "This is Dolly. She's visiting for the summer."

"Dolly," Mr. Riley said. "Haven't heard that name in a few decades. It's lovely. Nice to meet you."

"You too," she managed.

After that, things were a blur. Olive and Marley appeared, still costumed from earlier in the day, and then she was in the front seat of Ramona's car—some sort of SUV crossover deal—buckling herself in while Olive and Marley tried to help April fit into the back seat.

"Just deflate it!" Marley said, and April groaned.

Dylan laughed, relaxing a little more as Ramona settled into the driver's seat and started the engine.

"Dolly, huh?" Dylan asked.

Ramona froze, just for a second. "Sorry. It just popped into my head. I guess from when you mentioned it earlier."

"No, it's a good name."

Dylan glanced out the window as April finally fit herself in the car, a memory sliding into her brain.

Hello, Dolly . . . well, hello, Dolly . . .

She smiled at her reflection in the window, remembering the beach and fireworks, her first kiss with a girl in a cherry-print shirt. She wondered where that girl was now, where she lived, if she'd ever visited Clover Lake again.

"It worked though," Ramona said, pulling her out of her thoughts. She backed out of the driveway, all three passengers in the back seat still fussing about the tight quarters caused by the alien.

"What did?" Dylan asked.

"Your costume. My dad didn't recognize you at all."

"No? Does he know who I am? You know, normally?"

Ramona smiled. "Oh yeah. He loves Evenflow. Still listens to them at least once a week."

Dylan laughed, spread her hands over her skirt, and then felt the short ends of her blond bob.

"Well, hello, Dolly," she said softly, then settled back in her seat as Clover Lake's downtown swished by in a blur of golden summer evening light.

Chapter Ten

HELLO, DOLLY.

Dylan had said, *Well, hello, Dolly.*

Like she remembered.

Or remembered something, at least.

Ramona had nearly crashed the car into the Thompsons' trash and recycling bins—which they left on the street pretty much all week long despite garbage day being on Monday—when Dylan had said it.

When they'd arrived at Lakeland Lanes, the entire place had quieted upon their entrance—five people wearing wacky costumes in June certainly drew some stares and laughs, but no one seemed to recognize Dylan Monroe was among them. People said hi to Ramona and April and the girls, waved at Dylan politely, but she slipped into Clover Lake as a normal person, just like she wanted.

And she was having a blast.

And she was annoyingly good at bowling.

And she was laughing and slurping on a blue slushy and eating nachos and smiling, and she was clearly, *clearly* not affected by the whole *Hello, Dolly* thing one damn bit.

Which was fine.

It was *fine*.

Still, as Ramona sent another bowling ball into the gutter, she couldn't get the confounded song out of her head, nor could she shake this annoyed-hurt-angry feeling.

Maybe she just needed more nachos.

"You're terrible at this," April said. "Have you always been terrible at this?"

Ramona turned slowly and glared. "This from the grown woman wearing Olive's Halloween costume from when she was eleven."

"Oh my god, is that what it's from?" April said, looking down at the puffy nylon. "I just found it in a box in the basement and immediately thought, *Yes*."

"It's mine," Olive said. She was tapping away at her phone, sitting cross-legged on one of the bright orange chairs in their lane. "I got sick at your house after eating too many SweeTARTS and took it off there. I can't believe you saved it."

"You're precious in all ways, Olive Rebecca," April said.

Olive's fingers froze for a second, then she stood and tucked her phone into her bag before grabbing Marley's hand and marching the two of them toward the arcade without another word. Ramona watched her go, her own stomach tightening. Rebecca, while Olive's middle name, was also their mother's name. Not a word uttered too often in the Riley house.

"Sorry," April mouthed at Ramona.

She waved her friend off—not her fault, but the ghost of her mother entering the scene wasn't exactly helping her mood.

"Dylan, you're up," April said.

"Right, yeah," Dylan said, standing up from where she'd been sitting behind the computer, then heading to the ball return. She paused when she passed Ramona, set a gentle hand on her arm.

"You okay?" she asked softly.

Ramona's stomach went from tightly packed earth to an undulating ocean.

"Fine," she said brusquely.

She didn't mean to.

She knew she needed to let it go, this Cherry-Lolli-Dolly thing. It wasn't Dylan's fault they'd never exchanged real names, or that Ramona had told her she was on vacation too, or that Ramona looked quite different eighteen years ago. Or that Ramona was forgettable, unmemorable, a wisp of an event in the realm of Dylan Monroe's extensive and exciting life. Or that she was now descending into self-pity, which she very rarely allowed herself to do and never led anywhere productive, and only made her feel crabbier because she couldn't get over herself.

She plopped into a chair, folded her arms, and then unfolded them because she knew she looked like a petulant child. Also, because Dylan was watching her, her mouth slightly turned down, her bright pink bowling ball in her hands.

"You sure you're okay?" Dylan asked.

Ramona forced a smile. "Totally. See if you can get another strike."

Dylan didn't look convinced, but she turned away anyway, sent the ball down the glossy lane with a fervor matched only by the town's local bowling league team, the Clover Lanies, and knocked down eight pins in a seven-ten split.

"Damn," she said, but she was grinning, then scurried over to the ball return to try for a spare.

"You need a drink?" April asked from where she was now sitting at the computer.

"How many can you carry at one time?" Ramona asked.

April just laughed. "Margarita?"

"Extra salt."

"Got it."

April kissed Ramona on the top of her head as she passed, and Ramona took several deep breaths while Dylan waited for the pins to reset, trying not to notice how cute she looked in her bowling shoes and retro dress.

Because she did look cute.

Gorgeous and cute all at once, which was a dangerous combination, one that made Ramona feel even smaller, even more forgettable, and even more—

"Ramona, hey."

A deep voice.

Familiar and husky. A voice that when growled into Ramona's ear, all breathy and pleading, almost always led to very exciting things.

She turned to see Logan Adler standing next to her, a bottle of beer in his hands. Low-slung jeans that absolutely loved his thighs, a plain gray tee clinging to his torso for dear life, rugged brown boots not quite laced up all the way.

"Hey, Logan."

He smiled—perfect teeth, never even had braces, while Ramona suffered through years of orthodontia—and sat down next to her, one arm slinging behind her chair. He had the whisper of a beard, neatly trimmed and golden brown, just like the thick tresses that swooped over his forehead like a damn hair commercial.

He was gorgeous.

A paragon of human beauty.

And every time Ramona saw him, she couldn't stop thinking about his face between her legs and why in god's name she'd ever broken things off with him in the first place.

It was a problem.

Though maybe, in her current self-pitying, forgettable state, it was the exact opposite of a problem. Logan was sweet and safe, and god he was so, so good at cunnilingus.

"What's with the getup?" he asked, waving a calloused hand at her costume.

"You don't like it?" she asked.

"I love it," he said, grinning at her. "Very Wynonna Earp."

She laughed. "I think I'm more of a Waverly."

"Nah," he said, taking a sip of his beer. "Those chaps are badass."

He held her gaze—hazel eyes, lots of green and gold and some sort of magic that made her forget that his favorite band was Nickelback.

Made her forget about *Hello, Dolly* and fireworks and first kisses.

"What are you doing here, Logan?" she asked. "You hate bowling."

"Yeah, but Jared and Hollis don't," he said, motioning toward his buddies a few lanes down, guys Ramona had gone to high school with.

"Jared still going to ask Lorraine to marry him?" she asked.

"Next week, for her birthday," Logan said. "Far as I know." He leaned a little closer. "You wanna get out of here?"

She opened her mouth, but then a whoop went up in front of them—Dylan nailing the seven-ten split.

"Did you see that?" she asked, clapping her hands as she twirled around, her skirt flaring.

Her smile dipped when she saw Logan sitting there, his arm draped around Ramona's chair so that his fingers brushed her shoulder.

"That's a hard shot," he said, tipping his beer at her.

She nodded, walked slowly toward them. "I thought so."

Logan looked her up and down. "Marilyn Monroe?"

"Dolly," she said, and Ramona's stomach plummeted to her feet again.

"Logan. Nice to meet you."

"You too?" Dylan said, her voice tipping up at the end like a question.

"You new in town?" he asked.

Dylan's eyes flicked to Ramona's, eyebrows raised.

"She is," Ramona said. "Summer."

"You with this crazy movie?" Logan asked.

"Sort of," Dylan said. "Crew."

He nodded, not even a single flicker of recognition in his eyes.

"I know Dolly from a trip she took to Clover Lake years ago," Ramona said. "When we were teenagers."

The truth slipped out like an oil spill, but she didn't regret it. She waited for Dylan to realize the truth. Recognize her. Figure it the hell out. Anything that didn't make Ramona feel so invisible.

But Dylan just smiled. Nodded. "Right." She clasped her hands behind her and grinned, no curiosity in her expression, no wondering, not even a glint of confusion. As though she and Ramona were in on this secret identity plot. "Summer before tenth grade."

"Ninth."

Ramona stared at her, almost like a dare. Dylan stared back, expressionless but blinking rapidly, holding her gaze for about five seconds before she jutted her thumb toward the lane. "Do you think Olive would mind if I bowled her turn?"

It took Ramona a moment to get out "Not at all," but she managed it. She even put together some version of a smile—mouth upturned in what probably looked more like a grimace than a grin, but she wasn't the actress here.

Not by a long shot.

"She looks familiar," Logan said.

"One of those faces I guess," Ramona said flatly.

Logan narrowed his eyes at Dylan, but shrugged, then pressed his shoulder to hers. "So, about getting out of here."

Yes was on the tip of her tongue, because why the hell not. She watched Dylan fling a ball down the lane without a care—or memory—in the world.

Why the absolute hell not?

Chapter Eleven

NINTH GRADE.

Ramona had said it so matter-of-factly, so firmly. In the next five seconds, a million thoughts had flooded into Dylan's mind.

First—*Of course, yes, right, ninth grade, how could I forget, wink-wink.*

Second—*The summer before ninth grade.*

Third—*The summer. Before. Ninth grade.*

Her schooling had always been a little all over the place. She changed schools constantly and spent either seventh or eighth grade with tutors—she could honestly never remember which one.

But ninth grade, she remembered.

Dylan sent the ball down the lane with as much force as she could.

Ninth grade was when her father bought that giant house in Hollywood Hills in order to appease the social worker assigned to the Monroe family, and her aunt Hallie had lived with them from August to December, forsaking her own job in Athens, Georgia, for a semester, all to ensure Dylan went to school and ate more than canned pork and beans for dinner. Ninth grade was when she shot her first commercial, some teen-centric deodorant that smelled like strawberries and caused a rash to erupt in her armpits. Ninth grade was when she got cast in her second movie, *Glass House*, where she played a troubled child of two parents who couldn't keep it in their pants. And ninth grade was when she was knew, without a doubt, that she liked girls.

And the summer before ninth grade . . . that summer was how she knew.

Because of Cherry.

The name popped into her mind. She'd thought of it before, of course, the fake name of the first girl she'd ever kissed, that cherry-print shirt and fireworks on Clover Lake's shore, and—

Hello, Dolly.

She watched her ball obliterate the pins, the song filtering through her mind. Of course she remembered the song too . . . but . . .

She turned, looked at Ramona. Watched as she leaned into Rogan—Logan, Hogan, whatever the hell his name was—her dark hair falling across her freckled face, one thick thigh tucked under the other on the orange chair. April showed up, squeezing her alien's ass in between the two of them, plastic cups filled to the brim with fluorescent green margaritas splashing onto the shiny tiled floor. Some bro country all about trucks and beer played over the sound system. Ramona laughed at April, then licked a bit of salt from her cup.

Dolly.

Hello, Dolly.

No.

It couldn't be.

Cherry was a vacationer. A summer visitor just like Dylan and Hallie. She was—

Dylan blinked at Ramona, trying to picture this zaftig beauty as a skinny girl in the moonlight, tears shining on her face, a silly song on her lips.

Impossible.

Except was it?

Surely, Dylan would recognize the first girl she—

"Dylan?"

April's voice.

Dylan shook her head, the room coming into focus, as well as the realization she'd been staring at Ramona for a good minute or two.

"You okay?" April asked.

"Dylan . . ." Rogan-Logan said, then snapped his fingers. "That's why you look familiar. You're Dylan Monroe, holy shit."

"Well, fuck," April said.

"Nice going," Ramona said.

Dylan tilted her head at Ramona, trying to find Cherry in her features, find anything that would give her a clue about—

Ramona smiled at Dylan.

A sort of wince-smile, but it was enough.

A shock, like lightning flashing on a familiar scene, but with such intensity, you noticed all these little details you didn't notice before—the way a tree leaned to the left or how the mailbox's flag was a little rusty.

Because right there, on the left side of Ramona's face, was a dimple.

A dimple she'd noticed when they met in Clover Moon, but at the same time hadn't noticed at all.

A dimple she'd pressed her finger to eighteen years ago.

Her throat closed up, air refusing to fill her lungs.

"Dylan, it's okay," Ramona said, standing and coming toward her. "Logan won't make a big deal, will you?" She reached Dylan, placed a hand on her arm, then looked back at Logan.

"Nah," he said, taking another sip of his beer.

Quite the articulator, this guy, and while she knew it was rude—

she didn't even know Logan—the derisive thought was enough to distract her and open up her lungs a bit. She sucked in a breath slowly, nodded as Ramona squeezed her shoulder.

Dylan couldn't look at her.

Not in the face, or the eyes.

Not anywhere, really, because if she started looking now that she *knew*, she'd never stop.

Cherry.

The name was a firework in her chest.

"I . . . I'm not feeling so great, actually," she said.

"Oh," Ramona said. "What's wrong?"

"Just a headache," Dylan said, keeping her eyes averted. "Would you mind if we called it a night?"

"No, that's fine," Ramona said. "Let me text Olive and Marley." She got out her phone, wandered back to Logan, far enough away that Dylan could watch the two of them together. He leaned closer to her, like a moon in her orbit. Said something that made her laugh and made April roll her eyes.

Soon, Olive and Marley joined them, Logan disappeared, and they all piled into Ramona's car again, though Dylan insisted on April sitting in the front.

"More room for your ass," she'd said, making April laugh, but really, she just couldn't sit near Ramona. Not right now. She needed to think, to remember, to figure out how the hell she'd missed it these last two days.

Ramona was Cherry.

Her Cherry.

The girl she'd thought about a million times over the last eighteen years, her literal happy thought when shit went sideways, when her parents disappeared for days, when they got divorced then got back together, when Blair gave her shit on the set of *Spellbound*, when . . . when . . . when . . .

As Ramona pulled up in front of Dylan's small bungalow on the east side of town, the lake mere steps away, Dylan barely got out a *thanks* and *good night* before she was hurrying to her front door, ripping off her blond bob just as the tears started to swell into her eyes.

Inside, she pressed her back against the door. She could feel her pulse thrumming in her neck and tried to take a deep breath. But before her lungs fully settled, her phone buzzed in her pocket. *Laurel* flashed across her screen.

"Hey," Dylan said into the phone, grateful to have something to distract her from her heart, which currently felt as though it had claws and was scraping away at her rib cage.

"Hey yourself," Laurel said. "How's it going?"

Dylan sighed, slid down the door until she was sitting on the floor. "Ask me tomorrow."

"That bad, huh?"

"No. Yes. I don't know. First day on set didn't go as I planned."

"I heard."

Dylan thunked her head against the door. "Great."

"Look," Laurel said. "You're just in your head. Find a way to get out of it. Go out and do something fun. Lay on the beach. Play Frisbee."

"Frisbee."

Laurel laughed. "I don't know, what the hell do people do in a small town on summer vacation?"

"They go bowling."

"Jesus."

"It's not so bad," Dylan said, running her hands over the skirt of her dress. "Pretty fun, actually."

"Wait, you went bowling?" Laurel asked.

"I did. And it only fucked up my head even more."

On the other end, a pregnant pause before Laurel spoke again. "Okay, either something else happened, or I've been bowling the wrong way."

"You've been bowling at all?" Dylan asked.

"Fair point." Another pause. "What's going on, Dylan?"

Dylan pressed her fingers into her eyes, Ramona's pretty face flashing in her mind. It all sounded so silly now that she thought about it.

And maybe it was. Maybe that's what she needed to hear.

"I met someone here," she said.

"Did you, now?" Laurel asked, her tone suddenly playful.

"No, not like that," Dylan said. "A woman who lives here . . . I used to know her. Ramona. We met when we were kids." Laurel said nothing, so Dylan told her the whole story—that summer her parents were truly incapable of caring for her, coming here with her aunt, the cottage, the beach, the cove.

Cherry and Lolli and Dolly.

The kiss.

"Holy shit," Laurel said when Dylan was finished. "That's a pretty amazing story. That you ran into her again."

Dylan nodded, but Laurel's assessment didn't feel right—*ran into her*. It didn't feel like that.

It felt bigger.

Like . . . fate.

Stars aligning.

"So what's the problem?" Laurel asked.

Dylan closed her eyes, let herself go back to that night on the beach eighteen years ago. The mineral smell of the lake, the fireworks. The pretty girl. It was a good night. Maybe the best of her life.

And suddenly, Dylan did feel silly. Silly for not remembering as soon as she'd laid eyes on Ramona. But also silly for stressing about remembering at all. Ramona was her first kiss, the girl who made a horrible time in her life feel like light and laughter, if only for an hour or two. There was nothing bad about seeing Cherry again. No problem at all. It was just . . . surprising. Like Laurel said—amazing.

Now if only she had a clue what to do about it.

Chapter Twelve

RAMONA HADN'T SEEN Dylan in three days.

Which was fine.

Welcome, really, if the way she'd been feeling during bowling was any indicator. She'd needed these seventy-two hours to get her shit together, focus on what she truly wanted.

And what she wanted was to meet Noelle Yang.

That was it.

Period.

She didn't want to walk down memory lane with Lolli or Dolly or whoever the hell. She didn't want to think about first kisses or ice-green eyes or the way Dylan had bounced a little on her toes before sending a bowling ball down the lane. And she didn't want another dead-end tryst with Logan Adler, cunnilingus skills notwithstanding.

She just wanted to get a life, as everyone in her orbit had been imploring her to do for months now—years, if you were April Evans—and she was nothing if not accommodating to the people she loved.

She flung the rag she was using to wipe the counter at Clover Moon into the hamper in the back, unclenched her jaw. Okay, so maybe she'd been a little crabby these last three days, but it was only because she wanted to get things going with her life.

Her sad-sack, pathetic, small-town life.

She sighed and glanced at her watch—10:32 a.m. Close enough to her lunch, if you asked her.

"Owen, I'm taking my sixty!" she yelled toward the office, then didn't even wait for him to respond. She simply grabbed her bag from the break room and bolted out the back door, consequences be damned. Owen let her do whatever she wanted anyway, mostly because she was so damn reliable and steady.

Translation: sad sack and pathetic.

Outside, it was cloudy, the swollen sky threatening rain. She wasn't hungry for lunch yet, so she hoped the weather would hold off long enough for her to get over herself. She curved around the buildings, then hit Lake Street's busy summer sidewalk. She smiled and waved when people called her name but noticed most Cloverians' attention was on the town square.

Didn't take long to see why—the area was full of cameras and mics and people wearing black scurrying around like ants. Ramona rolled her shoulders back, then headed straight for the gazebo. She wasn't sure what she planned on doing when she got there. She assumed security was pretty tight, but she just had to *move*.

Forward.

Toward something.

As expected, there were security guards set up around the square, preventing anyone from setting foot on the grass. Still, Ramona spotted the action immediately—Dylan and Blair Emmanuel sitting in the gazebo, pressed close, looking cozy and cute and . . . very uncomfortable.

At least Dylan did as Blair pressed her palm to Dylan's shoulder and a woman in black jeans yelled "Cut!"

Actually, she yelled, "Cut, goddammit!"

Ramona got as close as she could, a large man with a tattoo of a Christmas tree on his huge pale arm keeping her about fifty feet away from the action. Still, she could see Dylan, see the panicked expression on her face, hear the not-great feedback the director—the incredible Gia Santos—was lobbing in her direction.

"Three days. Three days for the simplest scene on the planet," Gia was saying, "and you can't manage an ounce of emotion?"

Dylan opened her mouth. Closed it.

"You know how much money we've wasted already?" Gia said. "Time? Sanity?"

"I'm sorry," Dylan said. "I'm trying to get it right."

"Stop trying and do it," Gia said. "Or I'm pulling you."

Dylan blinked. "You're pulling—"

"Pulling you, yes. I didn't even want—" The director put up a hand. Took a deep breath. "Take your lunch. When you come back, you're Oscar worthy, or this is done."

The director stomped off while Dylan sat there with her sweet pink top and stained apron. Ramona's heart squeezed, but she told it in no uncertain terms to cut that shit out. In fact, she looked away from Dylan, scanning the set instead for Noelle Yang.

But her eyes seemed to have a mind of their own, drifting back to the gazebo. Blair was still there too, leaning her elbows on her knees. She said something to Dylan, too quiet for Ramona to hear, but whatever it was made Dylan's jaw tighten. Dylan stood up and jogged down the gazebo steps, closing her eyes briefly as she walked across the grass.

And when she opened them, her gaze landed squarely on Ramona.

Dylan stopped abruptly. Ramona lifted a hand, her heart picking up speed as Dylan waved back. Still, Dylan just stood there for a second before finally deciding to walk over. Ramona exhaled, straightened her posture, told herself to focus.

LA.

Noelle Yang.

Sad sack.

"Hey," Dylan said as she reached Ramona.

"Hey," Ramona said back. "How's it going?"

Dylan laughed bitterly. "I think you can see it's going badly."

Ramona winced. "Sorry."

Dylan pressed her fingers to her temples. "I don't know what my problem is."

"Can I help?"

The offer was out of Ramona's mouth before she could stop it, all her reliability coming back to bite her in the ass. But she *could* help Dylan. And in return . . .

Ramona swallowed hard. She wasn't used to this sort of transactional kind of relationship, didn't know how to even think about it without guilt splintering through her chest. It left her feeling slimy, as though she needed a hot shower and a harsh scrub.

Dylan looked at her, those green eyes searching hers. They searched her so long and so intently, Ramona started to squirm.

"Dylan?" she asked.

Dylan shook her head. "Sorry. I just . . ." She trailed off, rubbed her forehead. "Yeah. Yeah, I think you can help. Can we go to the diner?"

"Of course," Ramona said. "Anything you want to work on particularly?"

Dylan frowned. "I think I just want to talk?"

"Talk," Ramona said, her stomach fluttering.

Dylan nodded, her gaze soft as her eyes roamed Ramona's face. "About you. Your life. The town. I think it'd help me get into Eloise's brain a bit more."

Ramona opened her mouth, but nothing came out. All she managed was a nod, her feet turning and moving them back toward Clover Moon, though she doubted she'd be able to sit in a booth with a cup of coffee in her hands and talk to Dylan Monroe about her life. Life was emotions, dreams.

Love.

First kisses.

Her mind whirled, searching for some way around this, when Dylan stopped walking.

"Actually, will you come somewhere else with me?" she asked, her eyes toward the lake. "If I can find it."

"Find what?"

Dylan didn't respond at first, just looked at Ramona as though digging for gold behind her eyes. Ramona couldn't breathe, couldn't think, not with Dylan Monroe's green-glass gaze on her like that.

"A place we both know," Dylan finally said, then started walking toward the water.

Chapter Thirteen

TURNED OUT, THE place where Dylan and Ramona first met eighteen years ago was a real bitch to find. There was a path from the main beach, but it was little traveled and covered with brambles, and everything looked different in the daylight.

Of course, everything looked different than it did when Dylan was thirteen and starving for anything anyone would give her. Now, as she traipsed through the brush, thorns scraping her legs, Ramona behind her and silent, she couldn't help but wonder if she was just projecting a monumental event in her life onto Ramona, if maybe Dylan had imagined the whole night altogether.

A dream.

A desperate reach for something.

Some*one*.

But then the trees parted and the leaf-covered trail spilled out into a sandy cove. The space was a tiny semicircle, trees tucking the little plot of beach against the lake, barely enough room for a few towels and chairs. It was lovely and serene and real.

"This is gorgeous," Dylan said, toeing off her shoes. The sand was cool under her feet, the late morning sun hiding behind the clouds. "Just how I remember it."

Behind her, Ramona stopped walking. "You . . . you remember this place?"

Dylan turned to look at her, head tilted. She still doubted her recollection of that night, just a little, but if she was wrong, then so what? They'd laugh at her mistake, move on, and talk about the film.

But right now, she knew this unspoken memory between them was half of her problem these past few days during filming—she couldn't stop thinking about it, about Ramona. About how, if Ramona *did* remember, Dylan had already spent too long *not* remembering, and how shitty that must feel. She'd spent half the night after they'd gone bowling awake, replaying that July Fourth over and over, just like she'd done so many times in her past. And she knew she wanted to share that with Ramona. She wanted to share something with another person that had nothing to do with Dylan's parents or her job or what her connections could do for them.

She just wanted sun and water and the simplicity of a good memory.

"Do you?" Dylan asked. Her chest felt tight.

Ramona opened her mouth. Closed it. She wore a dress today, sort of vintage, sleeveless and yellow with a high collar. The color brought out her freckles, made her hair look darker.

"Ramona?" Dylan said, her hands on her stomach to try to calm her nerves. "Do you—"

"Of course I remember," Ramona said.

Dylan's breath left her lungs in one big gust. She bent over, rested her palms on her knees as though she'd just run a marathon. "You do?"

Ramona smiled. "Lolli."

"Shit," Dylan said, straightening and sending both hands through her hair. "Thank god."

Ramona laughed softly, then pressed her palms to her cheeks, which were turning a lovely shade of pink. But then Dylan started laughing too, and soon they were both laughing hard enough to pull tears from the corners of their eyes. Their bodies had moved closer as they'd giggled, and Dylan placed a hand on Ramona's shoulder for support as Ramona led them over to a low rock with a flat surface. They plopped down next to each other, and Dylan wiped at her eyes with a corner of her apron.

"Oh my god," she said. "I have no idea why I'm laughing so hard."

"Me neither," Ramona said. "In fact, I'm a little offended."

Dylan eyed her, and they started laughing again. But soon, they settled, both of them taking deep breaths as they looked out at the water. Dylan felt infinitely lighter already, but still, there were things to say.

"I'm sorry," she said, keeping her gaze on the lake. "That I didn't realize as soon as I saw you in Clover Moon."

Ramona's eyes narrowed a bit, but she just nodded. "I guess I'm just not that mem—"

"Don't you dare say it." Dylan turned to face her on the rock.

Ramona huffed a laugh, but this one held no mirth. She looked down at her hands, picking at her dark purple nail polish.

"Ramona, seriously," Dylan said. "That night . . . that night saved my life."

Ramona's head snapped toward her, eyes locking.

"It did," Dylan said. "Maybe not physically. But mentally? Emotionally? Yeah. I'm not being dramatic when I say that night was a lifesaver. Just because I'm a dumbass who can't put a face to my memories sometimes, doesn't mean you're forgettable. Not at all."

Ramona said nothing. Just shook her head and turned back toward the water. But a tiny smile pulled at her mouth.

"It was a good night," Dylan said. "Wasn't it?"

Suddenly, she needed reassurance too, needed to hear it meant as much to Ramona as it did to her.

Ramona turned back to look at her, small smile turning bigger, that dimple deepening in her cheek. "It was lifesaving."

She said it softly, three very simple words, but they felt like a firework in Dylan's heart. She nodded, then leaned her shoulder against Ramona's, just a little, and they sat like that for a while, watching the lake lap at the sandy shore, sharing a great memory.

It felt so . . . pure. That was the only word for it. Just good and simple and real. Like clean water and a cloudless blue sky. Dylan wanted to say more, wanted to ask Ramona more about her life during that time, but she didn't want to mess this moment up. It felt fragile and perfect all at once.

"Thank you," Ramona said after a while. "For telling me. I'm sorry I didn't mention it first. I just . . ."

"I get it," Dylan said, waving her hand.

Ramona nodded, then slapped her hands lightly against her legs. "Now. What are we going to do about your Eloise?"

Dylan groaned, but she felt a surge of relief at the subject change—that they could simply *be* with this history between them. Plus, she really did need to focus on work. The clock was ticking, and Gia expected her to come back in less than an hour as an entirely different person.

"I'm fucking it up," she said.

"You don't seem like you're having fun," Ramona said. "At least from what I saw today."

Dylan laughed, not happily. Despite being a little distracted lately after remembering everything about her and Ramona, she knew her acting problems went far beyond a first kiss memory. "An understatement."

"Why not?"

Dylan shook her head. "I don't know."

"I think you do."

"Oh, is that right?" Dylan said, glancing at Ramona. The wind whipped her hair into her face, that dimple pressing into her cheek as she smiled.

"Yeah," Ramona said gently, then said nothing else, forcing Dylan to actually *think*.

"Goddammit," she finally said. "You're right. I do know."

"So?" Ramona said.

"I just . . ." Dylan tucked her knees to her chest. "I don't think I can do it. This role. I'm the bad girl. I'm the mess. I'm the character who fucks up relationships and has a disaster family. I'm not Eloise."

Ramona laughed. "You don't think Eloise is a disaster?"

Dylan opened her mouth, closed it. "I . . . No?"

"She's a complete mess."

"Is she?"

"God yeah." Ramona adjusted, sitting cross-legged and facing Dylan now, leaning closer as she ticked off a list on her fingers. "Think about it. She grew up with a parent she couldn't count on and always had money stress, she has these huge dreams for a flower shop she really has zero hope of achieving, she's stuck in a town she loves, but love is tricky when you're forced into it, you know? Like, she can't leave. Has no means, no prospects. And the only girl she's ever really loved is a rich heiress to a publishing empire who now wants her to pretend to be her girlfriend around her snobby family. She's losing her shit here."

Dylan blinked, Ramona's passion and analysis stirring something in the center of chest.

Something exciting.

Something familiar.

But also, something a little sad, a little tender.

She studied Ramona, remembering what she'd said about her mother a few days ago in the woods, how she'd left when Ramona was—

Our mom left the summer I was thirteen.

"Oh my god," Dylan said quietly.

Ramona frowned. "What? You don't agree?"

"No, no, I do," Dylan said, then turned to look at the lake, her throat thick and crowding her airway.

The tears on Cherry's cheeks.

"Fuck," she whispered.

"I know, it's a lot," Ramona said, scooting closer. "But come on, you can do this. You know what it's like to have unreliable parents. To not have choices."

Dylan's eyes found hers. "So do you."

Ramona's brows lifted.

"That night," Dylan said. "When we were thirteen. Your mom had just left. Hadn't she?"

Ramona sighed, kept her eyes on Dylan. "Like I said. Lifesaving."

Dylan held her gaze for a second before looking away, needing a second to get herself together. To focus. This *was* a lot. She couldn't sift through her feelings, figure out what to do or say to Ramona. Finally, "Will you tell me about her?" fell from Dylan's mouth. "About your mom?"

Ramona stared at her for a moment, but then her shoulders relaxed. Dylan hadn't really meant to ask, but Ramona was lovely and sweet and hid such big feelings behind her eyes. Dylan could see them, swirling and gathering strength, because she saw the same kind of storm in her own face every time she looked in the mirror.

"My mom was beautiful," Ramona said, her gaze on the water.

"She'd have to be," Dylan said. The truth.

Ramona smiled a little but didn't glance at her. "She was born and raised in New York City, was always a big-city girl. She loved fashion and beauty and studied English literature at Sarah Lawrence."

"She sounds interesting."

"She was. She met my dad one summer when her family vacationed here."

Dylan's breath caught. "They fell in love."

"They did. He even moved to New York for her, but he was

miserable. My dad is not a city guy at all. He likes quiet and routine and for Owen to start making his usual omelet with tomatoes and colby cheese the second he walks into Clover Moon on Sunday mornings."

"So they moved here?"

Ramona nodded. "When my mom got pregnant with me. She said she wanted the small-town life, wanted a house with a backyard and a dog. So she left her job as editor of an online fashion magazine and came here." Ramona leaned over and raked her hand through the sand, filtering out tiny twigs and leaves. "Two daughters and thirteen years later . . ."

Dylan's chest was tight. "You still talk to her?"

"God, no," Ramona said. "She sent Olive and me birthday cards at first, but eventually, even those stopped."

"Jesus."

Ramona nodded, drew a circle in the sand. "I helped my dad raise Olive. Came home from RISD when he got in a bad accident and shattered his leg. He co-owned a landscaping business with his best friend, Michael, but couldn't do the work anymore. So he went back to school to become a teacher, and I . . ."

"You stayed here," Dylan said.

Ramona nodded. "I don't regret it. Olive was—*is*—worth it."

"I don't think you have to regret something to still want more," Dylan said. "To dream."

Ramona shrugged. "Maybe."

"Are you angry with her?" Dylan asked.

Ramona didn't say anything for a few seconds. Dylan let her sit in silence, worrying at her lower lip.

"Yeah," Ramona said finally. A whispered secret. "More for Olive than for me. I can tell Olive . . ." Ramona swallowed. "She doesn't remember her at all. Sometimes I think that's a good thing. But other times, I know Olive misses her. The idea of her, at least."

"Ideas can be intoxicating."

"Yeah," Ramona said. "And I don't know." She sighed, wiped at her cheek as though a tear escaped. "It's hard, knowing your own mother didn't want you. Didn't even want to stay in your life, even if she did have to leave. To be that . . . forgettable."

Dylan's heart sped up, a hummingbird behind her ribs. "We've already established that you're anything but forgettable, Ramona."

Ramona looked at her. "Really?"

"Really." Dylan's voice came out soft, a little breathy, and they watched each other for a few seconds, seconds that felt like hours, and Dylan found her eyes drifting over Ramona's whole face, down to her mouth . . .

She looked away. Her chest felt full, swollen with emotions and questions and the desire to tell Ramona about her own childhood, her own mother, her own dreams and worries and wounds.

But more than anything, Dylan wanted to kiss her, convince her she was memorable. "Ramona, I—"

Her phone buzzed in her pocket, startling her, and when she pulled it out and saw the time, panic took over every other emotion.

"Shit, I'm late," she said, catapulting to her feet. She had a text from Gia, the word *fuck* taking up most of the sentence.

"Go," Ramona said. She stayed sitting, smiled up at Dylan. "Good luck."

Dylan paused, opened her mouth to say something, but her words and feelings tangled together, a mess of emotions and memories.

And suddenly, she knew exactly how Eloise Tucker was feeling, sitting in that gazebo with a girl she'd kissed and loved a lifetime ago.

She smiled. "Will you come with me?" she asked, and Ramona's brows lifted.

"Come with you?" she asked.

Dylan nodded. "I think you just might be my inspiration, Ramona Riley." She held out her hand, and Ramona took it, letting

Dylan help her to her feet. Their chests brushed as she stood, breath mingling together.

Ramona laughed, her lashes brushing her freckled cheeks.

God, she was pretty.

And Dylan . . . well, Dylan had to admit it now.

For the second time in her life, eighteen years apart, she had a crush on Ramona Riley.

Chapter Fourteen

RAMONA WATCHED DYLAN with Blair—or rather, Eloise with Mallory—from right outside the gazebo with a studio pass hanging around her neck. And when Dylan said, *"I don't know how this will work,"* she said it with emotion and shyness, and Gia didn't yell cut, an event that seemed to momentarily shock both Blair and Dylan alike.

"What do you mean?" Blair finally asked as Mallory. *"Of course it will."*

"I just . . . " Dylan took a deep breath, looked down at her lap, and picked at her nails. *"I don't think I'm your family's type of people."*

"Exactly." Blair nudged Dylan's shoulder. *"You're sweet and unassuming and impossible to criticize."*

Dylan laughed. *"Impossible to criticize? Mallory, I live in a one-bedroom apartment over a hardware store. Your parents own three houses."*

"I don't care about any of that," Blair said. *"Plus, we can, I don't know. Dress you up. It's just for show. Ignorance is bliss, as they say."*

Here, Dylan frowned, opened her mouth, then closed it, the hurt on her face as Eloise apparent for a split second before she covered it with a smile.

"*Right,*" she said. "*Right, of course.*"

The scene went on, Mallory excited about how to make Eloise over for the fancy boat party, and Eloise putting on a good face, clearly telling herself that all this was fine. Ramona found herself sucked into the scene, transfixed by how Eloise and Mallory would eventually have to be real with each other, be themselves. Blair was a perfect Mallory, but Dylan . . .

Dylan was magic.

Granted, Ramona was probably a little biased, knowing how much Dylan struggled with the role and how badly she wanted to do well, but still.

She was *good*.

And when the scene ended and Gia shouted, "Thank fuck," and the crew laughed and clapped, Dylan's eyes found Ramona. A smile took over her face, like a sunrise over shadowed mountains. Ramona couldn't help but smile too, offer her a double thumbs-up. Dylan grinned even broader, then jogged down the gazebo steps, stopping just short of running into Ramona, as though her original plan had been to hug her.

Ramona's breath caught. She took a step back.

"Knew you could do it," she said.

Dylan shook her head. "I wasn't so sure. But thank you. And thanks for your help. I don't think I could've done it without you."

"That's not true at all."

Dylan tilted her head. "I think it might be."

Ramona didn't know what to say, but her stomach was in knots, nervous and fluttery and a bunch of other emotions she couldn't figure out. She still hadn't fully processed that Dylan had remembered her from eighteen years ago, albeit belatedly. It felt incredible, honestly, and April would probably chastise her for thinking so little of herself, but she didn't think that was it. It wasn't that the famous Dylan Monroe remembered their teenage encounter—it was that they'd somehow found themselves at Mirror Cove again after all this time. It felt magical, and, at the same time, inevitable. She didn't dare use the word *fate*, but she felt lighter somehow. Lighter than she had since Dylan showed up in Clover Moon. Lighter than maybe she had in a long time.

Ramona wanted to say as much, and she opened her mouth to tell Dylan how glad she was that they'd talked about it all, when she saw her.

Noelle Yang.

She was heading straight toward them, her salt-and-pepper bob sleek and perfect, a pair of maroon-framed glasses perched on her nose. A pale person with pink hair trailed behind her—an assistant, most likely.

"Dylan, good work," Noelle said as she reached them.

"Thanks, Noelle," Dylan said.

Ramona just stared. She knew her mouth was hanging open—*Noelle Yang was five feet away from her*—but she couldn't seem to close it. The designer was gorgeous, yet unassuming and practical. She was stylish and simple and perfect.

"I need your apron," Noelle said. "Vee here needs to clean it and then splatter it again for the diner scene tomorrow."

"Right, yeah," Dylan said, untying her apron.

"And don't leave set in those clothes again," Noelle said, waving at Dylan's blouse and shorts.

"Sorry," Dylan said.

"No worries. Just get them back to wardrobe ASAP." Noelle's eyes flicked to Ramona. "Cute dress," she said, and then turned and walked away as Vee held out their hand for the apron.

Ramona stood there, agog, the words *thank you* arriving on her tongue far too late. Still, she shouted them after Noelle, so loudly and awkwardly Vee literally startled, and Noelle didn't seem to hear Ramona anyway, her black-clad form already swallowed up by the crew.

"So," Dylan said once Vee had left with the apron. "What's on that normal-person list of yours?"

Ramona blinked at her, her processing time sluggish as she tried to remember what Dylan was talking about, what day it was, and how to spell her own name.

"What?" she asked. Her tongue felt too large for her mouth.

"The list you made the other day at April's tattoo shop," Dylan said. "I think it's time for Llama Face."

Ramona laughed, Dylan's joke working to clear her mind. "Llama Face is sacred."

"I haven't reached sacred level yet?"

"I don't know. It's a pretty elite level."

Dylan pursed her mouth, nodded. "Okay. What do I need to do to reach this god tier?"

Ramona felt her cheeks warm, and she tapped her cheek. "A hole in one."

Dylan frowned. "A hole in one?"

"Putt-Putt," Ramona said. "You get a hole in one at Dickie's, and I'll invite you into the Llama Face sanctum."

Dylan grinned and stuck out her hand. "You've got a deal."

"YOU'VE GOT TO be kidding me," Dylan said.

Ramona tilted her head back and laughed. Dickie's Miniature Golf was about five miles outside of Clover Lake, and it was infamous for its intricate courses and wild props and animatronics. Right now, they stood at hole one, staring down three rusty red loop-the-loops in a row. Meaning, a player had to aim exactly right for the first loop, then hope and pray to the Putt-Putt gods that enough force would shove the ball onto the second and third.

"This is deranged," Dylan said.

"It's iconic," Ramona said, setting her bright pink ball onto the green. She loved Dickie's, had been coming here since she was a kid, and the best part was, most summer people had no idea it was here. They frequented the newer, flashier course near downtown with the lake view and greens without mold growing in the corners.

"Whoever created this course is cruel," Dylan said. "They're a cruel person."

"And it's a par two."

"I don't know what that means, but it sounds bad."

"It probably means you won't be seeing Llama Face anytime soon," Ramona said.

Dylan narrowed her eyes. "Oh, so you're in cahoots with this cruel creator of impossible Putt-Putt courses."

Ramona just smiled. "Cahoots with Dickie? No. But I might've thought about how I usually take six or seven strokes on these courses to get the ball in the hole when I made the Llama Face deal."

Dylan flattened her mouth. "I *will* get a hole in one."

"No one has ever gotten a hole in one at Dickie's. Except maybe Dickie himself."

Dylan groaned as Ramona lined up her shot. "At least tell me about Llama Face."

Ramona swung her club, smacking the ball into the first loop hard enough that it followed the correct path, but then veered off to the right instead of zooming onto the next loop.

"Damn," she said.

"Okay, if I can get my ball onto the second loop, you tell me about Llama Face," Dylan said, setting her purple ball on the ground.

"It's not that thrilling of a story."

"Deal?" Dylan said, lifting a brow.

Ramona laughed. "Fine."

"Excellent."

"But you've never even played Putt-Putt before, so I think I'm safe."

Dylan ignored her, lining up her putter with the ball, studying the loops with narrowed eyes. She was very patient. Very . . . very . . . patient.

"Wow, you really want that story," Ramona said.

"I want the Llama Face." Dylan glanced up, eyes meeting Ramona's, a wry smile on her face.

Something happened in Ramona's stomach then—a low flutter. Too fluttery to be ignored and too low to be chalked up to nerves.

"Guess we'll see," Ramona said.

"Guess we will," Dylan said, then went back to her very focused analysis of the hole.

Ramona watched her, amused and intrigued. And when Dylan hit the ball and it made it onto the second loop—though not the third as it veered off to the left—Ramona groaned dramatically.

"Baby steps," Dylan said, then leaned on her club. "Story please."

Ramona sighed. "April used to be scared of llamas."

Dylan blinked. "Scared. Of llamas."

Ramona nodded.

"Do you have a lot of llamas 'round these here parts?" She put on an affected Southern accent.

"No," Ramona said through a laugh. "But we took a field trip to a farm in the fifth grade that had llamas, and April said they looked like alien goats and they freaked her out, especially when they opened their mouths and made noises and stuff."

"Opened their mouths," Dylan deadpanned.

"So on the bus on the way back, I offered her some exposure therapy."

"With a llama face."

"Naturally," Ramona said, smirking. "It worked too. She is no longer llama-phobic."

"There's got to be an official word for that."

"We'll look it up."

Dylan pursed her mouth, watching Ramona intently.

Ramona widened her eyes as if to say, *What?*

"I need Llama Face, Ramona."

"You'll live," Ramona said, lining up her club with her ball.

"I need it. Like air."

"You're breathing just fine."

"It's integral to my creative process for Eloise. Is it like this?" Dylan stretched her mouth open, top lip going one way, bottom going another. It was horrific and ridiculously cute.

Ramona swallowed her laugh, trying to remain stern. "Eloise would never be so uncouth."

"She would be if she was sweet as honey whiskey pie and trying to cure her BFF's llama phobia."

Ramona cracked then, laughing and giving up focusing on her shot. She straightened up, then leaned on her club as she looked at Dylan, who was so adorable in her begging, Ramona couldn't keep the smile off her face.

"Okay, maybe we can figure out a new deal," she said. "But I—"

She cut herself off when she saw some other Dickie's patrons a few holes ahead of them, a group of four. They were young, maybe college aged, and they were aiming their phones in their direction.

Well, in *Dylan's* direction.

"What is it?" Dylan asked, then turned to follow Ramona's line of sight, her smile dropping when she saw the oglers. "Ah, shit."

"It's fine," Ramona said. "They're just kids."

"Yeah, armed with these little computers that connect them to every single person around the globe." Dylan's jaw was tight as she turned back, her cheeks a little red. "Let's just play."

"You sure?" Ramona asked.

Dylan nodded. "This is my life. If I let every single asshole with a phone keep me from doing what I wanted, I'd never leave my house."

"I'm sorry. I thought Dickie's would be safer."

Dylan met her eyes then, her expression going soft. "It is. It's as safe as it can get." She waved her hands around to the otherwise empty golf course. "I'm still determined to see Llama Face."

Ramona smiled, nearly giving in right then and offering it up, but she had to admit, she liked this push and pull. This . . . flirting.

Because she was pretty sure that's what they were doing. Granted, other than with Logan, whose flirting strategy consisted of *so you wanna get outta here* and *take your shirt off*, she hadn't flirted with anyone in a while.

"Okay, hotshot," Ramona said. "Let's see what you got."

"Hotshot?"

"I live with my father," Ramona said. "Cut me some slack."

Dylan laughed, and then they played. They made terrible shots and got several holes in eight and holes in nine, but no holes in one as they made their way through the course, battling haunted windmills with moldering ghosts popping out of the rotating arms and clowns scarier than Pennywise, aiming at their gaping red mouths.

By the time they reached hole fifteen, Ramona's stomach was sore from laughing and the college kids were gone.

"This is it, I can feel it," Dylan said, wiggling her hips as she set up her shot. "A hole in fucking one."

"Dream on, Dylan Monroe."

Dylan stuck out her tongue but smiled, then eyed the giant plastic orange cat on the green, through whose animatronic paws she had to hit the ball. "Okay, I can do—"

"Dylan, who's your friend?"

Dylan froze, and when Ramona turned toward the deep voice just outside the course's peeling-paint fence, a flash went off in front of her face, momentarily whiting out her vision.

"Who are—" she started, but the flash ignited again, and she put up her hand instinctively.

"Dylan, come on, give us a name," the man said. He wore a maroon Dr Pepper T-shirt and sunglasses, and as he angled the camera for another shot, a second car rolled into the parking lot, spitting out a woman with frizzy blond hair and a green bomber jacket.

"Dylan, over here," she said, jogging toward the fence.

It took Ramona a second to realize they were paparazzi—actual, real paparazzi—and those college kids had probably called someone for ten bucks or free pizza or something else completely pathetic.

"Fuck," Dylan said under her breath. "We need to go."

"Yeah, okay," Ramona said, still dazed, and headed toward the gap in the fence that emptied into the parking lot.

"Not that way," Dylan said, grabbing her hand and pulling her away from the cameras.

"Right, sorry," Ramona said, but the flashes kept going, and Dylan's hand kept holding hers, the paparazzi's voices still pummeling them with questions.

"Who is she?"

"What's her name?"

"Are you two dating?"

"How did you two meet?"

Dylan answered none of them, just headed toward the wooden building that held the run-down arcade full of games from the seventies and eighties. As they climbed the steps, Dickie came out on the porch.

"Oh, no," Ramona said, but a smile tipped her mouth upward.

"What?" Dylan asked as they ran past Dickie, who was a famous *get off my lawn* sort with anyone who didn't pay a fee.

"Hey, jackasses," his cranky voice called. He stuck his hands in his cargo pants' pockets, rolled back on his heels. "You got exactly five seconds to either pay for eighteen holes or get the fuck off my land."

The paparazzi ignored him, still clicking away as Dylan and Ramona ran inside the building. Ramona looked back to see Dickie take out his flip phone, gnarled fingers poised to dial. "One . . . two . . ."

"God bless Dickie . . . what's his last name?" Dylan asked as they shot out of the front entrance and toward Ramona's car in the corner of the parking lot.

"I don't think he has one," Ramona said, laughing as the paparazzi spotted them and aimed their cameras in their direction. They threw themselves in the car, tires squealing as Ramona reversed. She slowed down on the way out though, giving Dylan plenty of time to present both of her middle fingers at the photographers as they drove away.

Dylan sighed once they were safely out of view and on the road back to town, head flopping against the headrest. "I'm so sorry that happened."

"It's not your fault," Ramona said. "I'm sorry—I know you don't like showing up on the gossip sites."

Dylan sighed, angled her head toward Ramona. "I'm not sorry for me. I'm sorry for you."

Ramona frowned, her hand tightening on the wheel. "What do you—"

Who's your friend?

Are you two dating?

"Oh," she said.

"Yeah," Dylan said. "Oh."

Chapter Fifteen

THE NEXT DAY, Ramona had to be at the diner earlier than usual. The first café scene was being filmed later in the afternoon, and Owen had asked for help getting things set up—or rather, clearing away all the stuff he didn't want the movie people to mess with. He'd insisted on serving breakfast as normal too, so there would be plenty to clean and arrange.

Also, it was Saturday, so Olive and Marley had begged Ramona to let them come along and help, excited to get a glimpse of a real movie set. Ramona wasn't sure how much actual help they would be, but she agreed, as long as they got out of the way when told.

Ramona stepped out of her room around seven, her stomach already in flight. She wasn't sure why—she didn't expect she'd get to be on set while they filmed, and while she hoped for an actual introduction to Noelle Yang sometime soon, she couldn't stop thinking about yesterday with Dylan.

Nothing about the two of them had shown up online so far. Ramona had checked sites like TMZ and the *Hollywood Reporter* every ten minutes last night. She had no idea how she felt about any of it. She certainly didn't want to end up in the papers or websites or Instagram Reels, but . . .

Are you two dating?

She couldn't get the question out of her mind. It was just so . . . preposterous. Silly. Impossible and ridiculous and . . .

Well, wasn't it?

She shook her head, focused on the day ahead. Smoothed her hands down her light-wash jeans, straightened the multicolored floral blouse she had tied at her waist. She headed down the hall to make sure Olive was awake, knocked on her door before turning the knob carefully.

"Hey, baby girl, are you—"

"Ramona, Jesus," Olive said. She sat on her bed with a bright orange shoebox in her lap, her hands holding what looked like a photograph, though Ramona couldn't tell what it was of before Olive dropped it back into the box and stuffed the lid on top.

"Sorry," Ramona said, frowning.

"Most people wait for a 'come in' when they knock."

"I didn't think you were awake."

Olive didn't say anything, just stood up and slid the shoebox under her bed, then headed to her dresser to put on a silver necklace, the pendant featuring tiny spotted mushrooms, a gift from Ramona for her fourteenth birthday.

"You okay?" Ramona asked.

"I'm fine," Olive said. "Just . . . you know. Last summer and all."

Ramona all but melted. "Yeah. It's a lot."

Olive nodded. "Good a lot. But a lot."

Ramona walked over to her, took the delicate chain Olive was struggling with, and fastened it around her neck. "You're amazing, you know that, right?"

Olive rolled her eyes but smiled.

"Amazing and wondrous," Ramona said.

"Oh, here we go."

"Wondrous and incredible. Astonishing. Staggering and stunning. Confounding. Breathtaking."

"Okay, okay, can we pick a new word already?"

Ramona laughed, ran her hands through Olive's straight brown hair. This was a game they'd played since Olive was little. One of them would lock on a word and then rattle off as many synonyms as they could think of. It was a teaching strategy their dad brought home from a seminar he'd been taking when Olive was around four, and Ramona had to admit, it certainly helped develop her own vocabulary along with Olive's.

She turned Olive around, set her hands on her shoulders. "I'm just proud of you," she said. "Don't forget that, yeah?"

Olive's expression dipped a little, but she nodded, looking down as she swallowed. Ramona started to ask what was wrong, but Olive's phone buzzed on her desk, and she slipped out of Ramona's hands to grab it.

"Wait, what?" Olive said, frowning at her phone.

"What is it?" Ramona said.

Olive didn't say anything, just flew out of her room and bounded down the stairs.

"Olive, hang on," Ramona said, following her.

"Marley says there are a ton of—"

But she didn't finish as she flung open the front door to a flurry of flashes and shouts.

"Ramona!" the voices called, at least a dozen people gathered on the Rileys' lawn. "Hey, Ramona, can we get a quote? When did you and Dylan start dating? Is it serious?"

Olive blinked, open-mouthed, Ramona right behind her, completely agog. It took her a good five seconds—which felt like an eternity with all the noise and clatter and clicking—to realize she should close the door.

She slammed it shut. Locked it.

Olive and Ramona stood in the foyer, breathing heavily, Ramona's back pressed to the door.

Finally, Olive broke the silence. "You're dating Dylan?"

"What?" Ramona said. "No."

Olive clicked around on her phone. "But you're all over the internet."

"I'm what?" Ramona dug her phone out of her back pocket, checked the same sites that were quiet last night.

They weren't so quiet anymore.

Pictures of her and Dylan at Dickie's were everywhere, particularly the one where Dylan was holding Ramona's hand to pull her away, but in this shot, it just looked like they were holding hands period.

"Oh my god," Ramona said. Her heart felt huge, as though it had left its spot in her chest and was zooming through her whole body.

"Ramona," her father said, ambling from the kitchen into the foyer. He was looking down at his phone. "Why am I getting texts from fellow teachers that my eldest is dating Dylan Monroe." He glanced up finally, eyes wide. "As in Jack Monroe's daughter?"

"Jesus," Ramona said, closing her eyes, but then her own phone buzzed.

And buzzed, and buzzed, and buzzed.

April: RA

April: MONAAAAAA

April: WHAT THE FRESH HELLLLL???

April: YOU WENT ON A DATE???

April: AND DIDN'T TELL ME???

"Okay, jerks," Olive said, still reading on her phone. "This article says you're not Dylan's normal type and that she must be slumming it."

"Oh, for god's sake!" Ramona said, then pushed off the door

and took off down the hall, closing herself in the powder room. She sat down on the toilet lid, muted April's still-buzzing texts. She just needed a second to think. To breathe. To get her head around this.

She knew this kind of thing happened to celebrities all the time—people wanted in to their lives, thought they were entitled to them even, but she never expected herself to be swimming in this fishbowl too. It was dizzying and overwhelming and, honestly, a little terrifying.

She knew she shouldn't, but she couldn't help herself. She opened one of the articles on her phone, eyes scanning the words.

> Dylan Monroe is summering in a tiny hamlet called Clover Lake (yeah, we've never heard of it either), and it looks like she's spending her time doing more than just filming her first rom-com (you heard that right— bad girl Killin' Dylan is playing America's sweetheart). Local girl Ramona Riley (she makes pie, everyone, and drives a very practical Honda) . . .

"I do not drive a fucking Honda," Ramona said. She had no idea how they got her name, but she knew it wouldn't be hard around there. Those photographers could've asked literally anyone in town—shaggy bangs, freckles for days, handmade clothes around curvy thighs. Ramona pressed her fingers to her temple, kept reading against her better judgment.

> . . . looks more the part of America's sweetheart, and even has the hips to prove it.

Ramona gritted her teeth. She was happy with her body—happy, or didn't think about it at all, honestly—but she knew the wider world didn't always look kindly upon curves and fat, despite the body positive and body neutrality movements flourishing through-out society. And Hollywood certainly wasn't regular society.

> After Dylan's explosive breakup with Jocelyn Gareth a few months ago (helicopters were involved, enough said), it's no surprise to find Dylan holding the hand of someone who is one hundred percent not her normal type. Maybe slumming it in New Hampshire will calm Jack and Carrie's wildling down a little. Good luck, Ramona Riley, and Godspeed.

Ramona swiped out of her browser, clicked her phone to dark, stuck it back in her pocket. She was tempted to toss it into the toilet and be done with the whole thing, but that felt extreme. Still, she couldn't read another word, and didn't want the temptation. Infuriating tears swelled into her eyes. She knew it was silly—these were gossip sites, for crying out loud. They weren't factual, and everyone knew it.

Still, despite this knowledge, everyone read them and oohed and aahed and believed every single word.

She took a few deep breaths, but the tears kept coming—she wasn't even sure why she was crying. She *wasn't* Dylan's normal type, and that was fine. She wasn't even actually dating Dylan Monroe, for Christ's sake. But she couldn't help this feeling of being invaded. And even more than that, she felt silly, filled with an embarrassment she couldn't seem to shake, which led to embarrassment over feeling embarrassed, a ridiculous cycle that pulled more tears from her eyes.

She swiped furiously at her face, willed herself to get herself together. She still had to be at Clover Moon in half an hour and had no idea how she was going to get out of her house. She pictured herself walking boldly through the journalists, acting as though they weren't even there, chin held high . . . Yeah no, she'd never pull it off. She'd lose her shit for sure, all that noise and clicking and yelling, and then they'd report on how she'd had a panic attack while getting in her car.

She dropped her head in her hands, tried to think. She'd just decided to duck out the back door and cut through the woods to walk to Clover Moon, when her phone buzzed again.

"God, what now?" she whisper-yelled, but fished it out of her pocket anyway.

Dylan flashed across the screen.

She sucked in a breath. She and Dylan had shared numbers that first day they'd met—or remet, more accurately—sitting on the couch in April's office, but neither of them had used that information yet.

She slid her finger across the screen. "H-h-hi."

"Ramona?"

She cleared her throat. "Yeah, hey."

"God, I'm so sorry."

"For what?" she asked stupidly.

"Oh, you haven't seen? Thank god, don't go on the internet, or—"

"No, I saw," she said. "Sorry, I'm just processing."

A beat of silence. "Right. I knew this might happen. I'm so sorry."

"No, *I'm* sorry."

Dylan sighed. "It's not your fault. It's mine, okay? I've got so many eyes on me since everything with Jocelyn, and everyone is just waiting for me to fuck up this movie. I shouldn't have dragged you into it. It was selfish and stupid."

Ramona nodded, even though Dylan couldn't see her. The lump in her throat was ballooning—Dylan's words should be comforting, but somehow, they just made her feel worse. She closed her eyes, swallowed about seven thousand times until her throat felt normal again.

"Ramona?" Dylan asked softly.

"Yeah, I'm here," she said. Coughed. "Um, listen, there are . . . well, a lot of photographers outside my door."

"What?"

"And I need to get to the café."

"Holy shit. I'm so, so sorry."

"It's fine. I just . . . I think I need to cut out the back maybe?"

"Goddammit. Fucking vultures. Hold on. Don't move. I'm on my way over."

"Dylan, no, that'll just make it—"

But Dylan ended the call, and Ramona couldn't help the fresh wave of tears that spilled down her cheeks.

Chapter Sixteen

DYLAN WAS SO mad, she was seeing stars.

Red stars.

Red stars exploding, shrapnel flying, landing on every single one of those miscreants standing outside of Ramona's door.

Breathe.

She needed to breathe.

If she didn't breathe, she'd never find her way out of the woods she was currently traipsing through, heading in the vague direction of Birch Street and Ramona's house. She wasn't sure the exact number, but she wasn't planning on going in through the front door either.

She spilled out onto Sterling, then checked her Maps app and kept heading east. She had to cut through some backyards, but this was preferable to the main road. At least it was until a very large, very unleashed dog in a very unfenced backyard spotted her, its barks like a security alarm.

"Hey, good dog," she said, slowing her quick steps, but the beast kept barking. She loved dogs, but small ones. Yippy ones, as Laurel called them, and this dog was huge and booming, with big sharp teeth and drool dripping down onto the grass.

"It's okay," she said soothingly. "I'm just cutting through. Just a little short—"

The dog lunged then, snapping its jaw at her flowy T-shirt and getting a piece of the hem. It yanked, jerking her forward, and Dylan heard her shirt rip. She lunged back, and her shirt tore even more, but at this point, she just wanted to survive this little encounter with Cujo. She let the dog have the chunk of cotton and took off running, angling around hydrangeas just starting to bloom and thorny rose-bushes. She didn't slow down until she spilled onto Birch, her lungs desperate for air.

She was not a runner.

She fucking hated exercise, actually, but speed walked on a treadmill in her house while reading scripts or watching mindless TV. That bit of cardio, however, did not prepare her for escaping territorial canines in New Hampshire. She rested her palms on her knees, catching her breath. Down the street, she spotted a crowd outside a little brick bungalow, her anger flaring again. She swung right, ducking into more backyards until she landed on Ramona's back porch, which was cute and filled with potted plants and flowers.

She knocked on the door, and Ramona flung it open before she'd even let down her arm.

"My god, what happened to you?" Ramona asked.

Dylan frowned, but then looked down at herself—shirt torn, cuffed jeans dusted with dirt, white sneakers filthy.

"I ran here," she said, still huffing for breath. "And escaped death by dog."

"And trees," Ramona said, plucking a twig out of her hair.

Dylan laughed, but then went sober when she remembered why she was here. "I'm so sorry."

Ramona sighed, and she stood aside to let Dylan in the house. "It's not your fault."

"It actually is," Dylan said, stepping into a cozy kitchen with dark green cabinets and butcher-block counters. "Killin' Dylan strikes again."

Ramona frowned, then went to a coffeepot by the sink and poured some of the dark liquid into a mint-green cup. She handed it to Dylan, then sat down with her own cup at the table. "Where does that name come from anyway?"

Dylan sank into the chair. All of her muscles hurt—Jesus, that speed walking had really fucked her over in terms of aerobic endurance.

"It's stupid," she said, folding her hands around the cup. "And from when I was an idiot in my early twenties and had no clue how to control my temper."

Ramona lifted a brow.

Dylan laughed. "Okay, so, sometimes, I still don't know how to control it." She winced. "Heard about Jocelyn's birthday party, did you?"

Ramona sucked her teeth. "Everyone heard about that, Dylan."

"Right, right," Dylan said, pressing her fingers to her eyes. "Well, losing one's shit on the set of *Spellbound* when your rock star father shows up to *support you*"—here she hooked finger quotes into the air—"and then proceeds to pretty much take over the entire day with his narcissism, resulting in his daughter blowing up and knocking over a prop table full of lit candles for a spell scene, will indeed get you a nickname like Killin' Dylan."

Now it was Ramona's turn to wince. "Well . . . at least I'd never heard that story before."

Dylan laughed, but it was bitter. "You're in the minority, trust me."

"Even I've heard that story," Olive said, coming into the kitchen, "and I was, like, ten when it happened."

"Oh, very nice," Dylan said, but she smiled at the girl.

"I've heard it too," Mr. Riley said, meandering into the room as well with his phone in his hand, clad in khakis and a short-sleeved plaid shirt. He looked like such a *dad*, Dylan felt a flutter of longing underneath her ribs.

"Mr. Riley," she said. "I'm really sorry about all of this."

He waved a hand, then tapped at his phone. "They're trespassing, and I've just found the state ordinance to reference if anyone gives me trouble, so if you'll excuse me, I'm going to go kick these charlatans off my lawn."

"You need to be riding a white horse when you do that," Ramona said. He winked at her, then came over and kissed her on the top of her head. Dylan melted a little, literally felt her insides go soft and warm. Luckily, her phone buzzed right then, a good distraction from her thickening throat.

But the name flashing across the screen did nothing to calm her down. In fact, it did the exact opposite.

Rayna.

"It's my publicist," she said. She'd already tried calling Laurel this morning, but her manager was on a plane on her way here, and her agent, Adriana, most definitely left this kind of drama to Laurel and Rayna. Rayna, who was a pit bull and had saved Dylan from many a scandal, but who was also sort of, maybe, definitely terrifying. Dylan clicked the red button, sending the call to voicemail, but it just rang again a second later. Dylan slapped the red button again.

As dread pooled in her stomach, the back door flew open, revealing April breathing hard and holding up her phone.

"Answer my texts, Llama Face."

"Oh, god, sorry," Ramona said, taking out her phone and tapping. "I'd turned off alerts."

"Turned off alerts?" April said, pressing her hand dramatically to her chest. "For *me*?"

They talked back and forth, an amusing verbal tennis match, but

Dylan's phone rang a third time, and she knew she couldn't put Rayna off any longer.

"Rayna, hey," she said, standing up from the table and wandering into the living room.

"Dylan, there are only a few things I really hate," Rayna said, her sexy-raspy voice deadly quiet. "Number one, roaches. They're nearly impossible to kill and carry diseases and, when you least expect it, they fly. *Flying roaches*, Dylan."

"Yeah, that's—"

"Number two, multiple forks at dinner. Who has the fucking time?"

Dylan stayed quiet this time.

"Number three, waking up to my client's name plastered all over the gossip sites when that client gave me no advance warning of said plastering."

"I'm sorry, Rayna," Dylan said. "I didn't think it would—"

"Were there cameras present, flashing in your face?"

Dylan sighed. "Yes."

"Then you knew it would." Rayna cleared her throat, and Dylan could hear the clacking of a keyboard, which meant Dylan was on speakerphone, most likely getting berated in front of at least two assistants and paying Rayna an exorbitant hourly fee for the experience.

"However," Rayna said—*click, click, click*—"this particular fuckup benefits you, so we'll call it square. Though next time you see a camera within fifty feet of you, I better hear about it. I don't care if the wielder is a four-year-old in pigtails playing with Mommy's phone."

"Wait, wait—benefits me?" Dylan asked.

"That's what I said."

"How does it—"

"Date her."

Dylan froze. "What?"

"Date. Her." Rayna was still clicking and clacking away.

"Her . . ."

Rayna released a belabored sigh. "The woman whose hand you were holding not twenty-four hours ago?"

"I wasn't—"

"I don't care. Gia's been on the phone with Laurel every day since filming started, and when Laurel is upset, I hear about it, and I don't like hearing about it, so—"

"Hang on, what?" Dylan said.

"Latching yourself publicly to an actual small-town girl can only help you at this point, particularly with the news of Jocelyn and Ruby's engagement breaking this week. I've already gotten dozens of phone calls for comment."

"Wait, *what*?"

Dylan felt dizzy, too many things flying at her at once. Jocelyn was *engaged*? Gia was calling Laurel? And . . . *date* her? *Ramona*?

She shook her head, wandered over to the fireplace mantel, her eyes scanning pictures of Ramona and Olive at various ages. There was one of Ramona holding a baby Olive on the couch . . . a very familiar-looking Ramona, all gangly and awkward, a half smile on her face, her eyes sad, dark circles underneath.

She was wearing a cherry-print T-shirt.

Dylan's breath caught, her heart climbing her throat. She turned to see now Ramona, still sitting at the table and laughing with April, who was talking a mile a minute, though Dylan couldn't make out about what.

Ramona's eyes met hers.

Dylan's stomach plunged to her feet, and she moved away from the mantel and the photograph, trying to focus on what the hell her publicist was saying.

"Okay, Rayna, just slow down a sec," she said, then sat on the edge of the squashy plaid couch, rested her head in one hand. "Why is Gia calling Laurel?"

There was silence for a beat, which was never a good sign with Rayna. There wasn't much she wouldn't come right out and say.

"You can ask Laurel about that," she finally said. "I'm in charge of image, not talent."

"Talent?" Dylan said, her chest tightening. "But the last scene we shot went really well, and—"

"Again, image," Rayna said. "So go ahead and hold what's-her-name's hand. Kiss her on the sidewalk. Invite her to the set so she can moon over your . . . talent."

Dylan's heart was going to break out of her chest. It really and truly was. Rayna definitely paused dramatically before saying the word *talent* there, and what the fuck was going on here?

"You want me to fake date Ramona?" Dylan asked.

"Hey, talented *and* smart," Rayna said. "Do it."

And then she ended the call, leaving Dylan alone, gaping in the Rileys' living room, trying to process what the hell just happened. Before she could figure anything out, her phone buzzed again.

Laurel: Just landed in Manchester. Meet you at the diner

Dylan's fingers hovered over her screen, but everything she could think to ask was just an amalgam of *what the actual fuck*, so she held off, hoping the walk to the diner from here would clear her head a bit.

If they could even get out the door without cameras trailing them the entire way.

Date her.

She dropped her phone in her lap, rubbed at her temples. She couldn't think about this right now. She needed Laurel, and she needed to get Ramona to work without the whole of Hollywood scum mauling her outside her own house.

So that was what she was going to fucking do.

⌒

THE WAY BACK to Lake Street via the backyards was a very different experience with three locals. Granted, Mr. Riley had succeeded in clearing off his lawn, but several photographers were still loitering on the public road just beyond their property line, and Dylan didn't want to take the chance.

She wanted exactly zero pictures of her and Ramona until she talked to Laurel and cleared her head.

Date her.

And on top of that little gem, Gia's daily calls to Laurel and the news of Jocelyn and Ruby's engagement cycled through her thoughts on a loop. The cool morning air helped, but what she really needed was a therapy session and an entire day burrowed under her covers.

At least their journey was quiet, peaceful even, and void of any sprinting through backyards. Dylan took several deep breaths and focused on the leaf-packed trees, the green canopy they created over the earth, the gentle *shush-shush* of their feet through the grass. No one spoke much, and Dylan was grateful for that, though April and Ramona whispered here and there. She was sure April had a thousand questions about the photos and their Dickie's outing, but she wasn't directing those inquiries toward Dylan right now.

Small favors.

"Hey, puppy dog," Olive crooned as they got to the yard that housed Cujo.

"Oh, hey, be careful," Dylan said, "that dog is—"

But Olive rubbed the dog's head, and it leaned into her hands, tongue panting and tail wagging happily.

Dylan sighed. Fucking figured.

"Nugget's a good dog, aren't you," Olive said, rubbing its ears and pressing her face close.

"Nugget?" Dylan said, lifting her damaged hem. "More like Demon."

"This is the dog that tore your shirt?" Ramona said, also petting the beast, who, if physically capable, would be purring right now from all the love and attention.

"Nugget would *never*," April said, joining in this little adoration party and patting the dog's butt.

"I hate you all," Dylan said, and kept walking, the others snickering and following her.

"You don't like dogs?" Ramona said, catching up with her.

"No, I like dogs just fine," Dylan said. She felt silly and stressed and wanted a cup of coffee the size of her head right now.

"Do you have any pets?" Ramona asked.

Dylan laughed, a bitter sound. "I'm not exactly reliable with caretaking. I kill every plant I've ever had. I really wanted a long-haired Chihuahua when I was a kid, but my parents could barely keep me alive, so . . ."

She trailed off, adding *embarrassed* to her list of emotions for sharing too much.

Next to her, Ramona was quiet for a bit, April and Olive whispering behind them. The morning sun was golden and sparkling through the trees, the air rain-washed from a summer storm the night before. The day was lovely and worked to calm Dylan down a little.

"Long-haired Chihuahuas are cute," Ramona finally said.

"You think so?" Dylan asked. "Anyone I've ever told that to immediately winces and starts talking about hyperactivity and how they hate little yippy dogs or some other reason why I shouldn't like them."

"You should get to like whatever you like," Ramona said.

Dylan watched her—head down, eyes on the grass, her hands in the pockets of her light-wash jeans. Her hair was pulled halfway back with a clip that had mushrooms all over it, and the sun sparkled on the deep brown, igniting a few red tresses.

Date her.

Dylan shook her head. Goddamn Rayna.

She couldn't.

Ramona *wouldn't.*

Except as she glanced at Ramona again, her stomach flipped and flopped like a preteen with a first crush. Granted, she knew she had a crush on Ramona—she was cute and sweet and smart, and crushes were all well and good, but she hadn't planned to do anything about it. And she certainly hadn't planned to do anything about it that provided a story for the gossip sites.

Hell, no.

"What?" Ramona asked, and Dylan realized she'd protested out loud.

"Nothing, sorry," she said, staring at the grass. Luckily, they reached Lake Street just then, and Clover Moon café was in view. Dylan picked up her pace, needing nothing more than to lock herself in a bathroom for some solitude.

As they left the cover of the trees, coming out into the open of the busy summer morning, the townsfolk and tourists . . . well, they noticed.

Of course Dylan was used to pulling glances wherever she went, but this was different. This was accompanied by whispers and crooned greetings toward Ramona, with knowing smiles and eyes shifting down to her fingers to see if they were tangled with Dylan's.

And dammit, Dylan was so close to taking her hand. Just to spite everyone. Show Ramona off as exactly her type—she couldn't believe that one post said she was *slumming it*—but she knew that would just lead to more pictures of the two of them together, and—

Latching yourself publicly to an actual small-town girl can only help you at this point, particularly with the news of Jocelyn and Ruby's engagement...

She sped up even more, claiming too much coffee this morning as she left the group behind and hurried into Clover Moon. The place went comically silent when she walked in, silverware clattering to plates and gasps emitting over coffee cups, but she just smiled and hurried to the single, gender-neutral bathroom in the back.

Locked herself inside.

The farmhouse decor with its hardwood floors and rose-colored glass globes around amber lighting was lovely, but Dylan barely noticed, because she did the worst thing she could possibly do in that moment and got on her phone. Googled Jocelyn Gareth. She didn't even need to put in Ruby's name, as the search engine autofilled it for her. She clicked on the first article.

Jocelyn Gareth and Ruby Chopra announced their engagement this week, as though the four-carat, vintage diamond on Ruby's hand didn't give it away. The happy couple doesn't have a date in mind quite yet, according to Jocelyn's manager, but the two have plenty to keep them busy. Ruby is slated to star in a romantic period piece, while Jocelyn will be entering the recording studio to lay down her debut album. Hollywood was delighted when the actress announced her musical ambitions, and even more so when she revealed that she'd signed with Evenflow Records, a company founded by rock legend Jack Monroe. Monroe still remains active in artist selection and production. One can't help but wonder at the connection between Jocelyn's latest creative endeavor and her fiery ex, Jack's daughter, Dylan Monroe. Regardless,

Hollywood rejoices at these particular wedding bells,
as the world is always in desperate need of another
happy queer couple. Congratulations, Jocelyn and
Ruby!

Dylan tossed her phone onto the floor, half hoping the damn
screen would crack. She clenched her fists, but there was no fighting
that hollowed-out feeling in the pit of her stomach, the very same
one she experienced when she'd found out, hours before Jocelyn's
birthday party at the Mondrian's rooftop pool, that her girlfriend
of eleven months had been talking to her father behind her back,
using her to get in his good graces, then sending him her demo, all
without Dylan's knowledge.

She didn't give two shits about Jocelyn and Ruby's impending
nuptials. She did, however, give a shit about being reminded of Jocelyn's betrayal and backstabbing. That was definitely not in her
morning plans, but it wasn't as though Hollywood would let her forget it.

A knock sounded on the door.

"Occupied!" Dylan said, and not kindly.

"It's me."

Dylan scrambled to unlock the door, then all but yanked her
manager into the tiny space.

"You are never allowed to leave me again," Dylan said.

Laurel laughed, tucked her hands in the pockets of her wide-
legged black pants. She eyed Dylan's phone on the floor. "Clearly
you can't be trusted."

"I told you I couldn't!" Dylan's screech echoed off the walls.

"Okay," Laurel said, presenting her hands, "you're going to the
bad place. Sit down and take a breath."

Then she all but shoved Dylan onto the closed toilet lid, but
Dylan didn't mind one bit. She *was* going to the bad place, one

where she couldn't breathe and couldn't think and she was naked on the home page of every single gossip site in existence.

In her mind, at least.

So she did as she was told. She took a breath. Several, in fact, as well as a few sips from the water bottle Laurel produced from her bag.

"What is going on with Gia?" Dylan asked when she felt like she could handle the answer.

Laurel frowned. "What do you mean?"

Dylan gave her a look, set the water bottle on the floor. "This makes me wonder how often you lie to me."

"I'm your manager—lying to you is part of the gig. You don't want to know everything, trust me."

"Yes, I do."

Laurel laughed, her dark coils bouncing. "No. You don't."

Dylan was starting to feel the need for more deep breaths. "Okay, well, Rayna spilled the beans anyway, so why is Gia calling you all the time? Our last scene was great."

Laurel sighed, leaned against the wall. "One ten-minute scene that took three days."

Her voice was soft, soothing, but her words were like knives nicking along Dylan's skin. Dylan opened her mouth. Closed it. She couldn't refute what Laurel said, but she had this now, she knew how to play Eloise . . .

Didn't she?

Suddenly, she wasn't so sure, her confidence melting like snow under a spring-warm sun. As she sat there, her cheeks reddening under Laurel's indictment of her abilities—however gently said— Gia's and Blair's voices over the past several days started filtering into her brain.

I can't believe I let them . . .

You get handed the role on a silver platter . . .

Pulling you, yes. I didn't even want . . .

Dylan pressed the heels of her hands to her eyes until she saw starbursts.

"Laurel," she said.

"Dylan."

She paused, wondering if she could just *not* ask the question, but no. The words settled on her tongue, inching toward her mouth. They were going to be free no matter what.

She took one more fortifying breath. Then . . .

"Did the studio even want me to play Eloise?"

She asked it quietly, with her eyes still covered, a kaleidoscope of color swirling behind her vision.

Silence at first.

A silence that stretched long enough that Dylan dropped her hands and looked up at her manager, whose pretty form was spotty and multicolored as Dylan's vision adjusted.

"Don't lie to me," she said. "I need to know what—"

"No."

Dylan's mouth snapped shut.

Well, now she knew.

"Then why . . ." she started but trailed off. She wasn't sure what she wanted to know now, wasn't sure it even mattered. She felt beat-up, a rag doll flung around by a thoughtless child. She knew she was lucky—she *did* know. She had a major role in a movie, and she never had to worry about money, and she shouldn't complain, shouldn't feel such a hollow place in her chest, but she couldn't help it.

She'd wanted this to be hers.

This movie, this role, this new chapter in her life.

But it turned out Blair was right.

"Then why did they cast me?" she finally managed to ask.

Laurel sighed again, but when she spoke, her voice was firm, sure. "Because you needed it."

Dylan looked up at her. "I needed it."

"You hadn't worked in months. You'd just broken up with Jocelyn, with the champagne in the Mondrian's pool and that helicopter fiasco—"

"I was there."

"You were drowning," Laurel went on. "You needed a new image. You *wanted* a new image, and my job is to get it for you."

Dylan shook her head, thoughts swirling. "How did Adriana even . . . *As If You Didn't Know* is major motion picture. Skylark is a major studio. Millions and millions of dollars. How?"

Laurel shrugged nonchalantly. "Adriana is good at her job, and I'm not too shabby myself. And you're a name. A big one. You think Skylark Studios would pass up turning Killin' Dylan into America's sweetheart? No, they wouldn't. And Gia got over it."

Dylan blinked. "So Adriana just . . . what? Pawned me off as some story?"

"I think Adriana would call it a pitch. But, sweetie," Laurel said gently, "everything in this business is a story."

Dylan opened her mouth to refute that, but realized she couldn't. Not one bit. Hollywood was a tapestry of tales, dreamed and woven and made. Hardly anything was organic, everything a carefully planned move. A strategy.

Even love.

"Rayna wants me to date Ramona," Dylan said, her hands pressed her to knees. She stared at a spot on the floor, a whorl of dark and light wood, waiting for Laurel to speak.

But Laurel said nothing. She let the words hover between them, and this too was probably a strategy.

"Say something," Dylan said.

Laurel sighed. "You know what I'm going to say, Dylan."

"Say something different, then."

"I can't do that," Laurel said. "I do what's best for your career. You already know Ramona. From your childhood, for god's sake. She was your first kiss. Is this such a stretch?"

A stretch.

Everything in Hollywood felt like a stretch. The tiniest bend of reality that still seemed to send the whole world askew more times than not.

But Dylan had to admit, professionally speaking, dating Ramona probably was a good idea. With all of Dylan's bad publicity, with the stakes of this film and her struggles with her role already, with the fact that Dylan did want a new image, she did want to broaden her scope, her reputation, her . . .

Her *story*.

Being with Ramona could only help. It would help her image, sure, but it would also help Dylan. After sitting with Ramona on the beach in that cove, talking with her, hearing about her life, Dylan had become Eloise. She'd done her job and she'd done it well. Ramona was an inspiration, a *muse*, if Dylan wanted to get dramatic about it.

But that was the thing—it wouldn't be dramatic. Dating Ramona wouldn't be wild and messy and packed with betrayal and pools full of champagne.

It would be calm.

Planned.

A story, that was it.

There was really only one problem.

She knew Ramona would never go for it.

True, she didn't know Ramona that well, but she didn't seem like the kind of person who would want to take part in a bona fide Hollywood shenanigan to reinvent Dylan's image. Ramona was *real*, and she was about real things.

Dylan closed her eyes, trying to figure out how to work this, if it even could be worked, but then she realized something.

She *liked* Ramona. Ramona Riley was the first girl Dylan had ever kissed, a person she actually enjoyed being with. It wouldn't be hard to spend more time with her. Hold her hand. Sure, she hadn't planned on acting on her crush, as every romantic relationship she'd ever had ended in disaster, but Ramona would be different.

Because Dylan could control the ending.

She'd ask Ramona out, pose it as summer fun, that was it. They were already hanging out so Dylan could experience some normalcy, why not add some hand-holding to the mix? It wouldn't even be a lie. Dylan was certainly attracted to Ramona, wouldn't mind at all if they kissed a little, but that would be it. If Ramona helped smooth out some of Dylan's admittedly rough edges . . . was there really any harm in that?

This was easy.

Innocent.

So, no, Dylan and Ramona weren't such a stretch. Ramona had her own life here, and Dylan's was in LA. This was simple. Or it *could* be simple if Dylan would just get out of her own head. She nodded to herself, as though she could shake the prickle of unease right out of her gut. That was just nerves. Just crush feelings. This would be fine. She'd date Ramona, they'd have fun together, and Dylan would prove all the assholes wrong with her portrayal of Eloise Tucker.

And when it was all over, it would be over.

"Okay," she said, standing up. "I'll do it."

Laurel smiled, said nothing, but she didn't have to.

Dylan turned to face the mirror, wiped away the mascara flakes under her eyes, smoothed the tangles in her hair from where her hands had knotted in the tresses.

Then she opened the door and went to find Ramona Riley.

Chapter Seventeen

"THERE'S OUR FAMOUS GIRL!"

Ramona had barely set foot in Clover Moon when the entire place erupted.

"Ramona, how did it happen?"

"Have you kissed her yet?"

"Does she wear colored contacts?"

Ramona blinked in the doorway as every single eye in the dining room landed on her, townsfolk shouting at her from their seats.

"Don't forget about us when you get married!"

"What's she like in bed, honey?"

This from Annette Fontaine, an octogenarian with a penchant for smut.

"Annette, for god's sake," Ramona said.

Annette just shrugged and went back to her omelet.

"Hey, darling!"

"Oh, Jesus," Ramona said, clutching at her chest. Penny Hampton, of *Penny for Your Thoughts*, had popped up next to her like a jack-in-the-box from hell.

"Sorry, doll," Penny said. "Would you mind if I asked you some questions?" She thrust her phone in Ramona's face, voice memo app recording.

"Penny, seriously?" she asked.

Penny nodded vigorously. Her shoulder-length copper hair—which Ramona was almost positive she dyed to match the color of an actual penny—didn't even move when she did, frozen into a football helmet style by an entire can of Aqua Net.

"I'm always serious about the town's goings-on," Penny said, "and this is the biggest news to hit our little hamlet since the movie itself."

"Oh, I doubt that," April said from Ramona's other side. "Nothing is bigger than when Howie Hanlin had to go to the ER in Manchester for sticking the handle of a hairbrush up his—"

"And I'll get back to you," Ramona said to Penny, grabbing April's arm and hauling her to the back of the diner. Olive had found Marley, and the two of them were hunched over Marley's phone at the counter. Ramona didn't want to think about what had them so engrossed, though she had a good idea.

It wasn't as though Ramona had done anything wrong, or that she was ashamed even. She'd played mini-golf, for god's sake. And while Clover Lake was small and everyone was always in everyone's business, Ramona wasn't quite used to this kind of prying.

Or attention.

Of course, after her mother left town, the town was abuzz, but they also had the wherewithal to shut up when Ramona and her dad were around, and they brought casseroles. Lots and lots of casseroles, as though Rebecca had died. And in retrospect, she kind of had.

She'd disappeared from their lives just as completely.

"This is amazing," April said as Ramona continued tugging her to the back. Ramona waved at Owen as he came out of the kitchen, and she and April headed for his office. As she closed the door, she heard his voice boom through the dining room.

"All right, folks, finish up! I need everyone out of here in ten minutes!"

A cheer went up, because Clover Lake was Clover Lake, excited over getting kicked out of a diner for a Hollywood film, and Ramona pressed her back to the door.

"So when's the next date?" April asked, folding her arms.

"Not you too," Ramona said. "I told you, nothing—"

"I know what you told me. I also know it's bullshit."

"It absolutely is not bullshit."

"Okay, well, it should be."

Ramona pressed her hands to her forehead. "I'm dizzy. I'm literally dizzy."

"Love will do that."

Ramona dropped her hands. "Be serious."

"I *am*. This is some serious Meant to Be shit."

Ramona scoffed. "That kind of thinking has never worked out very well for anyone in this room."

April's expression froze for a second, then her mouth snapped shut. "Right."

"Honey," Ramona said, exhaling heavily. "I'm sorry. I didn't mean it like that."

April's jaw was tight. "No, no, I'm fully aware that the person I thought was my Meant to Be discarded me like a piece of trash."

"Apes," Ramona said softly. "I just mean I don't think about Dylan that way. I can't. And you're not trash. You're perfect."

"Oh, I know." April agreed, and they both laughed softly before April grew serious again. "I'm not saying you have to believe in fairy tales," April said, lifting her eyes to Ramona. "But I want you to at least believe in *you*."

Ramona sighed, unsure how to respond to that. Luckily, she didn't have a chance. A knock sounded on the door, vibrating against Ramona's back and causing her to yelp. She clapped her hands over her mouth.

"Ramona? Are you in there?"

Dylan.

Ramona turned and flung the door open, then pulled Dylan inside.

"Whoa," Dylan said as she was hurled toward the couch.

"She's a little excited," April said, the energy in her voice back to normal levels, much to Ramona's relief. She winked at Ramona, then leaned against Owen's desk, which was completely covered in papers and sticky notes. The man hated computers.

"Sorry," Ramona said to Dylan. "This is just . . . unexpected."

"I know," Dylan said.

"But not unwelcome," April said.

"Okay, get out," Ramona said, opening the door again.

"What?" April said.

"I can't think with your constant two cents," Ramona said, waving her hand at the hall. "Out."

"Llama Face."

"Don't Llama Face me. Go.

"What do I get if I do?"

Ramona loved April. Would die for her, truly, but she swore to god. She rubbed her temples. "I'll watch *Serendipity* with you later. Again."

April narrowed her eyes. "Oh, well played." She ambled out of the room at a glacial pace. As soon as she cleared the doorway, Ramona pushed the door closed, and she was pretty sure it hit April in the butt before clicking shut.

"*Serendipity*?" Dylan asked.

"April's favorite movie."

Silence settled between them for a second before Dylan inhaled deeply and steepled her fingers, pressing the tips under her chin. "Can we talk? I mean, about something other than Kate Beckinsale movies."

Ramona swallowed thickly. "Um. Yeah. Sure."

Dylan motioned to the couch, then sat as Ramona made her way to the plaid monstrosity she was pretty sure Owen found in an alley. She sank down, the springs squeaking.

"So," Dylan said. "Exciting morning."

Ramona laughed nervously. "Yeah. To say the least."

"I'm sorry about that."

Ramona waved a hand. "You've apologized enough. Really."

Dylan nodded, fiddled with a loose string dangling from an artful rip in her jeans. She cleared her throat. Cleared it again.

"You okay?" Ramona asked.

"Yeah, yeah," Dylan said, wrapping the now free string around her forefinger. "I'm super."

"Super."

Dylan's laugh was shaky. "Okay. Yeah. I think I'm a little nervous."

"Nervous?" Butterflies swelled in Ramona's own stomach. "Why?"

Dylan took a deep breath, kept twining that string around her finger. "Because with all the excitement this morning, I . . . well, I started thinking."

They were larger than butterflies now. Some huge, winged creature flapping away in Ramona's gut. Yesterday at Mirror Cove flashed through her memory—yesterday and eighteen years ago—two girls, lonely, hungry, free with each other in a way they couldn't seem to find with anyone else.

"Oh?" Ramona said, but her voice squeaked like a prepubescent. She coughed, told herself to calm the hell down.

Dylan's finger was now nearly purple from the string cutting off her circulation. She unwound it quickly, flung it to the floor. "Yeah," she said, rubbing at her finger as it changed back to its normal color. "And . . . and I think we should go on a date."

Even though Ramona was half expecting this exact thing, she

was also half expecting Dylan to say they shouldn't hang out at all anymore, and she honestly wasn't sure which one she preferred. Her brain and heart battled it out—practicality and emotion, Noelle Yang against comfort in Clover Lake, thirteen-year-old Cherry versus thirty-one-year-old Ramona.

"Oh?" Ramona said. Again. Seemed like that two-letter word was the only thing left in her vocabulary.

"Just casual," Dylan said. "You know . . . fun. Not so different from what we've been doing, really. Just, you know . . . it's like . . . different because, I might, I don't know. Hold your finger."

"My finger?"

"I mean *hand*. Jesus." Dylan rubbed her forehead. "I'm very bad at this."

Somehow, Dylan's fumbling calmed Ramona down a bit—comfort that she wasn't the only one who was freaking out here.

Maybe it was a bad idea, a colossal mistake. There was really no chance for anything serious here—they came from two different worlds—and Noelle Yang hovered in Ramona's mind, an elegant ghost, a haunting of everything she wanted.

But she had to admit, she wanted this too.

It didn't have to be a big deal.

Fun, as Dylan said.

The whole town already thought they were dating anyway, and Ramona was tired of saying no to things. For all the ways April drove Ramona bananas, she was right about one thing—Ramona had put her life on hold for Olive and her family.

But she didn't have to do that anymore.

And if she wanted to hold Dylan Monroe's finger, goddammit, she would do it.

For herself. And for Cherry, that thirteen-year-old girl who felt so forgettable, so . . . *left*.

"Yes," Ramona said.

Dylan dropped her hand from her forehead. "Yes?"

Ramona smiled. "Yes."

Dylan smiled too, her hand twitching in her lap, as if she wanted to hold Ramona's hand right now. And maybe she would've, had April Evans not screamed "Yes!" from the other side of the office door at that very moment.

Ramona kept smiling serenely, kept her eyes on Dylan, then said calmly, "I'm going to kill her."

Dylan just laughed, then reached out and took Ramona's hand, lacing their fingers together and squeezing. It lasted only a moment before another knock sounded on the door—Laurel telling Dylan that Noelle was on her way for costume and makeup—but it was enough to send Ramona's stomach into a free fall.

Noelle's name echoed through her thoughts.

Casual, she told herself. *Fun.*

"Will you be here later?" Dylan asked as they stood up, their hands dropping away.

"Later?" Ramona asked.

"For filming?"

"Oh. No, I wasn't planning—"

"Please?" Dylan said. "I could use a friendly face while I inevitably do everything wrong."

Ramona looked down, tried to force Noelle Yang out of her head, but the more she tried, the more that was the only thing she could think about.

"Please?" Dylan said again, then twined her fingers back through Ramona's.

Ramona stared at their hands before lifting her gaze to Dylan's eyes. Those iceberg eyes, so clear Ramona felt like she was tipping into an icy pool, breath-stealing water closing over her head.

"Okay," she heard herself say, and in that moment, she wasn't sure she'd ever be able to say no to Lolli-Dolly-Dylan Monroe.

Chapter Eighteen

HOURS LATER, DYLAN stood behind the counter at Clover Moon Café—an apron around her waist, her hair up in a high ponytail, frayed denim shorts tickling her legs—keenly aware that she'd really only trained with Ramona at the diner that one time, and also that she was on the verge of melting down.

The diner didn't look all that different—townsfolk being paid as extras still filled most of the tables, pie still crowded the pastry case, and the air still smelled like coffee and french fries. The only differences, really, were the cameras everywhere, Gia barking orders, and Noelle currently adjusting Blair's sleek gray suit on the other side of the bar before they started filming.

Oh, and the fact that Dylan was hyperaware that she wasn't even last choice for the role of Eloise—she hadn't been a choice at all. She hadn't had time to properly process that information, what with asking out Ramona and all the havoc that had caused in the center of her chest, like a hurricane blowing in from the Atlantic. But now that it was time to do her job, she couldn't think of anything else.

She kept glancing at Blair—who looked perfect and professional as Mallory for their meet-cute scene—wondering if she knew.

Blair huffed a breath. "Why do you keep staring at me?" She

didn't even glance at Dylan when she spoke, just kept her eyes straight ahead as Noelle tugged on a shoulder pad that didn't seem to want to behave.

"I'm not," Dylan said.

"You are. What, you need a little more attention?"

Dylan flinched. "What the hell does that mean?"

Finally, Blair deigned a glance. "Don't be coy. It's much less annoying if you just own it."

"Easy, kittens," Noelle deadpanned, a pin protruding from one side of her mouth.

"Own *what*?" Dylan asked.

Blair just shook her head.

"You know," Dylan started, even though her brain was telling her to shut up, "we might not struggle so much in these scenes if it wasn't abundantly clear you'd rather swallow broken glass than engage in a romance with me."

Blair laughed. "That's not the issue, Dylan. I can do my job."

"And I can't?"

Blair closed her eyes, then looked at the ceiling. "Look, I'm not going to get into this right now."

"Please, get into it."

Blair turned then, disrupting Noelle's work as she popped a hand on her hip. "You really want to do this? You really want me to say that you're a spoiled, privileged brat who gets handed everything and still pisses it all away, while other people in this industry"— she pointed a finger at her own chest—"start from nothing, work their asses off, deal with racism and misogynoir and homophobia every single fucking day and still manage to do it with a modicum of respect for other people, still show up and know their lines and do their job like a goddamn queen? You really want me to say all that right now?"

Dylan's whole face felt frozen, her mouth hanging open, her eyes wide. Noelle had frozen too, her mouth pursed and her arms folded as she waited for Blair's tirade to end.

"I didn't think so," Blair said when Dylan said nothing. "Noelle, could we finish up somewhere else? I'm sorry for the interruption."

"No problem," Noelle said, and then the two of them moved off toward the front door.

Dylan stared after them for a few seconds. Blair's words floated through her brain like puzzle pieces flung into the air, the letters slowly falling and settling into some semblance of meaning.

And the completed picture wasn't pretty.

Then she heard a throat clear.

She turned to see Ramona standing about five feet away, an uncertain look on her face that told Dylan she'd heard every single word.

"Hi," she said. A set pass hung around her neck, but she jutted a thumb toward the back room. "I'm all done helping out here, so I'll—"

But Dylan didn't let her finish. She reached out and grabbed Ramona's hand, pulling her closer. She stopped before swallowing Ramona fully into her arms—even though she could use a goddamn hug right now—but she kept hold of Ramona's hand, her grip a little too tight.

"You okay?" Ramona asked softly.

Dylan didn't answer—couldn't, because that would mean Ramona really did hear everything Blair said. Instead, she just smiled, shook her hair out of her face.

"Any last-minute tips?" she asked.

Ramona's eyes searched hers. They searched for so long, Dylan started to worry Ramona had changed her mind, that she could suddenly see right through her, see that Dylan was made of nothing but glitter and glass, flimsy and breakable, all shine and no substance.

But then Ramona leaned closer, a small smile on her mouth. "Just remember Eloise is a mess too."

Dylan's breath tangled in her chest.

Too.

Eloise is a mess *too.*

But Ramona's voice was so soft, so sweet, Dylan didn't feel insulted or attacked. She felt . . . seen. She had a sudden and wild urge to kiss Ramona, or at least lean her head against hers. Get closer somehow. She couldn't remember the last time she'd felt like this—this *seen* feeling that didn't come with shame or guilt or fear, but simply . . .

She didn't know.

Couldn't even find a word for it.

"Maybe afterward," she said, thumb swiping over the back of Ramona's hand, "we can—"

But then she saw Laurel.

Right across from them by a booth, her phone aimed in their direction. She seemed to snap a picture, then looked at it with a smile on her face. Her eyes met Dylan's and she gave her a thumbs-up.

"Maybe we can what?" Ramona asked. She turned to see whom Dylan was looking at, but Laurel had moved on by then.

Dylan shook her head. She didn't think she could do this. Couldn't date Ramona under Laurel's gaze, Rayna's and Gia's, no matter how much she agreed that it would help her career right now. She just—

"Maybe we could hang out?" Ramona asked, her fingers tightening on Dylan's.

Dylan let out a breath. Let herself say "Yeah." Because she wanted to. It didn't matter who else was pushing her toward Ramona . . . Dylan wanted to push herself.

"Yeah," she said again. "Maybe we could hang out."

Ramona grinned, squeezed Dylan's hand again, and then she was walking away, and Gia was calling out that it was time to start, and cameras were moving into position, and lights warmed on Dylan's face as she wiped down the counter, this time as Eloise—a tired, discouraged Eloise Tucker.

And soon, the only girl Eloise had ever loved would walk through the café door, and then . . .

Dylan's eyes found Ramona one more time. She was standing in the hallway that led to the back, but still visible, still watching Dylan with a smile. Gia called, "Action," then all but glared at Dylan with her arms crossed as though waiting for her to fuck up.

And Dylan did stumble over her first line to her boss, Nate, played by character actor Michael Wiley, but it seemed to work as he was asking Eloise to cover a shift later that evening, which would put her on a fifteen-hour workday. Eloise was harried and exhausted, and Dylan's nerves fit right in with that. Miraculously, Gia didn't yell *Cut*, or sigh heavily or anything. She did continue glaring, and Dylan ignored her.

She did her job.

And when Blair walked into the café as Mallory, Dylan did exactly what she was supposed to do—act completely annoyed with this posh woman asking for an oat milk lavender latte with low foam and a shot of collagen.

"*Collagen?*" Dylan asked as Eloise.

Mallory nodded, her face hidden from view as she riffled through her tiny leather bag. "*Boosts skin's elasticity. You should really try it.*"

"*Thanks for that tip, but we don't have collagen.*"

Blair as Mallory finally looked up, and Dylan as Eloise took a step back, recognition washing over her. She let her mouth fall open, then close, remembering how she felt in the bowling alley when she realized Ramona was Cherry . . . how she felt when she realized

Cherry had just been left by her mother when they met . . . how she still felt every time she looked at Ramona—as though the world tilted, turned, twisted around just to bring them right here, right now.

"*Mal?*" Dylan said, her voice a whisper.

Mallory frowned, eyes narrowed, clearly not recognizing Eloise at first, but then her eyes widened. Still, it was too late, and Eloise was embarrassed.

"*Um, let me get that latte started for you,*" she said, then busied herself while Mallory sank onto a pleather stool in her thousand-dollar suit, watching Eloise work. When Eloise finally handed over the drink, their hands met.

"*Ellie,*" Mallory said.

Dylan pressed her eyes closed, let her lashes brush her cheek for a second before she looked up.

"*You remember,*" she said, her voice quiet.

"*I remember you,*" Mallory said.

"Cut!" Gia called out, then walked over to the two actors as the cameras reset. She looked at Dylan for a second, then just nodded and knocked on the bar top. "Ready to go again in five minutes."

Dylan didn't dare react, just pulled her hand from Blair's calmly and took a sip of water from her bottle under the counter. Her hands were shaking, and she couldn't help the smile that pulled at her mouth when she spotted Ramona in the hallway, who beamed at her like she'd invented moonlight. Except that smiling while drinking water didn't really mix, and a stream of liquid dribbled down her chin and onto her light blue blouse, staining it dark.

"Shit," she said, trying to brush it off, but that just spread it around even more.

"Don't do that," Ramona said, appearing at her side with a towel. "Dab."

Dylan laughed nervously but did as Ramona instructed. "I don't think that's going to help either." Her hands still shook, and she couldn't tell if it was from adrenaline or nerves or the fact that she'd just fucked up her costume. Eloise couldn't very well have a huge spill all over her shirt after very obviously *not* having one the second before.

"Noelle!" Gia called.

Dylan glanced at her director, who was back to glaring.

"Great," Dylan muttered so only Ramona could hear her.

"It's okay," Ramona said. "You're doing great."

"Yeah?"

Ramona met her eyes, smiled. "Yeah."

"Okay, what do we have here?" Noelle asked. She put her hands on her hips, eyed Dylan's shirt over her orange-framed glasses. "Easy."

Then she disappeared into the back as quickly as she'd come.

"I guess that means she'll fix it?" Dylan said.

Ramona didn't answer, just stared after Noelle, her mouth slightly open.

"Ramona?"

She startled. "Yeah? Sorry," she said as Noelle hurried back into view, a blue blouse in her hands.

"Always bring at least three of everything for this very reason," Noelle said as she started unbuttoning Dylan's shirt right there.

Which . . . was not a big deal. It was a shirt. Dylan had on a bra underneath, of course, and when costume mishaps happened on set, you changed in front of everyone. It was standard, and no one in Hollywood gave two shits.

But Ramona wasn't Hollywood.

"Um" was all Dylan could think to say as the cool air in the café hit the bare skin of her stomach and chest. Ramona's cheeks bloomed red, her eyes flitting down to Dylan's boobs before darting away. She pressed her mouth together, cleared her throat. It was sort of adorable, if Dylan were being honest. Still, she needed to fill the awkward silence with something as Noelle yanked off her stained shirt.

"Noelle, this is my friend, Ramona," she said, nodding in Ramona's direction.

Ramona's eyes went wide. "H-h-hi."

"Hey, there," Noelle said, smiling as she tugged the blouse onto Dylan's body. "You're from here?"

Ramona nodded, then straightened her shoulders. "Lived here all my life. With one exceptional year."

"And what was that?" Noelle asked. Her fingers worked quickly on the mother-of-pearl buttons, then she moved on to tucking the shirt into Dylan's shorts, a task Dylan could've easily done herself, but Noelle was famously meticulous, so Dylan let her do her thing.

"What was what?" Ramona asked.

"What was your exceptional year?" Noelle asked.

"Oh." Ramona swallowed, ran her hand over the back of her neck. "I was at RISD for a while."

Noelle brightened at that. "Were you? I went to RISD."

Ramona smiled. "I know."

"What's your medium?" Noelle asked, finally finishing with Dylan. But before Ramona could answer, Gia bellowed that it was time to go again. Ramona hurried off set, and Noelle adjusted Dylan's shirt a bit more, calling Vee over with an iPad to compare it to the shirt in the scene before.

And then they were off again. Dylan Monroe receded, and Eloise Tucker took over, fumbling and blushing and spilling coffee around a girl she'd all but given up as lost.

Chapter Nineteen

RAMONA COULDN'T STOP shaking.

She wasn't sure if it was adrenaline from officially meeting No-elle Yang, or the fact that Noelle was perfect and lovely and asked about her life, or the fact that Dylan had no idea about this said life, at least not anything that Ramona really wanted or dreamed.

But *Noelle Yang*.

Ramona also couldn't stop smiling. She leaned against the hall-way wall, half watching the scene, half replaying the admittedly very short conversation she'd just had with her actual hero.

Her fingers itched to create something—a tea-length dress cov-ered in tiny solar-powered lights, chiffon underneath that rustled when the wearer moved, a gentle *shhh* paired with the sparkle and shine. That was what she'd put Eloise Tucker in for her big party that took place toward the end of the book. Off-white satin with a blush-pink, light-infused swirl over the whole dress, capped sleeves and a sweetheart neckline, like a queer Audrey Hepburn.

It was perfect, this picture in her mind. She knew a large part of a costume designer's job was to simply select existing garments that fit a character—but Noelle designed plenty of her own pieces too, and that was what Ramona loved most. That a piece that existed because Ramona made it so, the creation, drawing and sewing into being.

As she watched Dylan and Blair act out their roles, Dylan perfectly flustered and unsure, Blair like a comet on its sure path, her chest felt like it was full of sparklers, that excitement and longing that she just couldn't shake.

And she didn't want to. She let her mind wander, dozens of designs taking shape in her mind, rich fabrics for Mallory and simple elegance for Eloise. Then she drifted off into other books she'd loved, queer stories that she could see so clearly on the screen, the clothes that surrounded the actors bringing them to life, making them *real*, the magic of a simple blazer or pair of jeans or the most elaborate suit or dress her imagination could conjure. It *was* magic, and she—

"Hey," Dylan said, suddenly beside her and beaming. Sweat dotted her brow, but her smile could've lit the entire room. All around them, things were being broken down, crew packing up. Ramona glanced at her watch and realized hours had passed while she stood in the hallway, daydreaming.

Because that's all it really was . . . a daydream.

Wasn't it?

"You're done?" she asked Dylan.

Dylan nodded, still grinning. She took both of Ramona's hands between them. "And I kicked ass and I want to go celebrate. You with me?"

Ramona felt that same sparkly sensation in her chest—because she wanted this too.

"Yeah," she said, squeezing Dylan's hands. "I'm with you."

DYLAN WOULDN'T TELL Ramona where they were going. After they left Clover Moon, she sent Ramona home with instructions to wear something comfortable, which for Ramona meant a pair of mauve overalls with a black tee underneath, cuffed over a pair of lavender Docs with flower-shaped buckles.

"At least give me a hint," Ramona said after Dylan picked her up in her rental car. They drove out of town and hit I-93 North.

Dylan shook her head. She was dressed in light-wash jeans and a maroon tee with *Lonely Only for You* in white script across the chest. "You'll love it. Is that enough of a hint?"

"I also love hot dogs with mayonnaise, so . . . not really."

Dylan laughed. "Are you serious? Mayonnaise?"

"It's delicious!" Ramona said. "Mix in a little ketchup too, some salt and pepper. A delicacy."

Dylan shook her head but kept smiling. Ramona smiled too, glanced out the window. It was early evening, the sun just starting to spread gold over the summer trees, turning the green leaves a softer yellow. It was lovely, and Ramona felt a swell of excitement as they headed deeper into the country.

She hadn't been on a date in so long. With the excitement of the set and Noelle, it hadn't truly hit her until now that she was on a date at all. Not just a hookup with Logan, which usually featured a cold beer seconds before they tumbled into bed, but a real date.

With Dylan Monroe.

Ramona nearly laughed. It was absurd, really, that she, this small-town waitress, would be on a date with an honest-to-god celebrity.

Maybe slumming it a little will calm Jack and Carrie's wildling down a bit . . .

The gossipy article's words came back to her like a hand to her face, swiping the smile right off. She went quiet, focused on the scenery out the window. She wasn't even sure where they were. She'd lived in New Hampshire all her life but, honestly, didn't venture beyond Clover Lake very often, and if she did, it was south to Concord or Manchester for the bigger shops or the airport. She led a small life, and nothing made that more apparent than sitting next to Dylan Monroe.

"Almost there," Dylan said softly, smiling at Ramona as she turned off the interstate, as though she could tell Ramona was a bit caught in her feelings.

"And *there* would be?" Ramona asked.

"Nice try." Dylan turned onto a secluded state road, which they stayed on for about a mile before turning left at a wooden sign that read THE EARTHSTARS.

"What's this?" Ramona asked, the dirt road bumping under the car's tires.

"You'll see."

"Earthstars are actually a type of mushroom," Ramona said.

"Is that so?" Dylan asked. The trees started to clear, and Ramona saw a flash of red up ahead.

"They're one of my favorites," she said. "Their name is really cool, but they also have this beautiful shape, like a flower and a starfish combined, and . . . they . . ."

But she trailed off as the trees completely cleared, revealing a red wooden building—more like a large cottage—nestled in the forest, green trees hugging the structure. A sign arched over the top of the teal front door.

THE EARTHSTARS MUSEUM

"Wait . . ." Ramona said as Dylan pulled into a parking space. There were a few other cars in the gravel lot, and Ramona noticed there were tiny hand-painted mushrooms along the wooden railing that bordered the path to the door. "Is this . . ."

She looked at Dylan, who was watching her and smiling pretty damn smugly.

"Is this a mushroom museum?" Ramona asked.

Dylan's smile widened. "I think it might be."

Ramona glanced back at the building. "I didn't even know this existed."

"It just opened a few weeks ago. I found it on the internet during my lunch break today," Dylan said, setting the car in park and unbuckling her seat belt. "You want to go inside?"

Ramona laughed, unbuckled her own belt. "Um, yes."

Inside, it was cozy and cool, decorated in a cottage-core style, and Ramona couldn't keep her jaw in place. Dylan paid for two tickets at a tiny glass booth, and the wide-eyed teenager working there handed Dylan a museum guide in the shape of the quintessential red-and-white fly agaric mushroom. She handed it to Ramona, who spent a good ten seconds marveling at the details on the glossy front cover.

"I think there's even some information inside," Dylan said.

Ramona laughed again. "Sorry, it's just so pretty!"

Dylan's shoulder pressed against hers. "So . . . you like it?"

Ramona locked onto those icy eyes, and her breath did something bubbly in her chest. "Yeah," she said quietly. "I love it."

Dylan exhaled, a sweet smile on her lips. "Good."

Ramona nodded. "Yeah. Good."

She had to look away then, Dylan's gaze too intense and her lungs too lighter-than-air to get a decent breath. Instead she took in the museum, which was two stories and all honey-colored wood, from the floors to the guardrails by the displays to the ceilings. This first level was mostly one large open room, and all around the perimeter were glass cases full of local flora and fauna and, of course, fungi.

Ramona opened the guide, searching for some of her favorites.

"Oh my god, they have a basket stinkhorn!" she said.

"They have a what?" Dylan asked.

"And a *Cordyceps*!"

"Okay, why don't we—"

"Holy shit, a violet-toothed polypore."

Dylan laughed, then Ramona felt her take one of her hands, twine their fingers together. Ramona's breath caught, but she couldn't seem to move her eyes away from the mushroom guide.

"Let's walk," Dylan said.

As Dylan started to lead her into the main room, she noticed the teen in the glass booth had their phone surreptitiously pointed in their direction.

"Dylan," she said, but Dylan just kept moving, and so Ramona let herself be led inside the magical world of mushrooms. She still couldn't believe this place existed, not an hour from her own house, and that Dylan had found it.

For *her*.

Ramona's stomach had joined her chest in that bubbly feeling—Dylan had researched, remembered that Ramona loved mushrooms, and found something that was purely *Ramona*.

She couldn't think of the last time someone did something like this for her. Truly just for her, because Ramona didn't think Dylan was also obsessed with fungi.

Her throat felt impossibly thick all of a sudden, her fingers growing sweaty around Dylan's. Still, Dylan held on, leading her to the first display and stopping.

"Tell me about this one," she said.

Ramona focused on the mushroom behind the glass, a brilliant orange yellow growing from the trunk of a tree that the building itself seemed to be built around.

"Chicken of the woods," Ramona said.

"Did you say *chicken*?"

Ramona laughed. "Isn't it cute?"

"It looks like a brain."

"It's edible! But don't eat a bunch at first, because a lot of people have stomach issues with them."

Dylan snort-laughed. "I don't think you have to worry about that."

Ramona grinned. "Not appetizing?"

"Did you hear my brain comment?"

Ramona just shook her head as they wandered to the next display. There were several other people in the room, fellow mushroom enthusiasts, but Ramona also noticed they were paying a lot of attention to Dylan, a few phones out, whispering to one another.

"I think we have an audience," Ramona said quietly.

Dylan lifted her brows, looked around the room. Then she waved at everyone, smiling beatifically. "It's fine," she said. "Part of the gig. Better to just acknowledge them once, then ignore them. What's this one?" She motioned to the next mushroom, but Ramona felt uneasy, the hairs on the back of her neck prickling from the attention.

"Um," she said, trying to focus on the mushroom, which wasn't hard once she realized what it was. "Mauve parachutes."

"You do realize you just said that in the same tone one might coo over a new puppy."

Ramona nudged Dylan's shoulder. "Just look at them. These are actually my very favorite mushroom." She pressed closer to the glass, staring at the tiny, flowerlike fungi with the mauve-colored umbrella-like cap, delicately fanning over a thin, darker pink stalk. They grew on the forest floor, usually in bunches like a bouquet.

"They look so vulnerable," Dylan said.

"They do," Ramona said. "But they're really tough. They shrivel up when it's dry to wait for rain, then they open back up to life. They have marcescence."

"Mushroom newb over here."

Ramona grinned. "It's a mycological term that indicates reviving ability."

"So they basically die . . . and come back to life?"

"Sort of. And look." She tapped on the glass. "They're just so beautiful. Like flowers. They're also called purple pinwheels. And nature just *made* that. It's a miracle."

She knew her mouth was hanging open, like she was watching an eclipse or some other rare phenomenon, but in a way she was. She sighed happily, ready to move on, but when she looked at Dylan, Dylan was looking right back at her, her own mouth open a little too.

"What?" Ramona asked.

Dylan just shook her head. "Nothing. Just . . ." She shrugged, then took Ramona's hand again and ambled with her to the next display. She let Ramona prattle on and on, even seemed interested, and when they left two hours later and headed for a local fast-food restaurant that purportedly had the best seasoned fries on the East Coast—all researched and discovered by Dylan—Ramona felt like she was a kid who'd just visited her favorite theme park.

Or . . . maybe she was a small-town girl who'd just experienced the best date of her life.

Chapter Twenty

RAMONA DIDN'T SEE Dylan at all the next day. She knew they were filming at the diner, but she and April had promised to take Olive and Marley shopping for dorm room supplies in Concord, the closest town with big commercial stores most likely to have everything they needed.

"Wait, you didn't kiss?" April said as they strolled through the bedding aisle at Target. April pushed the cart, which was already half-full of plastic hooks, a lamp with a purple shade, two shower caddies, shower shoes, and a jumbo pack of ramen.

"There wasn't really a great opportunity," Ramona said as she investigated which pack of twin sheets was the cheapest but also wouldn't feel like Olive was sleeping on sandpaper.

"You're both terrible gays, you know that, right?" April said, leaning on the cart's handle.

Ramona laughed. "She walked me to my door like a gentleperson, though."

"And . . ." April rolled her hand for more details.

"And . . . Dad opened the door."

"Clam-jammed by Mr. Riley."

Ramona laughed again. "He turned so red. Said he thought he heard something and was worried it was the paparappi again."

"You mean paparazzi?"

"No, he said paparappi."

"Oh my god, why is he so cute?"

Ramona shook her head. "Anyway, it was fine. We had so much fun—"

"I mean, nothing spells romance like fungi."

"But I'm not even sure I . . ."

Ramona sighed while April lifted a brow.

"You're not sure you what?" April asked.

"I just . . ." Ramona picked a pack of white sheets with tiny purple flowers all over them. "She's Dylan Monroe."

"Oh, is that her name?"

"She's famous, Apes. She's not like me. And she's leaving at the end of the summer."

April groaned. "Not everything has to end in wedding bells, Llama."

"No, I know, I just . . ."

But Ramona wasn't sure how to end the sentence. Truth was, she was supremely disappointed—and a little embarrassed—when her father crashed the end of her date, but she'd spent the entire night and this morning convincing herself it was for the best. Not that she was opposed to a kiss or two, but Dylan wasn't like Logan. She was . . . Ramona didn't know. But she wasn't Logan.

"Let me ask you this," April said as Ramona put two packs of sheets in the cart. "While you were mooning over mycelium, did it feel like you were with a famous person, or did it just feel like you were with a person?"

Ramona opened her mouth but closed it quickly. Other than the brief moment with everyone staring at them—and Dylan smiling and waving like Hollywood royalty—she never even thought of

Dylan's fame again. Didn't have to, because Dylan was just . . .
Dylan. Not *Dylan Monroe*, or Killin' Dylan, or Jack and Carrie's
wildling. She was a girl who'd meticulously planned a date for Ramona. She was romantic and sweet and . . .

Ramona liked her.

Goddammit, she did.

"That's what I thought," April said.

"Oh, shut up," Ramona said, laughing, but then grew serious
and took April's arm. What she'd said about April's failed engagement in Owen's office yesterday still weighed on her mind. "Hey."

"Hey," April said slowly, lifting her brows.

"You know I love you, right?" Ramona said. "And I support
whatever you want or feel or think, and however you process what
happened with Elena. Always."

April's eyes went a little soft. "I know, Llama Face."

Ramona squeezed her arm. "I want you to believe in you too."

April's expression dipped, but just for a second before she
grinned. "There are few things I believe in as strongly as my badass
self," she said, before pinching Ramona lightly on the cheek and
then pushing the cart to the next aisle.

Ramona huffed a laugh as she followed her, but she'd barely
rounded the corner when she smacked right into April's back. April
had gone stock-still, blinking at a person in front of her.

"Leigh?" April said.

"April, oh my god," the person said. They were thin, and had
brown skin and wild dark curls, hair cut short on the sides. They
had on torn jeans and white sneakers, a worn band tee. "Ramona,
hey. Should've known I wouldn't see one of you without the other."

Ramona smiled at Leigh Reynolds, who was now standing in the
comforter aisle at Target, a navy quilt in their arms. April launched
herself into Leigh's arms.

Leigh Reynolds had been their friend in high school. There

were only a handful of out queer kids in their class, so the three of them had naturally flocked together, moving as a pack through their four years at Clover Lake High. Leigh was a lesbian, nonbinary, and had also been April's first sexual experience. She'd slept with Leigh when she was seventeen, continued to sleep with them until she met and fell in love with Elena, and now here they were again.

Ramona could never quite keep it straight, to be honest, because Leigh Reynolds was a fuckboi and knew exactly how to get into any girl's pants they wanted to, with enthusiastic consent. Ramona had never gone that route—she hadn't had the time, despite the fact that Leigh was empirically hot—but April couldn't resist.

After graduation, Leigh had left Clover Lake, went to medical school, and became an anesthesiologist. They worked at a hospital in Chicago now, at least the last Ramona had heard. Every now and then, they'd come back to town, slip into April's bed, then head back to Illinois.

"My god, Leigh, warn a girl!" April said, grinning.

"You know I like to keep you on your toes," Leigh said. "Came back for my mom's birthday this weekend."

"Such a good kid," April said, patting Leigh's cheek.

Leigh just winked, and Ramona stifled a laugh. She could almost hear April's panties dropping.

"Hey, there you are," Olive said as she and Marley appeared in the main aisle. Olive had a pile of lavender towels in her arms, and Marley flipped a pack of gauzy plum-colored curtains from hand to hand. "Did you find a purple comforter?"

"Oh," Ramona said, then looked around at the shelves. "Not yet."

"Holy shit, Olive Riley?" Leigh said. "You grew up."

Olive's eyes went wide. "Leigh, oh my god," she said, then threw her arms around Leigh too.

Leigh laughed, then glanced at Marley. "Hey, Mar-Mar, god, what is in the water here?"

"We're shopping for their college dorm room," April said.

"No way," Leigh said as Olive pulled back.

"Very way," Marley said. "Ollie wants all purple shit."

"Purple shit is a compromise between my pink and your blue," Olive said.

"How very bisexual of you," Leigh said.

Olive's brows lifted, and she glanced at Ramona, who just lifted her brows right back. Marley very pointedly looked at the floor.

Olive cleared her throat. "Which one do you like, Mar?" She waved at the plastic-wrapped comforters on the shelves.

"Whichever one you do," Marley said. She put her curtains in the cart too, but then Ramona noticed her eyes following Olive, gazing at her best friend instead of the comforter options. When Marley's gaze snagged on Ramona's, her cheeks went red and she got out her phone, busying herself with scrolling.

"I like this one," Olive said, grabbing a deep purple comforter with lavender leaves all over it. It was reversible, the colors switched on the other side.

"That's pretty," Ramona said. "It'll match everything we've got so far."

"Like Barney threw up," April said, and Leigh laughed.

"Oh, ha ha," Olive said. "Marley, what do you think?"

Marley didn't answer. Her eyes were wide on her phone, her fingers pressed to her mouth.

"Mar?" Olive said. "You okay?"

Marley lifted her head, but she didn't look at Olive.

She looked at Ramona.

"What's wrong?" Ramona asked.

"Um . . ." Marley said, but then Olive all but stomped over and took her phone, eyes scanning whatever had Marley so spooked.

"Holy. Shit," Olive said after a few seconds.

"God, what now?" Ramona said, but she was laughing as she plucked her phone from her bag's front pocket. Honestly, she'd expected this—there had been a ton of tiny cameras on her and Dylan yesterday, and if she was going to hang out with a famous person, she was going to have to get used to some pictures of herself on the internet. It's not like she'd ever be doing anything scandalous in public. The most risqué thing would probably be a swimsuit shot if she and Dylan ever went swimming and, honestly, she looked amazing in her two-piece.

"What's going on?" Leigh asked.

"Oh, Ramona's dating a star," April said.

"I am not. Well, not really."

"A star?" Leigh said. "Is this about all this movie insanity I came home to?"

"Oh yeah," April said. "Dylan Monroe."

"God," Leigh said. "She's hot."

"Right?" April said as she got out her own phone and started swiping and tapping.

Ramona ignored them both, tapping her name along with Dylan's into her browser's search window.

"Fuck," April whispered, always faster with the tech. "Ramona, hang on."

"What? Why?" She tapped enter, and several articles popped up on TMZ, Page Six, and PopSugar. She clicked on one, immediately faced with a picture of herself and Dylan holding hands at the Earthstars Museum. Nothing horrible—she looked cute in her overalls, it was true.

But then she saw the headline.

CHILDHOOD SWEETHEARTS REUNITE

Her stomach immediately went cold. She felt someone's hand on her back—April's probably—but everything else in the store faded away, blurred as though she'd just taken some hallucinogenic drug as she read the article.

> Dylan Monroe's efforts at starring in a romantic comedy might not be too far from the actual truth, as our wild girl seems to be living her own real-life, clutch-at-your-heart romance. As it turns out, Dylan and Ramona of Clover Lake (move aside, Anne Shirley) met each other eons ago when they were thirteen on the lakeshore during a fireworks display. As if that wasn't swoon-worthy enough, the two shared a memorable first kiss, then never spoke again.
>
> Until.
>
> You guessed it.
>
> Dylan arrived back in Clover Lake for *As If You Didn't Know*, and now it appears Dylona has been born. Or shall we go with Ramlyn?

That was all there was. A hundred words tops, but it was enough to obliterate Ramona's mind, her smile, her entire understanding of what she and Dylan were doing. Her heart felt huge, swollen and beating too fast, or maybe too slow, she couldn't tell. It was just wrong, unnatural, and she was in the middle of the bedding aisle at a fucking Target.

"Is this true?" Olive asked.

Ramona looked at her sister, Olive's eyes full of both wonder and hurt.

"Ollie," Ramona said, her name for her sister when she was small and could fit in her arms.

Olive just shook her head, looked away. It was true they told each other everything. Olive even knew about Logan—granted, she didn't know specifics, but she was old enough to understand that sex between consenting adults was perfectly normal and healthy, and Ramona had made damn sure to raise Olive in a sex-positive environment, no matter how much their father squirmed when condoms were mentioned at the dinner table.

Still.

Olive didn't know this, and Ramona didn't know what to do about that wounded look on her favorite person's face, especially when her heart felt shredded and raw.

Because *no one* knew this story.

No one except April and Dylan.

She turned to her best friend, felt her brows lower. She didn't want to believe it. Didn't even want to think it.

April's expression was nothing but concern . . . until it shifted.

"Mona," she said softly. "I didn't. I swear to god."

Ramona felt herself relax. She knew April wouldn't—why the hell would she? There was no reason, and April was her ride or die, her everything from the day they met.

"I'm sorry," Ramona said, then covered her mouth with her hand, talking through her fingers. "I know you wouldn't."

April smoothed her hand down Ramona's hair, squeezed the back of her neck. Leigh just stood there quietly, eyes soft, didn't ask what was happening, didn't take out their own phone to find out.

"I just don't understand," Ramona said.

April sighed. "There is another person who knows that story."

Ramona shook her head. "I know, but why would she . . ."

She trailed off. She couldn't even begin to imagine why Dylan would share the tender details of their first meeting with the media. Didn't *want* to imagine. But Dylan was the only explanation. Dylan, whom Ramona liked. Dylan, whom Ramona had really wanted to kiss last night. Dylan, who researched a mushroom museum for her.

Dylan, whom Ramona really didn't know at all.

Chapter Twenty-One

THEY WERE TAKING a break between filming café scenes when Dylan heard a strange hush descend over the dining room.

The crew was still busy, but the Clover Lake locals who were playing extras and seated at the tables had gone eerily still, and when Dylan looked up from her place behind the counter, most of them were looking right at her.

"What did you do now?" Blair asked. She was sitting at the bar, scrolling through her phone in a white eyelet blouse and tailored denim shorts. Dylan, as usual for the Clover Moon scenes, was unkempt with straggly hair and a greasy apron.

"Nothing," Dylan said. "Well, I took one of their own on a date last night, so I assume it's about that." She breathed through the unease in her gut, the *knowing* that there would be photos of her and Ramona on the internet and the guilt that came with it.

But she liked Ramona.

She'd had an amazing time with Ramona. She'd learned about mushrooms while also realizing she might have a touch of trypophobia, as the more porous fungi really freaked her out, but it was still one of the best nights she'd had in a long time.

Maybe ever.

And god, she'd wanted to kiss Ramona last night. She'd cursed the heavens when Mr. Riley interrupted their good night, but she'd smiled and all but skipped to her car afterward, because she was happy.

She was on fucking cloud nine.

And none of that had to do with the fact that she knew pictures of the two of them would be good for her career, or that the whole dating idea had come from her publicist for image reasons.

She was simply happy to know and be with Ramona Riley.

"Well, aren't you the secret romantic," Blair said, still looking down at her phone.

"What?" Dylan asked. She grabbed a towel and started wiping down the counter, a habit by this point.

"Not that I usually put much stock in these gossip sites, but this is a good story. If it's true, of course," Blair said.

"I can't believe you read that shit," Dylan said.

Blair laughed. "Like I said. I don't, but my partner sent this to me. Thought it was interesting."

Dylan put down her rag. "Wait. You have a partner?"

Blair gave her a look. "Yes."

"How did I not know this?"

Blair went back to her phone. "Because I practice a little something called privacy."

Dylan sighed. "Okay, fine. I give. What did your *partner* send you about me?"

"Their name is Harlow. They work in graphic design and we're moving in together when I'm done here."

"I didn't ask."

"I know," Blair said softly, glancing back up at Dylan and tilting her head. "Just thought maybe you should."

They stared at each other for a second, and for the life of her, Dylan did not get this person. Blair hated her, told her she was a piece of shit, then turned around and offered personal information both passive-aggressively and also in a way that seemed like Blair might have really wanted Dylan to ask about Harlow.

"That's . . . a nice name," Dylan said.

Blair smiled. "They chose it themself."

Dylan nodded as Blair handed over her phone. Dylan took it carefully—the last thing she needed was to break Blair Emmanuel's property during this fragile moment of peace. She looked down at the screen.

And blinked.

Then literally rubbed her eyes.

Because she couldn't be seeing what she thought she was seeing. She'd breathed in some sort of mushroom spore last night, and it was causing hallucinations, surely, because the headline *Childhood Sweethearts Reunite* right above a picture of her and Ramona couldn't be real.

Please, holy shit, let it not be real.

She refreshed the web page, but her stomach plummeted to her feet when she saw the screen was the same, headline and all. "Fuck," she breathed out.

"So is it true?" Blair asked.

Dylan didn't answer. Couldn't. She scanned the article, short but devastating.

How?

Who?

Why?

A million questions jumbled around in her brain, like rocks in a tumbler.

Ramona?

No. Ramona would never share this memory with gossip sites. Dylan was pretty sure April knew the story too, as Ramona and

April shared everything, but April didn't seem like the type either. Maybe it was Olive, if she knew, or even her friend Marley. But Ramona's whole circle seemed fiercely loyal to one another, the sort of relationships Dylan had never experienced herself. No, this had to have come from her own side. She combed through her tangled thoughts, trying to remember if she'd ever written this memory down or told someone or—

"Laurel," she said. "God*dammit*."

"You okay?" Blair asked.

Dylan shook her head. "No. Definitely not." She handed Blair her phone, then plucked her own out of her back pocket to call Laurel, but of course, at that moment, Gia rallied everyone back together. Every curse word in existence kaleidoscoped through Dylan's head, but there was nothing she could do about it.

She had to work.

She had to be professional.

No matter how much she wanted to scream that she had an emergency, do whatever she had to do to get out of here and figure this out, she knew she couldn't. She was already on such thin ice.

She took a few deep breaths, then went back behind the counter. Blair watched her, brows furrowed, but Dylan didn't know what to say. She didn't know how to process the fact that this story about her and Ramona was—

Fuck.

Ramona.

She'll see it.

She probably already had.

"All right, people," Gia called out. "Let's try to get this done in one take. My wife is coming into town, and I'd rather not bore her all night complaining about the incompetence of my actors."

Dylan barely registered the dig—surely meant for her alone,

despite the fact that there were four actors in this scene, when Mallory's boat shoe–wearing brother wanders into the diner with his girlfriend.

"Inspiring as always," Blair said.

Dylan managed a smile, her fingers still gripping her phone. She tapped on Ramona's name in her messages.

I'm so sorry, she texted.

It was paltry, maybe not even worth sending, but she had to do something.

"Dylan," Gia said. "Phone away. Let's go."

Dylan hit send, then tucked her phone out of sight so she could work.

〰️

FOUR HOURS LATER, Dylan all but ran out of Clover Moon, her phone pressed to her ear. Gia was pissed—they did not, in fact, get the scene done in one take, but seven—and Ramona hadn't texted Dylan back, leaving her on read, which made Dylan's stomach feel as though it were full of writhing snakes.

"Laurel, what the actual fuck?" Dylan asked when Laurel answered her phone.

"It wasn't me," Laurel said.

"Well, it sure as hell was someone." Dylan crossed the street, stopping near the square and the gazebo. It was early evening, the sun just starting to dip into the lake, downtown's lights spreading a golden glow over the twilit sidewalks. People filled the streets, heading to dinner or getting ice cream, shoulders bared to the warm air.

"Dylan, it's a good story," Laurel said.

"It's *my* story," Dylan said. "And Ramona's. Not some publicity stunt, and I—"

"You're *in* a publicity stunt, Dylan," Laurel said. "The second you asked that woman out. In all my time with you, I've never seen more serene pictures of you on the internet. Never. You didn't resist them. You didn't put up a fight like you usually do. You didn't tell them all to fuck off and get a life. You're telling me you didn't *know* cameras were on you at that museum?"

Dylan sent her hand through her hair, pulling at the strands until her scalp stung. She sank onto a bench, kept her face down as people passed by, her name whispered into the air.

"Is that what you're telling me?" Laurel asked again.

"No," Dylan said softly.

"I didn't think so," Laurel said just as softly.

Dylan exhaled. "Was it Rayna?"

A pause. "Probably."

"But you told Rayna," Dylan said. "Why the hell would you tell Rayna?"

"She called to check in about you and Ramona. I told her I didn't think it would be a problem as you already had a romantic history."

"Fuck, Laurel," Dylan said, pressing her thumb and forefinger into her eyes. "We were thirteen. Thirteen-year-olds don't have romantic histories!"

"You do now," Laurel said. "And like I said. It's a good story. It's sweet and innocent, and let's be honest, you could use a bit of both."

Dylan shook her head, but she knew everything Laurel said was right—it *was* a good story. And of course Dylan knew cameras were on her and Ramona at the Earthstars Museum. Hell, she even *waved* at them, like she was on the fucking red carpet.

She checked her messages again—still nothing from Ramona.

"I've got to go," she said, then ended the call before Laurel could use any of her usual tactics to calm Dylan down. Dylan didn't want to calm down.

She just wanted to talk to Ramona.

She tapped on her name, but the call went straight to voicemail. She didn't have April's or Olive's numbers, so she did the only thing she knew to do and went to Ramona's house. It was close enough to walk, but Dylan wasn't too proud at this moment to run, cameras be damned.

And she was sure they were on her. She heard her name through the breeze, Ramona's name too, and the whole situation made her head and heart feel as though they'd switched places in her body.

You're in a publicity stunt, Dylan.

Dylan slowed to a calm but brisk walk, which probably made her look even more ridiculous.

She could fix this.

She *would* fix this.

At the Rileys' front door, she straightened her tee—an old Evenflow shirt she often wore to set, because she didn't give a shit if it got lost or stolen or ruined. She knocked on the door, a green-leafed wreath circling the small glass window in the center. She held her breath, thought of what she could possibly say when she saw Ramona, but as the door latched open and Mr. Riley appeared, she still had nothing.

"Hey there, Dylan," he said.

"Hi, Mr. Riley."

"She's not here."

Dylan's mouth opened but closed again. Ramona's dad stood in the doorway, wearing the most dad clothes Dylan could imagine—khaki pants and a short-sleeved navy button-up—and he held a cup of what smelled like Earl Grey tea, wore glasses on the end of his nose. It was all so *normal*, tears swelled into Dylan's eyes.

Then they raced down her cheeks, not even bothering to ask Dylan's permission. They simply *ran*, as though set free from captivity.

"Oh, Dylan," Mr. Riley said. "Honey, it's okay."

The *honey* just made it all worse, a veritable flood, and Dylan could only stand there swiping furiously at her face.

"Come in," Mr. Riley said, opening the door wider. "I'm sure she'll be back soon. I'll make you some tea."

Dylan shook her head, sniffing snot back into her nose. If she went into that house now, she'd probably end up sobbing against Mr. Riley's chest. "That's okay, but thank you. I'm going to go try and find her."

Of course she said all of this between hiccups, which just made her look all the more pathetic.

"Let me at least get you a tissue," Mr. Riley said.

Dylan laughed, then nodded, and Mr. Riley disappeared for a few seconds before returning with a whole box of lotion-infused Kleenex.

"Thanks," Dylan said, taking the gift without argument. She plucked a white tissue from the box, wiped at her face.

"No problem," he said. "You know, Ramona usually likes to go to the lake when she wants to think. Ponder life, I guess."

Dylan paused in her cleanup. "Yeah?"

He nodded, a small smile on his lips. "It's a big lake, of course, and I'm not sure exactly where she is, but you know, if you needed some ideas."

Dylan smiled back, then threw her arms around Mr. Riley in a quick hug. He patted her back, and, after a few more effusive thank-yous, Dylan took off down the street with her box of Kleenex.

She knew exactly where she would find Ramona Riley.

Chapter Twenty-Two

RAMONA WAS RELIEVED that the moon was full and bright. The sun had just disappeared for good, her phone was turned off, and she wasn't nearly ready to leave this beach.

This cove.

Their cove.

The thought stung, but she hadn't known where else to go. She couldn't sit in her childhood bedroom and cry, and she couldn't be around people right now, even April, who would do her best to comfort Ramona, but Ramona didn't want comfort right now.

Comfort was for tomorrow.

Right now, she wanted to be pissed and hurt and confused and sad.

She sat cross-legged on the cool sand, the lake's gentle waves whispering against the shore.

Shh.

Shhhhh.

The sound did help to calm her a bit, made everything feel delicate and soft, as though she were under those waves, water shimmering above her. The moon spread silver over the surface, sparkling and dancing.

It was a perfect night.

Clear and warm with just enough cool breeze to keep her hair from sticking to the back of her neck.

But everything else was a mess. Dylan, Ramona's whole sad little life. She shouldn't even be here. She should be at home, spending time with her sister, who was leaving in a couple short months, but no, because Ramona's most soft and secret memory was in a tabloid.

A *tabloid*.

She sighed and scooped up a handful of sand, tossing it at the water as hard as she could. It was completely unsatisfying, the dirt scattering in the breeze and mostly back onto her bare legs. She stood, hunted around in the sand for a good rock, then hurled it at the lake. It landed with a plop that still did nothing to ameliorate the pressure in Ramona's chest. She switched to skipping the rocks, hoping the more skips she could achieve the less she'd feel like screaming at the sky.

She'd been at it for a good five minutes when she heard a branch crack behind her. She whirled around, hoping a racoon hadn't ventured out of the woods to crash her pity party.

But it wasn't a racoon.

She would've preferred a racoon to who was actually standing on the beach in her cove.

Her fucking cove.

"Hi," Dylan said, breathing hard as though she'd run here. She had a box of Kleenex under her arm. Ramona opened her mouth to ask why, but then decided she didn't care.

She turned back to the water, side-armed another rock over the surface.

"You're good at that," Dylan said.

"I know."

Dylan laughed softly. "I've never been able to skip rocks very well. I always—"

"What do you want, Dylan?"

Ramona didn't turn around. Didn't look at her. Didn't even really want an answer. Still, infuriatingly, she felt her throat go a little thick.

"I . . . I wanted to talk," Dylan said, her voice closer now.

Ramona released a bitter laugh. "I think you've done enough talking."

Dylan was close now, standing in front of her. She was gorgeous even with her red-rimmed eyes. The moon made her hair look silvery, her Evenflow tee loose over her cuffed jeans.

"I'm sorry," Dylan said.

Ramona's face crumpled, but she smoothed it out fast. Her heart, however, wasn't so easy to keep in check. "So it was you?" Her voice was soft, too small.

Dylan took a tiny breath. "Indirectly, yeah."

Ramona didn't even know what that meant. Didn't care. All that mattered was that Dylan had shared their story with the world without even asking her.

"I'm so sorry," Dylan said again.

She seemed closer now, her booted feet only an inch from Ramona's sandy toes.

"Why?" Ramona asked.

"Why am I sorry?"

Ramona shook her head, let her silence say what she really meant.

Dylan sighed, set the tissue box in the sand. Ramona frowned at it, the familiar blue-and-green flowers on the cardboard.

"Is that from my kitchen?" she asked.

Dylan laughed quietly. "Yeah. Long story."

Ramona kept her eyes on the box, the pattern blurring in her vision. "That memory was ours."

Dylan was quiet for a second. Ramona saw her fingers twitch by her side, as though she wanted to take Ramona's hand, but Ramona stuffed them into her pockets.

"I know," Dylan said softly.

Ramona felt the first swell of tears.

"I told someone close to me, and they made a mistake," Dylan said.

"*They* made a mistake?" Ramona replied sharply.

"*I* made a mistake," Dylan said. "I should have realized they might . . . I don't know. Use it."

"Use us," Ramona said.

Dylan's expression was so soft and open, that first damn tear escaped and slid down Ramona's cheek. She couldn't help feeling betrayed, like this was all some game to Dylan.

"We don't have to do this," Ramona said, sniffing. "We can just stop, and I won't—"

"Ramona," Dylan said. She lifted her hand slowly, and Ramona didn't flinch or back away when she swiped the tear from Ramona's face with her thumb. "That's not what I want." She trailed off, looked down, biting her lower lip. "My job . . . who I am . . . I know it can be complicated. But that story *is* ours. And it's important to me. I need you to believe that."

"Is it?" Ramona asked, her voice a whisper, even though she didn't mean it to be. She was shifting though, her anger giving way to something else, something light and gauzy, like lake water under a full moon.

"Yeah," Dylan said. "Lifesaving, remember?"

Ramona exhaled. That word—*lifesaving*—like tiny flickers of light through her rib cage. This might be complicated, but it was also *good*. And she didn't want to stop. She wanted Dylan in her life, and Dylan Monroe was never going to be simple.

Somehow, they'd moved even closer, Dylan's tee brushing the front of Ramona's blouse. And this time, Ramona reached out first, both of her hands taking Dylan's, twining their fingers together.

Dylan exhaled heavily. "You believe me?"

Ramona could only nod, could only focus on their hands, the sensation of touching Dylan, being close. It obliterated doubt and anger, replaced it with something fragile and desperate. Maybe a little scared too, because she *did* believe Dylan. And that belief—that *trust*—was scary as hell.

"I was going out of my mind today," Dylan said, curling their hands and resting them on her chest.

Ramona lifted her eyes to look at her. "You were?"

"The idea of hurting you. It was unbearable."

"Dylan," Ramona said softly.

"Last night," Dylan said, "I really wanted to kiss you."

"I wanted you to kiss me," Ramona said. Her heart felt huge, thrumming at every pulse point.

"This is better though," Dylan said. She lifted their hands, pressed them to her mouth. "To kiss here, in our cove."

"Our cove." Even closer now. Impossibly, defying physics. Ramona wanted to be closer still, crawl inside Dylan and set up a home, which was wild and terrifying and silly.

"Ours," Dylan whispered, right before she closed that gap between them and brushed her lips over Ramona's.

Soft.

Gentle.

So terrifying and so, so not silly at all.

Ramona kissed her back, just as soft and gentle, opening her mouth only a little to capture Dylan's upper lip between hers. Dylan sucked in a breath, a tiny moan making its way out of her mouth and into Ramona's.

And Ramona felt it everywhere. Soft and gentle wasn't enough, not by a long shot, and the slow pulse spiraling through her body turned electric with that one little sound, a firework blasting into the sky.

She untangled their hands, a barrier between them, and then slid her fingers into Dylan's hair, pulling her closer. Dylan was only a little taller than she was, her arms fitting perfectly around Ramona's waist.

They obliterated any space left between them. Ramona tilted Dylan's head just so, needing to kiss her deeper, harder. Ramona teased Dylan's mouth open, swept her tongue over her top lip. Dylan gasped and responded, pulling Ramona tighter, letting her tongue meet hers, soft and wet and perfect. Her arms tightened around Ramona, but then her hands slipped under her blouse, fingertips soft on the bare skin of Ramona's back. That touch—skin on skin—made Ramona feel wild. She wanted that feeling everywhere.

"Hello, Dolly," Dylan whispered against her mouth.

Ramona laughed, pulled her even closer, framing Dylan's face and angling her head so she could kiss down her neck.

Dylan groaned, and the sound shot straight to between Ramona's legs.

"You're . . . fuck . . . you're really good at that," Dylan said as Ramona kissed her neck, making her way to a sensitive spot just below her ear. Still not too wild. Not as wild as Ramona suddenly felt, as wild as she wanted to be.

But then Dylan whispered "Cherry," and Ramona went feral. She made herself pause, pulled back to look at Dylan, her lips already kiss-swollen, her pupils blown wide.

"We're on a beach," Ramona said.

Dylan frowned. "Yeah. A cove."

"Our cove."

Dylan trailed her fingers up Ramona's bare back, stopped at her bra strap, then drifted back down. "Our cove."

"It's stupid."

Dylan froze. "Stupid?"

"God, sorry." Ramona shook her head, rested her hands on Dylan's shoulders. "Not stupid."

"I thought it was kind of romantic."

"It is." Ramona pressed her forehead to Dylan's. "It is so romantic. Or it was until I kissed you and now all I want to do is . . ."

She trailed off, suddenly shy.

Because what if Dylan didn't want to . . . well, do what Ramona wanted to do? What if she wanted to go slower? Which was fine, god, of course it was fine, and it had been so long since Ramona had mixed feelings and sex. Logan was . . . not a mixture. He was a very simple solution, and everyone before him was only a fling, a summer romance, a—

Ramona blinked down at their feet in the sand, her forehead still against Dylan's.

Just casual. You know . . . fun. Not so different from what we've been doing, really . . .

That's what Dylan had said when she'd asked Ramona out.

And this *was* fun, but somehow, in the center of Ramona's chest, it felt anything but casual. And as Dylan lifted Ramona's chin with a finger, thumb swiping at her cheek, those eyes looking so deep into her, it didn't feel like Dylan thought it was casual either.

"Tell me what you're thinking," Dylan said softly.

Ramona felt herself trembling, tried to steady her muscles, but Jesus, Dylan's voice. Soft yet gravelly. Rough but somehow silky. She wanted it to trail over her skin. Scrape down her stomach and whisper between her thighs.

"I . . . I'm thinking I want you to take me back to your place," Ramona said, her own voice as quiet as the lapping lake. A plea.

Dylan looked at her, eyes hooded, her mouth parted. "You sure?"

"Never been so sure," Ramona said, her fingers digging into Dylan's shoulders.

Dylan responded by wrapping her arms back around Ramona's waist, pulling her close and kissing her, lifting her off the ground a little.

Ramona gasped, opened her mouth to Dylan, reminded herself to tease Dylan later about being so strong and buff and literally sweeping her off her feet, but right now, she just wanted to kiss her.

She wanted to kiss Dylan Monroe. Her Lolli. And so that's what she did.

Chapter
Twenty-Three

DYLAN HAD NEVER been so thankful to be in a small town. If they'd been in LA—especially if they'd been at the beach—it would've taken an hour to get back to her Silver Lake house, and most likely, traffic would've been very, very cruel. In Clover Lake, the walk from Mirror Cove to the house she was renting was relatively short, though still plenty torturous.

She held Ramona's hand the whole way, thankful for the shade of darkness as they hurried through the woods. She didn't want to think of anyone else. Not cameras or Rayna or her reputation or the fact that Gia was properly pissed at her for how distracted she was on set again.

She just wanted this.

Ramona Riley's hand in hers.

"Wait, wait," Ramona said, pulling them to a stop in the middle of the trail.

"Wait?" Dylan asked, laughing. "Exact opposite of what I'm thinking right now."

Ramona smiled, but then waved her free hand through the air. "It's Moon Lover's Trail."

Dylan blinked, but then the name came back to her. "Number two on the list."

"And here we are," Ramona said, "under a full moon."

Dylan looked around—it *was* lovely. The trail widened at this point, almost like a tiny alcove in the woods, trees on all sides, the rest of the trail narrowing ahead of them. The moon sprinkled silver over the entire space, making everything look a little magic.

"Here we are," Dylan said, then pulled Ramona closer and kissed her. She kissed her long and deep, hands sliding down Ramona's ass. She meant it to be a little more romantic than an ass grab, but god, Ramona drove her crazy.

"Not exactly what I had in mind when I put it on the list," Ramona said as she pulled back, her voice gloriously breathless. "But I'll definitely take it."

"Same," Dylan said, then kissed her again. Ramona groaned, her thigh hooking around Dylan's hip.

"God," Ramona said, gasping into Dylan's mouth.

"Yeah," Dylan managed, biting her bottom lip and pulling her closer. She was so soft, flawless, her curves fitting Dylan's hands perfectly, like Ramona was made for her, for this moment. "I need to get you home."

"Not home," Ramona said, hands scraping through Dylan's hair.

"I mean my home," Dylan said, mouth trailing down Ramona's neck. She smelled like summer, like grass and lemons and starlight, whatever the hell that smelled like, but it felt right. Everything with Ramona felt right.

"Bed," she said. "I need to get you to a bed."

"Then get me there," Ramona said, breathless, and god, she was everything.

Dylan groaned against her neck, then forced herself to stop, laced their fingers together again, and all but took off running.

Ramona laughed, running with her, and by the time they scrambled through the town and up the front steps of Dylan's little mint-green bungalow at the edge of the lake, Dylan was very, very close to ripping off Ramona's clothes and taking her right there on the porch.

She unlocked the door and let them inside. The room was mostly dark, lit only by the light above the stove in the open kitchen, the full moon streaming in through the windows. All the furniture and art on the walls looked metallic in the silvery glow.

"Do you want something to drink?" Dylan asked, setting down her keys on the glass-and-teak end table by the sofa. "Or eat?"

Ramona just smiled at her. Laughed lightly, like a bell tinkling. "Yeah," she said softly, but then she took Dylan's hand and led her toward the hallway, weaving past the closed doors until she found the main bedroom at the end of the hall, which was clearly Dylan's from the unmade bed and suitcase that looked like it had exploded all over the room.

Dylan felt a swell of nerves as they entered the room. It wasn't like she didn't know what she was doing in the bedroom—she was pretty experienced with people who had vaginas, but this was . . .

Well, it was Ramona.

It was *Cherry*.

And it was the first time, and Dylan was always a little nervous the first time. Her last first time had been with Jocelyn, of course, over a year ago, and Jocelyn was such a dominant top, Dylan barely had to make any decisions at all.

Which she liked.

But she also liked being the one who called the shots. When it came to sex, she'd known she was a switch for a long time, she just hadn't had the opportunity to top anyone in a while. Before Jocelyn, there was Jackson, and he was a bit of a top himself, a little too *I'm a man* for her taste. And now with Ramona standing in front of the bed, so soft and sweet and, Jesus, so, so sexy, Dylan knew exactly what her taste was.

Exactly what she wanted.

Whom she wanted.

And god, Ramona was gorgeous. She just wanted to lay her out on the bed and look at her. Study her like a work of art.

"So . . ." Ramona said, drawing closer, her hand still holding Dylan's. She twisted up her mouth, shy, and so fucking cute Dylan had to grin.

"So," Dylan said, then pulled Ramona into her arms. She tucked a piece of hair behind Ramona's ear, kissed her once. "Can I tell you what I want?"

Ramona sucked in a breath. "God, yeah."

"And you tell me if I ask for anything you don't like, okay?" Dylan said. "I want to know what you want too."

Ramona just nodded, bit that perfect bottom lip of hers.

Dylan and Jocelyn had safe words, traffic light words, really—*red* for stop and *yellow* for slow and *green* for go—and Dylan always liked that. She appreciated that Jocelyn, so bossy and in charge in the bedroom, made space for Dylan's comfort. Sexually, she'd learned a lot from Jocelyn, despite the awful way it ended, despite the fact that Dylan had no idea whether Jocelyn ever really liked her for *her*, or just what Jack Monroe could give her.

Still, as she stood in her moonlit bedroom, Ramona in her arms, she wanted to give the same to Ramona. Make space, even if they didn't end up needing any safe words or had the most vanilla sex in the world—vanilla sex with Ramona would be amazing, she had no doubt.

"Can we talk about some safe words, then?" Dylan asked.

Ramona's brows went up. "Yeah. Absolutely."

Dylan nodded, then explained about the stoplight words. She felt her cheeks warm as she did so, not because she was embarrassed, but because she couldn't help but picture Ramona's head tilted back, her lovely throat exposed, crying out, *Green, green, green,* while Dylan made her come.

Jesus, she was sweating.

"That sounds perfect," Ramona said. Then slipped her fingers under Dylan's tee. "Now can I please take this shirt off?"

Dylan laughed. "Green."

Ramona smiled, then lifted Dylan's tee above her head, threw it in a corner. The ceiling fan was on, cooling Dylan's heated skin. She had on a lacy blush-pink bralette that was a touch too small, her C-cup breasts spilling over the top. Ramona drifted her fingers over her skin, slid a thumb down to Dylan's already peaked nipple.

Dylan couldn't stop the moan that came out of her mouth but tried to focus. "Your turn," she said, playing with the top button of Ramona's blouse.

"Very green," Ramona said.

Dylan made quick work of the shirt, spreading it wide to reveal Ramona's black bra with the scalloped edging. Her tits were large and perfect, and Dylan wanted them in her mouth immediately.

But.

She wanted something else first.

"I want you to show me what you like," she said, fingertips drifting over Ramona's collarbone.

Ramona tilted her head. "Show you . . ."

"Show me." Dylan pulled Ramona's blouse off all the way, let it drop to the floor. "And I'll show you."

Ramona looked at her for a second, then realization seemed to dawn. Dylan's face flamed even hotter, but god, she wanted this. She wanted to see Ramona spread out on that bed, and study exactly how she liked to be touched, hear her come while Dylan's fingers played in her own wet heat.

Ramona unbuttoned her shorts, pulled the zipper down, let

them drop to the floor before she stepped out of them. She leaned forward then, kissed Dylan, opened her mouth and slid her tongue inside, swirling it in a way that made Dylan groan.

She pulled back, whispered, "Green," against Dylan's mouth. Then—god, *then*—she turned around and crawled onto the bed, hands and knees, her ample ass moving away from Dylan when all Dylan wanted was to get her teeth into that flesh. Her underwear was plain, light blue cotton and the sexiest thing Dylan had ever seen.

Ramona kept crawling until she reached the fabric headboard, then pushed up to her knees.

"Jesus," Dylan said.

Ramona looked at her over her shoulder. Dylan didn't even think she meant to look so fucking sexy, but she did. She certainly did.

"What?" Ramona asked as she grabbed a pillow.

"You're perfect," Dylan said.

Ramona smiled, then adjusted the pillows before turning and settling down on the bed, half sitting up against the headboard. Dylan stood at the end of the bed, slack-jawed as Ramona stared back at her.

Then . . . Ramona started to touch herself.

Slowly.

Just a hand sliding down her throat to her collarbone, but dear god, she was beautiful.

"Ramona," Dylan said. It was all she could say, her brain short-circuiting as Ramona's fingers dipped into her deep cleavage, then over to cup her full breast. Soon both hands were on her tits, and Dylan could see her hardened nipples through her bra.

"Pinch your nipples," Dylan said softly, and Ramona did. Let out a little moan as she did so. "Fuck." Dylan felt her cunt flood, so wet and ready.

"Will you take off your bra for me?" Ramona asked. "Please."

Dylan smiled. "So polite."

"I know who's in charge here."

Dylan had to press her legs together, because god. This woman. "You first."

Ramona smiled, sat up a little to unhook her bra. The material fell away and Jesus Christ. Her tits were perfect. Heavy and round, her nipples rosebud pink and hard.

Dylan watched her fingers play—pluck and pinch and roll—and she was nearly panting as she pulled her own bra over her head, her tits swaying with the movement. Ramona's eyes roamed over her, mouth open a little.

"Will you touch yourself for me too?" Ramona asked.

"Yeah?"

"Yes," Ramona said. "Please."

There was a little whine to her voice, and Dylan couldn't have said no if she'd wanted to.

And she definitely didn't want to.

She unbuttoned her jeans, shucked them off so fast, she nearly tripped getting them off her feet.

Ramona laughed sweetly. "Easy, tiger."

"Rawr," Dylan said, and Ramona laughed even more. But soon the laughing stopped when Dylan put one knee on the bed. Her underwear wasn't exactly her sexiest—a pair of white hipsters with tiny rainbow tacos all over them, a random purchase from the internet because she thought they were queer and funny. She had no idea this was how her day would end—quite the opposite, actually. Still, Ramona's mouth dropped open a bit, her eyes finding the space between Dylan's legs, then lifting to her tits again.

"You're gorgeous," Ramona said.

Dylan smiled, lifted her other leg to the bed so she was on her knees, then trailed a hand up her thigh. She needed to touch herself

like this too, needed something while she watched Ramona continue to feel herself up, hands gliding over her skin.

Dylan scooted closer, staying on her knees, then sitting back on
her heels. She heard Ramona's breath catch as she opened her legs
as wide as they'd go.

"You like that," Dylan said. Not a question. Ramona just swallowed, nodded, her eyes flitting from Dylan's chest to her cunt, back
and forth. "Spread your legs for me."

Ramona obeyed, her mouth slightly open, hands still on her tits.
Her knees parted, and Dylan groaned at the sight before her—
Ramona's pussy, still covered by her underwear, a wet spot at the
center.

"Fuck," Dylan said. "I need you to touch your cunt. Like, immediately."

"Thank god," Ramona said, then slid one hand down her soft
stomach, over her mound and underwear.

"Exactly like you want it, baby girl," Dylan said, transfixed by
where that hand was going next.

"God," Ramona said, her back arching a little. "I really like that."

"Oh, yeah?" Dylan said. She put one hand on Ramona's knee,
making her gasp.

"Yeah," Ramona said, her voice breathy, raspy. "Please."

"Show me, Ramona," she said. "Show me how you like to be
fucked."

Ramona moaned as her fingers dipped lower, spread over her
pussy, fingers rubbing and curling. Dylan watched, her pulse like a
hummingbird's wings, her own cunt throbbing. Ramona's fingers
moved over that wet spot, and Dylan wanted to press her nose there,
her tongue, make it wetter.

"God," she said. "You look so good."

Ramona's breath quickened as she rubbed harder. "I need . . ."

"Tell me," Dylan said. "What do you need, baby?"

"More," she said, her voice desperate now.

Dylan reached over Ramona, swiped her thumbs over the skin above her underwear. Ramona groaned, and Dylan hooked her fingers into Ramona's waistband, then tugged her underwear down her legs. Ramona had to stop touching herself for a second to get them off, but holy shit was it worth it.

Dylan tossed the undies into the dark, then spread Ramona's legs again, pushing her knees wide.

"Fuck," she said. Ramona's cunt was gorgeous. Hair trimmed, but still present, a dark scattering of curls over a soaked pussy. She took Ramona's hand, placed it on those wet lips again. "Keep going."

"I need you," Ramona rasped, her fingers starting to move. "Please, Dylan, touch yourself for me too."

Dylan angled to take off her own underwear—who was she to deny Ramona anything she wanted—then situated back on her heels, legs spread as wide as they'd go.

"Oh my god," Ramona said, rubbing harder. "Please."

Dylan set one hand back on Ramona's knee, then slid her fingers into her own folds.

"God, I'm wet," she said.

"Good," Ramona said, her fingers dipping inside herself. "Please, show me, Dylan."

Dylan watched Ramona's fingers fuck herself—two, and slow at first, getting faster as she got more needy. Dylan slid fingertips down her own cunt, then back up, spreading her wetness to her clit. She liked it gentle at first, using her pussy lips to stimulate her clit.

She arched back, gripped Ramona's knee even tighter, spreading her wider. "Fuck. Baby. You look amazing."

"Yeah," Ramona said, her fingers moving quicker. "Dylan, god."

Dylan couldn't take it—she nearly came just from her name on Ramona's tongue, rubbing her clit faster, circling and pressing just like she needed. Ramona watched her, mouth open, breathing heavily.

"Oh my god," she said. "I'm gonna—"

"Do it," Dylan said. "Come for me, baby girl."

"Fuck," Ramona yelled, her tits bouncing as she fucked herself harder. She was gorgeous, crying out as she came, her body tensing and undulating.

"Fuck, Ramona," Dylan said, her own fingers working desperately, her orgasm building as she watched Ramona writhe and moan, fingers deep inside her cunt.

She dipped inside herself, and that's when it hit her, hard and fast, almost a surprise. She nearly fell over from the force of it, gripping Ramona's knee, hand sliding down her thigh as Dylan curled over herself, *fuck, fuck, fuck* falling out of her mouth over and over, her own legs clenching around her hand. She heard Ramona come again, her free hand gripping Dylan's until they both settled, breathing hard.

Dylan met Ramona's eyes, which were glazed and blinking slowly, both of their mouths still open to get as much oxygen as they could.

"That was . . ." Ramona said.

"Yeah," Dylan said. "It was." She scooted back for a second, but only so she could lie on her stomach, spread Ramona's legs even farther apart. "And I'm not nearly finished with you yet."

Chapter Twenty-Four

RAMONA YELLED AN expletive at the ceiling.

Really yelled it. As in, the neighbors would hear if the windows were open—she hoped there were no windows open, because she could not stop making noises as Dylan pressed her mouth to Ramona's cunt.

Soft at first.

A kiss.

But Jesus, it could've been the kiss to end the world, start and end wars, rearrange stars and planets.

"Dylan . . . fuck," Ramona said, her hips lifting to get more friction.

Dylan pressed her hand to Ramona's lower belly, pushed her back down to the bed, then lifted her own head to look right at her.

Ramona whined at the loss of contact.

Literally *whined*. Ramona had never whined about anything in her life. She was a planner, a decider, had to be when pretty much raising a kid since she was thirteen. She didn't have time to whine or complain or second-guess anything.

But now, with Dylan's mouth hovering above her, not quite

touching, she couldn't think, couldn't do anything but make these needy noises she barely recognized.

"Such a brat," Dylan said, smiling, then pressed a kiss to Ramona's thigh.

Ramona laughed. "I'm not, I just . . ."

"You just what?"

"I . . ." She squirmed, lifting her hips again only to be pushed back down. Again.

"Tell me," Dylan said. "Tell me what you want."

"I want your mouth."

"Tell me *exactly* what you what."

Ramona groaned again, Dylan's breath ghosting over her slick skin.

"Now," Dylan said firmly. "I won't touch you again until you do."

Fuck. Ramona felt herself get even wetter with Dylan's dominant tone, those eyes looking at her with such command—she could come just from all this, she was pretty sure. She'd never had this kind of sex, if she was being honest. Logan was more of a wham-bam kind of guy, and while he wham-bammed quite well, he wasn't very mysterious. Wasn't into talking. Everyone she'd ever slept with, in fact, wasn't really into talking. The women she'd been with were mostly tourists, summer flings where they simply made each other come.

Which, of course, was nice, but she'd never been with someone like Dylan.

Someone who asked Ramona to fuck herself.

Someone who told her what to do.

Made her say what she wanted.

"Ramona," Dylan said. "Tell me."

Ramona felt dizzy, addled by this woman between her legs. She could barely think what she wanted, to be honest. *You* was on the tip of her tongue, but Dylan had asked her to be specific. Still, she wanted so many things, wanted to be touched so many different ways.

And then Dylan bit her thigh.

It was a soft bite.

A nibble mostly, but holy shit.

Ramona gasped, her cunt flooding as her hips reached for the ceiling of their own accord. "Oh my god. Do . . . do that again."

Dylan lifted a brow. "Yeah?"

"Please. God, yeah, please."

"What is it that you want exactly?" Dylan said, her voice teasing.

"Goddammit, Dylan."

Dylan laughed, dragged her tongue and mouth over Ramona's thigh.

No teeth though.

"Say it," Dylan said.

"Bite me," Ramona said. "Please, I want you to bite me."

And then Dylan did. She opened her mouth and scraped her teeth down Ramona's thigh, moaning against her skin, then caught Ramona's flesh between her teeth.

Bit down.

"Harder," Ramona said on a gasp, her hands pressed to her face. Jesus, it felt so good, that line between pleasure and pain. She wanted *more*. "Please, god, please."

"Please what?" Dylan said against her skin.

"Fingers," Ramona managed to get out. "Inside me, please."

"Good girl," Dylan said, pressing a kiss to her leg. "See how easy that was?"

Ramona laughed, but it was shaky, barely supported by air, all her brain cells concentrated on Dylan's mouth and hands and teeth.

Dylan didn't make her wait long. She spread Ramona's pussy with her fingers, dragged her tongue up the center, then swirled it around her clit.

"Fuck," Ramona yelled. "Oh my god, yeah."

"Yeah?" Dylan said, then did it again. Except this time, while she flicked her tongue over Ramona's clit, she slid two fingers inside her pussy.

"God," Dylan said. "You take it so good. Such a gorgeous cunt." Then Dylan put her mouth exactly where Ramona wanted it.

"More," Ramona said. "Please, more."

"More what?"

Ramona groaned, back arching. "Fingers. Just want to be filled."

"That's a good sl—" Dylan started, but then stopped, pausing in her ministrations.

Ramona blinked for a second, her cunt clenching around Dylan's still fingers, letting that word she knew Dylan was about to use settle. She'd never been called a slut before in bed. Never even thought about it . . . but . . . fuck.

She liked it.

She liked it a lot.

"Hey," Dylan said, her nose grazing Ramona's thigh. "Give me a color."

"Green," Ramona said. "Green, green, green. Say it, please."

"Yeah?" Dylan said. "You want to be my good slut?"

Ramona was right—she liked it so fucking much.

"Yes," Ramona said. "God, yes."

Dylan slid another finger inside her, tongue back on her clit.

"Teeth," Ramona said. "Please. Bite me, Dylan, please. Leave a mark."

"God," Dylan said, her thumb replacing her tongue on Ramona's clit. "Such a desperate slut for me."

Ramona could only nod, her need at a fever pitch now. Dylan's teeth went back to that same spot on her thigh, bit down and hummed against her. Paired with her fingers in Ramona's pussy, her thumb circling, Ramona felt insane.

She literally felt crazy with want, with need, with desire. She wanted to be fucked and fucked hard and told what to do and called a slut, and she wanted to come on Dylan's fingers and see a bruise on her thigh, and she wanted and wanted and wanted.

"Harder," Ramona said. "Everything, please, Dylan."

"Such a good girl," Dylan said against Ramona's thigh.

And god, Ramona loved that too—the praise paired with a little mean. Jesus, Dylan Monroe was going to kill her. Actually, physically kill her.

Dylan's free hand roamed down the outside of the thigh she was biting, and when she slapped Ramona's skin lightly, Ramona yelled again, expletives and *yes* and *green* and anything she had to say to get Dylan to keep going.

"Come for me, baby girl," Dylan said, then bit her again, sucked at her flesh, fucked her deeper and harder with her fingers.

"Oh . . . my . . . god . . ." Ramona rasped, hips flailing, nails scraping through Dylan's hair. She couldn't parse the sensations—tongue and fingers and teeth, the crack of Dylan's palm on her skin. Her body felt like lightning, constant bolts sizzling from the sky to the ground, waiting for the thunder to boom.

And fuck, when it finally did, it crashed through her like an earthquake. She screamed, whole body arching off the bed, nails digging into Dylan's scalp, but she couldn't *not* dig, couldn't *not* scream, it was so good, life-changing, the kind of orgasm she'd seen only in porn and assumed was half-fake. Her body felt like light, like electricity and nothing else, her pulse replacing bones and blood and muscle. She came again . . . then again as Dylan kept fucking her, until she finally felt her ass settle onto the bed as though she were rejoining her body from some other dimension. That's what it felt like—dramatic and wild and almost impossible.

"Jesus Christ" was all she could say, her lungs working like she'd just finished a marathon. Hell, maybe she had. She wasn't sure. Couldn't even tell someone her full name right now if they asked.

Dylan slid up her body, kissing as she went and pulling giggles from Ramona's throat. She was so sensitive, every nerve a live wire, which only increased when Dylan straddled one of her thighs, her hands on either side of Ramona's head, lovely face above her.

"So," Dylan said.

Ramona laughed, her cheeks growing a little warm. "So."

"That was good?"

"God," Ramona said, then couldn't help but grab Dylan's face and pull her down for a kiss. "That was good," she said against her mouth. "So good."

Dylan smiled, their teeth clacking together gently. "I agree."

"Yeah," Ramona whispered, keenly aware that Dylan's perfect cunt was pressed to her thigh and very, very wet.

And just like that, she felt feral again, could spend all night coming, she was pretty sure, but she wanted something else right now. Something she'd never asked for, never even thought of really, not until she was in Dylan's bed.

"Use me," she said. A whisper. Barely audible. She set her hands to Dylan's waist, lifted her leg just a little so Dylan felt the movement.

Her brows lifted. "Yeah?"

"Yeah," Ramona said, her voice needy and breathy again. "Please."

Dylan kissed her, then slid down her neck, licking and biting. "You want me to use my slut?" she whispered into her ear, so quiet, but it felt like a shout.

"Fuck," Ramona said. "Please."

"My beautiful slut?" Dylan palmed one of Ramona's breasts, squeezing before she concentrated on the peaked nipple, her hips starting to move over Ramona's leg. "Perfect. Just a little slut here to make me feel good."

"Yes," Ramona whined, arching her back as Dylan pinched her nipple. She gripped Dylan's hips, moving her more on her thigh. "Anything you want."

"Just you," Dylan said, setting one hand between Ramona's breasts and sitting up a bit. She rolled her hips, a slow undulation over Ramona's thigh. "Fuck. You feel so good."

Ramona had no words then, could only moan as Dylan used her body, breasts bouncing as she moved faster. Ramona kept one hand on Dylan's hip, lifting the other to her tits. She hadn't gotten her hands on them yet and she needed to, needed it like air, like water. Dylan's breasts were heavy in her hand, her pink nipples hard.

"God," Dylan said, sitting up all the way now, which meant Ramona could see her pussy sliding over Ramona's skin. Waxed with a little thatch of hair on her mound, lips pink and lovely and soaking wet.

"I want to touch you," Ramona said. "Please, please, can I touch you."

"Yeah," Dylan said, hips slowing so she could lift up a little. Ramona slid her hand, palm up, under Dylan . . . and fuck, when Dylan pressed back down again. The feel of her pussy, wet and soft. There was nothing like it. Ramona angled a bit so her fingers could play at Dylan's entrance.

"Fuck, yeah, god," Dylan said. "Go inside me."

Ramona happily complied, fingers sliding into Dylan's wet heat, tight and silky. Her other hand grabbed Dylan's ass, urging her to fuck herself on Ramona's fingers even harder, clit sliding over Ramona's palm.

"Oh my god," Dylan said, moving faster. "Baby. I'm gonna—"

"Come," Ramona said. "Please, come on my fingers. I need it."

"Yeah," Dylan said, her head thrown back. "Beg me. Beg me to come."

"Please, god, Dylan, please come. Wanna feel you. Please."

"Fuck, Ramona." She pumped her hips, leaned over for more friction, hand going to Ramona's throat. She didn't squeeze though. Just rested there, a weight Ramona suddenly loved. Ramona reached as deep as she could inside Dylan, curled her fingers, pressed her palm upward.

Dylan gasped, grabbed Ramona's wrist, her body convulsing. Her cunt clenched around Ramona's fingers as she came. "God, fuck," she said, hair in her face, her chest flushed red. Still, Ramona didn't stop, wanted her to come again, come on top of her. She used her free hand to pull Dylan close, their breasts touching, Dylan's face buried in her neck as she came again, Ramona's name a muffled gasp against Ramona's neck.

Finally, Dylan stilled, breathing heavily. Ramona could barely get enough air either. Her fingers were still inside Dylan, but her other arm was around Dylan's waist. She drifted her fingers up Dylan's back, then into her hair. Dylan lifted up so Ramona could free her fingers, and for a second, Ramona worried her touch had been too intimate right after, too *sweet*, and that Dylan was headed to the bathroom, but then Dylan settled next to her, wrapped her arm around Ramona's waist.

"You," she said, then took Ramona's hand—the one that had just been inside Dylan—and licked her fingers clean.

Ramona laughed. "I'd say that's a big *you*."

Dylan smiled, then kissed Ramona's palm before releasing her. Then she snuggled closer, her chin resting on Ramona's shoulder.

"Was that all okay?" she asked.

Ramona grinned. "Um, yeah. It was more than okay. Was it okay for you?"

"Jesus, yeah," Dylan said. "You're . . . god, you're incredibly sexy."

Ramona couldn't stop smiling.

Dylan leaned in to kiss her. Then they just kept kissing, soft hands roaming, making out for what felt like hours. Then, after they both used the bathroom and got some water, Dylan pulled the down comforter over their naked bodies, breath mingling, Ramona's hands tangled in Dylan's hair, mouth on hers again as though they'd both been made for this exact moment.

Chapter Twenty-Five

DYLAN SLEPT SO hard, it took her a few seconds to realize that the incessant knocking sound was not a dream. She pried her eyes open, blinked at the wavy hair that was splayed across her chest and over her face a little. She looked down at the dark head burrowed under her arm—actually, in her armpit—and the hand resting directly on her right tit.

Ramona.

God, so she hadn't dreamed it.

For a moment, she really thought she had—the mind-warping sex, Ramona in her bed, kissing for hours into the night, then eating peanut butter and jelly on Ritz crackers in bed at two in the morning because that was all Dylan had in her kitchen, followed by even more incredible sex until they finally fell asleep near sunrise, limbs tangled like kittens.

Thank god it hadn't been a dream. Dylan closed her eyes, then ran her fingers over Ramona's hair. She'd nearly drifted off again when something else proved itself very real—the incessant pounding on her front door.

"Mph," Ramona said without moving. She was so adorable, Dylan couldn't help but smile.

"Go back to sleep," Dylan said, not moving either. "Whoever it is will go away."

But a minute later, the knocking continued, and Dylan's phone had joined in the fun, buzzing on the nightstand over and over.

"Goddammit," she said, reaching over to grab it. The screen was loaded with text notifications—never a good sign—and the first one that unfurled in its full glory was from Laurel.

I'm sorry, I'm sorry, I'm sorry.

That was alarming enough, but the other seventy thousand texts were from her father. And her mother. And then her father again.

She blinked at the screen, hoping all that sex had blown her mind to the point of hallucinations.

But then . . . a voice, spoken loudly but muffled on the other side of the front door.

"Dill Pickle?"

"Fuck me," she said, then sat up, Ramona's hand flopping from Dylan's boob to her lap.

"Readydid," Ramona mumbled, her eyes still closed, which Dylan translated to *already did*, which, dammit, was so ridiculously cute, Dylan wished she actually was hallucinating.

"Pickle!"

Ramona finally lifted her head, hair a mess, eyes bleary. "Did you order pickles?"

Dylan laughed. "God, if only. Stay here." She leaned over and kissed Ramona on the top of her head, then got out of bed and threw on her robe.

The knocking continued, as did the nicknames, but she paused before heading out into the living room to text Laurel.

Dylan: You're fired

Laurel: A comedian this morning

Dylan: I contain multitudes

"Dylan Page Monroe!"

"Jesus god," Dylan said, scrubbing a hand down her face. She set her phone on the cream-colored dresser, then tightened her robe's sash as she went into the hall. She closed the bedroom door as quietly as she could before walking to the front door, where she could see her parents' silhouettes through the wavy inlaid glass. She flung open the door and fake smiled at Jack Monroe and Carrie Page.

"Dill Pickle!" Jack said, pulling his daughter into his arms. He was dressed in his usual black tee and low-hanging black jeans, chipped black nail polish and ear-length brown hair streaked with gray. Same rocker style he wore in the nineties, same thin frame, just a few more lines on his face.

"Sweetheart," Carrie said when Jack released Dylan, patting her face. Her mother had a silver pixie cut, heavy black eyeliner, and about a thousand gold chains around her neck, different pendants hanging at different lengths, everything from tiny skulls to weed plants and birds to a heart engraved with the initials JDC.

Jack, Dylan, Carrie.

A gift from Jack a few years ago when they got married.

Again.

"Mom, Dad," Dylan said. "What are you doing here?"

She tried to keep her voice level, but her pitch was high with panic. Whatever the answer to her question, it couldn't be good.

"I'm producing the soundtrack," Jack said. "I thought I told you that."

Dylan blinked, the word *soundtrack* suddenly a foreign word in her brain. Gobbledygook.

"Soundtrack," she repeated. "Soundtrack?"

"And we wanted to meet your new girl," Carrie said as she stepped farther into the house, her black combats clomping loudly on the hardwoods.

"New girl," Dylan said, because apparently all she could do was repeat words, like a toddler learning how to talk.

"What's her name?" Carrie said as she lifted a fake orchid from a milk-white vase and smelled it. "Ramona?"

Meaning joined the words, a slow unveiling of the full picture.

Ramona.

Soundtrack.

Laurel's apologies.

"Soundtrack," she said again.

Jack grinned. "Pretty cool, yeah? Just compiling artists, though I was thinking about having Jocelyn do an original. Attach a fresh sound to the film, you know?" He wandered around her living room as she spoke, completely clueless about how his words landed.

"Jocelyn," Dylan said again, still unable to move past repetition. Her mouth was dry, and she couldn't tell whether her heart was going so fast she could no longer feel it or if it had stopped beating altogether. She wished she were wearing actual clothes, because if so, she'd simply walk out the door, actually fire Laurel, and then find another place to stay under a pseudonym like Black Widow or Jessica Rabbit.

Hell, maybe she'd just quit the movie altogether. Work at Dickie's. Or the Earthstars Museum. She could get over her trypophobia long enough to sell some tickets. No problem. And she and Ramona could—

Fucking hell.

Ramona.

Her new girl.

Ramona was in her bedroom, sweet and soft and sleepy. And here were Dylan's parents, two hurricanes ready to blast through everything Dylan was trying to—

You're in *a publicity stunt, Dylan.*

She closed her eyes, took a few deep breaths.

"Breakfast," she said.

Carrie glanced at her from where she was inspecting the fabric of the couch pillows. In her older, more sedate years, Carrie Page had gotten severely picky about her surroundings. All the art frames in her house with Jack were white or cream colored, the walls never darker than a storm gray, and every linen had to boast a thread count of at least a thousand.

Serene surroundings, serene mind was Carrie's mantra, which Dylan supposed was an improvement over the cacophony of Carrie's younger rock and roll days, where eighty percent of the photos capturing Dylan's mother featured smeared red lipstick and flaky mascara.

"You haven't eaten?" Carrie said now.

Today was a rare day off from shooting—Gia's wife being in town and all—and Dylan had no idea what time it was, but the light outside didn't look brighter than nine or so.

"We ate on the plane," Jack said, "but I'd love to get a cup of terrible coffee in this little hamlet." He rubbed his hands together, and now Dylan panicked about where to take them.

Couldn't go to Clover Moon, which was closed for a few days due to filming anyway.

Definitely couldn't ask Ramona—couldn't risk her parents realizing Ramona was all but twenty feet away. The last time Jack and Carrie met someone she was seeing, that someone got a recording deal and Dylan ended up saddled with a ten-thousand-dollar fine in damages.

She'd find somewhere—she knew there were a few other places to eat on Lake Street, though the idea of walking through downtown Clover Lake with her infamous parents made her want to puke. Still, she had to get them out of here.

Now.

"Five minutes!" she said, then rushed quietly to the hall bathroom, where she'd never been so thankful in all her life that she'd left some clothes on the floor when she'd changed for a swim the other day. She threw on the dirty cutoffs, bra, and a T-shirt featuring a skeletal hand on a tarot card with its middle finger lifted in the air. But even in her desperation, she couldn't bear to pull on dirty underwear, so she just went without, hoped her morning breath wasn't too noticeable, and yanked her hair into a messy top bun.

"Let's go," she said when she emerged.

"Brunch!" Carrie said, looping her arm through Dylan's as Jack opened the front door.

"Whatever," Dylan said. She looked back at her closed bedroom door, her heart crawling up her throat, but there was nothing for it. It was this or let her parents ruin everything.

"I'm so excited to hear all about your big movie," Carrie said as she pulled Dylan out the front door and onto the sidewalk. As they walked under the summery morning sun, Dylan tried to focus on her mom and dad prattling on and on, but even with her lakeside house half a mile behind them, she couldn't stop thinking about leaving Ramona.

It would be fine.

She'd text her. She'd text her right now. She dug into her pocket—

Her hand froze. Then dipped into her other pockets, front and back, but she already knew—she'd left her phone on the dresser in her bedroom.

"Fuck," she said.

"What's that, love?" Carrie asked.

Dylan didn't respond as they turned onto Lake Street.

Chapter
Twenty-Six

RAMONA OPENED THE door to Dylan's bedroom, the flat sheet from the bed wrapped around her naked body.

She could've slept for hours longer—she didn't think she and Dylan had fallen asleep until around four in the morning—but when she woke up to an empty bed, she didn't want to be that girl who slept till noon the first time she stayed over. Besides, it was nearly ten already, and her stomach was growling.

"Dylan?" she called.

She blinked into the bright morning sun streaming through the front windows. Looked around for Dylan but didn't see her anywhere. It was a small house, only two bedrooms and one hallway bathroom between them, and the kitchen, living room, and dining room were all one open area. There were only so many places Dylan could be.

"Dylan?" she called again, checking the other bedroom. The bathroom door was open, the space dark inside. She went to the front door, sheet dragging behind her like a badly designed toga, and stepped onto the empty front porch, nothing but two wicker chairs and a table between them. The morning was warm, a slight breeze that always blew this close to the lake.

Dylan's rental car was in the driveway.

"Dylan?" she said, a little louder this time, just in case Dylan was out in the yard or checking yesterday's mail or . . .

But the tiny cul-de-sac where the house sat was quiet, void of any neighbors out and about, and certainly void of any famous movie stars picking flowers or petting a neighborhood dog.

Ramona went back inside before anyone saw her—she knew Mrs. Murphy who lived two houses down was a notorious gossip—and closed the door behind her.

"Dylan?" she said one more time, panic lacing her voice, but there was no answer.

Dylan Monroe was not here.

Ramona found her bag on the couch, dug out her phone. She had several missed calls from April, none from Olive. None from Dylan either. She tapped on Dylan's number and pressed the phone to her ear.

A second later, she heard a vibration in the bedroom. There, on the dresser, was Dylan's phone. She had no idea how attached Dylan was to her phone—she remembered Dylan mentioning that it got her in trouble a lot, so the fact that she'd left without it might not be all that unusual.

Because Dylan had left.

She'd left Ramona alone in her own house, no note, no text.

Nothing.

Ramona sank down onto the bed, sat there for a good five minutes trying to process what to do or how she felt. Maybe Dylan had gone out to get breakfast for them. Made sense, as she knew Dylan didn't have much in the house. Ramona nodded to herself and got dressed. Used Dylan's toothpaste on her finger to scrub her teeth clean. Made Dylan's bed and picked up Dylan's own discarded clothes on the bedroom floor, set them in the hamper by the dresser.

Then she settled on the living room couch and read a thriller on her e-book phone app.

She sat there and read four chapters.

Sat there for an hour.

One hour and eleven minutes.

Finally, she slipped her phone into her bag, then stood and left Dylan's house, leaving the door hanging wide open as she went.

"WAIT, WAIT, WAIT," April said, "let me make sure I've got this right."

She sat on her couch, a squashy lavender-gray color with black-and-white throw pillows featuring tragic women's faces—Marilyn Monroe, Judy Garland, Sylvia Plath. Ramona was tucked into one corner, a cup of coffee in her hands, Sylvia in her lap. One of April's cats, Bob the Drag Cat—named for one of April's favorite drag queens—was curled up next to April. Her other cat, a notoriously cranky lynx point Siamese named Bianca del Kitty for another drag queen, glared at Ramona from her perch on the back of the over-sized armchair by the fireplace.

Ramona had gone straight to April's after leaving Dylan's, knowing April would pepper her with questions, which was what she needed right now. Questions and answers.

"Don't make me say all of that again," Ramona said.

"No, no," April said. She was in a white undershirt-style tank top, which Ramona had never seen her wear before, and a pair of plaid boxers. "I wouldn't dare. But . . . mind-blowing sex, right?"

"Check."

"And no sign of Dylan in her own house?"

"Check, check."

April frowned. "Let's go back to the sex."

Ramona laughed, flopped her head back onto the cushion. She

stared at the ceiling, which was plaster and painted the same light aqua color as the walls, because April was nothing if not unconventional. Framed art covered nearly every inch of the walls too, all different colors, styles, mediums. Some of it was April's, some not. After Elena left, April had become a plant gay as well, greenery thriving and draped all over her tiny bungalow.

"It was good," Ramona said.

"Excuse me, I believe you said mind-blowing. Dare I say, DNA-altering?"

"Oh, god," Ramona said, covering her face. "This is just like Elena, and Dylan is going to pulverize my heart, and I'm totally screwed."

"Wow, my life has a lovely outlook," April said flatly.

Ramona groaned into her hands. "Sorry. I'm being dramatic."

"A bit. But DNA-altering sex will do that. Trust me, I know."

Ramona groaned louder.

"Plus, this is not like Elena," April said. "I highly doubt another narcissist of her level even exists in the world, and if they do, goddess help us all."

Ramona peeked at April through her fingers. "She called me a slut."

April's brows lifted. "In a fun, kinky way, I hope."

Ramona's face flamed, and she dropped her hands. "Of course."

April smirked. "And you liked it."

"God, I did," Ramona said, "but now she's disappeared, and I'm not sure whether to report her missing or be pissed off that she ghosted me in her own house."

"There's got to be an explanation."

"Maybe," Ramona said. "Maybe I should—"

But she froze when another person sauntered into the room from the hallway that led to the two small bedrooms. Not just any person.

Leigh.

"Morning," they said, looking bleary and mussed. Their hair was a complete mess, at least five inches tall, and they wore April's favorite Sleater-Kinney T-shirt.

"Um" was all Ramona could say.

"Coffee's in the kitchen," April said.

Leigh sauntered off, and Ramona pointed at April's tank top. "That's Leigh's."

April shrugged and sipped her coffee. "I ran into them again after I locked up the shop and was craving ice cream."

"They were at Sugar Sandy's?"

"Eats Chocolate-Chocolate Monster like it's laced with Molly. You remember that about them."

Ramona shook her head. "You two didn't waste any time."

April grinned. "They're only here for a few days. And let me tell you, they have learned some *skills* since the last time."

Ramona lowered her voice. "I thought if I wasn't allowed to hook up with Logan, you couldn't hook up with Leigh."

"No such deal was ever made, darling. You said if you dated, then I had to date, and this"—she plucked at the chest of Leigh's tank top—"is not a date. It's just sex. I'm not in love with Leigh, nor do I want to be. Cloverians really need to expand their ideas about sex and pleasure." She leaned forward. "I have to tell you, Leigh does this thing with their thumb that—"

"You're here early, Ramona," Leigh said, reappearing with coffee and plopping into the armchair, eliciting an annoyed mew from Bianca.

"It's after eleven o'clock," Ramona said.

"Is it?" Leigh said, then nothing else, sitting with one ankle propped on their knee as they sipped their coffee, looking exactly like the quintessential fuckboi they were.

"Ramona is having some girl trouble," April said.

"April," Ramona said.

"What? Leigh is an expert at girl trouble."

Leigh smiled over their coffee mug. "Giselle?"

"Who?" April said.

"Dylan Monroe's character on *Spellbound*," Leigh said. "Fucking loved that show."

"Oh, god, that's right," April said. "Hottest vampire ever."

"I used to write smutty fanfic about her and Cressida," Leigh said.

"Well, that I have to read," Ramona said.

"It's terrible," Leigh said. "Definitely not my best work."

"All the more reason to read it," April said.

"The sex scenes were hilarious. Like, positions no human could ever get themselves into."

"Good thing they're a witch and a vampire, then," April said.

Ramona laughed, but the sound was tight. She checked her phone—still nothing. "Can we get back to me?" she asked. "What do I do here?"

"What's the situation?" Leigh asked, then April proceeded to explain what happened.

"How mind-blowing are we talking?" Leigh said.

April snorted a laugh, and Ramona flipped her off.

"What?" Leigh said, grinning. "It's a relevant question. Like, you want to see her again kind of mind-blowing?"

"Mona *likes* Dylan, Leigh," April said. "An alien concept to you, I know."

"I like people," Leigh said.

"Yeah, their cunts."

Leigh smirked. "Well, cunts are very likable."

"Cheers to that," April said, lifting her coffee mug.

"I'll have you know, I had a real live girlfriend last year," Leigh said.

April's jaw dropped open. "Leigh Reynolds caught feelings."

"It was awful," Leigh said, shaking their head, their gaze distant as though remembering a nightmare.

April just laughed, while Ramona stood up abruptly. On any other day, she'd be joining in the fun here, but right now, she was about to crawl out of her skin.

"I've got to find her," she said. "Make sure she's okay."

"She's fine," Leigh said. "She's hot and famous."

"Physically, I mean," Ramona said. "What if something happened to her? What if she went out for bagels and, I don't know, fell in the lake?"

"Fell in the lake," April deadpanned.

"Maybe she can't swim," Ramona said, her panic growing and pushing out any anger or hurt. Because Dylan wouldn't do this. She wouldn't just *leave* Ramona without a word. Not after their night together. Not after the Earthstars Museum. Not after already hurting Ramona, however unintentionally, by spilling their story to a tabloid.

"I've never seen anyone just fall into the lake," April said.

"They might if they were on a pier," Ramona said.

"Why would she be on a pier?"

"I don't know!" Ramona said, her voice reaching screeching levels. "Why would she not be in her own fucking house when I woke up?"

"Okay," April said calmly, presenting her palms. "Okay, you're right. Maybe she fell in the lake."

Ramona threw her bag's strap over her shoulder, headed for the door. "Someone must've seen her. She's Dylan Monroe. She can't go anywhere without a camera pointed at her face."

"Hey, hang on," April said, standing up too. "We'll come with you."

"What?" Leigh said.

"We'll come with you," April said again, glaring at Leigh.

"Right. Yes. We'll come with you," Leigh said, though they didn't budge from the chair.

"Just let us get dressed," April said, grabbing Leigh's arm and pulling them up.

"Fine, but hurry," Ramona said as she tried calling Dylan again. She wouldn't mind someone going with her, to be honest. She felt a little shaky, adrenaline and worry and Dylan's phone going to voicemail over and over again coalescing into a terrible, awful combination.

Chapter Twenty-Seven

PREDICTABLY, BRUNCH HAD turned into a complete clusterfuck.

Dylan had tried to get them to go out of town, maybe call a Lyft and head to a nice little roadside diner off the interstate, frequented by truckers too tired to notice Jack and Carrie in all their glory. But no, they'd barely turned onto Lake Street when Carrie spotted Pierce Apothecary, a nice restaurant that did brunch every day in the summer until three p.m.

So now here Dylan was, sipping on Bellinis while every single eye in the place stared at them, along with a constant stream of patrons stopping by and telling Jack and Carrie how much they loved their music and how *Citrine*—Evenflow's debut album, which rocketed the band to fame in the early nineties—changed their life or saved their life or made their life worth living or some shit.

Then they had to fawn over Carrie next, who of course came second after *the* Jack Monroe, and people always had to mention something about how hard it must've been raising a child back then, and how lovely Dylan turned out, and Dylan wanted to scream *Fuck you* at the top of her lungs, both for Carrie's sake for always being seen as a mother first and a serious musician in her own right second, and for the fact that it *had* been so hard to raise a child back then her parents essentially *didn't*, and Dylan hadn't turned out lovely at all.

She'd turned out a complete dumpster fire who had to literally sink her teeth into her lower lip to keep from cussing out her parents' adoring fans in the middle of a small New Hampshire town.

Add all this together with leaving Ramona in her bed and not knowing Ramona's number so she could text her from her mom's phone, and it amounted to Dylan polishing off an entire bottle of prosecco—very little peach juice added—all by her lonesome.

"Maybe you should slow down, darling," Carrie said during a rare lull between adoring fans.

"Slow what down?" Dylan said, topping off her glass with the last of the wine. Her head was already fuzzy, and she knew, way back in the tiny corners of her brain, that her mother was probably right, that she didn't make the best decisions when intoxicated, but the numbness felt goddamn great right now, and if she didn't embrace it, she'd feel way too much and probably end up on top of the table shooting finger guns with her middle finger at the entire town of Clover Lake anyway.

She was a mess sober, and she was a mess drunk.

How lovely she'd turned out indeed.

"So, Dill Pickle," Jack said, shaking some hot sauce onto his now-cold egg white omelet. "Tell us how the film is going."

"Oh, swell," she said, letting the wine's bubbles pop down her throat. "Just swell."

"How's Blair?" Carrie asked, tearing into a piece of bacon with her teeth. "She's so beautiful, that girl."

"That she is," Jack said. "We always thought you might end up with her, the way you two danced around each other during *Spell Locked*."

"Spell what?" Dylan asked.

"Spell *Bent*, sweetheart," Carrie said.

"Sure, that's what I said," Jack said, then winked at Dylan, who decided not to correct her parents on either of their completely wrong points. Not like she'd spent six whole years on *Spellbound* or anything. No big deal.

The server put down another bottle, which Dylan immediately tipped into her glass, sans any peach juice this time.

"Dill," her mother warned. Her mother, who'd *learned her lessons the hard way* and who only ever drank club soda with blood orange slices and coconut water.

"I'm *fine*," Dylan said.

"Oh my god, Jack and Carrie," a voice said.

Dylan looked up, recognized the woman standing at their table with her phone in her hands, coppery hair and too much eyeliner.

"Hey there," Jack said jovially.

"Penny," the woman said, sticking out her hand. "I write a small blog called *Penny for Your Thoughts* here in Clover Lake."

"Oh, how adorable," Carrie said.

"Thank you!" Penny said. "We've so enjoyed having Dylan in town. She's very exciting and we just love her and Ramona together."

"Yes, *Ramona*," Carrie said. "Tell us more about her. Dylan is very mum about the whole thing."

"Mother," Dylan said, teeth clenched.

"I have some pictures here!" Penny said, swiping up on her phone.

"What?" Dylan said. "I don't think that's—"

"Lovely," Carrie said, angling to see now, as though Dylan weren't even there. As though she'd disappeared, nothing but *Jack and Carrie's daughter* now. Nameless and invisible, just some tiny girl falling asleep on an open box of half-eaten pizza.

"Goodness, our daughter is gorgeous, Jack," Carrie said.

"She is that."

"And this Ramona!" Carrie said, tilting her head and slipping on her reading glasses to look closer at Penny's phone. "Not your usual type, but she's really love—"

"That's fucking enough!"

A yell.

A bit slurry, but still, the volume was there, the scratch in Dylan's throat evidence that she'd said it out loud, not just in her head.

And this time, it was enough to make her parents stop.

"Dylan," Carrie said. "You're being very rude."

"Oh, *I'm* being rude?" Dylan said, then stood up. The room spun, and then spun a little more. Dammit, she loved bubbles, but they did not love her. Ever. "I think you've got that backward, Mother."

Carrie frowned, sent a confused look to Jack, a pause in their constant and dizzying combo of fawning all over Dylan and ignoring her completely. The silence was long enough for Dylan to realize just how silent it was—the entire restaurant quiet and staring at the family with interest, tiny *holy shit* smiles on their faces, cameras out.

Always the fucking cameras.

"Goddammit," Dylan said, just as loud. Her mouth felt dry, her head already ached. She pushed her chair back so she could dig herself out of the seat by the window she'd been stuffed into when they'd arrived. The chair felt extremely heavy, and she fumbled with it enough that she fell against the window, her shoulder pressing into the cool glass.

She cursed, then lifted the chair into the air and above her mother's head as she stumbled-tripped around the table.

"Dylan!" Jack said sternly, standing up too.

The restaurant patrons gasped.

Phones were everywhere.

In the back of her fuzzy brain, Dylan knew this was all wrong, very wrong, so wrong she'd hate herself in about six hours' time, if not before, but right now, it felt like the only thing she could do. She had to get out from behind the table, had to get out of this restaurant, and this was the only way to do it.

Simple as that.

"I just need some air," she said.

Or maybe yelled.

She couldn't quite tell. Didn't care.

"Sweetheart," Carrie said. She was standing too. Following Dylan as she headed toward the front door, dragging the chair behind her.

"Don't call me that," Dylan said, hand on the heavy oak door.

"What?"

Dylan paused, turned around. "I'm not your sweetheart, Carrie. I'm not your perfect little daughter and I'm not swell and the show I played a lead on for six years is called *Spellbound*. Spell. *Bound*."

Carrie blinked at her, hurt filling her expression.

"No," Dylan said, leaning against the door with her back, then pointing at Carrie's face, the same ice-green eyes as Dylan's tearing up. "You don't get to look like that. You *don't* get to look all—"

But she never got to finish her sentence, because the door flung open then, someone out on the street trying to get in, and Dylan went flying backward as all her weight had been resting against the solid wood. She stumbled, tried to catch herself, but she also had a chair in tow, and she ended up hitting the pavement hard, her ass first, but then she felt the skin of her elbows scrape, the chair landing perfectly upright and in a way that caged her in.

And that's when it hit her.

It was official—she'd truly gone and lost it, Killin' Dylan done in by a cute girl, great sex, and brunch with her too-famous parents. She felt her eyes fill up as she stared into the blue summer sky. She didn't want to move. Wasn't sure it was even worth it.

"Oh, honey," she heard Carrie say, disappointment lacing her mother's voice.

And then, another voice.

"Dylan?"

A face, replacing the cerulean sky, freckled and beautiful and perfect.

"Ramona," Dylan managed to say. It wasn't a question. A lament, maybe.

"God, are you okay?" Ramona bent down, her hands going to Dylan's face—cradling it, really. "Did you hit your head?"

"That was a spectacular fall," someone said. April maybe. Though when Dylan angled her neck to see, there was a third person there she'd never seen before. At least she didn't think she had. Head full of dark curls, large black boots, definitely queer. A half-bored, half-curious expression on their face as they looked down at Dylan.

Maybe Dylan had hit her head. And if she didn't, perhaps she needed to. Because she was lying on the sidewalk underneath a chair, drunk off her ass and wishing for a meteor to land on her right the hell now.

Except a meteor would also hit Ramona, and she liked Ramona.

"God, I like you," she said, lifting her hand to touch Ramona's face. "So much."

"She's drunk," someone else said. Definitely April this time.

"Dylan, my darling," her mother said, though there was no warmth in the term of endearment. "Why can we never have a simple conversation when you're upset?"

"Holy shit," April said. "I didn't see you there. Carrie Page. You're Carrie Page."

"There she is. *The* Carrie Page," Dylan slurred. "Jack's around here somewhere too, so don't worry about me. Nope. I'll just lie here in the middle of the street while you all lose your fucking minds over the two worst parents on the planet."

A beat of silence.

Long enough for Dylan to wonder if she'd said that out loud, and fuck, the silence must mean she had. She wasn't sure she'd even meant to, but there it was. The truth. Fine. Great. Let it fly.

"Help me get her up," Ramona said.

"Not sure that's wise," said Curls.

"We can't leave her here," Ramona said, picking up the chair and handing it off to someone.

"Sure you can," Dylan said, but Ramona was already hefting her upright, hands under Dylan's arms. The world tilted, as did Dylan's stomach, her brain, everything.

"I got you," Ramona said, circling one arm around Dylan's waist and looping one of Dylan's own arms around her shoulder.

"Mona, you can't walk with her like that all the way back to your house," April said.

"We'll call you a car," Carrie said flatly.

"No," Dylan said. Her head felt so heavy. "Wanna walk, fresh air."

"Bad idea," Curls said.

"Dylan, for god's sake." This from Jack, who'd just come outside with his hands on his hips.

Her *father*. Authority figure and everyone's hero. Oh, wait, *formative* hero. Can't forget how *formative* he'd been for everyone.

"You're being extremely rude and hurtful," he said firmly.

"Oh," Dylan said, squinting at her dad. She thought she might be getting drunker by the second. "Did I say that out loud too?"

"Uh, yeah," April said. "Awks."

"Super awks," Dylan said, then shot a finger gun at April.

"We really need to get her somewhere safe," Ramona said, still holding tight to Dylan.

"Oh, oh, Mom and Dad," Dylan said. "This is Ramona. Isn't she pretty?" Dylan leaned her head against Ramona's.

Carrie pressed her mouth together. "You need to get to bed. And drink some water, take some ibuprofen."

"Second that," Curls said.

"They're a doctor," April said, motioning to Curls. "Dylan's in good hands."

"Righto," Dylan said. More finger guns. God, she couldn't stop shooting finger guns at everyone. Her mother was right. She needed to be put away, hidden, the shameful only daughter of icons.

"My car isn't too far," Curls said. "Left it downtown last night."

"Perfect," Ramona said. "Thanks, Leigh."

"Fine," Carrie said. "Thank you all, so much. Dylan, we'll call you later."

"Oh, can't wait for that," Dylan said, sans finger guns this time, because she was very suddenly and very violently not feeling awesome. Her stomach crawled everywhere, jittering up her throat and then into her arms, fingertips, then back again. She felt herself swinging away from Ramona, stumbling down the cobbled sidewalk as people watched. Or, rather, as they watched through their phones, cameras recording.

Laurel was going to kill her. Rayna was also going to kill her, then find a witch to resurrect her just so she could kill her again. Gia, god, who the fuck knew what Gia would do? Fire her, probably. Fuck. She was a mess. Made terrible decisions. How did she always make such terrible decisions?

"I think she's going to puke," Curls said.

"Am not," Dylan said.

"Do it now, rather than in my car, please."

"Am *not*," Dylan said again, but then she froze on the curb, pressed a hand to her stomach. And as it turned out, Curls was right.

Chapter Twenty-Eight

DYLAN WOKE UP in Ramona's bed.

At least, she thought it was Ramona's bed. It was dark outside, the blinds on the windows shut tight, but no light seeped through the cracks. White noise whirred from some machine on the nightstand, and she was burrowed so deep in a nest of soft sheets and blankets, she was sure she'd never been so cozy in her life.

She rolled over to her back, and her head nearly split in two.

Okay, so, not the coziest she'd ever been then.

Her stomach roiled a bit, but a few deep breaths calmed it enough for her to sit up, then gulp from the glass of water on the nightstand. As the liquid slid down her throat, it was as though it washed away the muck blurring a window. The entire day filtered back to her—leaving Ramona in her house, her parents, her parents again, lots and lots of wine, an uneaten brunch, and then . . .

Fuck.

Lots of humiliating things.

Humiliating things that were most likely, definitely, absolutely all over the internet by now. Laurel was probably blowing up her phone, which she remembered she didn't have, and had never been so happy to be unplugged.

All that shit could wait until her stomach and brain remembered their places within her body. She set the now-empty glass back on the table, then rubbed at her throbbing temples. She just wanted to go back to sleep, but her mouth tasted horrible and her bladder screamed at her. She slipped out of bed and cracked open the door. The house was quiet, and there was a bathroom in the hallway. She peed and washed her hands, then found a bottle of blue Listerine under the sink and swished it around her mouth until her cheeks stung. Finally, she crept back into bed and the cozy cocoon.

Just as she nearly slipped to sleep again, the door cracked open. Ramona's silhouette, holding a plate.

Dylan sat up. "Hi."

"Hi."

Ramona shut the door behind her, then ventured into the room, set a plate of buttered toast and scrambled eggs on the nightstand. She clicked on the tiny blue lamp, sending a dim, watery glow throughout the room.

"Thought you might need some food," Ramona said.

"Thanks," Dylan said, though she didn't feel she'd quite reached the hangover food stage of her idiocy.

"Okay," Ramona said, then turned to go.

Dylan reached out and grabbed her wrist. The least stupid thing she'd done in the last eight hours.

"Wait," she said. "Please."

Ramona did, but she didn't make a move to sit or even turn to face Dylan. She just let Dylan hold her arm, thumb brushing against the inside of her wrist.

"I'm sorry," Dylan said. "I'm an idiot."

Ramona shook her head, but Dylan saw the ghost of a smile on her profile. "You're not."

"You're too nice."

"April says the same thing."

"Something we agree on."

Ramona finally turned, the motion slipping her arm free from Dylan's grasp. She sank onto the bed, leaving plenty of space between them.

"I think you're selfish," Ramona said. "Not stupid."

Dylan felt the color drain from her face. "I think I prefer stupid."

Ramona nodded, serious. "What happened this morning, Dylan? You left me alone in your house after . . ."

She trailed off.

Took a deep breath.

Her hair was in braided pigtails, her bangs shaggy over her freckled forehead, and she wore jeans and a royal-blue T-shirt that said *RISD* in white script. Dylan stared at those four letters, realizing for the first time since they'd met—met *again*—that Dylan hadn't asked about her experience there, hadn't thought about what she'd given up to take care of her family. Hadn't wondered if she still wanted to work in apparel design or if she was content with what she was doing now.

Dylan pressed her eyes closed, rubbed at her temples again.

"You're right," she said. "I'm sorry. I don't have a good excuse for this morning except that my parents make me crazy." She looked up, met Ramona's eyes. "I didn't want you to meet them."

Ramona frowned. "Flattering."

"No, no." Dylan took her hand. Ramona let her. "Not because of you. You're perfect. They just . . ." She sighed. "They're Jack Monroe and Carrie Page. They take up all the space in a room, make me feel like I'm still six years old vying for their attention. Or they smother me and make me feel like shit because I'm so fucking angry with them."

Ramona squeezed her hand.

"I *am* selfish," Dylan said. "When it comes to them, I go into fight or flight, and I do stupid things like drink too much because that always seems like a good solution, and it never goes well because I'm terrible at moderation when I'm emotional, and I forgot my phone, so I couldn't text you that I was getting them out of my house so they couldn't ruin everything with us." She shook her head. "So *I* couldn't ruin everything with us."

"Dylan."

"But I did anyway."

Ramona closed her eyes, long lashes on her cheeks. "You didn't ruin it."

Dylan's lungs felt as though they were functioning normally for the first time since she opened her front door this morning. "No?"

Ramona shook her head, a small smile on her mouth.

"Well, just give it time," Dylan said, and Ramona laughed. "Someday I'll probably have to offer you some really big grand gesture."

"Oh yeah?" Ramona said, smiling. "Like what?"

Dylan watched her for a second, eyes trailing over Ramona's face. "You'd need something romantic. But soft. Not super public or flashy. But still big enough that you knew I meant business."

"Like a mushroom museum?"

Dylan laughed. "Maybe. But I already did that."

Ramona squeezed her hand. "You did."

"So I can't do that again. How lazy."

Ramona laughed.

"If I'm the one who fucked things up," Dylan said, "which, let's be honest, I would be, I'd want to do something where you wouldn't feel trapped."

Ramona frowned. "What do you mean?"

"So many grand gestures in books and movies are like . . . I don't know. They feel intrusive sometimes. Like, 'Hey, here I am, the person you're furious with! Talk to me!'"

Ramona laughed. "You have a point."

"So I'd do something where you had a choice. I would . . ." She trailed off, but then the perfect grand gesture drifted through her thoughts. Perfect for Ramona. Elegant and romantic, one of Dylan's most favorite places in the world. "I've got it."

"What is it?"

"I'm not giving away my secrets."

Ramona tweaked her thigh, making Dylan yelp.

"Tell me," Ramona said, tickling her way up Dylan's leg to her stomach.

Dylan laughed, curled in on herself. "Fine, fine, I give!"

Ramona relented, then looked at her pointedly.

"Okay," Dylan said. "We'd have to be in LA though."

Ramona's expression sort of froze. "LA?"

"Hypothetically," Dylan said.

Ramona waved her hand in a *go on* gesture.

"I'd go to the Griffith Observatory," Dylan said. "Every day at sunset. It's gorgeous then. Soft and romantic and perfect. And I'd post a picture on my Instagram every day that I went. No caption, or maybe a caption only you would understand, and I'd wait there for you every day for five days until the observatory closed."

"Only five?"

Dylan smiled. "I figure that's enough time for you to know if you wanted to see me."

"What if I didn't see your Instagram?"

Dylan just grinned. "Come on. You'd check my Instagram."

"I would?" Ramona said.

"You would," Dylan said. "At least *I* would."

Ramona laughed, then grew serious. "I'd rather not have to wait for a grand gesture."

"Me neither," Dylan said, then tugged on her hand, tugged and tugged some more until they were both lying down, facing each other. Dylan tucked Ramona's hair behind her ear, then traced the delicate shell, the lobe, drifting over to her nose and mouth. "Can I kiss you?"

"You better," Ramona said, and so Dylan did.

Soft and slow.

A savoring.

Opening her mouth gently, tasting Ramona's bottom lip, then her top before touching her tongue with her own.

Ramona gasped, softly, adorably, but in a way that made Dylan feel immediately feral, wild with want. She kissed harder, licking into Ramona's mouth, tracing her teeth.

"God," Ramona said into the kiss.

"Yeah," Dylan said, then kissed her again, pulling her tighter against her and trailing her hands down Ramona's back, then under her T-shirt. "Take this off."

Ramona sat up enough to take off her shirt, which she did slowly, lifting it above her head and revealing her gorgeous tits held in a pink lace bra.

Dylan groaned. "You're gorgeous."

Ramona tilted her head. "What next, Ms Monroe?"

Dylan lifted her brows. "You like being told what to do."

Ramona giggled, literally giggled, and it was both the cutest and sexiest thing Dylan had ever heard.

"Turns out I do," Ramona said.

Dylan smiled. "Take off your pants. Then take off mine."

And Ramona did.

She slid off the bed and shucked off her jeans but left on her yellow cotton underwear. Then she yanked the covers back, unbuttoned Dylan's cutoff shorts, and slid them down Dylan's legs.

"Oh," she said when she saw that Dylan didn't have on any underwear.

Dylan felt her cheeks go warm, but she laughed. "Surprise."

"And a nice one at that."

"Shirt next," Dylan said through a laugh, sitting up so Ramona could take off her tee. "Good girl."

Ramona smiled. "Now?"

"Straddle me," Dylan said, and god, Ramona did. Thick thighs over Dylan's hips, perfect and soft. The contact was almost too much, Dylan's cunt already wet and throbbing for more. "God, I want to do so much to you. *With* you." She slid her hands up Ramona's legs, dipped her thumbs into the crease where her hips joined her thighs.

Ramona tipped her head back. "Please. Anything."

"Anything?"

"Anything," Ramona said again, her hips moving.

"You remember our safe words?" Dylan asked.

Ramona nodded, then leaned over and kissed her, whispered, "Green," against her mouth.

"Jesus," Dylan said, hands on Ramona's soft waist. "Take your bra off."

Ramona reached back, no hesitation, unclasped the garment, and let it fall onto Dylan's stomach. Dylan didn't even move it, couldn't, her hands trailing up to Ramona's heavy breasts, cupping and squeezing, plucking at those pink nipples.

Ramona moaned, her head arched back again, her chest already flushed with want, hips rolling. Dylan sat up enough to get her mouth on Ramona's breast, teeth scraping over her nipple, then soothing the bite with her tongue.

"Oh my god," Ramona said.

"You like that?"

"So much."

So Dylan did it again, licking and biting and sucking, first one breast, tonguing her nipple to a hard peak, then the other.

"Your mouth, god," Ramona said. "I need it."

"That's a good girl."

Dylan pushed Ramona's tits together, buried her face between them and inhaled, licked, kissed.

"Do you have any toys?" Dylan asked against her skin, her voice raspy.

Ramona nodded. "Drawer."

"Show me."

Dylan released Ramona's tits and rested back on the pillows. Ramona leaned over, not even bothering to get off Dylan or the bed, which was exactly how Dylan wanted it. She held on to Ramona's hips as Ramona slid her nightstand's drawer open. She took out a soft bag and set it on Dylan's stomach, tossing her bra to the floor as she did so.

"Open it," Dylan said.

Ramona did, and inside was a purple dildo, textured with a mosaic of designs.

"Well, that's very interesting," Dylan said, and Ramona laughed. "What else?"

Ramona got out a clitoral stimulator, a bright pink dildo that had a suction cup on the base, and a red vibrator that had an insertable part and a base shaped like a butterfly that stimulated the clit and entire vulva.

"Which is your favorite?" Dylan asked.

Ramona smiled down at her toys, her cheeks flushing a gorgeous pink.

"Tell me," Dylan said, sliding her hands up Ramona's thighs.

Ramona held up the red butterfly. "This one."

"Good," Dylan said, smirking. "Looks fun."

Ramona laughed. "It is. You want to tell me why I need it right now?" She rolled her hips a little, making Dylan gasp and then laugh too.

"You need it," Dylan said, squeezing her thighs, "because I want you to come while going down on me."

Ramona's eyes widened, then she smiled. "I think I can do that."

"I know you can."

Ramona put the other toys back in the drawer, then Dylan sat up again and kissed her. Kissed her deep and long, pulling at her lower lip with her teeth, tugging to the point of pain, but Ramona just moaned, kissed her back, her hands going to Dylan's tits.

"Yeah," Dylan said, and Ramona unhooked her bra, then dipped her head to get one of Dylan's breasts in her mouth. "Fuck." Dylan sucked in a breath, tilting her head back. Ramona's mouth was magic, tongue swirling and teeth grazing her skin, lips full and soft. Dylan needed them on her cunt as soon as possible.

"Baby," she said.

"Tell me," Ramona said. "Tell me what you want."

"You," Dylan said, her thoughts going fuzzy as Ramona's work on her tits continued. "Your mouth. Now."

"Thank god," Ramona said, lifting her lips to Dylan's. "Because I'm dying to taste you."

Dylan gasped a laugh, then watched as Ramona got off her, slipped her underwear down her legs. She was a goddess—silky skin, a perfect triangle between her thick thighs. Dylan wanted her mouth on Ramona's pussy too, but one thing at a time.

"Put your toy in," Dylan said.

Ramona licked her bottom lip, a shy smile on her lips. She picked up the toy from the bed.

"I bet you don't even need any lube," Dylan said. "So wet for me already."

"I am," Ramona said. "Soaked."

"Show me."

Ramona slid her fingers between her legs, dipped inside in a way that made Dylan groan. When she pulled her hand away, her fingers were glistening. She stepped closer to the bed and offered them up. Dylan sat up, grabbed her wrist, and took her fingers into her mouth.

"God," Dylan said, sucking and licking. "Tastes so good."

"I want to taste you," Ramona said, her voice a perfect whine. "Please."

"Get that toy in your cunt, then," Dylan said, releasing Ramona's now-clean fingers.

Ramona didn't smile shyly this time. She set one leg on the bed, then positioned the toy at her entrance. It slid in so easily, inch by inch, the butterfly base coming to rest against her pussy.

"God," Dylan said. "I could watch you do that all day."

Ramona laughed, but it was breathy, desperate. "Feels really good."

"Fuck yourself with it," Dylan said. "Just for a minute."

Ramona obeyed, holding on to the base and moving the toy in and out of her cunt. She moaned, grabbed Dylan's knee with her free hand, hips working into the toy.

"Jesus," Dylan said. "You're ridiculously sexy."

Ramona couldn't even respond, her chest flushed. Dylan wanted her to come, and soon.

Dylan scooted up a little so she was sitting up against the pillows. Then she spread her legs.

Ramona had stopped moving the toy inside her, her eyes fixed on Dylan's cunt.

"God," she said. "Perfect."

"Put that mouth to better work," Dylan said, her words terse but her tone soft.

"Yes, ma'am," Ramona said, and Dylan swore to god, she could come just from Ramona staring at her, fucking herself, and doing exactly what Dylan told her to. It was all the sexier because Dylan knew Ramona loved it too, loved giving up control. It was what they both needed right now, what they wanted, and Dylan had never felt so safe.

She wanted Ramona to feel the same.

"Give me a color," she said.

Ramona smiled. "Oh, very, very green."

Dylan grinned back. "Just checking."

"Though we do have to be quiet," Ramona said.

Dylan's eyes went wide. "Is your father here?"

"No, he's out with some friends, and Olive is spending the night at Marley's, but I'm not sure when my dad will be back. I'd rather he not walk into the house to the sound of his daughter screaming."

Dylan smirked. "Plan on screaming, huh?"

Ramona's eyes glittered. "With you? Yeah."

They watched each other for a second, Dylan's heart swelling in her chest. "Come here."

Ramona stepped closer, leaned down while Dylan arched up, lips meeting gently at first, then growing more wild, more fevered. Dylan loved this, loved how sex with Ramona could feel feral one second, then soft and romantic the next.

She'd never had that with anyone else.

The kiss went soft again, then wild, a cycle that made Dylan want to cry, and also fuck Ramona until she really did scream, all at the same time. It was dizzying and perfect and real.

She pressed her fingers to Ramona's toy, pushing it in a little farther, angling it so it hit Ramona's clit.

Ramona groaned into Dylan's mouth, and that was perfect and real too.

"Dylan," Ramona said, and Dylan knew what she needed. What she wanted.

"Go," Dylan said, then kissed her one more time, before pushing her hips away, then slapping her gently on the ass as Ramona turned.

Ramona laughed and went to the end of the bed, then crawled

onto the mattress slowly, her eyes fluttering closed as the toy moved within her. She settled between Dylan's legs, her eyes glazed as she got a closer look.

"Kiss me," Dylan said.

And Ramona did. A single kiss to the center of her cunt, and god, that first touch. Nothing like it. Dylan's back arched. Even with how soft the kiss was, it felt like a firework lighting up the sky. Ramona moaned and kissed again, harder, before she slid over to Dylan's thigh, dragging her tongue over her skin.

"Oh, so you're a tease," Dylan said.

"I think you like it," Ramona said.

"God, I do," Dylan said, sliding her hand through Ramona's hair. "You know just what I like."

Ramona hummed against her thigh, moving closer to the center again. But then she bypassed where Dylan really wanted her, teeth scraping across Dylan's other thigh. And god, as much as Dylan wanted Ramona to fuck her hard with her mouth, she liked this too, this slow build. She watched as Ramona's own hips worked over the toy.

"Is that thing charged?" Dylan asked.

Ramona lifted her mouth from where it was, right next to Dylan's lips. "Of course."

"Turn it on."

Ramona didn't hesitate, needy little thing, and slipped her hand between her legs. Dylan heard a faint buzzing sound, felt a soft vibration through the mattress.

"Fuck," Ramona said, resting her head against Dylan's thigh for a second. "Oh my god."

"That's right," Dylan said. "That's what you needed."

Ramona just nodded, biting at her bottom lip.

Dylan tightened her hands in Ramona's hair, directing Ramona's mouth toward her own cunt. Ramona went eagerly, mouth finally right where Dylan wanted it. Ramona moaned against her, and Dylan moaned right back as Ramona kissed and licked, tongue swirling up to her clit, then back down to her entrance.

"Jesus Christ," Dylan said, her hips bucking, fingers still curled in Ramona's hair. "God, baby, you're so good at that."

Ramona kept up her work, but soon her breathing grew erratic. Dylan watched her eyes flutter closed, mouth closed over Dylan's cunt.

"You going to come for me?" Dylan said.

Ramona hummed a yes, her tongue wild now, sliding into Dylan and back out.

"God," Dylan said. "You're perfect. My perfect little slut. Come for me. Come with your face in my cunt."

Ramona moaned even louder, her hips spread on the bed, undulating for more friction against her toy.

"That's a good girl," Dylan said, hand tightening in her hair. "Come while you tongue fuck me."

Ramona's sounds were at a fever pitch now. Dylan couldn't keep from making her own noises, the idea of Ramona coming like this bringing her so close herself. Ramona's tongue was so deep inside her. She slid it out, swirled it over Dylan's clit before diving back in again.

Ramona groaned, her body locking up as she came, but she didn't break contact with Dylan. She stayed buried in her pussy, Dylan's nails scraping through her hair.

"Fuck," Dylan said. "Yeah, right there, baby." She came suddenly, the feeling slamming into her and radiating down her legs and ass, all the way to her toes. She heard Ramona come a second time, her tongue dragging over Dylan's clit before sucking it into her mouth.

"Christ," Dylan said, tried not to yell, but it was hard. Ramona's touch was almost too much, she was too sensitive, but she couldn't stop either, never wanted to stop, and she came again, so hard her vision went dark, knees closing around Ramona's ears. She stayed like that for a second, breathing hard at the ceiling, completely boneless.

Ramona's toy still buzzed as she kissed Dylan softly now, but then she pressed her forehead to Dylan's lower belly, her breathing going ragged again.

"You come so easy for me," Dylan said, her fingers still tangled in Ramona's hair. "Do it again."

Ramona could only nod, her hands on Dylan's hips, mouth hovering above her mound.

"Come on, dirty girl," Dylan said. "One more for me."

"Fuck," Ramona said, hips working frantically now. "Dylan."

"That's right," Dylan said, her hands curling tighter into Ramona's hair.

Then she tugged.

Just a little, but Ramona moaned.

So she tugged harder . . . then harder still as Ramona writhed, fucking gorgeous, a goddamn goddess. When she broke, it was beautiful, her cries soft and muffled against Dylan's stomach, her body still pressed to Dylan's cunt.

"Fuck," Ramona said, then reached down to turn off the toy, laughing as she did so. Then she collapsed against Dylan's belly again.

"Yeah," Dylan said, resting her hand on Ramona's head.

They lay there like that for a few minutes before Ramona lifted her head, their eyes meeting and watching each other.

"Come up here," Dylan said.

Ramona got up, took out her toy, and set it at the end of the bed. Then she crawled onto the mattress, aligning herself with Dylan's body. Dylan pulled the covers over them, then wrapped her arms around Ramona's waist.

She needed her close.

She kissed Ramona's nose, tucked her head beneath her chin.

Her heart was still going a bit wild in her chest, but it felt larger than it did before, a river swollen with rain. This might be the safest she'd ever felt. The healthiest. This moment, this bed, in Ramona's bedroom. There were so many things pressing in on her—her parents, the movie, her career, Laurel and Rayna's constant plotting and rearranging of her image—but none of that mattered right now.

Nothing mattered but Ramona and Dylan.

Cherry and Lolli.

Dylan felt invincible with Ramona in her arms like this, and at the same time, soft. Like light and water and air.

"I don't want to be an idiot with you," she said, mouth pressed against Ramona's temple.

Ramona's arms tightened around her. "I don't want to be an idiot either."

"You could never," Dylan said.

Ramona lifted her eyes to Dylan's, her mouth dropping open to say something. Instead, she kissed Dylan, just once, then buried her face in Dylan's neck. Soon, her breathing became steady, but Dylan stayed awake, listening to Ramona sleep, fingers trailing through her hair.

Chapter Twenty-Nine

DYLAN WAS STILL fast asleep, arms splayed above her head like a little kid, when Ramona heard Olive come home.

It was morning, light streaming through the blinds, and Ramona had been awake for a good half hour, her brain too busy to sleep any more. As carefully as she could, she worked her way out of the covers, then scooted to the end of the bed so as not to wake Dylan. She grabbed her robe from the back of her door, tied the terry cloth sash around her waist, then sneaked down the hall to Olive's room.

She knocked.

Waited.

Knocked again.

"Fine," Olive said.

While not the warm greeting she was hoping for, Ramona took what she could get, cracking open the door to find her sister sitting on her bed, scrolling through her phone.

"Hi," Ramona said.

"Hi," Olive said, deadpan.

"Did you have fun?"

"Sure."

Ramona sighed, stepped farther in, and closed the door. "Ollie."

"Look, it's fine," Olive said. "I don't tell you everything either."

Ramona wasn't sure how to process that. She'd always assumed Olive did in fact tell her everything, because that's the way she and Olive had always been. They were Lorelai and Rory from *Gilmore Girls*, complicated parental issues and all, granted without the teen pregnancy and Lorelai's constant horrible decisions.

Ramona had spent the last twelve years trying to be the best big sister, best mother, and best friend Olive could possibly want, but she knew she'd failed. Because she couldn't be all of that to one person, all the time. Sometimes, she'd had to get angry with Olive. She'd had to back up their dad when he grounded her. She'd had to fuss at her about homework, pick up her gross softball socks from the living room floor, and she'd had to show Olive how to use a condom, just in case. But Ramona didn't know if Olive had ever actually used a condom. Olive had never told her either way, but that didn't mean no, because Ramona was the mom.

The mom *figure*, at least.

Something in her heart ached, a sort of mourning for the sisterhood they'd missed out on. The friendship. All the things that had to recede while Ramona tried to be everything to Olive.

Ramona walked over to the bed. "Can I sit?"

"I guess."

Olive was in jeans and a tee, her knees pulled tight to her chest. She clicked her phone dark and stuffed it under her butt.

Ramona settled next to Olive, her back against the headboard. "I didn't tell you about meeting Dylan when I was younger because . . ." She trailed off. Sighed. "Because it was mine."

Olive frowned at her. "What do you mean?"

Ramona rubbed her forehead. She wanted to be honest, but she didn't want to hurt Olive either.

"When Mom left," Ramona started, "my whole life changed."

Olive looked down. "I know."

"I know you know. But I never want you to feel the weight of that, Ollie. It wasn't your fault, it wasn't mine. It was *hers*. And I wouldn't give up our life together—mine and yours—for anything. Okay?"

Olive nodded, her lower lip trembling a little.

"But that night I met Dylan," Ramona went on, "Mom had just left. Dad was wrecked, you were a baby. And I couldn't fix any of it."

"You were just a kid."

"Who had to grow up really fast," Ramona said. "And that memory about Dylan was like this little pocket of time where I was just a girl."

"Standing in front of the daughter of really famous rock icons?"

Ramona laughed, slung her arm around Olive's shoulder. "Yes. Exactly. Though I didn't know it was her at the time."

"Really?"

Ramona shook her head. "I'm not sure I would've even recognized her name then, though I did know her dad's band. But we didn't share names."

Olive's eyes popped. "You didn't?"

"Nope. Fake names."

"Okay, I have to know this story now. Will you tell me? Please?"

Ramona smiled, leaned her head against her sister's, and told her the tale of two lonely girls on a moonlit beach in July.

"That's a pretty great story," Olive said when Ramona was done.

"I think it might be," Ramona said.

"And . . . she's in your room right now, right?"

Ramona stiffened, but then sighed. Not like she could deny it. "Maybe."

"Definitely."

Ramona laughed.

"Dad would be scandalized," Olive said. "Sex under his roof!"

"Who said anything about sex?"

"Please. I'm eighteen."

"No," Ramona said. "You're eight. You're eight and you want a She-Ra party for your next birthday."

"Hey, I might actually want a She-Ra party for my next birthday."

"Mermista," Ramona said, knowing she was Olive's favorite from the show.

Olive laughed. "God, she's so hot and mean."

Ramona laughed too, wondering not for the first time just how straight her sister was . . . or just how queer. But Olive would figure that out in her own time. She'd realize sooner or later that Marley was totally in love with her, if she didn't know already, and she'd have to decide for herself what to do about it.

She'd have to decide everything for herself come August.

"Hey, can I ask you a question?" Olive asked.

"Always."

Olive waited a few seconds before speaking again, fiddling with the end of Ramona's robe sash.

"Do you . . . ever . . ."

She trailed off, and Ramona felt herself tense, knowing exactly the direction this question was going before it went there, like a scent on the wind.

"Do you ever think about Mom?" Olive finally asked.

Ramona exhaled as quietly as she could.

"Of course I do," she said just as quietly. A whisper.

"And?" Olive asked, sitting up a little to look at her sister.

"And what?"

"And . . . don't you wonder? Where she is? How she's doing?"

Ramona sat up too, pulled her robe tight around her throat. "No."

"No?" Olive asked.

"No," Ramona said, her tone even firmer. "I wonder about her, sure, but not specifics. She doesn't deserve that, Olive. She hasn't earned it."

Olive flinched, her mouth opening, but closing again without a sound.

"It's normal to wonder," Ramona said, trying to soften her tone this time, but it was hard. Her mother brought up so many feelings, reactions, instincts. It was nearly impossible to control, this tightness in her chest, this anger and sadness and resentment and, somewhere under there, gratitude.

That she left.

Because if her mother hadn't wanted them, Ramona was glad she hadn't stuck around to remind them every single day. And at the same time, she felt hot with rage that her mother had left, that she hadn't considered anyone worth more than her own comfort, hadn't *tried* to make things better, gone to therapy, couples counseling, family therapy. Hell, anything.

Anything but leaving, thereby indelibly marking her daughters as unwanted.

Forgettable.

At the mention of Rebecca Riley, Ramona was always a riot of emotion, her pulse in her throat, her ears, her temples, tears right at the surface. But she had to hold it together. Had to be strong for her sister, who was eighteen and young and vulnerable.

"But it's useless to wonder too long," Ramona said. "Too hard."

"Why?" Olive asked. She'd taken her phone out from under her legs, flipped it around in her hand. "She's our mother."

"Who left."

"It doesn't change who she is."

"Yes, it does." Ramona's voice was loud. Louder than she meant it to be, but she needed to put this to rest.

An unbearable sadness fell over her. An emptiness.

"Yes, it does," she said again, quieter this time. "She left. She gave up. She gave *us* up. I'm here, Olive. I'm the one who . . ."

But she stopped herself, not sure how to even finish that sentence. She didn't want credit. She didn't want praise or acknowledgment. She didn't even want a fucking thank-you for all she'd given up.

She just wanted to protect Olive.

And she wanted to protect herself.

She felt on edge now, her chest tight, her throat aching. "I need to go check on Dylan."

Olive just nodded, her eyes glazed, focused on nothing in front of her.

Ramona stood up and kissed her sister's forehead, then left the room before she lost it completely. But when she got to her room and crawled back into bed next to a sleeping Dylan, who roused when Ramona burrowed under her arms, she pressed her face against Dylan's neck and let everything go.

Because she could here.

She was safe.

"Baby," Dylan said, her voice muzzy with sleep. But she didn't say anything else. Didn't ask what was wrong. Didn't pry. She just held Ramona and kissed the top of her head, whispering, "It'll be okay," as Ramona cried.

And goddammit, Ramona believed her.

Chapter Thirty

LATER THAT MORNING, Dylan headed back to her house to change and face the proverbial music. She walked, taking shortcuts through the woods she remembered from last week when she'd sprinted to Ramona's house after the first pictures of them appeared online.

She smiled as she passed by Nugget's yard, not even sparing him a glance as he barked once at her and then simply watched her go by.

Ramona.

Her smile broadened, making her cheeks ache. She didn't even feel panicked as she thought about all the texts and missed calls waiting for her when she got home. Both Laurel and Rayna were probably blowing up her phone, but it all slid off her back, at least for now. For this moment, walking through the sunshine on a June morning, the lake glittering in the distance, all she wanted to think about was Ramona.

Dylan couldn't put it into words, what she was feeling. This fluttery, nervous, happy feeling. Or rather, she *could*, but the word was ridiculous, way too fast, so she just let herself feel all the word-defying feelings as she walked.

When she got to her house, though, all those feelings popped like bubbles in flat champagne.

A car she didn't recognize sat in the driveway, Massachusetts plates. A rental, most likely, and from the bright red color and two-door convertible style, it had to be her parents'. Laurel used her firm's car service here, and no one else Dylan knew would drive such an ostentatious vehicle through small-town America.

She stopped at the bottom of the porch stairs, staring at the front door. She knew she had to go in, but she needed a plan first.

Ignorance.

Now that word wasn't ridiculous at all. It was perfect. She'd walk in, say a bright hello, gather her things and claim she had to get to the set, which was true. La-di-da. Nothing the matter here!

Except when she walked in, a fake smile already in place, the first thing she saw was her mother, perched primly on the edge of the couch, a glass of water in her hand.

She was just . . . sitting there.

No TV blaring, no music playing. No phone scrolling.

"Um, hi," Dylan said.

Carrie offered a small smile. "Dylan."

"Where's Dad?"

"He's at the house."

"You rented a *house* here?" Dylan asked. Now the panic was surging, rising and cresting. There was no way she could deal with her parents being in Clover Lake for longer than a few days, not while she filmed, not while she tried to build something with Ramona that was more than a publicity stunt.

"We did," Carrie said calmly. "Just for two weeks. Your dad wanted to get a sense of things for the soundtrack."

Dylan clenched her teeth. "Is Jocelyn coming to town for her original song?"

Carrie just looked at her coolly. "At some point, yes."

"What? Seriously?" Dylan rubbed her forehead. "Mom, I don't want her here, and it's not fair that you just swoop in and—"

"Dylan, stop," Carrie said.

Dylan did, more from Carrie's icy tone than the command itself. Her mother stood up, gold necklaces swaying on her pale chest. She wore a lacy maroon blouse and torn black jeans. Elegance and rock and roll, just like always. She walked up to Dylan, then put her hands on her daughter's shoulders.

"Sweetheart," she said softly.

Dylan looked down. She'd never known what to do when her parents showed her affection. On the one hand, she craved it like water. On the other, her skin felt too small for her body, and her jaw tightened without her consent.

"Look at me," Carrie said.

Dylan sighed, forced her eyes on her mother's matching set, icy green, nearly transparent.

"I know your dad and I messed up a lot when you were young," Carrie said.

Dylan frowned. Because they'd never had this conversation. Not once. Not when all their separate therapists recommended family therapy. Not when Carrie and Jack got out of rehab or remarried or divorced. Not when Aunt Hallie took Dylan away from them for a month in the summer when Dylan was thirteen.

Never.

"Mom," she said, unsure she wanted to have it now.

"Just let me say this," Carrie said, then took a deep breath. "Your dad and I messed up a lot. And I get that you're angry about that. You're hurt. And you should be. I'm sorry, Dylan, I can't express how sorry we are. If I could change it all for you, I would."

Dylan's throat went thick, aching as though a snake had curled around her windpipe.

"But at some point, baby . . ." Carrie trailed off, her lower lip bobbing. Her hands went to Dylan's face, cupping her cheeks like she was a little girl. "At some point, you're going to have to choose. You either forgive us, and you accept the life we're trying to build now. Together. With you. The efforts we're making, however imperfectly. The work we all need to put in to be a family. Or . . ." Her eyes filled with tears. "You don't. And we'll stop trying to make you."

She leaned forward and kissed Dylan on the forehead, whispered *I love you*.

And then she left.

Chapter Thirty-One

THE NEXT FEW weeks passed quickly. Dylan kept her head down, her mouth shut, and concentrated on filming and Ramona.

That was it.

After the initial fallout of her drunken sidewalk episode—photos on myriad online gossip sites, Gia and Rayna both going apoplectic when they first talked to her about it—Laurel and Rayna managed to spin the story in a romantic light.

A lovers' quarrel between Dylan and Ramona, the sites reported—a distraught, lovesick Dylan Monroe and a small-town girl rescuing her from her own demons.

Blah, blah, blah.

It was sweet, and the gossip sites ate it up, but it was hardly the truth. Not a single mention of Jack and Carrie other than them visiting their daughter on set in a show of *solidarity*, and Ramona seemed to trust Dylan when she told Ramona those sites weren't worth looking at in the first place. She was sure April did, probably Olive and Marley too, but after the night they'd shared in the Riley house, Ramona hadn't brought up anything the internet said about the two of them.

And Dylan certainly didn't want to discuss it, particularly how dating Ramona—the romance, their history together, even the side-walk rescue—had done nothing but help Dylan's image.

Just like Laurel and Rayna said it would.

But it didn't matter.

None of that mattered, because Dylan *liked* Ramona.

So damn much.

She liked holding her hand, she liked taking her out to dinner, she liked kissing her on the couch while they tried to watch a movie, and she liked taking her to bed when they both decided there were much more interesting things to do than watch a movie.

God, she really, really liked Ramona in her bed.

The sex was incredible, yes, but Ramona also just made Dylan feel so soft. She woke up every day and knew exactly how to be Eloise Tucker. She knew how to hold Blair's hand as Mallory, knew how to smile shyly, and she knew how to let her smile reach her eyes on Mallory and Eloise's first fake date. She knew how to be wary of Mallory's rich family, how to act jealous when Mallory fumbles around an old ex, how to drum up some real tears when Mallory pretty much tells Eloise she could do so much more with her life.

In short, she knew how to fucking *act*.

And Gia wasn't the only one who took notice.

"Can we talk through this scene?" Blair asked one morning, the day before the Fourth of July.

It was a big day on set as they prepared to film a hugely important scene, the one where Mallory and Eloise share their first real kiss. They were at the house the studio was using as Mallory's family's home—a gigantic and beautiful craftsman on the north end of the lake surrounded by the woods, greenery and summer flowers blooming all around the property, the blue water sparkling in the background. Inside it was expertly decorated, all spa blue and linen, white cabinets and gray quartz counters, the light gauzy and fresh and . . . well, *rich*. In reality, the house belonged to some finance bro named Jason Bonner who lived in New York City most of the year and barely frequented the house even in the summer months.

"Yeah, of course," Dylan said to Blair, making a note in her own script. They sat at the patio table on the back porch, already done with wardrobe and makeup, the lake glittering in front of them as the crew finished setting up the huge fundraiser taking place in the backyard in this scene. The immaculate lawn was filled with round tables covered in white and sage-green linens, a buffet table was overflowing with gorgeous food they wouldn't really get to eat, and a sign declaring the noble cause—a foundation that helped foster children who had aged out of the system—fluttered in the breeze between two oaks.

"I think I'm actually nervous about it," Blair said.

"Because of the author?" Dylan asked. They both looked out at the yard, where Iris Kelly, the author of the book the film was based on, was chatting with the actors who played Mallory's parents, her hands flying as she spoke. She had wild red hair and wore a long green skirt that hit midcalf, brown ankle boots laced up on her feet. Her partner—a stage actor in New York City, Stevie Scott—stood next to her and smiled. Iris was an executive producer for the film but didn't have much involvement other than consulting. Still, she'd created Eloise and Mallory, so Dylan was a little on edge about her performance.

"Maybe," Blair said. "I think it's mostly . . ." She trailed off, her pen tapping on her own script. "I don't know."

"That we have to *kiss*?" Dylan asked, drawing out the last word like a middle schooler.

"Oh, I can kiss," Blair said. "I think it's more that I have to pretend to like you." She laughed as she said it, her tone jovial.

Blair and Dylan had been getting along pretty decently since Blair had laid into her a few weeks ago. Maybe they'd just needed to clear the air, and Blair's points, Dylan had to admit, were all very valid. Dylan wouldn't say they were friends, but they were friendly. Cordial. Which was enough to get through a day of filming without Dylan feeling the need to pluck out her entire head of hair with a pair of tweezers.

"I think I'm having a hard time getting it," Blair said.

"Getting what?"

"Why Eloise is so into Mallory."

Dylan blinked, then frowned.

"I mean, Mallory's got money, right?" Blair went on. "She can do anything with her life, pretty much. Go anywhere. Give Eloise the world. So I get the material side to it. That's easy. But Eloise is sweet and gentle, and Mallory is haughty and high-maintenance and an emotional mess, and I just . . ." She sighed. "I don't know. Need to dig deeper."

She looked back down at her script, but Dylan just stared at her, her heart suddenly thick and loud under her ribs.

"What do you think?" Blair asked. She was dressed in an immaculate suit—fuchsia, with a white lace blouse and bright orange heels Dylan was pretty sure cost about the same as this lake house. On the other hand, Dylan—Eloise—was in a cheap cotton sundress, sky blue, and ballet flats that pinched her toes.

"They're too small," she'd told Noelle when she'd been in wardrobe this morning.

"They're supposed to be," Noelle said curtly. "There's the whole scene where Eloise's feet are killing her and Mallory throws her shoes into the lake."

Dylan frowned. "Can't we just *act* like they're killing me?"

Noelle just smiled without her teeth. Dylan knew the designer was known for authenticity on set, but Jesus.

"These really hurt, Noelle," Dylan said, rubbing her toes.

"Look," Noelle said, sighing and pressing her fingers into her eyes. "My assistant went waterskiing over the weekend and now has a fractured fibula, whatever bone that is. All I know is that Vee can't walk, so they can't work, and I'm a little pressed. So, please, Dylan, just put on the shoes."

Dylan had kept her mouth shut after that.

Now, as Dylan sat in her too-tight flats and ruminated on the vast chasm between Eloise and Mallory—a chasm that was contrived and scripted and one hundred percent supposed to exist—her breath felt suddenly short and uneven.

"You okay?" Blair asked. "You just went white as a . . . well, a white person, but you're even whiter now."

Dylan forced a laugh. "I'm good."

"So what do you think?"

Dylan swallowed. "About?"

Blair sighed. "Never mind."

"I'm just not sure what you mean," Dylan said. "Eloise loves Mallory because . . . because she's . . ."

But she had nothing.

Her mind went blank, heart thrumming in her temples, taking up all the space. This was ridiculous—Mallory and Eloise were fictional. Made-up. Their creator was walking by the lake right this very second. There was absolutely no reason for this sudden panic building in Dylan's chest like a violent storm.

"Because she's . . ." Blair said, rolling her hand for Dylan to go on.

Dylan opened her mouth, determined to say something, anything, but then Ramona appeared at the back door, a set pass around her neck.

"Hey," she said. "There you are."

Dylan cleared her throat. "H-hey."

"Oh, good, Ramona," Blair said, sitting back in her iron chair and crossing her long legs. "Help me out here. You've read the book, right? Why does Eloise like Mallory so much?"

Ramona, who'd been visiting the set a few times a week when her schedule at Clover Moon allowed for it, just laughed. "What?"

"I need some insight," Blair said.

Ramona flicked her eyes to Dylan, a small crease in her brow. Dylan's panic surged, and she shot up from her chair. "Do you want to meet Iris Kelly?"

Ramona's eyes widened. "For real?"

"Yeah, she's here," Dylan said, slipping her hand into Ramona's and squeezing. She looked out at the yard and spotted Iris's red hair ambling toward the house. "She's heading this way."

"Oh my god," Ramona said. "She's gorgeous."

Dylan laughed. "She is. Bohemian vibe."

"Yeah," Ramona said, her voice breathy. Dylan just watched her watch Iris approach, those long lashes, her pink mouth open a little, thinking about how Iris wasn't the only gorgeous one.

Which sounded cheesy and silly but perfect in her head. She started to say it out loud, but then Iris froze at the bottom of the porch steps.

"Dylan Monroe, oh my god," Iris said, climbing the steps.

"Hi," Dylan said, waving.

"You're even more beautiful in person," Iris said, smiling with her hands on her hips. "I'm a huge fan."

Dylan frowned. "Are you?"

Iris just laughed, then glanced at Ramona. "Hey, I'm Iris."

"Oh, sorry," Dylan said. "This is Ramona Riley. My—" But she cut herself off. *Girlfriend* was on the tip of her tongue. It was right there, but she and Ramona hadn't had that conversation.

Hadn't used that word.

And this was just supposed to be a summer thing.

Wasn't it?

"Hey, *I'm* a huge fan," Ramona said. "I've read all your books. They're amazing. So funny and tender and sexy and smart. Sorry, I'll shut up now."

"Please do, authors hate hearing how wonderful we are," Iris said, then winked. "I'm so excited to be here on set. Everything looks gorgeous. My partner, Stevie, is wandering around here somewhere." She waved a hand at the yard. "She's fascinated with film."

"I saw her in last year's Shakespeare in the Park," Dylan said. "She was an incredible Katherina."

"She'll be so happy to hear that," Iris said, beaming.

"Iris, hi," Blair said, appearing next to Dylan and sticking out her hand.

"Hi, Blair Emmanuel, good god, you're lovely," Iris said, shaking her hand.

Blair just laughed. "I've got some questions for you about Mallory and Eloise. Do you mind?"

"Not at all," Iris said. "That's what I'm here for."

"Oh, god, sorry, Blair," Ramona said, resting her hand on Blair's shoulder. "I got so distracted."

"No worries. Totally understandable." Then to Iris, Blair motioned toward the patio table. "Shall we?"

Dylan watched Iris and Blair settle at the table, her chest still a little too tight for comfort.

"Should we sit too?" Ramona said. "I'd love to hear what Iris has to say about—"

"Dylan," Noelle said, appearing from the house's back door. She was frowning, a tape measure curled around her neck like a scarf, iPad tucked under one arm. She walked up to them and started fiddling with the hem of Dylan's dress. "I think we need a wardrobe change."

"What?" Dylan asked. "Why?"

Noelle didn't answer right away, just mumbled to herself as she circled Dylan, her brows pressed together.

"Yep," she said. "I need something . . . more."

"More what?" Dylan asked. "Please don't put me in a child's shoe."

Noelle didn't respond, just narrowed her eyes at Dylan's very simple dress. "Damn Vee and their fibula. Could really use their opinion on this."

"Opinion on what?" Dylan asked, smoothing her hand down the garment. "It's a good dress."

"But not good enough, maybe," Noelle said.

"Isn't Eloise, like, not into fancy clothes?" Dylan asked.

"Yeah, but she's at this fancy event and she's nervous, so she'd probably tried a little harder than normal."

This was from Ramona, who said it fast, then pressed her hands to her reddening cheeks.

"God, I'm sorry," she said. "None of my business."

"No, but you're right," Noelle said. "That's what I was thinking too. It's not . . . desperate enough." Noelle tapped her chin with her iPad's stylus. "Maybe something in stripes. What do you think?"

It seemed to take Ramona a second to realize Noelle's question was directed at her. Dylan had to nudge her shoulder.

"Oh, me?" Ramona asked.

"You," Noelle said, not even looking at her. She was still glaring at the blue cotton.

"Um, well."

Dylan watched as Ramona closed her eyes and took a deep breath.

"I think you're right," she finally said. "It needs more."

Noelle nodded, then snapped her stylus into the holder on the top of her iPad. "Come with me, both of you."

"Both . . . both of us?" Ramona asked.

Noelle just waved them on as she headed toward the door. "I need to change Dylan, and I need someone else's input other than my own exhausted brain."

And with that, she vanished into the house.

"Better follow her," Dylan said, taking Ramona's hand and starting toward the door. "Trust me, what Noelle wants, Noelle gets."

Ramona's eyes glittered as they followed Noelle into the airy house and toward the main bedroom, which was doubling as wardrobe and makeup.

"Is this really happening?" Ramona asked when they stepped inside the room.

"Is what happening?" Dylan asked.

"I mean . . ." Ramona shook her head. "Noelle Yang. Talking to me. Asking my opinion."

"You're a fan of Noelle's?"

Ramona's starstruck expression faded. She frowned, opened her mouth, but nothing came out. "I—"

"Okay, here's what we've got," Noelle said, motioning toward a metal rack of dresses. "What do you think? Muslin? Stripes?"

Ramona snapped her mouth shut, then squeezed Dylan's hand once before she released it, and walked over to Noelle. Soon the two of them were talking fabrics, cut, hem length, Dylan all but forgotten. Dylan watched Ramona, fascinated, pride swelling in her chest.

Pride, and something else she couldn't quite put her finger on.

Don't be so naive, Dylan.

That's what Jocelyn had said to Dylan at Jocelyn's birthday party. The party Dylan had planned and paid for. The party where they broke up because Jocelyn chose that moment to announce her record deal with Evenflow Records, Jack Monroe to produce. A deal Dylan had never known about before that moment. A deal she didn't even know her girlfriend had wanted.

Everyone wants something. Everyone has an angle.

Dylan shook her head, swallowed down her doubts, and watched her girlfr—

Watched Ramona pick out her dress.

Chapter Thirty-Two

"THE BLUE-AND-WHITE-STRIPED DRESS," Ramona said.

"Why?" Noelle asked.

Ramona took a breath. She stood in the center of the room, afternoon light streaming through the windows, making the white linens on the giant bed glow. The walls were gray, the furniture midcentury modern, a boring room, to be quite honest, but the *clothes*.

There were clothes everywhere. Metal racks on wheels filled the room, packed with garments of every color, every fabric, every price point. Some of the pieces—for Mallory's character and her family, Ramona was sure—cost more money than Ramona made in six months. Louis Vuitton, Versace, Dior, Chanel—the legends in fashion, all right there, inches from Ramona's fingertips. She didn't dare touch any of it, though she was dying to know what thousand-dollar silk felt like.

Still, even the caliber of the clothes couldn't distract her from the fact that she was standing with Noelle Yang in a wardrobe room.

Standing and *talking*.

Standing and giving her *opinion*.

Standing and being *asked* for her opinion.

"I think it looks more polished," Ramona said, taking the cotton dress off the hanger and holding it up. It was sleeveless, but modest, with a scoop neck that would show off Dylan's collarbones, and an A-line skirt that should hit right above her knees. Wide navy and white stripes gave it a summery, nautical feel. Perfect for a yacht-loving crew like the folks who would be at this fundraiser.

"We know at this point that Eloise is insecure about Mallory's wealth and status," Ramona said. "With an event this big, she'd probably try to find something that gave the illusion of money. Something simple, but a little more sophisticated than a sundress."

Noelle nodded, took the dress from Ramona, and held it up in the natural light. "Yes, I think you're right."

Ramona had to press her lips together to keep from squealing— Noelle Yang just said she was right.

"Dylan, let's get changed," Noelle said, waving her toward the en suite bathroom. "And we'll need different shoes."

"Thank god," Dylan said, already pulling a strap of her dress off her shoulder.

"Could you find some flats in navy?" Noelle asked, looking at Ramona over her glasses. "Or should we do a heel?"

"A heel, definitely," Ramona said.

Noelle nodded. "In the closet. Size seven."

"I'm an eight," Dylan said.

"Size seven," Noelle said again, not even looking at Dylan.

"You're going to kill me. Tight flats are one thing, but too-small heels?" Dylan asked, hands on her hips.

"Fine," Noelle said. "Seven and a half."

Dylan threw up her hands, then took the dress from Noelle and disappeared into the bathroom. Noelle smiled and winked at Ramona, then started riffling through the racks again.

Ramona laughed as she stepped into the massive closet for the shoes. She felt like she was in a dream, her chest full of bubbles as though she'd sipped on some funky drink made by Willy Wonka.

But as her eyes locked on a pair of pumps with a low kitten heel, the perfect shade of navy, seven and a half like Noelle wanted, she knew it was real. The faux leather under her fingers was cool, cracked, and perfect.

"How about these?" she asked, stepping out of the closet and holding them up for Noelle to see.

"Excellent," Noelle said.

Ramona walked over to her, held out the shoes. But Noelle didn't take them.

Not at first.

Instead, she tilted her head, eyes narrowing on Ramona's face. "What was your name again?"

Ramona's heart plummeted to her feet. She had to force her voice to stay steady as she said her name. "We met at Clover Moon a few weeks ago," she added.

Noelle pursed her mouth. "Ramona, right. Dylan's girlfriend."

"Oh," Ramona said, her face warming. "Well. I don't know. We just . . ."

"And you went to RISD."

Ramona's eyes widened. "Yes, I did. Though I didn't graduate."

"Your medium?"

"Apparel design," Ramona said.

One corner of Noelle's mouth turned up. "I thought so."

Ramona smiled, and then the bathroom door opened, Dylan stepping out looking perfect in the striped dress.

"What do we think?" Dylan said, smoothing her hands down the skirt.

"We think your girlfriend is a little genius," Noelle said.

Dylan's eyes popped, flew to Ramona, who could only stare back.

"She's not . . ." Dylan said. "Well, she is a genius, but we're—"

"Yes, yes, you can have your little DTR talk later," Noelle said, walking over to Dylan and tugging on the dress here and there. "What I need right now is an assistant."

Silence.

Dylan stood stock-still as Noelle plucked at her, and Ramona wasn't sure what to say. Still, Ramona's heart was full-on galloping in her chest, which was understandable considering how much the word *girlfriend* was flying around. She and Dylan hadn't used the word, and they had always said from the start that this was just summer fun.

And it *was*.

But if it was so much fun, Ramona didn't think the word *girlfriend* should feel so terrifying.

And so . . . right.

Autumn was nearing—Olive would be leaving soon, the movie wrapping—and Ramona didn't want to look too closely at any of it.

Couldn't.

"So?" Noelle said, eyes flicking to Ramona. "What do you say?"

Ramona blinked. "Say?"

"I need an assistant for the rest of filming," Noelle said, pulling out a needle and thread from the apron around her waist. "You're smart. Your instincts are good. The studio was going to send someone over from LA, but I'd prefer to have a say. Pay is shit and the hours are long, but you can't beat the experience."

Ramona felt all the color drain from her face. She felt dizzy. Had to grab on to the corner of the armchair by the window so she didn't fall over. She glanced at Dylan, who was simply watching her with an expression Ramona couldn't quite parse—half-curious, half . . . wary? No. Just surprised.

Because that's all Ramona could think of right now—shock. Awe. Wonder. Pure impossibility.

"I'm sorry?" she said.

Noelle smiled. "You heard me." She slid the needle through

something at the back of Dylan's dress. "But if you've got a job that keeps you from committing, or—"

"Yes," Ramona said.

Loudly.

Nearly yelled it.

Noelle barely blinked. "Perfect. We'll go over the details later, but for now, go tell Gia we need five minutes. She won't stop texting me, and I'm about to throw my phone into the lake."

Ramona hesitated, but only for a second. She knew this was a moment, a test of sorts—could the new assistant, a small-town girl, talk to the scary director? Noelle could easily text Gia back, surely, but she probably wanted to know she could count on Ramona to do her dirty work and the shit tasks, because that's what an assistant did.

That's what Noelle had done, working her way up and through Hollywood.

"Right," Ramona said, squaring her shoulders and heading for the door. She wanted to look at Dylan again. Wanted to send her a *holy shit* nonverbal, but she was still processing the entire last half hour and wasn't sure what Dylan was thinking.

She wasn't sure what *she* was thinking either, how'd she explain her emphatic *yes* to Noelle's offer. They hadn't really talked about RISD since that night they went bowling, and it felt as though so much had happened between them since then.

Still, *yes* was the only answer Ramona could give to Noelle. She knew it. Dylan probably knew it too. Even April knew it, the news reaching her by some sort of astrological magic or best friend osmosis.

Ramona floated through the house and outside, spotting Gia gesticulating wildly at a crew member. She paused on the top porch step. One deep breath, and then she went and did her job as Noelle fucking Yang's assistant.

"OKAY, OKAY, TELL me again."

Ramona was sitting at April's kitchen table with Olive and Leigh later that night, reliving the details of the day over and over. April, in particular, couldn't stop freaking out about this development.

Ramona laughed, took another bite of one of the vegan bao buns Leigh had made them all for dinner—who knew pulled jackfruit could be so delicious—and shook her head. "I've already told you a million times," she said, licking the garlicky sauce off her finger.

"I know, I know," April said, wiggling in her seat. "I just can't get over it." She put on an affected air, pursing her mouth and lifting her pinkie finger and then speaking, inexplicably, with a British accent. "'So? What do you say?' I mean, it's classic!"

"Noelle did not stick out her pinkie finger like a douche, for the record," Ramona said. "Nor is she from the UK."

"In my mind, she's the fucking queen," April said.

"The queen's dead," Leigh deadpanned.

"What did Dylan say about it?" Olive asked. "Was she excited?"

Ramona opened her mouth, then snapped it shut. The truth was, she hadn't spoken to Dylan since everything happened in the wardrobe room. She'd told Gia that Noelle needed five minutes, to which Gia said, *Who the hell are you*, to which Ramona managed to splutter out the words *assistant* and *Noelle* and *new*, not necessarily in a logical order, but the sentiment was conveyed nonetheless.

The rest of the afternoon was a blur of running around the set, fixing loose buttons, and driving to and from Concord not once, but twice to procure a scarf Noelle needed and then a pair of socks for Mallory's dad.

Socks that would barely be seen on-screen.

When she wasn't driving or answering Noelle's calls while in the car, she was following Noelle around set like a shadow, then double-checking all the costumes for the next day's shoot, which was a boat scene on the water. By the time seven o'clock rolled around, they were still filming, but Noelle told her to go home.

"That's enough insanity for your first day," Noelle had said, and honestly, Ramona had to agree. Her feet were killing her—she definitely had not worn the right shoes to be running around on grass—she hadn't taken a single sip of water or eaten a thing in five hours, and she was late for dinner at April's.

Not that April didn't understand.

In fact, April would've probably sent her back to set, if Noelle would take her, anything to make sure Ramona had a shot at LA.

A shot. At LA.

The words sounded foreign in Ramona's thoughts, much less the concept itself. She couldn't quite picture it—couldn't see herself anywhere but Clover Lake, if she was being honest—but she wanted it nonetheless.

That life.

The kind she lived today, wild and stressed and hungry, helping create a story. It was hard, but god, it was so *good*.

Exciting.

And she had no idea if Dylan felt the same.

"I haven't really had a chance to talk to her about it," Ramona said. "Busy day and all." She checked the time on her phone—nearly nine o'clock, and no text from Dylan. Before everything with Noelle, they'd planned to come to April's for dinner together, but Ramona knew filming was unpredictable.

April lifted a pierced brow. "Ramona."

"April."

April sat forward, clasped her hands around her beer glass. "Does she still not *know*?"

"Know what?" Leigh asked.

"That Ramona here is a costume design hopeful," April said.

"Of course she knows," Olive said. "How could she not? She's your girlfriend."

Ramona sat back, huffed a breath. "That's the third time I've heard that word today, yet Dylan and I have never used it."

"But she is, right?" Olive said.

"Summer fling?" Leigh asked.

Ramona sighed. "I don't know *what* Dylan and I are exactly, and now, with this assistantship, I just . . ." She took a sip of beer. "It feels complicated."

"What's complicated?" April said. "You like her, she likes you, and you want to work in costume design."

"Which I very pointedly hid from her when we first met," Ramona said, "because I'm an idiot and had no idea I'd be making out with her a few weeks later—"

"More than making out," April said, waggling her eyebrows like a cartoon character.

"And now, if I tell her the truth," Ramona barreled on, "it just looks like I was hiding it."

"You *were* hiding it," Leigh said. "Pointedly."

"Yes, thank you," Ramona said.

Leigh lifted their glass in salute.

Ramona rubbed her temples. "I need to tell her, but she's sensitive about this."

"About what?" Olive asked.

Ramona let her hands flop to the table. "About people she dates using her for her fame and connections."

God, it sounded so horrible when she said it out loud. She'd told herself a million times over the last few weeks—and at least a thousand since this afternoon—that she wasn't doing that. Yes, hanging out with Dylan might have started like that, a way to possibly meet

Noelle, but then Dylan asked her out and they kissed and slept to-gether and went on dates and Ramona had barely thought about costume design in the last few weeks.

Barely.

"You mean like Jocelyn Gareth?" Olive asked.

Ramona frowned, Dylan's most recent ex's name settling heavy in her stomach. "What about Jocelyn?"

Olive rolled her eyes. "You need to read PopSugar more often."

"I'd say less is best," Leigh said.

"Jocelyn got a recording deal with Evenflow Records," Olive said. "Jack Monroe's label? And she did it all behind Dylan's back. I mean, allegedly. But that's what the whole rooftop party and heli-copter mess was about. At least, that's what social media says."

Ramona just blinked, glanced at April. "Did you know about that?"

April shook her head. "No. I mean, I knew about the helicopter—everyone knows about that—but I never heard about the record deal thing."

Ramona felt sick. A few weeks ago, on that walk through the woods, Dylan had talked about people using her—even lovers and friends—but she hadn't mentioned any specifics. Ramona had no clue it was Jocelyn. And she had no idea it had anything to do with Dylan's father.

Suddenly, Dylan's reaction to her parents showing up a couple of weeks ago made a lot more sense.

"Oh my god," Ramona said, her throat going thick.

"Hey, that's not what you're doing," Olive said, reaching out and squeezing Ramona's arm.

"Isn't it?" Ramona asked quietly. "I mean, I wouldn't have this job with Noelle without Dylan. That's what it comes down to. Dylan, who I'm sleeping with. Dylan, who thinks I simply studied apparel design at RISD for a year and then came home to take care of my family."

Everyone was silent. They knew she was right. They knew this looked as bad as it did in her head, even worse actually, because now everyone agreed with her.

"Apparel design isn't all that different from costume design," Olive said quietly, and god, Ramona loved her for it.

She dropped her head into her hands.

"Okay, okay, don't panic," April said, then got out her phone. "Let's see what Madame Andromeda has to say."

Everyone at the table groaned.

"Oh, please, you know you all read her when you're freaking out about something," April said, scrolling.

"We really don't," Leigh said.

"All right," April said, ignoring them. "Libra this week . . ."

She trailed off as she read, forehead wrinkled in concentration before her brows shot suddenly into her hair. Then she put the phone face down on the table.

"You know what, Madame Andromeda is a hack," she said. "Who wants dessert?"

"Absolutely not," Ramona said. "What did Andromeda say?"

"She said you're the most beautiful girl on the planet," April said.

"Right," Ramona said. "Don't make me break out Llama Face."

"Shit, I forgot about Llama Face," Leigh said, leaning forward on their elbows. "Let's see it."

"Not until April reads me my horoscope," Ramona said, folding her arms. "And there are seven words I never thought I'd say."

"She said you're doomed."

All three of them looked at Olive, who had declared this lovely fortune. She held her phone in her hand, eyes on the screen.

"Doomed?" Ramona asked.

"Basically," Olive said.

"Just read it," April said, sitting back in defeat.

"*As a Libra, you crave balance and fairness,*" Olive read, "*but this week, as Saturn moves into emotional Pisces, you find yourself ruled by the heart. This is a welcome respite from your usual logical methods, but be careful. The heart is wild, and left untamed, it can place you in situations where you find yourself risking heartbreak. You'll have to decide whether or not it's worth it.*"

They were all quiet for a second, Andromeda's words echoing through the room.

"Well, shit," Leigh said, standing up. "This definitely calls for some black bean chocolate mousse." They went to the fridge and pulled out a tray of tiny glass jars, each one full of silky-looking chocolate and topped with blueberries and shaved almonds.

Ramona just stared as Leigh placed a pot in front of her.

Heartbreak.

You have to decide . . .

"Hey, everyone," Dylan said, coming in the side door. She still had a full face of makeup, but she was dressed in jeans and a plain gray T-shirt instead of the fateful striped dress. "Sorry I'm late. Gia was on a tear tonight."

"Hey," Ramona said, standing up and pulling Dylan into her arms.

She held on a little longer than was necessary. When she pulled back, Dylan met her eyes, her brows lowered a little. She tucked Ramona's hair behind her ear.

"Congrats on the job," she said softly. "Didn't get a chance to tell you earlier."

Ramona forced a smile, searching Dylan's eyes for . . . she wasn't even sure. Anything.

"Thank you," Ramona said when all she found was Dylan's calm expression, no smile, but no angst.

Which really wasn't like Dylan at all.

Dylan looked at her for a second, brushed her thumb over her cheek before she sat in the chair next to Ramona's. Leigh handed her a plate full of bao buns and Dylan dug in, marveling at how much jackfruit could taste like pork, just like they all had earlier. She was beautiful. She smiled. She ate. She complimented the food. She asked Olive about college preparations and April about recent tattoos she'd done and Leigh about why the hell anyone would ever want to put black beans in chocolate, and then they all talked about how they hated the Fourth of July and its illusory celebration of American independence, which led to laments about the next election's possibilities.

It was a perfect night, really. There was humor and food and shared camaraderie over genuine fears, laughter and stories and strong coffee.

But the entire time, Dylan never really looked at Ramona again. She didn't ask her anything, didn't say anything else about Noelle, and neither did the rest of their party.

Unease slithered through Ramona, slow and steady, like an oncoming sickness.

She reached out and took Dylan's hand while they all drank coffee, and Dylan let her. Their fingers tangled together, a perfect fit, but Dylan still wouldn't look at her, and Ramona had never craved a pair of eyes on her own so much in her life. She felt feral with want, and as she sat there, other wants bubbled to the surface, wants she'd been avoiding, been brushing off.

Dylan with her friends like this, with her sister. Dylan with *her*. Ramona wanted all of that. She wanted more than the summer, and she wanted more than just a fling. She wanted, and she wanted, and she wanted.

And she wanted to tell Dylan the truth. And she would. She *would*. She just had to figure out the right time.

~

DYLAN WAS QUIET on the way back to her house.

She and Ramona walked, holding hands through the twinkle-lit downtown, red, white, and blue decorations already hanging in the square for the Fourth celebrations tomorrow. The entire way, Ramona didn't break the silence, her mind too busy trying to figure out how to broach the subject of Noelle and RISD and all the things Ramona wanted.

The shape of her dreams.

A shape that had morphed in the recent weeks to include Dylan Monroe.

She still hadn't figured it out when they walked into Dylan's house, the glow from the stove the only light.

Dylan dropped her bag, then went straight to the refrigerator and poured a glass of water. She drank the whole thing down in five gulps.

Ramona stood by the couch, watching her. Thinking.

Dylan, when we first started hanging out, I had hoped you could introduce me to—

God, no.

Dylan, I've pretty much worshipped Noelle Yang since her first film—

Jesus Christ, the idea here was to *not* sound like an opportunistic asshole.

Because that's not what Ramona was at all.

Was she?

She shook her head. Took a breath.

Dylan, I want to be a costume designer. I always have.

There. Simple. To the point. Left Noelle out of it altogether, which seemed best. Maybe Dylan would simply say, *Great, babe, anything I can do to support you.*

Ramona swallowed about a billion times. Clasped her hands in front of her. Then behind her. Then folded her arms, but no, that looked confrontational, so she let them dangle by her sides like deadweight.

Dylan . . .

Her brain told her to say it.

Dylan . . .

Her tongue wouldn't cooperate though. She swallowed some more. Linked her hands in front of her again.

Meanwhile, the real flesh-and-blood Dylan stood watching her, that cool expression she'd worn all evening on her face.

"Come here," she said.

Ramona hesitated, but only for a second. She'd give Dylan the moon right now if she could. She walked over, stood in front of Dylan by the center island.

Dylan set her empty glass on the counter, her eyes never leaving Ramona. She watched her for so long, head tilted, eyes soft and hooded, Ramona started to squirm.

She started to sweat and breathe heavily.

She started to think maybe Dylan already knew, or at least knew that Ramona had used her.

But that wasn't true.

Ramona . . . fuck.

Ramona *loved* Dylan.

That was the truth of it.

But she couldn't just say that. Not right now, not with so many other things she needed to say first, but she couldn't say those things either. She didn't want to say anything right now. She just wanted to *do*. To act, to show Dylan that she was hers.

Ramona was *hers*.

She stepped closer, set her hands on Dylan's waist, and pulled her against her body.

Dylan let her, eyes still watching her.

Then Ramona kissed her cheek. First one, then the other, going slow. Giving Dylan plenty of time to stop. She kissed her nose then. She moved to her eyebrows, listening to Dylan's breathing stutter and start. Ramona worked her way around Dylan's lovely face, trailing to her neck, below her ears, her throat.

Ramona let her hands roam too, up Dylan's rib cage and around to her spine, then down over her ass and around her hips again. She wanted to touch every inch of her skin, every nerve ending, every goose bump her fingertips pulled to the surface. She kissed Dylan's neck, reveling in the soft moan Dylan released. Ramona's fingers stopped on the button of Dylan's jeans, pausing before she kissed Dylan's mouth.

"Give me a color," Ramona said softly.

Dylan paused, eyes fluttering closed, then said, "Yellow."

Ramona knew that meant *caution*, to go slow, so that's what she did. She cupped Dylan's face in her hands, then kissed her mouth. Soft. Closed. Gentle and barely there, letting Dylan take the lead.

Ramona loved their sex life. She'd experienced things with Dylan she hadn't with anyone else, things she never even thought she'd be into. But she was. She loved getting tied up and being called names and having to beg Dylan—*Ms. Monroe*—over and over to make her come. It was wild and exciting and *safe*, and Ramona loved every moment.

And she loved this too.

This slow dance, emotional and quiet and close.

"Dylan," Ramona whispered against her.

Dylan's breath hitched, her mouth opening to Ramona's, letting her in. Their tongues met, both women moaning at the contact, and Dylan finally grasped Ramona around the waist, pulling her closer and closer. The kiss grew deeper and more desperate, teeth and gasps and hands in each other's hair. In this moment, Ramona didn't think she'd ever wanted anything like she wanted Dylan right now—naked, sprawled underneath her, her mouth pressed between Dylan's legs.

"Baby," Ramona said, fingers skimming Dylan's waistband. "Give me a color."

"Green," Dylan said, her mouth right under Ramona's ear. "So green. Dark, bright, fluorescent, whatever."

Ramona laughed. "Thank god."

Then she pulled Dylan over to the plank-style, driftwood kitchen table. Ramona didn't want a bed right now, didn't want the couch. She wanted Dylan right there on this table, wanted Dylan to see that Ramona wanted her there, wanted her anywhere, any way, anytime.

Ramona didn't waste time getting Dylan's clothes off. She lifted off her T-shirt, unhooked her bra, and had her jeans off her legs in under ten seconds.

"Efficient," Dylan said.

Ramona just laughed, then pushed Dylan to the edge of the table, her ass, still in her purple underwear, hitting the wood.

"Bossy tonight," Dylan said.

"I just know what I want," Ramona said, looking her in the eyes. Dylan canted her head. "Do you?"

"I do," Ramona said firmly.

They both watched each other for a second.

"And what's that?" Dylan asked. Her voice was soft, even small.

"You," Ramona said. No hesitation. No coy smile. She knew. "I want you, Dylan Page Monroe."

Dylan didn't respond right away. Not with her mouth, at least. But her hands worked, unbuttoning Ramona's lipstick-print blouse, sliding her bra straps down her arms before unhooking the clasps.

Then she plucked at both of Ramona's nipples before she moved on to her jeans. Ramona gasped, body arching toward Dylan for more. But Dylan simply unzipped her jeans, shucked them down her legs, and then did the same with her underwear.

Soon Ramona was naked, and Dylan trailed her eyes up and down her body, devouring her. Ramona felt herself get even wetter just from that look, those icy eyes somehow smoky.

Finally, when she'd had her fill, Dylan pushed the chairs out of the way and slid herself onto the table, leaned back on her elbows.

Then she spread her legs, a slow, exquisite reveal.

"You got me," Dylan said.

Ramona didn't wait any longer. She pressed her thighs between Dylan's legs, hands on Dylan's hips to pull her even closer, kissing her hard, then soft, then hard again. She wanted everything—the wild rollick and the slow dance, feral and gentle all at once, a kaleidoscope of everything she felt.

Ramona cupped Dylan's breasts, pulling at her nipples as they kissed, Dylan's moans making her crazy. Making them both crazy.

"Please," Dylan said against her mouth, and Ramona loved that too. The begging. Usually she was the one to beg, but these turned tables were exciting. "Ramona, please."

"Please what?" Ramona asked, happy to stay here, kissing Dylan's perfect mouth, sliding down to get her mouth on her tits.

"You know what."

"I want you to say it," Ramona said, taking Dylan's nipple between her teeth.

Dylan slid her hand into Ramona's hair, right at the back of her head, then pulled her head up to look her in the eyes. The tug stung in the best way, Ramona's mouth open as she looked up at the most beautiful woman in the world.

"Put your mouth on my cunt," Dylan said.

"Ask nicely," Ramona said. She didn't want to give up quite yet, the power she so often begged to relinquish to Dylan. But tonight, she wanted it. Not to exert over Dylan, but to share.

To share everything.

Dylan leaned forward, bringing her mouth right against Ramona's. "Please, Ms. Riley, put your mouth on my cunt."

Ramona smiled, then licked into Dylan's mouth. Once . . . twice, before she pulled away so she could push Dylan onto her back. Then she just looked.

Because this.

This was how Ramona had wanted her—spread out, vulnerable, laid bare. Just like Ramona had felt all night.

How she always felt around Dylan, if she was being honest.

"God," Ramona said, sliding her hands down Dylan's thighs. "You're gorgeous."

Dylan's only response was to arch her back, those tits bouncing with the movement, nipples peaked and hips bucking at the air for friction. Ramona didn't want to make her wait any longer. *She* didn't want to wait any longer. She pressed her face between Dylan's legs and inhaled, her nose right against that wet spot at the center of her underwear.

Dylan gasped.

And Ramona licked.

A slow slide of her tongue up toward Dylan's clit.

"Fuck," Dylan said, drawing out the vowel, breathy and needy.

The sound made Ramona crazy, just as desperate to devour her. She kept licking, swirling, sucking the cotton into her mouth, tasting Dylan through the barrier while Dylan writhed on the table.

Soon, though, the underwear was in the way. Ramona wanted more, so she stopped what she was doing, pushed Dylan's legs together, and pulled down her underwear as fast as she could. It got stuck on Dylan's ankle, but Ramona didn't care, spreading Dylan out before her again.

"Oh my god," Dylan said, right before Ramona's mouth touched her, then said it again even louder when Ramona made contact. Skin to slick skin. "Baby, that's so good."

Ramona moaned against her, licking and kissing, sucking Dylan's clit into her mouth until her body locked up, back arched, one of Ramona's hands cupping her breast and pinching her nipple.

"Jesus," Dylan said when she relaxed back onto the table. She looked down at Ramona. "You."

Ramona smiled, but she wasn't done yet. Not by a long shot. She loved making Dylan come any way she could, every way, but right now, she wanted something more.

Closer.

"Stay here," she said, then turned and walked into the bedroom.

Chapter Thirty-Three

DYLAN SAT UP, still bare-ass naked on the kitchen table, her bones rubbery and loose. She watched Ramona walk into the bedroom, that perfect ass bouncing as she went.

She missed her already.

Which sounded ridiculous.

And completely sane all at the same time.

Dylan didn't know how to talk to Ramona's about her new job with Noelle. Didn't know how to ask for more details, because she was terrified to know the answers.

Over the past few weeks, she and Ramona had shared more of their lives—they'd talked about Dylan's experiences growing up, and Ramona had told her more about Rebecca Riley, and how it had felt when her mother left and never looked back, about the birthday cards she'd received for herself and Olive. Cards that petered out after about four years. Cards she'd hidden from Olive, a guilt she carried.

They'd shared so much, and yet Dylan never really asked about Ramona's dreams. What she *wanted*. She was Ramona of Clover Lake. She seemed to belong here—she seemed to be happy here.

And really, any question about the future, be it jobs or dream cities to live in, made Dylan feel lost and empty.

Lonely.

Because she didn't want this to end with Ramona, no matter how it had started.

"Babe?" she called, because she needed Ramona closer. Needed her pressed to her skin, her breath in her ear.

"Patience!" Ramona called back, but then appeared in the doorway.

Dylan sucked in a breath.

Ramona was still gloriously naked—those full breasts and soft tummy, thick thighs Dylan almost always wanted closing around her ears—but she also had on the underwear-style harness she'd left here a few nights ago.

And situated in the O-ring was Frankie.

Frankie was Dylan's favorite dildo. She had a quirky habit of naming all her dildos and sex toys with monikers she felt carried Big Dyke Energy. Frankie, which had this perfect ridge about halfway down that made Dylan crazy, seemed like exactly the kind of dildo someone would wear to fuck someone good and proper. Ramona found this story hilarious, but she also couldn't deny Dylan's logic, especially after the first time Dylan had used it to fuck her into oblivion.

"Jesus," Dylan said as Ramona walked toward her, her cunt already throbbing and ready. "Did you put on the bumper?"

"I did," Ramona said, stepping up to the table, sliding her hands down Dylan's thighs.

"Good," Dylan said, grabbing Ramona's hips. "Because I want you to come inside me."

Ramona just tilted her head, her eyes soft. Dylan reached out and pushed Frankie against Ramona, watching as her eyes fluttered closed as the bumper—a textured silicone cover for the base of the dildo, kind of like a glove—rubbed against her clit.

"Good girl," Dylan said.

That's what she wanted right now. Ramona's mouth against hers while they fucked, breaths mingling and indistinguishable.

Dylan spread her legs and scooted to the edge of the table, then pulled Ramona as close as she could get her. Ramona held Frankie, positioning the dildo at Dylan's opening. Dylan had to lean back a little, but soon they got the angle right and Ramona slid inside her.

Dylan moaned, her head tilting back. The cock was so thick, almost too much, but just right at the same time.

"God," she said, lifting her head and pulling Ramona's hips toward her, pulling her even deeper inside her. She slid her hands down Ramona's ass, squeezing her flesh, while Ramona tangled her hands in Dylan's hair, angling her mouth to fit against hers.

They kissed, whispering *fuck* and *more* as they pumped their hips into each other. Sweat slicked beneath their fingers, and Dylan had the fleeting thought that they'd have to make sure they cleaned this table thoroughly, but that was later, that was after, and this was now, which was all Dylan wanted.

She wanted *this* and *now* and didn't want to think even ten minutes into the future, when Ramona wouldn't be inside her, wouldn't have her forehead pressed against her, wouldn't be breathing heavily with her own pleasure, wouldn't be whispering Dylan's name like a prayer.

Dylan felt herself growing wild, desperate to come, but not wanting to at the same time, because she didn't want this to end.

She didn't want any of it to end.

"Baby," Dylan said, because her orgasm was building anyway, a slow swell, her heart pounding faster as her fingernails dug into Ramona's ass. "Fuck."

"I want you to come," Ramona said, her hands tightening in Dylan's hair. "Come for me. You're so beautiful when you come for me."

"God," Dylan said, pressing her mouth to Ramona's. She wanted to come like that, breathing her in. She swirled her hips, pulling Ramona deeper, making sure that bumper hit her in just the right spot. "With me. Please."

Then it was just sounds, honeyed breathing and moaning until Dylan lit up, a flash flood through her blood and muscle and bone. She cried out into Ramona's mouth, and Ramona did the same, her body stuttering into Dylan's as she came too.

They stayed like that for a while, just breathing, hearts hammering together on that kitchen table, clinging to each other and not daring to move.

Not daring to break the beautiful spell of *now*.

Chapter Thirty-Four

TWO DAYS LATER, reality intruded.

They had spent most of the Fourth in bed, which was just fine with Dylan. She had no desire to see anyone but Ramona, and when Ramona suggested they meet Olive and April and Leigh at the beach for fireworks that night, Dylan agreed because she wanted to give Ramona anything she wanted.

She wanted to give her the world.

If she could.

Later, they had sneaked away to their cove and kissed under the moonlight, just like they had eighteen years ago. This time was different though. This time they whispered their real names against each other's mouths. This time, they didn't let go. This time, they left together, fingers tangled.

It had been a perfect night. A perfect day. A perfect month with Ramona, and Dylan never wanted it to end.

But the next morning, both of their phones started buzzing at seven a.m.

"What the actual fuck," Dylan said. Her hair—or maybe it was Ramona's—was spread across her face, and her eyes felt gummy.

Ramona stirred next to her, gloriously naked, and slapped at her own phone on the nightstand.

"It's me," she said.

"No, it's me," Dylan said, not moving. "Death awaits the caller."

Ramona squinted at her phone. "Mine's a text."

Dylan's phone stopped buzzing, only to start up again a second later.

"Fuck, it's Laurel," she said.

Ramona sat up, her hair a beautiful mess. "How do you know?"

Dylan still didn't move. "Repeat calls. Gotta be her."

"You better answer, then."

Dylan just groaned and closed her eyes again. Repeat calls from Laurel were never a good thing, and she'd enjoyed her day off yesterday in sex-addled, romantic bliss far too much to start this bullshit so early.

"Who's yours?" she asked, her phone already starting to buzz a third time.

Ramona was quiet for a second.

Dylan cracked open an eye. Ramona blinked at her phone, then caught Dylan's gaze.

Smiled.

"It's Noelle," she said softly. "She needs me to run to Concord for some boots."

Dylan nodded, but she felt her shoulders go tight, even lying down in the bed. They still hadn't really talked about Ramona's new job. Dylan had wanted yesterday to go on and on, simple as that, but now that same terror from before was back, that small sensation in the center of her chest that made her feel like she was shrinking.

"You should get going then," she said. It just came out. She knew she needed to be honest, needed to just *tell* Ramona what she wanted, what she wondered, what she was so afraid of. But being honest with people about how much she cared about them had never been easy for her. Deflecting, as her therapist would call it, was natural, a reflex.

And as her phone buzzed for the fourth time, she knew she didn't have the time or energy to get into this emotional minefield with Ramona right now. She sat up and grabbed her phone—sure enough, Laurel's name flashed over the screen—while Ramona got out of bed and headed for the bathroom.

"Yes, darling?" Dylan said into the phone after sliding her finger across the screen.

"Hey, wanted to give you a heads-up," Laurel said, wasting no time. She was used to Dylan's deflections by now, and rarely called attention to them unless absolutely necessary.

"About what?" Dylan asked. "Should I be nervous?"

"Depends. Are you over Jocelyn Gareth?"

Just the name made Dylan's stomach tense. Not that she'd tell Laurel that.

"*Over* her?" she said.

Laurel sighed. "You know what I mean."

"Why are you—" Dylan froze. Closed her eyes. "She's coming to set, isn't she?"

"She is. Today. I just got the confirmation. She's been out in North Carolina with Ruby's family."

"How lovely." Dylan pressed her fingers into her eyes and squeezed.

"Look," Laurel said softly. "I'll be on set today too. You don't even have to speak to her, but . . ."

Dylan groaned. "But I should."

"It would be a good look, yeah."

"God, I don't need this right now," Dylan said. "My parents are still here too, which means she's going to be parading around with Jack, talking about romantic song lyrics to match *my* kissing scenes."

Laurel was quiet for a second. Ramona came out of the bathroom in a plain lavender tee tied at her waist and formfitting black pants that hit at her ankle. She looked retro and adorable, and Dylan wanted nothing more than to pull her back into bed.

But then Laurel sighed loudly into the phone, bringing real life crashing down once again.

"Dylan, this is your job," she said. "I know Jocelyn hurt you, but that's on her. You wanted to remake yourself after everything that happened with her and the Mondrian. So do it."

Dylan felt her shoulders drop. "Yeah. Yeah, okay."

"I'll see you in an hour?"

"Okay. Thanks, Laurel."

She ended the call, dropped her phone in her lap. Laurel was right. She had to suck it up, stop letting other people's issues become her own.

"You okay?" Ramona asked, slipping her phone into her back pocket.

Dylan nodded, scrubbed a hand over her face. "Jocelyn's going to be here today."

Ramona's eyes widened. "Oh."

"Yeah."

"Are you . . . is that . . ."

"A problem?" Dylan asked, then laughed bitterly. "No. I don't know." She looked at Ramona. "I never told you what she did, did I?"

Ramona's mouth opened, then she sank down onto the bed, sitting on one leg. "No. But Olive mentioned something about a record deal with your dad."

Dylan nodded. Of course Olive would know about it. The whole world knew about it. Ramona only hadn't known about it because she didn't read the gossip sites. Or at least, she hadn't before she met Dylan.

"I'm sorry I didn't tell you myself," Dylan said. "It's just . . . I didn't react well. The Mondrian and the helicopter. The champagne and the pool. It wasn't my proudest moment."

She reached out and took Ramona's hand.

"It's okay," Ramona said, staring at their fingers.

Dylan squeezed. "Good. And it'll be fine with Jocelyn. I can be professional. I have to be, right?"

Ramona looked at her. Smiled, though there was something sad in her eyes.

"Are *you* okay?" Dylan asked.

Ramona blinked. "Me? Yeah, I'm . . . I'm fine. But hey, can we talk tonight?"

Dylan tilted her head. "Talk?"

"Just . . . yeah. Just, like, talk. Maybe go to dinner?"

"Of course. I always want to talk to you," Dylan said, though somehow she didn't think Ramona meant simply shooting the breeze over some fried calamari.

But Ramona nodded, took a deep breath as she stood up. "Good. Great. I'll . . . I'll see you on set? We're at the lake house again, right?"

"Yeah," Dylan said as their hands slid apart. "Kiss?"

Ramona came over to her side of the bed, leaned down, and kissed her, framing Dylan's face in her hands.

"You're talented and beautiful and good," Ramona whispered against her mouth.

Dylan's throat nearly closed up, aching with the effort to hold back a sudden swell of tears.

"Thank you, baby," she said, her voice shaky.

"And you know what else I think?" Ramona asked.

"What?"

Ramona grinned. "I think that you've earned Llama Face."

Dylan eyes popped. "No." She pressed a hand to her chest. "Have I really?"

"Oh, yes. Definite earnage going on here."

Dylan wiggled her ass in the bed, eagerly set her hands in her lap like a little kid. "I'm so ready."

Ramona sat on the edge of the bed and took a deep breath. "You have to see it from the side."

"Deal. Yes. Go," Dylan said, glee filling her up.

Ramona laughed, then turned so Dylan faced her right side. Then she hooked her thumb under her top lip and her forefinger over her bottom lip. She pulled her lips out, opened her mouth and stuck out her tongue, then made a sound like . . . well . . . a llama.

Dylan just watched in awe. It was, indeed, a llama face. A laugh burst out of her, because it was also the funniest and cutest and most ridiculous thing Dylan had ever seen.

She clapped, while Ramona stood and took a bow.

"Excellent," Dylan said, still clapping. "A-plus. Oscar-winning performance right there." She beamed at Ramona, affection like she'd never felt for another person flooding into her chest. "Encore!"

"Oh no," Ramona said. "Llama Face only comes out at very special and very specific times."

"Hmph." Dylan pouted, folding her arms. "Fine. I'll accept that under duress."

"Fair enough," Ramona said, smiling down at her. They watched each other for a second, soft expressions on both faces, and Dylan felt her affection surge even higher, brimming to the top of her head and the tips of her toes.

Ramona's smile widened, as though she knew it, and then bent down to kiss Dylan goodbye.

"Beautiful," she whispered against her mouth one more time, then was gone.

Chapter Thirty-Five

RAMONA HAD NEVER been so tired in her life.

Eight-hour shifts on her feet at Clover Moon—and sometimes longer—were nothing compared to the exhaustion of being Noelle Yang's assistant. Ramona rarely stood still, ate her lunch standing up with a tape measure hanging around her neck, and had taken so many trips to every neighboring town, she'd had to use Noelle's studio credit card to fill up her gas tank twice.

And all this in just one day.

She never had time to think about Dylan. Or Jocelyn and Dylan. She never even caught sight of the blond starlet, and half hoped Jocelyn Gareth had simply decided not to come by the set. Still, Ramona barely had time to pee, let alone to talk to her girlfriend's ex.

Her *girlfriend*.

For once, she didn't correct her train of thought. It was what she wanted, and she was ready to tell Dylan she wanted it too.

Now, as she stood in the main bedroom of the Bonner lake house—Mallory's family home—sifting through ties for one to match Mallory's brother's cream linen suit, she smiled at the idea. It was dark outside, and they had one more scene to film at this house, an evening party that actually led to the third-act breakup for Mallory and Eloise, preempted by the revelation in front of the partygoers that they've been faking their relationship.

"How about this one?" Ramona said, holding up a purple silk tie with tiny darker purple leaves all over it. "It'll complement his eyes and drive home the point that he's into appearances."

Noelle lifted a brow from where she was sitting on an armchair, her iPad in her lap. "And why's that?"

Ramona considered the tie. "It's unique. And Hunter likes being rich. Likes being a man who people underestimate. This tie will go well with the cream and emphasize that he's a bit of a snob."

Noelle tilted her head. "Very good."

Ramona beamed, but tried to hide it. Yes, she was exhausted, and her feet were killing her, and she was worried about Dylan, and she couldn't remember the last time she'd had a sip of water, but she was *happy*.

This job was thrilling.

It was everything she wanted. Well, not everything. She'd much rather have her own assistant while she sat with her iPad and planned out costumes, but she knew this was the way to get there, and she loved every energy-draining second.

"Why did you drop out of RISD?" Noelle asked.

Ramona's smile vanished. She cleared her throat, set the tie on the bed, and started looking for a shirt to go with it. "I had some family obligations."

"Like what?"

Ramona had learned quickly that Noelle was blunt and didn't really care about crossing personal lines. Not when it came to doing her job well.

"My mother left when I was young," Ramona said. "And my father had an accident that put him out of work when I was nineteen. I had to come home to care for my little sister."

Noelle nodded. "Noble."

"No. Just necessary," Ramona said, fingers skimming a row of dress shirts on a rack.

"It's a shame you couldn't finish," Noelle said, tapping at her screen with her stylus. "Though something tells me you don't regret it."

Ramona smiled softly. "I could never regret my sister."

Noelle smiled back. "Fair enough." Then she snapped her stylus into its holder, sighed as she considered Ramona. "I think you should come work for me."

Ramona froze, an off-white silk shirt in her hands. "As in . . . after this film?"

Noelle stood up and took the shirt from Ramona. She laid it on the bed next to the tie, nodded. "You're smart. You're hardworking. And you've got a passion for the work. You're *me* twenty years ago."

"But . . . you . . . I've only worked for you for, like, two days."

"Sometimes that's all it takes." Noelle straightened, looked at Ramona over her glasses. "I'm based in LA, so you'd have to relocate, but I can help find you a place to live, and I pay a decent wage. You'd work with me on films, some plays from time to time when I get tired of Hollywood bullshit. Work your way up."

Ramona could only stare.

Noelle smiled. "A shock, I see. But I can tell you want this. Like I said, you're me." She squeezed Ramona's shoulder, just once. "Think about it. Talk to your family. This film wraps in two weeks— Vee is more interested in the makeup side of things, so they're moving on once they're up and about—so I'll need you in LA by the end of the month. I'd like an answer in one week, and I don't expect you'll give me the wrong one."

Ramona could only nod.

"I'm not sure if Dylan factors into it at all, considering, but feel free to talk to her too," Noelle said. Then she went back to the chair, back to her iPad, immediately lost in her work, while Ramona stood there, processing.

She processed for what felt like hours, just standing by a clothes rack in the middle of some rich guy's bedroom doubling as a wardrobe, Noelle's words filtering back and over and through her brain.

LA.

Work.

Film.

Plays.

Dylan…

…considering…

"Noelle," she said, turning toward the designer. She held a floral skirt in her hand she didn't even remember picking up. "What did you mean *considering*?"

Noelle glanced up. "What?"

"You said you weren't sure how Dylan factored into it, *considering*. Considering what?"

Noelle didn't even blink. "Considering your arrangement."

Something in Ramona went cold, a warning.

"Arrangement?" she asked.

Noelle slipped off her glasses. "Yes, arrangement." She sounded impatient, but Ramona just waited for her to go on. "Dating to smooth over her image? Isn't that what you two are doing? At least, that's what Gia wanted."

The cold spread now, radiating out from her stomach to her limbs, her heart. "Gia."

"After you two got caught at that miniature golf place," Noelle said. "Gia said you'd agreed to date for publicity and you might be on set here and there. Happens all the time. Did you know Ryan Locke and Fiona Whalen's entire marriage was a stunt? I get dating, but a legal bond?" She shook her head and slipped her glasses back on. "Hollywood needs therapy."

Ramona closed her eyes, squeezed them hard until color exploded behind her lids. Opened them back up, but Noelle was still there, she was still here, and Noelle's words still echoed against the spa-blue walls.

"Hang on," she said, holding on to the bed's fabric footboard. "Are you . . . What are you saying?"

Noelle glanced up, alarmed. "Oh, shit."

"Are you saying Dylan has been fake dating me for . . . what? A publicity stunt?"

"Fucking hell," Noelle said, standing up. "You didn't know."

"Wait. You're really saying . . . Dylan . . . fake . . . me . . ." Ramona's words tripped and gasped, the air thin, her lungs rebelling.

"Sit down," Noelle said, grabbing Ramona's arms and easing her down onto the bed. Then she hurried into the bathroom and emerged with a glass of water. Ramona held it, but didn't drink. She was too busy trying to breathe, trying to get the words that were tumbling through her brain to slow down.

"You really didn't know?" Noelle asked.

Ramona could only shake her head. No need to ask, *Know what?* or *What do you mean?* Noelle had been clear enough. And Noelle wasn't prone to gossip. She hated that shit—was famous for her no-nonsense approach when it came to Hollywood drama, especially on one of her projects. She wouldn't have said any of this if it weren't true.

Ramona's memories swirled back a few weeks ago to Dickie's, then the photos of her and Dylan online, how riled Dylan was about it, and then . . .

"Just casual," Dylan said. "You know . . . fun. Not so different from what we've been doing, really. Just, you know . . . it's like . . . different because, I might, I don't know. Hold your finger."

"Finger?"

"I mean hand. Jesus." Dylan rubbed her forehead. "I'm very bad at this."

Except she wasn't. Apparently Dylan was very, very good. God,

Ramona had thought it was all so adorable, how Dylan had tripped over her words when she'd asked her out. How romantic it was when she'd taken her to the Earthstars Museum.

How she'd waved at the phones pointed in their direction.

Fucking *waved*.

When only the day before, she'd nearly lost her mind over the three paparazzi at Dickie's.

"I didn't know," Ramona said quietly.

"My god," Noelle said, pressing her hand to the base of her throat. "I'm sorry, Ramona. It wasn't my place. I thought you—"

"No, no," Ramona said. "Don't apologize. This isn't your fault."

Noelle sighed. "What do you need right now?"

Ramona looked up at Noelle. *The* Noelle Yang, Oscar winner and so tough and smart with her no-bullshit attitude. But here she was being kind, asking Ramona what she needed after learning that her girlfriend was actually her fake girlfriend.

A single laugh burst out of Ramona. She slapped a hand over her mouth, but it was all just so absurd. And right now, if Ramona didn't laugh, she'd cry or scream or storm out of the wardrobe and onto the set and do something that would certainly make her famous in Hollywood for reasons she didn't care for, and that's not what she wanted.

That's not who she was.

She was strong. Resilient. And she did what fucking needed to be done, no matter the condition of her heart.

She always had.

She took a sip of water, then kept going and gulped the whole glass down.

"I need to work," she said once the cup was empty. She stood up, rolled her shoulders back. "Thank you, Noelle. For everything. But right now, I just want to do my job."

Noelle nodded, a glint of admiration in her eyes. "Fair enough."

She took the glass from Ramona and set it on the dresser, then walked over to her iPad and started tapping. "I'm sending the brief for the scene at Eloise's house to your phone. Make sure everything's ready."

"Of course," Ramona said as she took her phone from her back pocket. She tapped on Noelle's AirDrop, ignoring her shaking hands, ignoring the sting in her eyes.

Then she did the only thing she knew to do right now and got to work.

Chapter
Thirty-Six

YOU'RE TALENTED AND *beautiful and good*.

Ramona's words looped through Dylan's head during the day, pulling her shoulders back and filling her lungs with air. It had been a tough shoot so far, long as hell. They were wrapping up every scene that took place in the Bonner house, which included polishing the first kiss scene, as well as the breakup scene that occurred at night, golden twinkle lights glittering through the backyard and along the private pier.

Still, the work had gone smoothly so far, and Dylan felt calm and capable. Confident, even. Shockingly, Gia had given her an approving nod when she'd swiped a thumb over Blair's cheek during their kissing scene, soft and sweet, Blair's eyes liquid, love and lust radiating between them. Which was one hundred percent bullshit and was also one hundred percent perfect. Even Gia couldn't deny it, and Blair laughed and batted Dylan's hand away after the scene ended, but she too seemed pleased.

So as the sun sank into the lake, spreading pink and lavender and gold across the lawn while Dylan sat at the patio table and reviewed her lines for the breakup scene, she was feeling pretty good. She was feeling like herself, and like she couldn't wait to see Ramona later. She had barely caught a glimpse of her all day long, the woman was so busy.

She smiled, thinking about Ramona kicking ass. She knew they needed to talk about the job with Noelle, but she also knew Ramona wasn't Jocelyn. She wasn't anyone Dylan had ever dated.

And then Jocelyn Gareth herself walked out the back door, Jack Monroe at her side.

"Fuck," Dylan said under her breath.

"Dylan," Jocelyn said, all her perfect teeth showing. She was dressed in a terracotta pantsuit à la Julia Roberts in *Pretty Woman*, loose and flowing, perfect for her lithe form. "I was hoping to run into you."

"Were you?" Dylan asked, standing and pulling her dress to the side so she could walk. At least she was dressed impeccably for the upcoming party scene, wearing a strapless tulle gown embroidered with red, pink, yellow, and blue flowers.

Talented and beautiful and good.

She folded her hands in front of her, determined to stay calm. Professional.

"Of course," Jocelyn said.

"Dill Pickle here is really killing it on this film," Jack said.

Dylan gritted her teeth at his use of the nickname in front of her ex.

Jocelyn's eyes glittered. "I'm sure she is."

"Dill, I brought Jocelyn by to see this breakup scene," Jack said. "I think an original song would fit perfectly after the break, in a sort of montage."

"Great," Dylan said.

"Great," Jocelyn said.

"Great," Jack said.

Dylan would rather be chewing on tinfoil right now.

"So," Jocelyn said, "I hear you're dating."

Dylan narrowed her eyes. "I hear you're engaged."

Jocelyn laughed and held out her hand, a diamond sparkling on her ring finger. "I am. Ruby is wonderful."

"So is Ramona," Dylan said. Jack's eyes flicked between them, his brows lowered.

"She's made of strong stuff, then," Jocelyn said with a smile, an insult aimed at Dylan rolled up in a pretty compliment for Ramona.

"She's made of *real* stuff," Dylan said, even as she knew she just needed to shut up. Be the bigger person instead of jumping into a pissing match over current partners with her ex, but Jocelyn made her feel so fucking small.

"Okay," Jack said, clapping his hands together. "Jocelyn, why don't we find a good spot to watch the action?"

"Sounds great, Jack, thank you," Jocelyn crooned.

The two were about to head off, and Dylan knew she should let them, but then she saw her.

Ramona.

Her Ramona.

Stepping out of the back door with a cute cream-colored apron around her waist, needles and thread and sewing scissors tucked into the pockets.

"Ramona, hey," Dylan said, hurrying over to her. "Come meet an old friend."

Ramona opened her mouth, a frown creasing her forehead, but Dylan simply slipped her fingers between Ramona's and pulled her toward Jocelyn, who had stopped at the sound of Ramona's name.

"Jocelyn, this is Ramona Riley," Dylan said. "Ramona, Jocelyn Gareth."

Jocelyn smiled angelically, held out her hand. "The girlfriend."

Ramona hesitated, then took Jocelyn's hand, shaking it only once before dropping it. She didn't smile. Didn't look at Dylan. In fact, she looked a little miserable, her face pale and her lower lip red and textured, as though she'd been chewing on it.

"Hey," Dylan said softly, squeezing her palm, "are you all—"

"I'm not the girlfriend," Ramona said, cutting Dylan off. Her eyes were fixed on Jocelyn. She untangled her fingers from Dylan's. Her words took a few seconds to land, like the first snowflakes falling from the sky, tumbling from a huge height to the ground.

But when they finally settled . . .

Dylan felt everything in her go cold.

"Oh?" Jocelyn said.

Behind her, Jack cleared his throat.

"No," Ramona said. "I'm just . . . I'm no one. Good luck with the song. Excuse me."

Then Ramona turned and started walking away.

Without a word to Dylan, without even glancing in her direction.

Dylan's instincts took over, spurred on by a cold fear.

"Hey, hey, wait," she said, hurrying after Ramona and grabbing her arm at the top of the porch stairs.

But Ramona pulled back, forcing Dylan to drop her hold and lift her hands in surrender.

"Hey," Dylan said again. "It's just me."

"Is it?" Ramona said, her eyes filling with tears.

"What are you talking about?"

They were attracting attention, crew members and cast alike. Blair was in the yard, all gussied up for the scene in a classic black strapless dress. She frowned in their direction, as did Gia, who was talking to one of the sound technicians. Still, Dylan couldn't walk away, couldn't leave this for later, no matter how much she knew she should. Ramona was looking at her like she didn't even recognize Dylan.

"What happened?" Dylan asked. "What's wrong?"

Ramona shook her head. "Dylan."

Dylan just blinked at her, reached for her hand. "What? Baby, please—"

"Don't," Ramona said, pulling her hand away. "Don't call me that. Let's just—"

"Then tell me what's wrong."

Ramona sighed, then finally looked at her. "You really want to do this here?"

"Yes. Whatever *this* is. Yes, I want to do this here."

Dylan's internal alarms were blaring, crimson light circling through her whole body.

Stop.

Do not proceed.

Red. Red. Red.

But she'd never been able to handle strong emotions with a level head, with *caution*, especially this kind, when she didn't even know what the emotions were. Her early life with her parents had triggered an almost constant state of fight or flight in her day-to-day functioning, never knowing what was coming next, and that uncertainty was like a cancer eating away at her heart, her thoughts.

"Fine," Ramona said, turning to face her, her arms folded. But then her expression crumpled, her eyes red-rimmed.

Dylan's heart collapsed in on itself. "Ramona," she said softly, stepping closer and cupping Ramona's elbows gently. "What is—"

"Did your publicity team tell you to date me?"

The words didn't make sense at first; they were the last thing Dylan expected Ramona to say. And then . . . they made far too much sense.

"What?" Dylan asked, even though she knew. She knew, and panic had replaced all of her cells. Because this wasn't right, this wasn't how this day was supposed to go. This wasn't how Ramona was supposed to ever feel, she wasn't supposed to ever know—

Dylan's swirling thoughts jolted to a stop.

She wasn't supposed to ever know.

That was what she'd planned. Because she liked Ramona, wanted her, and now she realized how stupid she'd been. How *wrong*.

"Ramona," she said softly so no one else could hear her. "Let's go somewhere and talk. Please."

Ramona just laughed humorlessly. "I guess I have my answer."

"Please," Dylan said again. "I can explain."

"Oh, I'm sure you can," Ramona said, but shook her head. Her eyes were dry, but swollen with emotions all the same. Hurt and anger and so many things that made Dylan want to wrap her up in her arms.

But she couldn't.

Ramona wouldn't let her.

"Let's just talk, please," Dylan said again.

Ramona took a step back. The set was quiet, all eyes on them, but Dylan didn't even care right now. She didn't care about anything but erasing that look in Ramona's eyes.

"The thing is," Ramona said, lifting her arms and then letting them slap back at her side, "I haven't been honest with you either."

Dylan felt her heart stutter. "What do you mean?"

Ramona eyes finally filled then, but she kept them on Dylan. "We're wrong, Dylan. We just hurt each other."

"Don't say that," Dylan said, stepping closer to her. "Look, yes, Rayna and Laurel wanted me to date you, but *I* wanted to date you too. For me, for *you*, for—"

"I want to be a costume designer."

Dylan closed her mouth, let the words sink in. They didn't seem barbed—seemed like a basic fact about Ramona that Dylan should know. A fact she *did* know. But then the meaning settled over her—*costume*.

Not just apparel.

"So you . . ." Dylan said, blinking, trying to make it make sense. "You want to . . ."

"Work in costume design," Ramona said, folding her arms. She closed her eyes, then opened them again. A tear escaped and she swiped it away, but her gaze was still steel and glass. "Like this. Like Noelle Yang. I've always wanted that."

And then it all came together.

Click.

The pieces sliding into place.

Ramona and Noelle. Noelle, whom Ramona had met through Dylan, and how nervous Ramona always seemed around the designer. The assistantship. Who knew what else—Dylan certainly didn't. She didn't know this woman standing in front of her at all. Hadn't asked so much, because she was scared of the answers, and she had a right to be. But unlike Jocelyn, Dylan had hurt Ramona too . . . and that just made it all worse.

Ramona was right.

They hurt each other. Lied to each other, didn't trust each other. And they both had good reason. Dylan knew she shouldered just as much of the blame for this moment as Ramona, but right now, a numbness spread through her limbs, radiating out from her heart. She felt it happening, when fight or flight shut down, and she simply turned off.

"Dylan," Ramona said. Not softly. Not gently. Just her name. Utilitarian and emotionless.

But there was nothing else to say, was there?

So Dylan hiked up the dress that Ramona herself had no doubt prepared for this scene—this breakup scene where everything came out between Eloise and Mallory and everything went to hell—and walked away.

Chapter Thirty-Seven

RAMONA WOKE UP still exhausted.

She'd barely slept. After getting home close to midnight, she hadn't even had the energy to change clothes, much less cry about what had happened on set. She'd passed out fully clothed, but kept waking up with a start, each time thinking the entire fight with Dylan had been a dream, only to feel a pit open in her gut when she realized it wasn't.

This happened at least three times. By the time she finally dragged herself out of bed around seven, she felt as though she hadn't slept at all. She'd never been so happy for a day off in her life, for multiple reasons. She couldn't bear to face Dylan right now, anger and hurt swirling through her in a sick amalgamation. Then there was Noelle's job offer, her dream come true, but she couldn't get her brain around it, couldn't seem to shove Dylan out of the way long enough to be *happy*, and that just caused her anger and hurt to surge even more.

She needed coffee. Needed something to fill her up instead of all these fucking feelings.

Downstairs, she found Olive standing by the coffee maker, the brew already burbling, and looking down at her phone.

"You're up early," Ramona said.

Olive startled, dropping her phone to the tile floor. She bent down to pick it up, her face pale.

"You okay?" Ramona asked.

"Yeah, yeah, I'm just . . ." Olive trailed off, tucking her phone into her back pocket. "I didn't think you'd be up yet on a day off."

"Couldn't sleep," Ramona said, taking a mug out of the cabinet. "What about you? You and Marley have plans today?"

Olive said nothing, and that's when Ramona noticed her duffel bag on the kitchen table, her last name and softball number from Clover Lake High monogrammed in a curly red script over the cream canvas.

"Are you going somewhere?" Ramona asked.

Olive swallowed, and Ramona's already unsettled stomach cramped with worry.

"What's going on, Olive? Tell me right now."

Olive closed her eyes.

"Ollie," Ramona said sharply. She sounded like a parent, she knew, but her panic was rising.

Olive sighed, looked down at the floor. "I found her."

For a second, Ramona just stared at her.

Found her.

Found . . . her.

The words flitted around her head, trying to land.

And then they did.

Found. Her.

"Where?" Ramona asked, her voice barely a whisper.

"Brooklyn," Olive said. "She does fashion consulting there."

Ramona's breath felt nonexistent, her lungs a vacuum. No sound. No light. No air.

"How long?" she asked. "How long have you known?"

Olive bit her lower lip, then lifted her head to look at Ramona. "Since April."

Ramona blinked, trying to process the information. It all came together in bits and bursts, the last few months. "That's who you've been texting with? Every time I would walk in the room and you put your phone away?"

Olive didn't say anything. She didn't have to.

"And now you're going to see her?" Ramona asked. She couldn't help the hurt that tumbled through her, colliding with the hurt already there from Dylan, the hurt that had been there for eighteen years, since her mother walked out on her.

Olive looked at her. "She said she sent birthday cards."

Ramona just stared back.

"For years," Olive said. "And you never told me or showed them to me."

"For *four* years," Ramona said. "Then they stopped. And I didn't show you because you were a baby, and by the time you were old enough to even understand what they were, she'd stopped sending them."

"I still deserved to see them!" Olive said.

"You really want to talk about what we deserved?" Ramona asked, her eyes filling and spilling over. She'd held tears back for so long—all night, eighteen years. But now, as her sister, the most important person in her life, glared at her as though betrayed, she couldn't stop the tears. Her throat shoved them upward, her eyes pushing them out, finally released.

"She *left* us," Ramona said. "Never looked back."

"She *did*," Olive said. "She's sent cards and wants to see me and—"

"Did you find her? Or did she find you?"

Olive opened her mouth but snapped it shut again.

"Exactly, Ollie." Ramona stepped forward, took her sister's hands. Looked in her lovely brown eyes. "Because we've always been here. Right here. She's always known where to find us."

Olive shook her head, tears spilling down her own cheeks. "You don't get it."

"I do," Ramona said. "I'm hurt too. I miss her too."

"But you *knew* her." Olive's voice broke. "You knew her, had pictures with her you remember, and I never got that. All I got was—"

She cut herself off, looked down as she cried, but Ramona heard her words anyway.

All I got was you.

Ramona held Olive's hands tighter, tears pouring silently now. She tried not to feel hurt, she really did, because she knew, better than anyone, that a sister didn't replace a mother.

But she'd never had time to *really* know that, had she? She'd had too many responsibilities, too much to do for Olive or with Olive or for her dad. She'd never slowed down enough to process it, and she felt like it was all hitting her at once now—the emotions themselves and realization that she hadn't done the emotional work to sort through them.

And Olive deserved that chance, even if it tore Ramona in two.

She squeezed Olive's hands once more, then let her go.

"Okay," Ramona said.

Olive sniffed. "Okay?"

"I can't stop you. You're eighteen and if . . . if you want to see her, you should go."

"Come with me," Olive said, fresh tears spilling over.

But Ramona couldn't. She wasn't ready, couldn't even begin to fathom seeing her mother right now after so long and zero effort on Rebecca Riley's part to reach out.

No.

This was one thing she couldn't help Olive do.

"I can't, sweetheart," Ramona said. "I wish I could, but I just can't."

Olive nodded, but her tears kept coming.

And then Ramona did what she did best—she took her sister in her arms and held her until she stopped crying.

Chapter Thirty-Eight

OLIVE WAS GONE for three days.

In that time, Ramona worked. She worked and she kept her head down and tried not to go anywhere near filming, if she could help it. They were doing a lot of shots outside recently, as the weather was perfect for it, which meant Ramona spent a ton of time in her car running errands or sorting clothes at the Bonner house, as they were still using the main bedroom for wardrobe and makeup. She had a suspicion that Noelle might be keeping her out of Dylan's path, but that didn't sound much like the shark Noelle Yang was known to be, so Ramona just took it as a small blessing from the universe.

Because she didn't want to see Dylan.

Didn't even want to think about her.

She couldn't quite wrap her brain around everything that had happened the last few days. Dylan, Olive, Noelle's job offer. It all swirled in her mind like soup, a sludge that gummed up her insides.

Plus, news of Dylan and Ramona's breakup was everywhere.

Every gossip site.

Someone had recorded their argument and put it on TikTok and Instagram.

Even *People* magazine had a small article about it, the majority of which focused on Dylan Monroe's tragic flair for drama, most likely stemming from her fraught upbringing.

Ramona's heart ached when April alerted her to the article's existence—she immediately wanted to call Dylan, to ask how she was, but she didn't. She couldn't.

Dylan didn't care about her.

Not like Ramona thought she did, at least.

And maybe Ramona didn't care about Dylan the way she'd thought either. After all, she'd kept her closest dreams from Dylan, the thing that, along with Olive and her mother leaving, had defined her entire life.

"You were just scared," April said when Ramona said as much. "That doesn't mean you didn't love her. It just means you've been hurt, Mona."

Ramona ignored most of that, particularly the L-word.

Everything was a mess, and Ramona just wanted to work. She wanted to do her job and try to clear her head about LA. She hadn't even told April about Noelle's job offer, hadn't told anyone, and every time she slowed down for a second to ponder it herself, she couldn't breathe.

She wasn't sure why.

It was her dream, right there, on a plate held out to her with two hands, and yet she felt the moment she reached for it, it would vanish like a wisp of smoke.

Three days after Olive left, after Ramona finished sorting all the suits at the Bonner house for a lakeside shoot the next morning, she drove home, wanting nothing more than to crawl into bed and sleep for days. When she closed her front door behind her, her dad was sitting in his favorite squashy armchair in the living room, reading.

"Hey, Dad," she said.

"Hey, honey," he said, slipping off his glasses and looking at her. "You look exhausted."

She dropped her bag, then slumped down on the couch, rubbed her eyes. "An understatement."

He *hmm*'d, then closed his book. "Have you heard from your sister?"

Ramona shook her head. She hadn't texted Olive. Hadn't called her, even though she'd wanted to every free second of every day. But she wanted to give her space too—and, maybe more selfishly, was scared to hear what was happening with her mother. Scared it was going horribly. Scared it was going wonderfully, because if that was the case, what did that say about Ramona? She felt like she was thirteen years old again, lost and lonely and left.

Her dad sighed. "I know this is hard for you."

Ramona really didn't want to get into it. "It's fine."

But her voice sounded dead, unconvincing, even to her.

He sat up, rested his elbows on his khaki-clad knees. "It's hard for me too."

Ramona looked at him, her father, the parent who stayed, who tried his best, who still had a limp from his accident that brought Ramona home all those years ago. His heart must have been broken when his wife left him, left *them*, but their family had never really gotten into talking about the emotional side of it all. They'd been too busy surviving. Any emotional needs Olive had growing up, Ramona took care of, or at least, took care of as best she knew how.

"She left you too," Ramona said, stating the obvious, yes, but she'd never really let herself think about that side of it. "I'm so sorry, Dad."

He frowned, his eyes suddenly shiny. "I'm the one who's sorry, baby."

Her chest immediately went tight, her throat clogging with tears. "Dad, you—"

"No, let me say this," he said. "I put too much on you. I know I did. With me. With Olive."

"She's my sister. You're my father."

"And you're my child," he said firmly. "I was lost, I'll admit that, and didn't know what else to do, especially after the accident. But I hated it every day, Ramona. I hated that you had to come home. Had to give up your life like you did. I wish it could've been different. That I'd had another option."

He blinked, looked down, and Ramona was sure her father was on the verge of crying.

"Dad," she said. "Look at me."

He did, wiped at his face.

"I love my life," she said. "Every second I've spent with you and Olive. I wouldn't change anything." And it was true. Getting to be part of her sister's life like she had, not everyone got that. Not everyone got to see such an amazing person, a beautiful, kind, smart person bloom into being right before their eyes.

"I know that, honey," he said. "But the fact is, you've sacrificed too much. And now with all this hullaballoo with Dylan Monroe."

She cracked a smile. "*Hullabaloo?*"

He laughed, shook his head. "I just want you to be happy."

"I am," she said softly. And that was true too.

And it wasn't.

She took a deep breath, picked at a string on a rip in her jeans. "Noelle Yang offered me a job in LA."

She said it fast, the first time she'd said it out loud at all since Noelle's offer.

Her dad blinked, his mouth falling open slowly. The words hovered between them for a second, the reality of them.

"Of course she did," he finally said. "And you're taking it."

It wasn't a question, but when Ramona opened her mouth, there was still doubt on her tongue.

"I'd have to be in LA by the end of the month," she said. "And Olive"—her throat went a little tight—"Olive's not due at Vanderbilt until the middle of August."

She couldn't miss it—couldn't leave in July, letting Olive and her dad settle her into her dorm room without Ramona. It was a *moment*, one of those Ramona wanted to be a part of, and she couldn't seem to see around it.

Her dad simply shrugged. "So take her with you. She'd love to see LA and where you'll be living. Then you two can fly home, my treat, and you can drive with us to Tennessee. Fly out of Nashville later on."

Her eyes brimmed. Such an easy solution, but it felt so huge in her heart. And there was also April, her best friend since she knew what a best friend even was. Ramona wasn't sure she could get on without her. LA was so big, a different world from her small-town life. She'd be lost.

She'd disappear.

"Dad," she said quietly, looking down at her hands. "I'm . . . I think I'm scared."

His eyes went soft. "You'd be a fool not to be. But this is your time, sweetheart. You've spent years choosing other people over yourself. Enough, baby. You're taking the job."

He said it gently. Not a command, just a fact.

And in that moment, Ramona knew the only answer to Noelle's offer was yes. She'd miss her town, her father, her best friend, her sister when she came home during school breaks, but Ramona had to go. She and April would always be just that—Ramona and April. When April was still at RISD, after Ramona had come back to Clover Lake, they still talked and texted all the time. And nothing could keep Ramona from checking in on Olive at Vanderbilt, probably to an annoying degree.

Her dad was right—it was time.

She nodded, and then they simply sat in silence for a while, father and daughter, the reality of Ramona leaving settling between them, bittersweet and right.

"I'm going to go to bed," she said finally, standing. "I need to process all of this."

"Of course, honey." He stood too, then held out an arm. Ramona went happily, letting herself be held by her father.

"I'm proud of you," he said into her hair, rubbing her back like she was a little kid. "Always have been, always will be."

"Thanks, Daddy," she said, her throat thick. She breathed him in, Old Spice and cotton, that Dad smell that made her feel young and soft and innocent.

They'd just broken apart when the front door opened and Olive walked into the house, her duffel bag on her elbow, her cheeks flushed, and her eyes a bit red.

Ramona and her dad parted, but he kept a hand on her arm, his fingers tightening in anticipation.

"Hey, Ollie," Ramona said softly. "How—"

But before Ramona could ask a thing, Olive dropped her bag and hurried across the room, diving in between them, her face buried against Ramona's chest as she started crying.

She caught her dad's eye, his expression just as sad as hers felt, but neither of them asked about Rebecca or the visit. They just held Olive between them, their little family of three, and told her they loved her.

Chapter Thirty-Nine

"*I DON'T CARE if we're from different worlds.* You *are my world.* Wherever you are."

Blair said the words with heart.

With feeling.

Tears brimmed in her eyes as she held Dylan's face between her hands. Dylan's own tears trailed down her cheeks as she gripped Blair's wrists, their foreheads pressed together.

"*I'm yours,*" Dylan said. "*In any world. Every world. Always.*"

The moment of Eloise and Mallory's reconciliation was romantic and taut. The entire crew around them seemed to be holding their breath right along with the paid extras as the two actors stood in the middle of Clover Moon Café, which Mallory had filled with a thousand purple irises, Eloise's favorite flower. Eloise had opened the restaurant door that morning to a sea of purple, a powdery floral scent filling the space.

And in the center stood Mallory in a pair of worn jeans and a tee, ready with all the reasons she and Eloise should be together, despite the chasms in their lives.

The scene was cute, a grand gesture for the big screen, but it was powerful too. Weighted. Because Blair was goddamn good at her job, and every single one of Dylan's emotions had been living at the surface for days, ready to spill over for this very moment.

It had been two weeks since her split with Ramona, and since then, she'd only caught glimpses of her, a flash of dark hair and curves, always carrying clothes, always hurrying, never looking up or around at anyone.

Which was just as well.

Dylan didn't know what to say to her. Didn't know if she wanted to say anything. Anger and hurt simmered just under her skin, but there was something else there too.

Her own mistakes.

Her own lies.

Her own . . . *missing*.

Because she missed Ramona so much. More than she'd ever missed anyone in her entire life. When she and Jocelyn had broken up, even when all the drama and publicity about it slowed down, she never longed for Jocelyn like this. Never felt her arms ache from emptiness, her bed too big for her solitary form. But there was nothing to do about it. She'd hurt Ramona. Ramona had hurt her, and Dylan had never known how to get around those feelings to the other side.

She wasn't sure there even was another side.

"*Kiss me*," she whispered against Blair's mouth now.

And goddammit, she tried not to think about Ramona. She'd tried this entire shoot, the penultimate scene of the movie and the last day of filming in Clover Lake, to *not* think about Ramona, about reconciling, about taking her in her arms and kissing her, but she couldn't help it.

And maybe that was a good thing, because Dylan was *good*. This scene was emotional and intense, and even Gia was speechless as she and Blair kissed, hands in each other's hair, tears on their cheeks.

"*Always*," Blair whispered.

"*Always*," Dylan whispered back.

"And cut," Gia said, her voice the softest and gentlest Dylan had ever heard.

Everyone remained quiet while Gia checked the monitor, hand on her chin as she watched what had just been filmed. Dylan's hands were still tangled in Blair's curls as they both waited.

"And . . ." Gia said, looking up and smiling. "That's a wrap."

Cheers went up in the crowd, and some people even threw their caps into the air if they had them.

"Good work, everyone," Gia said, then shot a finger gun at Dylan, which was the closest she'd probably ever get to a compliment from Gia Santos.

Dylan smiled back as she pulled away from Blair. She clapped along with everyone else, nodded when people asked if she'd be at the wrap party in a few hours at Four Leaf, the only bar in town and, really, the only place big enough to house the entire crew. Her chest felt tight and bubbly at the same time—she'd done it.

She'd had a few bumps in the road, her name on the sites more than she'd like over the last six weeks of filming, but she'd done it. She'd become Eloise, portrayed a character wholly unlike her, and did it *well*.

And she was happy.

She *was*.

But she'd learned long ago that emotions were never only one thing. Fear could exist with excitement, and anger could exist with love, and hurt could exist with longing, and all those things could exist together.

She looked around the room, spotted Iris Kelly, the book's author, who had flown back to Clover Lake for the last scene and wrap party. She saw Owen, the diner's owner, shaking hands with Gia. She saw Noelle Yang near the back, clapping and beaming along with everyone else. And with all the pride and relief in her heart right now, Dylan couldn't help but let in a wave of sadness that Ramona was nowhere to be seen.

IT DIDN'T TAKE very long for the wrap party to get wild. That was usually how these things went, the relief over being finished, the stress that had built up for weeks and weeks finally allowed to release.

Dylan sat at a table in Four Leaf, nursing a club soda. She hadn't been drinking lately, and she'd never felt better physically or mentally. She knew she used alcohol as an escape, something her therapist had pointed out very brutally last week during a Zoom session, and it was a habit that could quickly spiral out of control if she didn't do something about it. She'd fallen into her parents' old habits, an ironic twist of fate that left her feeling like an idiot, like a weakling. Eli had said she was none of those things, that she simply had never been given other tools to process her emotions, and that was something they needed to work on.

So here she was, drinking fizzy water with lime and trying to *process her emotions* with some good old-fashioned introspection.

"Hey," Blair said, sitting down at the table with her, a glass of red wine in her hand. "When do you head out?"

"Tomorrow," Dylan said. She was going back to LA, back to life, back to her cavernous house alone. True, when everything started with Ramona, she'd never expected it to last past filming. And when she realized she liked Ramona way more than she'd ever dreamed was possible, she never really thought past Clover Lake.

She hadn't thought through so many things. There was still so much shit in her life she needed to work out, including years of pointless enmity with Blair. Despite the tentative peace they'd formed over the past couple of months, Dylan wanted to make it right.

Because she'd been wrong. So, so wrong.

"Blair," she said.

Blair took a sip of wine, blinked at her. Then widened her eyes when Dylan stayed silent. "Yes, Dylan?" she asked, laughing a little.

But Dylan didn't smile. She took a deep breath, leaned forward in her seat. "I'm sorry."

Blair's thick brows lifted. "What?"

"You were right," Dylan went on. "That day you told me off in Clover Moon."

Blair just stared at her.

"I was—*am*—spoiled and entitled," Dylan said, looking down at her half-empty glass. "I was a brat on *Spellbound*'s set, and I treated you like I was a brat, and I'm sorry. You deserved better than that."

Silence for a second, then Blair took another sip of wine, set it down.

"Well, shit," she said. "Words I never thought I'd hear Dylan Monroe say."

Dylan gave her a small smile. Her heart was pounding, palms sweating, but this was right, so she pushed through the anxiety and just *let herself feel it*, as Eli said. She'd spent her life fighting negative emotions, because negative emotions always meant chaos for her as a kid—they were like harbingers of disaster, rather than what they really were. Just feelings. Normal responses to shitty situations.

"I know," Dylan said. "And I'm sorry for that too."

Blair nodded.

"I think you're amazing," Dylan said. "You're talented, smart, and classy. You're pretty badass."

Blair smirked and lifted her glass. "I'll drink to that."

They both took a sip, but then Blair sobered a little. "Look, Dylan, I appreciate this. Thank you."

Dylan shook her head. "It was a long time coming."

"Yeah, it was. But for what it's worth, I recognize your—" Blair sighed, hesitated. "I get that the way you grew up wasn't easy."

"That's no excuse to be a dick."

Blair laughed. "No. But it explains it a little, at least."

Dylan laughed too, and then they sat there, people dancing and whooping around them, finally a comfortable peace between them. A real one. Air cleared, shit owned.

And god, it felt good.

It felt good just to be honest, to take responsibility for her choices. Dylan had been putting shit on her parents for so long, and sure, they held their share of the blame for a lot of things, and like Blair said, that explained a lot, but this was Dylan's life.

Not Jack's or Carrie's.

And Dylan decided its shape and path.

"Hey, you two," Iris Kelly said, approaching their table. She had on a pair of navy high-waisted pants covered in yellow suns and moons and a green crop top. Her red hair was long and thick, tiny braids woven throughout. "I've been looking for you. May I?" She gestured to the other chair at the table.

"Please," Blair said, sliding her wineglass out of Iris's way.

Iris sat, took a sip of her own white wine. "I just wanted to tell you both how wonderful you were. Truly, I couldn't have imagined a more perfect Eloise and Mallory."

"Really?" Dylan asked.

Iris laughed. "Really. That surprises you?"

"A little," Dylan said, laughing too. "Took me a while to find Eloise."

"She did it though," Blair said, winking at Dylan.

"She absolutely did," Iris said. "Thank you both. This has been a dream come true for me."

"Thank *you* for writing a kick-ass queer romance," Dylan said, lifting her club soda.

"I'll drink to that too," Blair said.

Iris beamed and they all clinked glasses and took a sip, then Iris glanced around the room.

"Where's your girlfriend, Dylan?" she asked. "Ramona, right?"

Blair just widened her eyes at Dylan, as though waiting for the answer too, even though Dylan knew she already knew what had happened between them.

"I'm not sure," Dylan said, her stomach tightening. "She's not my girlfriend."

"Oh," Iris said, making a *yikes* face. "Sorry. Put my foot in my mouth. I tend to do that."

Dylan waved a hand. "It's fine."

An awkward silence filtered between them.

"Okay, I'm just going to keep my foot in my mouth and ask what happened," Iris said.

Dylan managed a weak laugh, then shrugged. "We just . . ." She trailed off, shook her head. "I fucked it up. Wasn't honest, was destructive. The usual self-sabotaging behavior."

Iris pursed her mouth. "I know something about that."

Dylan perked up at that. "Do you?"

Iris laughed. "Oh my god, yes. My partner and I had a rocky road to getting together."

"Stevie Scott, right?" Blair asked.

Iris grinned, as though just her partner's name filled her with light. "That's her."

"So what happened?" Dylan asked, suddenly ravenous for some camaraderie.

"I fucked it up," Iris said, smiling at Dylan. "Wasn't honest, was destructive. The usual self-sabotaging behavior."

Dylan smiled back, and then Iris told them about her and Stevie's journey, which started out as a disastrous one-night stand, turned into fake dating so Stevie could save face in front of an ex, and resulted in falling in love.

"That's wild," Blair said, "but I went through something similar with my partner."

"You did?" Dylan asked.

Blair nodded. "When Harlow suggested moving in together a few months ago, I totally freaked out."

"Sounds about right," Iris said.

"It's just so huge, you know?" Blair said. "A million doubts flooded my brain—what if they didn't like me once we lived together? What if they hated the way I made coffee, or that I need, like, three blankets when I sleep even in the middle of summer?"

"Oh, that is annoying," Iris said, but nudged Blair's arm with a smile.

Blair grinned. "Letting someone in is always a little scary. No matter who you are or what you've been through. But it's always worth it."

"And *I* will cheers to that," Iris said, lifting her glass.

Blair laughed, clinked her glass with Iris's again, but Dylan was lost in thought. Maybe Iris and Blair were right. Maybe most people were just terrified that they wouldn't be loved if someone saw them for who they really were. As Dylan sat there in Four Leaf, she realized that pretty much summed up her entire life.

She was scared.

All the time.

That no one would ever really love her.

Not Dylan Monroe. But *her*.

And it wasn't just Ramona. It was her parents and past friends Dylan shoved out of her life for that very reason, every lover she'd ever had.

"Well, shit," she said, then gulped at her club soda, letting the bubbles burn her throat all the way down.

Chapter Forty

TWO DAYS LATER, Dylan pulled through the gate and into the diamond-patterned driveway of a modern white house in Laurel Canyon. Greenery hugged the property, and myriad tiny plants were built into the wide stone stairs that led to the front door.

It was evening, and Jack and Carrie's house in LA was softly lit and quiet, the sky a lavender blue. The glassed-in balcony overlooked an infinity pool, and a modern copper fountain burbled near the front walkway, succulents and greens nestled all around.

Dylan sat in her car for a few minutes. She assumed her parents had been alerted to her use of their gate code, but the front door remained closed. She hadn't talked to either one of them all that much since her mother's declaration at Dylan's rental in Clover Lake a few weeks ago. She wasn't even sure when they'd left Clover Lake. Her father, of course, witnessed her and Ramona falling apart, but the only direct contact she'd had with them was a text from Carrie the day after the breakup—We love you.

That was all it said.

And Dylan hadn't even responded, because she'd never known

how to respond to her parents' acts or words of love. She didn't trust them. Wasn't sure she knew *how* to trust them.

The only thing she did know was that she was tired. She was tired of feeling angry, of feeling hurt and wounded all the time. She was tired of blaming Jack and Carrie for everything that was wrong with her life.

And at the end of the day, right now, she just wanted her parents. Not Jack Monroe and Carrie Page, two people the entire world recognized and idolized.

Just Mom and Dad.

She took a deep breath, then opened her car door. Stepped out on the pristine walkway, all white stone and bright green grass. She made it to the front door without turning back, so she counted that as progress.

Baby steps, as the cliché saying went, but right now, she'd take every win she could get.

She stared at the giant oak door for what felt like a long time, the water from the fountain whispering behind her. She couldn't remember the last time she'd been here, though her parents had lived in this house for ten years. Her throat went a little thick at the thought—she felt suddenly young and unsure.

Like that toddler sleeping on the pizza box in a destroyed hotel room.

But she wasn't that kid anymore.

And her parents weren't those parents.

She reached out and rang the doorbell. Before the chime even stopped ringing through the house, the door flew open, and there was her mother, that short silver hair and all her gold chains, her icy eyes wide and liquid, as though she'd been standing in the foyer, waiting for Dylan to make the first move.

They stared at each other for a second, and then Dylan stepped forward and fell into her mother's arms.

THEY SAT OUTSIDE on the patio, all of them sipping on some sort of mango green tea Carrie was obsessed with, enjoying the last bites of a spicy coconut curry Jack had made himself. The late July breeze drifting through the hills was warm, the sky cloudless and full of stars.

It was a perfect night, by all accounts, and Dylan couldn't remember the last time she'd felt this comfortable with her parents.

The evening hadn't started off quite so easily.

After that initial embrace, Dylan and Carrie had made it to the living room—a giant space with a huge cream sectional, sage-green and coral pillows, the room emulating a calm coastal day. Jack had poured them all a glass of the tea, and then they'd talked.

Really talked.

Sometimes voices were raised.

Sometimes they cried.

Sometimes they all got quiet, because they didn't know what to say or how to say it. The realization that the past was the past washed over them more than once, a hard reality that they couldn't change any of it.

But they communicated. With words that meant something, and they all shared and they all listened. Dylan still responded with some passive-aggressive jabs here and there, and Jack still tried to act as though love were enough to wipe away past transgressions, and Carrie still tried to explain away those past transgressions, because none of them were perfect. But this was the first real conversation the three of them had experienced.

Ever.

It was hard and only a start, but it was *good*.

Now, as Dylan sat at the table with her parents, she felt completely drained. She was exhausted, but in a good way. In a *fresh start* kind of way.

"So what's next, Dill Pickle?" Jack said, dipping a hunk of bread into his bowl of curry. "You really blew everyone away with this last project."

Dylan smiled, her hands folded on her stomach. "I don't know if I blew them away."

Jack shook his head. "You did, you did. You really showed them."

Dylan was tempted to ask, *Showed them what?* but she knew. It wasn't a secret how she had been viewed in Hollywood—how she was still viewed by the majority of the industry—but she hoped *As If You Didn't Know* would change all that once it was released.

She was proud of it.

Proud of herself.

"Maybe I did," she said, and Jack winked at her.

"Laurel and Adriana have anything lined up for you next?" Carrie asked.

Dylan sighed. She hadn't spoken directly to anyone on her team since she'd been back in LA. Honestly, she needed a break from it all, from their plotting and their plans for her, even though she knew they were just doing their jobs.

Her lack of honesty regarding Ramona was on her.

Still, there were a few scripts in her inbox that Adriana had sent her way, all from casting directors for the exact kinds of projects Dylan was looking for. There was even one for a biopic about Marlene Dietrich, who was famously bisexual and loved to don a pantsuit in the 1920s and '30s. It was the role of a lifetime, and Dylan wanted it. She just had to get her head—and heart—on straight first.

"I don't know what's next," she said, sipping on her tea. "Still figuring some things out."

"Things," Carrie said, shooting Jack a look.

"Yes," Dylan said slowly. "Things."

"Things as in . . . people?" Carrie asked. "One person, maybe?"

"Subtle, Mom," Dylan said.

Carrie spread her hands in surrender. "I'm just saying."

"She seemed like a sweetheart," Jack said. "Wish we could've spent more time with her."

Dylan rubbed her temples. "I think talking about Ramona is a bit too much for tonight."

"That's fair, honey," Carrie said, nodding. "We just want you to be happy and you seemed . . . happy with her."

Dylan didn't say anything.

But Carrie was right.

Dylan had been happy with Ramona. So fucking happy. She'd never felt like that with any of her past lovers, never ached for them so much after everything ended. Never racked her brain so much about what she could've—*should've*—done differently.

Letting someone in is always a little scary. No matter who you are or what you've been through. But it's always worth it.

Blair's words echoed through her thoughts for the millionth time since the wrap party.

It's always worth it.

Dylan gulped some more tea, her throat dry—not from a sudden realization, but from this constant *knowing.*

She wanted Ramona Riley in her life.

By her side.

Her hand in hers, their lives tangled together. She'd known it before they broke up, but she also knew, without a doubt, that she had to work on herself first. And even now, as she was doing that work, she wasn't sure she'd ever be worthy of Ramona, that she'd ever be able to mesh their lives together the way she wanted.

She groaned, dropped her head into her hands.

"Oh, honey," Carrie said, leaning forward and placing a hand on her arm. "You'll figure it out."

Dylan shook her head. "I don't know if I will. She's too good for me."

"Nonsense," Jack said.

"I fucked up. She won't forgive me."

"You never know until you *ask* for that forgiveness," Carrie said, squeezing her arm.

"She's in Clover Lake," Dylan said, slumping back in her chair. "Her whole life is there."

Both Jack's and Carrie's brows lifted. They looked at each other, eyes wide.

"What?" Dylan asked, shifting in her seat. "What is it?"

"Pickle," Jack said slowly, "Ramona's in LA."

The words didn't register at first. Didn't make sense.

"She's what?" she asked.

Jack laughed a little nervously. "She's in LA."

Dylan just stared at her father.

"She took a job working for Noelle Yang," Carrie said. "I heard it from Noelle herself when I called her about a gown for the premiere. You didn't know?"

Dylan's mouth opened, then closed again. She'd had no idea. She hadn't really seen Ramona for more than a split second since their breakup, and no one on the film's set mentioned her to Dylan. It had been like some unspoken rule, some protection Dylan never asked for.

Dylan sat there, trying to figure out how she felt about this new development. There was some hurt over the fact that she'd been in the dark about this huge opportunity, that Ramona hadn't told her. But as she slowed herself down, really let the emotions just *be*, as Eli would say, she realized how unfair that hurt was. Her feelings were what they were, sure, but she'd never asked Ramona about her dreams. Never looked beyond her own issues to really see what Ramona's might have been. And god, right now, sitting with her parents in Laurel Canyon, she wanted to know them. She wanted to know them all. She wanted to know what Ramona dreamed about costume design, and she wanted to know about this new job with Noelle. She wanted to know why Ramona never felt comfortable telling Dylan the truth, and she wanted to tell Ramona how sorry she was.

She wanted Ramona.

"Shit," she said, pressing her hands to her mouth. "You think—"

"Yes," Carrie said emphatically. "Yes, I really do think."

Dylan just stared at her mother, her mind whirling with *what* and *how* and *if.*

If.

That was the big one. *The* question.

And there was only one way to answer it.

Chapter Forty-One

"SO THIS IS LA," April said.

Ramona stood on her tiny apartment's even tinier balcony, squashed between her best friend and her sister, and gazed out at the evening vista that was her new home. The sun was just starting to set, sending pink and purple and orange across the sky.

"Strip malls and pine trees," Olive said.

"With mountains in the distance," April said in an ethereal voice, spreading her free hand over the view.

Ramona laughed. "How about constant sunshine and perpetually seventy-five degrees?"

"Ugh," April said, but she was smiling as she held out her arms to the sun. "No one needs this much cheer. Give me some moody clouds and a stormy lake any day."

Ramona shook her head, but when she took a deep breath, it was shaky.

She was here.

She *lived* in LA.

She had a job working for Noelle Yang.

Her actual dreams had come true, and yet, everything still felt nebulous, unreal. She had arrived in town only a few days ago, and she'd been so busy unpacking and trying to set up the apartment in Silver Lake that Noelle had helped her find, she'd barely had time to process it all.

She hadn't really been able to process anything since the night she'd decided to take the job, the night Olive came home from visiting their mother.

Olive had taken a few days to tell Ramona what happened, and even then, there hadn't been all that much to say. Olive shared that Rebecca—that's what Olive had called her, *Rebecca*—was very nice, but clearly wasn't interested in being a mother.

Ever.

"She never said as much," Olive had said. She and Ramona were in Ramona's room, packing up her things for LA. "It was just a feeling I got, you know? Like, she'd take me out to dinner, but then just talked about herself a lot."

"She didn't ask about you at all?" Ramona asked, teeth already clenching.

"No, she did," Olive said, folding a pair of Ramona's jeans. "It just felt . . . I don't know. Like she asked because she knew she should, not because she actually cared." Olive shrugged. "Maybe I'm reading into it too much."

Ramona zipped up a suitcase that was already full, then moved closer to her sister. She smoothed a hand down her hair. "I'm sorry, honey."

Olive had looked at her then, her eyes shiny. "I'm sorry too."

Ramona frowned. "For what?"

"I don't know," Olive said. Her lower lip trembled a little. "Just . . . thanks. You . . . you've given me everything I need. You and Dad."

Ramona had to fight to keep the tears at bay right then, but when Olive fell into her arms, hugging her tight for a long time, she let them fall anyway. And in that moment, everything was worth it.

Olive had always been worth it, but Ramona felt it so keenly then, a gratitude that she got to know this person in her arms, got to help her become who she was.

Now, Ramona smiled at Olive, happy to have her in LA, if only for a short time. Her apartment was pretty much set up, Noelle didn't need her for another three days, and she couldn't wait to explore the city with her two favorite people.

"What should we do over the next few days?" she asked, turning around and pressing her back to the balcony railing.

"I want to see the Hollywood sign before I leave," Olive said.

"Some studios would be fun," April said, scrolling through her phone. "Oh, the tar pits. Oh, wait, I've got it." She looked up and grinned. "Celebrity house tours."

She quirked an eyebrow at Ramona, who tried to ignore both April's and Olive's charged silence at the mention of *celebrity*.

"No thanks," she said coolly, then turned around to look at the city again. She very much doubted Dylan's house would be on such a tour, as those things usually included classic Hollywood icons like Cary Grant and Rita Hayworth.

But Jack Monroe and Carrie Page?

They might be on a tour like that, especially if it was a more modern excursion through LA.

"Mona," April said. "You're really not curious?"

Ramona didn't answer. It wasn't that she wasn't curious.

She definitely was.

She hadn't seen or talked to Dylan in nearly a month. Hadn't gone to the wrap party in Clover Lake. She had prepared the costumes for the film those last two weeks with such meticulousness, all Noelle had to do was pick them up and hand them to whatever actor they were intended for. And Noelle, being a classy person, did just that. She never asked Ramona to deal with Dylan once she was in a costume, and Ramona appreciated that courtesy more than she could verbalize. A badass like Noelle Yang certainly didn't have to think of Ramona's heart when dealing with work, but she had.

And Ramona was forever grateful.

Because, no, her thoughts and feelings regarding Dylan weren't about curiosity.

They were about survival.

She couldn't let herself drift back into memories and what-ifs, because she didn't think her heart would survive it if she did. She wasn't worried about crying or simply feeling sad.

She was worried about disappearing into those feelings.

Right now, it was too fresh, and her heart was too battered, too tender to face that kind of battle. She was healing, wasn't ready for combat, and she knew it would take time—maybe a long time—to get over Dylan Monroe.

Because the fact was, Ramona loved her.

Loved her so much she sometimes couldn't breathe, couldn't see straight, couldn't remember what she'd been doing when the memory of a kiss or mushrooms or the way Dylan liked to link her pinkie with Ramona's when they walked down the street washed over her, a surprise tsunami. No matter what had happened or how it ended, no matter that Dylan had fake dated Ramona to smooth over her image problem, Ramona had fallen in love with Dylan.

And she needed time to fall out.

She took a deep breath, then focused her brain on dinner for the night. "How about—"

"The Griffith Observatory," April blurted loudly.

Ramona turned to look at her best friend, who was staring down at her phone, her brows wrinkled.

"What did you say?" Ramona asked.

April looked up at her. "The Griffith Observatory."

Ramona's breath stilled in her chest, her lungs suddenly refusing to fill.

I'd go to the Griffith Observatory. Every day at sunset. It's gorgeous then. Soft and romantic and perfect.

"The . . . the Griffith Observatory?" Ramona asked. "Why are you talking about the Griffith Observatory?"

April handed over her phone. Olive pressed closer to Ramona, looking over her shoulder at the screen.

At first, she only registered pictures of the sky—tiny squares, three across, the LA skyline at sunset. But then she realized she was looking at Dylan's Instagram page, and her hand flew to her mouth.

Because these were pictures of the Griffith Observatory at sunset.

And I'd post a picture on my Instagram every day that I went. No caption, or maybe a caption only you would understand.

Underneath each picture, there were only two things in the caption—a cherry emoji and a lollipop emoji.

"Oh my god," Ramona said.

"What?" Olive asked. "What does it mean?"

"I don't know," April said. "But I feel like those emojis can't be a coincidence."

"Emojis?" Olive asked, squinting at the screen. "What does a cherry and a lollipop have to do with anything?"

"Cherry," Ramona said. "Cherry and Lolli." She looked up at her sister. "That's what Dylan and I called each other the first time we met when we were thirteen."

Olive's mouth opened, then closed again. She squeezed Ramona's arm, a gentle weight that Ramona needed right now.

And I'd wait there for you every day until the observatory closed for five days.

"Oh my god," Ramona said.

"What?" April asked.

Only five?

"Oh my *god*," Ramona said again.

"What, what?" April said, her voice nearly a screech.

I figure that's enough time for you to know if you wanted to see me.

Ramona counted the photos—today's photo, posted just twenty minutes ago, was the fifth one. Ramona felt frozen, locked in place by a million emotions.

It was true that she needed time to fall out of love with Dylan Monroe. And no, she didn't want to think about Dylan for too long, too much.

But that was before.

Before these pictures.

Before five minutes ago that changed everything.

Because yes, goddammit, yes, she loved Dylan Monroe.

And if she was reading this right, remembering right, and she *knew* she was, Dylan Monroe loved her too.

She looked up at April and Olive, who were waiting, their own breaths shallow, their eyes wide. And then she asked the only question that mattered right now, the only thing that mattered in the entire universe.

"How long does it take to get to the Griffith Observatory?"

Chapter Forty-Two

DYLAN STOOD OUTSIDE on Griffith Observatory's deck, the white stone cool under her forearms. She had on light-wash jeans, a plain black baseball cap over her long hair, and a fitted black T-shirt with the word *Nonchalance* spelled across the chest in white capital letters. It was a David Rose shirt from *Schitt's Creek*, one of her favorite shows ever, but it was also incredibly ironic.

She felt anything but nonchalant right now.

This was her fifth night in a row at Griffith. Her fifth time using her parents' annual pass to get into the observatory. Her fifth time watching the sun set over the city from the deck. Her fifth time waiting . . . waiting . . . waiting, jumping every time someone came out onto the deck. And as it was summer, the town swollen with tourists, this happened approximately every five seconds.

Still, it wasn't the waiting that bothered her. She'd always loved it here. She remembered her parents bringing her here once or twice during the more stable times in her childhood, and her aunt Hallie loved the observatory too. She'd bring Dylan any time she was in town, and they'd spend hours on this deck after the sun went down, staring at the night sky through the telescopes, dreaming up stories for the constellations.

But on this fifth night, the last night she'd told Ramona she'd wait for her—the last night she'd told *herself* she'd wait for her—her stomach was in knots. Suddenly, this entire plan seemed silly and childish. Too hopeful for reality.

Of course Ramona didn't pine over Dylan's Instagram.

Of course Ramona wouldn't come and meet her here, even if, by the smallest of chances, she did happen to see Dylan's posts.

Dream on, Dylan Monroe, she told herself.

Still, she would wait. She'd wait and wait until ten p.m. when the observatory closed, and Harold, the night security guard, found her on the deck once again and escorted her from the building, tipping his hat and saying, *Have a good night, Ms. Monroe*, even though she had covered most of her face and he never let on that *Ms. Monroe* was anyone all that famous.

She sort of loved him for that.

"Good ole Harold," she whispered into the evening air. It was nearly dark now, a Friday night, the observatory busier than usual. Families and couples wandered over the deck, holding hands, laughing, and still she waited.

She sighed, started thinking about what would come next, about how she'd have to give this up after tonight. Give Ramona up. Move on and all that. The thought made her feel lonely, a hollowness in her chest she could physically feel, but she could do it.

She could do anything.

And maybe, that was the point of all this, in the end.

Dylan Monroe could do anything she wanted. She could act in a rom-com. She could act in a horror film or biopic or a miniseries about spies. She could recognize her mistakes and own them. She could become friends with Blair Emmanuel.

She could forgive her parents.

She could forgive herself.

She could start fresh, remake, redo, be, become.

She smiled a little and gazed out at the city, a sort of contentment mingling with that cavernous feeling in her core. But still, she waited.

She waited, and she waited, and she—

"Dylan?"

At the sound of her name, she didn't react. Not right away. There were so many people out here, someone might have recognized her despite her best efforts. Best to ignore it. Still, those two syllables sent her stomach fluttering. And then . . .

"Dylan."

Not a question.

A statement. Wrapped in a soft, familiar voice.

She straightened, turned just a little, just enough to see her.

Ramona.

She stood about five feet away. Her hair was loose and wavy, bangs a little longer than the last time Dylan had seen her, sweeping over her forehead.

She wore a cherry-print T-shirt.

"Hi," Dylan said.

"Hi," Ramona said. She folded her hands in front of her.

"You're here," Dylan said.

Ramona's chest lifted with a deep breath. "I am."

Dylan took a tentative step toward her. "I was starting to think it wasn't meant to be."

Ramona didn't refute it, she simply tilted her head, her eyes liquid and deep brown. "You really came here every night for the last four nights?"

"Five, if you count tonight," Dylan said.

Ramona shook her head, looked down, her lower lip trembling. Dylan let her have a minute. She needed one herself, because for all her dreaming of this very moment, she had no idea what came next, how to tell Ramona everything in her heart.

But then suddenly, she did. And the next step was so simple, so perfect. So right.

"Ramona," she said. Another step.

Ramona looked up, her eyes shiny.

"I'm so sorry," Dylan said. One more step, and she was right in front of Ramona, close enough to touch. She didn't though. Didn't dare. She hadn't earned that privilege yet. "I'm so, so sorry for everything. I should've told you what my publicity team wanted. I should've told you that I'd agreed to it. But I swear on every single weird mushroom that resembles a brain on the entire earth"— Ramona cracked a smile, but it was small and fragile—"I *wanted* to date you."

Ramona didn't say anything for a second, so Dylan went on.

"I wanted *you*," she said. "Yeah, it started casual, some summer fun, but that changed so quickly for me."

"It did?" Ramona asked.

"God, yes," Dylan said, her throat going a little thick. "You . . ." She took a shaky breath. "You are impossible not to love, Ramona Riley."

Tears spilled down Ramona's cheeks, silent and beautiful. Dylan wanted so badly to wipe them away, take Ramona's face in her hands, but she still didn't dare.

"I'm sorry too," Ramona said. "I should've told you about costume design, about my dreams. I just . . ." She took a deep breath. "I never wanted to make you feel how so many other people had made you feel in the past. I *did* want to meet Noelle. And I *did* think you could help me with that. But from the moment you walked in Clover Moon Café that day, walked back into my life, I knew it was never about Noelle or costume design or any opportunities that knowing you might get me."

"No?" Dylan said. Her heart felt huge and tender in her chest.

Ramona shook her head, took a step closer. Their chests

brushed, and she placed her hands on Dylan's wrists, slid her hands down until they tangled with Dylan's fingers. Dylan nearly cried in relief, the contact, the physical touch like a gasp of air.

"It was about us," Ramona said. "You and me. Cherry and Lolli."

Dylan smiled, her own tears breaking free now.

"Ramona and Dylan," Ramona said.

"Dylan and Ramona," Dylan said, and then she did take Ramona's face in her hands. And she did wipe away her tears. And she did kiss her. And she kissed her and kissed her and kissed her, until Harold came up to the deck and escorted them both out into the world.

Chapter Forty-Three

TEN MONTHS LATER

RAMONA SAT IN a turquoise Adirondack chair on a pier over-looking Clover Lake, the twilit sky reflecting purple and pink on the water. The late May air was perfectly crisp and carried the scents she'd missed so much these last months living in LA—a loamy forest, that mineral-lake smell from the water. Behind her, the sound of her father laughing with Jack Monroe as they grilled hamburgers and debated guitar legends made her smile, which only broadened when she spotted Olive and Marley share a small kiss in the canoe they'd taken out on the lake to watch the sunset.

"I didn't think Olive would ever get wise," April said, sliding into the Adirondack chair next to Ramona's and handing her an open bottle of beer.

Ramona laughed. "Amazing what sharing a tiny space will do."

"Right?" April said. "Junior year at RISD, I think I slept with my roommate before even learning her last name."

Ramona clinked her beer against April's. "To roommates."

April rolled her eyes. "I think *room*mates is a bit of a stretch to describe you and Dylan," she said, but drank to the toast regardless.

Ramona just smiled bigger. She and Dylan had recently moved in together in LA. Dylan had sold her house in Silver Lake in favor of renting a smaller bungalow in Hollywood Hills—the price was still astronomical, and Ramona's share felt like a drop in the proverbial bucket, but at least the house was cozy, felt more like a home to Ramona than her apartment had or Dylan's cavernous white house, which hadn't even felt like Dylan.

They'd barely moved in when Ramona's work on Noelle's latest project wrapped up, and she and Dylan flew east to stay in this waterfront house at Clover Lake for the next month—adorable and sky blue with navy trim, right near the cove where they'd first kissed all those years ago. Ramona was looking forward to a quiet summer with Dylan, with her family and April, whom she'd missed so much.

Once settled in LA, the homesickness was overwhelming at first. While happy to be reconciled with Dylan, they still lived apart, and Noelle's next film project after *As If You Didn't Know* was a period piece that took far more designing than buying, which Ramona loved. It was also completely exhausting, taking most of her energy during the day, and sometimes deep into night and early morning hours.

Still, every sleepless night was worth it, every skipped meal, and she knew she did good work for Noelle. Meanwhile, Dylan took a couple of months off to read scripts, went to a lot of therapy, and worked on her relationship with her parents. It was hard work, and sometimes Dylan didn't know how to express just how hard it all was, but luckily, patience was one of Ramona's virtues—that, and the fact that she was so wild about Dylan Monroe, she'd take her as a disaster, as a paragon of mental health, and every gray area in between. She was proud of Dylan, proud too of Jack and Carrie, to whom Ramona had grown quite close—they were even staying with Ramona and Dylan in Clover Lake for the next week.

Now, Ramona watched her sister climb out of the canoe, holding Marley's hand, a familiar ache in her chest she could never quite shake. It was a sweet ache though, one that meant she loved her

sister, her dad, her family. Olive had had a great first year at Vanderbilt, had fallen in love, come out as bisexual. Ramona couldn't be
happier for her.

"Did you read Penny's latest post?" April asked, handing over
her phone.

"Oh, lord," Ramona said, setting her beer on the chair's arm and
taking April's device. "Does it read like the *Hollywood Reporter*?"

April moved her hand in a teeter-totter motion. "Slightly
classier."

Ramona shook her head, then started to read the latest edition
of *Penny for Your Thoughts*.

> Happy May, my dear Cloverians, that lovely month of
> warm(ish) weather and the calm before the storm of
> the Summer People™ arrives. While we're all still wait-
> ing with bated breath to find out who Natalie Jacobs
> will choose to walk down the aisle with—her longtime
> boyfriend Dave, or Logan, everyone's favorite golden
> boy furniture maker who professed his undying love to
> Natalie just weeks ago—the mayor has asked every-
> one to please stop betting money on the union. These
> are people's hearts, Cloverians! Have some dignity.
>
> Meanwhile, this summer proves to be much quieter
> than the last. Much to my own personal disappoint-
> ment, no Hollywood studios and film crews are on
> their way here to shoot a movie. Though we are all ex-
> tremely excited about next month's national release
> of *As If You Didn't Know*, last summer's dramatic rom-
> com that had our local darling, Ramona Riley, riding
> high on her own romantic escapades.
>
> Well, move over, Natalie, because Ramona and
> Dylan Monroe—yes, that Dylan Monroe, who fell for

our dear Ramona last summer and then mucked it all up in the last days of shooting—are back in Clover Lake after reuniting at the end of last summer in La-La Land. They've been living in romantic bliss in sunny California for the last ten months while Ramona worked for the legendary Noelle Yang on a project that this author hears is going to get plenty of Oscar nods.

Dylan, however, has been quieter on the career front. The gossip rags have posted lots of photos with her and her parents—and our Ramona!—out at brunch and at parks and shopping, like any normal family might do. She hasn't yet officially signed on for another project since *As If You Didn't Know*, but this author has heard rumblings that she's recently committed to a Marlene Dietrich biopic, which would be a career maker for anyone in Hollywood.

Well, I say, bring on the bisexuals!

Ramona chuckled at Penny's flair, but wondered, not for the first time, how the hell Penny learned all this information. She was gossipy, but, as far as Ramona could tell throughout Penny's entire time running her blog, she was also wildly accurate.

"She's clairvoyant, I swear to god," Ramona said, handing April back her phone.

"Who's clairvoyant?" Dylan said, walking down the pier toward them, a can of sparkling water dangling from her fingers. She wore a pair of cutoff shorts and a purple bikini top. There were only two chairs, so she slid into Ramona's lap, kissed her on the cheek.

"Penny," Ramona said. "She knows all about the Marlene Dietrich biopic."

Dylan just shook her head. "*Variety* hasn't even announced that yet."

"As I said, clairvoyant," Ramona said.

"Speaking of," April said, clearing her throat and tapping on her phone.

"Oh god, no, please," Ramona said, pressing her face into Dylan's bare back.

"This week in Libra land . . ." April started, but then Ramona snagged her phone before she could continue. "Hey!"

"What we really need is some Scorpio action," Ramona said, scrolling through Madame Andromeda's page to Scorpio's horoscope.

"I think not," April said, trying to grab the phone back.

Ramona held it out of her reach, eyeing her suspiciously. "You already read it."

"I did not."

"You read it, and you don't like what it says," Ramona said.

"Lies!" April said, still waving her hand around for the phone.

Dylan just laughed at them and sipped her drink.

"Ahem," Ramona said, holding the phone high into the air and squinting at the text. *"As a Scorpio, you crave mystery and intrigue and magic, but that often leaves you feeling like no one can quite understand you. Keep in mind that what we need most in life is often the last thing we can imagine wanting. To truly be happy, we must sometimes step outside of the proverbial box."*

Ramona lifted her brows at her best friend. "That sounds like you need to take some risks, April Evans."

April stood up and grabbed her phone from Ramona, huffing as she stalked off toward the house.

"I love you!" Ramona called after her, giggling.

April just flipped her off.

"I really need to hear this ex-fiancée story," Dylan said.

Ramona wrapped her arms tighter around Dylan. "I'll leave it to April tell you that grisly tale of woe."

"I'm intrigued."

"Oh, it's intriguing all right."

"I take it she and Leigh aren't MFEO?"

"Leigh's a player," Ramona said. "And no, Leigh is back in Chicago."

Dylan laughed and Ramona just grinned, held her tighter. The water rippled under the sun, and Ramona let out a sigh of contentment so long and happy, Dylan chuckled and kissed her neck. Ramona lifted her chin for a real kiss.

"I'm glad you came along to shift my perspective and deepen my understanding of my life's purpose," Ramona said against her mouth.

Dylan laughed. "Um, what?"

Ramona smiled. "The day I learned you were coming back to Clover Lake, that was my horoscope. *Be prepared for challenges and opportunities that could shift your perspective and deepen your understanding of your life's purpose.*"

"So I was a challenge, huh?"

"A beautiful"—*kiss*—"life-changing challenge."

Dylan grinned, then stood and held out her hand to Ramona. Ramona took it, waiting as Dylan fiddled with her phone. A second later, a song burbled out of the tiny speaker, tinny and quiet, but perfect at the same time.

Hello, Dolly, well, hello, Dolly . . .

"Dance with me?" Dylan asked.

"Always," Ramona said, then smiled as Dylan settled her hands on Ramona's waist. Ramona looped her arms around Dylan's neck, pulling her close. She breathed her in, summer air and citrus, laughing as Dylan sang the words in Ramona's ear, quiet and awful.

"Wow, you're terrible at singing," Ramona said.

"Shh, don't tell my parents," Dylan said, twirling Ramona in a circle.

"I'll keep all your secrets, Dylan Monroe."

Ramona could feel Dylan smile against her cheek. "And I'll keep yours, Ramona Riley. Every secret and every dream."

They stayed like that for a while, just Cherry and Lolli, whispering secrets and dreams while the sun dipped closer and closer to the water.

Acknowledgments

This book was so fun to write. I hope you love Dylan and Ramona as much as I do, dear readers. Thank you for following me on this new series journey. Thank you for reading, sharing, and recommending! Thank you, librarians and booksellers, for being generous, kind, and enthusiastic ambassadors of romance.

Thank you, as always, to my agent Rebecca Podos, a fearless and constant champion. Thank you, Angela Kim, my editor, who supports, encourages, and helps me make these stories the best they can be. Thanks to my team at Berkley, including Kristin Cipolla, Tina Joell, Elisha Katz, Tara O'Connor, and everyone at Berkley who has helped bring this book into the world.

Thank you, Katie Anderson, for your flawless cover design. And thank you Leni Kauffman for your cover illustration—as always, you breathe beautiful, colorful life into these characters, and I'm forever grateful.

Thank you, Brooke, for being my first reader, as always. Your enthusiasm gives so much comfort and confidence! Thank you, Meryl for your tireless support, humor, and love—and so.

Thank you, Zabe, Emma, Crash, Mary, Mary, and Christina, for being a ding dang awesome group of writer pals.

Thank you, Craig, for always carving space for these stories in our lives. Thank you, Benjamin and William for being excited for every new endeavor even though you're still far too young to read these books. I absolutely adore the people you are becoming.

I started off thanking my readers, and I'd like to end the same way. Thank you, thank you.

Keep reading for an excerpt of

Get Over It, April Evans

The next contemporary romance by Ashley Herring Blake

APRIL EVANS KNEW she was prone to astrological panic.

She'd always put a lot of stock in the stars, knew when some planet's position was messing with everyone's communication skills, and had three different Zodiac-themed tattoos. Still, she'd like to think *panic* was the wrong word, despite what her parents would say about it. She was simply dealing with at least twenty complicated feelings at any given time, just like any triple Scorpio.

But right now, as she stood in her own driveway and handed her house keys over to a divorced MILF with shiny brown hair named Trudy, while her two kids poked their fingers through the holes of April's cat carriers, April definitely felt a sense of astrological doom.

"So garbage day is on Monday," she said to Trudy, even though these sorts of details were posted on the refrigerator. "And if you have any trouble with the faucet in the hallway bathroom, just shoot me a text."

"Perfect," Trudy said, tucking the keys into her linen shorts. "I know the kids and I are going to love summering here. Your house is adorable. So eclectic!"

April smiled without her teeth, her eyes gazing up at her admittedly adorable mint-green bungalow. She'd bought it nearly eight years ago, the first year her tattoo shop made a profit, and now she was a landlord, renting it out to a Clover Lake summer person for the next three months because she could no longer afford her mortgage.

She looked at all her houseplants on the front porch, which Trudy had promised to water, but she nevertheless had a sinking feeling in her gut they'd all be dried out and brown by August.

Just like her life.

Okay, fine, that was dramatic, but in her defense, her horoscope for the last month had been nothing but darkness and gloom, words like *change* and *risk* and *decisions* constantly floating before her eyes. She shivered, thinking of Madame Andromeda's declaration about her life just this very morning.

Lately, you've been feeling small and overlooked. As a Scorpio, this is unfamiliar territory. So this week, try to view challenges as bright new opportunities to grow—there is always something beautiful hiding in the unexpected.

She was fucking tired of *unexpected*. And while she was a devout believer in Andromeda's clairvoyant insights, this proclamation was simply a sugar-coated way of saying *Buckle up, bitch.*

And she'd really, really rather not.

"Mommy, can't we keep the kitties?" one of the Trudy's kids asked. The smaller one named Coltrane or Copeland or something else that sounded like a jazz musician's last name. The tiny imp pressed her face against the carrier's door. Bianca del Kitty, April's grouchy lynx point Siamese cat she'd had for seven years, hissed, while Bob the Drag Cat, her beloved orange dum-dum, lounged in his own carrier like he was at a spa.

"I don't think so, honey," Trudy said, but then lifted her eyebrows at April. "Any chance you need a couple of cat sitters for the summer?" She placed a hand on top of each of her children's heads. "They'd take good care of them."

April nearly clutched at her chest, appalled. This woman had taken her house—granted, April had freely offered it to her—but she would not take her fucking cats.

They were literally all she had at this point.

Two cats, one broken-down business, and a partridge in a pear tree.

In reality, she knew she had a lot more than that, like disapproving parents and a failed engagement, a best friend who lived three thousand miles away and hadn't responded to her last three texts, and a love life that made her want to drill a hole through her skull. Add *uncertain financial future* to the list, and she was a cornucopia of angst and, well, astrological panic.

"I'm good, thanks," she said as calmly as she could, then said a quick goodbye before she could add *catnapping* to her list of grievances. She grabbed the carrier handles and hauled them to her ten-year-old turquoise Mini Cooper, which was already stuffed to overflowing. She didn't look at her house as she backed out of the driveway, nor did she mentally acknowledge the lump rising in her throat. And she definitely didn't glance at Wonderlust Ink as she drove through downtown, her tattoo shop that she'd only just closed four weeks ago.

Permanently.

She'd been fighting against the decision for over a year. Just six months ago, she'd let Mac go—her only employee, who was now working at a fancy shop in Concord—but that hardly fixed April's financial woes. A small-town like Clover Lake had only so many regular clients, and the summer crowd was no longer keeping her in the black. She'd lived in the red for the last two years, but when she started struggling to pay for high-quality ink and other crucial supplies, she knew it was time to throw in the proverbial towel.

So, about a month ago, she'd referred her regulars to Mac, flipped the sign to *Closed* on her shop door, and proceeded to spend the next week on her couch eating Cheddar Jalapeño Cheetos and trying to will Paris and Rory from *Gilmore Girls* to kiss.

Needless to say, they never smashed, and April had to face the reality of her situation, which was how she ended up renting out her home, packing her bags for the summer, and taking a job teaching an art class at Cloverwild, the fancy new resort opening in just a few days on the north shore. The position came with room and board—a tiny lakeside cabin complete with a cabinmate—and the owner, Mia Gallagher, had asked absolutely zero questions about April's suddenly wide-open schedule when she'd applied.

April hadn't exactly told anyone about closing her business. Not her parents, not her best friend Ramona. Only Bianca and Bob knew her secrets, and they weren't talking. In Clover Lake, it was only a matter of time before the news broke, but she'd like to maintain her dignity as long as possible.

She pulled into a parking spot in front of Clover Moon Café, then stepped out into the warm June sunshine. The New Hampshire weather wouldn't get truly hot until July, so she cracked the windows, promised Bianca and Bob she'd only be a second, then ducked into the café for some coffee. She'd enjoyed a cup this morning, sitting in her quaint kitchen for the last time and soaking up the way the pale sunlight streamed through her vintage-style windows, but she needed another hit to get through this day.

She stepped inside, the bell over the door dinging, and took in the familiar vibe of Clover Moon, all rustic wood, navy and green accents, and mismatched chairs. She slid onto a barstool and smiled at the owner, Owen—a bald man in his fifties and covered in tattoos, a lot of which April did herself.

"Usual latte, please," April said. "Oat milk if you've got it."

"I've got it," he said, wiping down the counter in front of her. "Triple?"

"Do I look like a woman who wants a small amount of caffeine right now?" April asked, plucking at the bags under her eyes.

Owen pressed his lips together. "I'm going to shut my mouth and get to work on a quad shot oat milk latte."

"Good man," April said, then rested her elbows on the counter. Behind her the diner buzzed with activity from the usual clientele—Violet Chalmers sipping on a mocha latte spiked with a few dribbles of Baileys that she kept in her purse; Duke Hansard and his brother, Jake, with their daily helping of sausage links wrapped in buttermilk pancakes, then smothered in strawberry syrup; Logan and Natalie Adler fighting about what to name their soon-to-be-born twins. Personally, April liked Natalie's most recent faves, Maple and Oak.

"Hey, darling, how are those cutie patootie cats of yours?" Penny Hampton asked, popping up next to April like an annoying neighbor in a sitcom.

April startled but managed a smile. "They're little demons."

Penny laughed, clicking her long russet-colored nails on the plastic menu in front of her. "Good company, I imagine."

April said nothing, not sure how to take that. Plus, the last thing she wanted was to show up as some story in Penny's gossip blog, *Penny for Your Thoughts*.

"Any juicy news from Ramona lately?" Penny asked, eyeing April over the tops of her tortoiseshell reading glasses. Her hair was copper red—just like a penny—and April was pretty sure she was wearing bright green contact lenses, which were new.

"Not lately, no," April said, widening her eyes at Owen to hurry it up. He just smirked at her, happily steaming milk.

When people started plying April for Hollywood news, it was time to get the hell out of Dodge. Mostly because she had no idea what Ramona was up to these days. At least, not the details. She knew Ramona was immersed in a historical romance for Netflix with her boss, Noelle Yang. She knew Dylan, Ramona's movie star girlfriend, was just about to wrap filming a biopic that she'd been working on for over a year, in which she played Marlene Dietrich. But specifics? Those details were spotty at best, like bad cell reception on the south end of the lake.

She glanced at her phone, eyes drifting over her and Ramona's last text interaction. Several blue bubbles sent from April, asking Ramona if she thought getting a tattoo of a tattoo gun was a little too on the nose. And underneath the last text—the last text with no response from Ramona—were the words *Read 8:41 PM*.

That was two days ago.

April really didn't want to use the L-word—*lonely*—but ever since Ramona had moved to LA to work as a costume designer nearly two years ago, the word haunted her like Ms. Havisham's ghost. Ramona was crushing it as Noelle's assistant, taking on more and more responsibility with each project. It was everything Ramona had ever wanted, everything she deserved after giving up her whole life when she was nineteen to help raise her little sister after her father's car accident, and she certainly didn't need her small potatoes BFF whining about loneliness and a struggling business.

Still, over the last few months, her texts with Ramona were sporadic at best, and she couldn't remember the last time they'd Face-Timed. She did know, however, that they hadn't seen each other in person since last November, when Ramona and Dylan had come back to Clover Lake with Dylan's '90s rock icon parents for Thanksgiving. Even then, their time was taken up with Ramona's family, and April hadn't wanted to impose.

Her own Thanksgiving was a quiet affair with Dr. and Dr. Evans, sipping red wine around her mother's immaculate table while trying to deal with her father's insistence that she invest Wonderlust's profits—that was a laugh—in the stock market and her mother's constant hints about *settling down*. April didn't think Jacqueline

Evans, a Capricorn through and through, would appreciate April's long-term plans of becoming a cat lady, or how she'd recently decided to give up dating altogether, because what the hell was the point, so instead she'd sipped her drink and gotten a little too tipsy, which had only invited further disapproval from her parents.

Then, after walking home in a red-wine haze because her dad hadn't wanted to drive in the inch of snow that had fallen the night before, she'd promptly opened up her favorite dating app looking for . . . well, *something*, and was met with the same boring people asking her the same boring questions.

Casual dating had been her bread and butter for the last three years, after her engagement had imploded in spectacular fashion, but it all felt so tiresome to her—the first dates that she never had any interest turning into a second, getting naked in front of someone new, the whole song and dance afterward, when all she wanted was go home and sleep in her own bed.

She wasn't really interested in anyone she dated—and hadn't been since Elena. No matter how much she tried to open her mind to possibilities, no one stimulated her imagination or affections, no one made her stomach flutter with that first-crush feeling or caused her heart feel like it was going to bust right through her rib cage. No one made her smile uncontrollably or wake up in the morning marveling at how fucking lucky she was.

Lately, the only thing she woke up to was a hairball vomited up by one of her cats on the kitchen floor.

But even if some Riley or Simon or Anna *had* inspired such feelings, April had been there, done that, and consequently been crushed into oblivion when the only person she'd ever fallen madly in love with left her after three years together for a twenty-two-year-old artist named Daphne Love.

She'd rather not relive that experience, thanks, no matter what

Ramona, her mother, or the entire town of Clover Lake thought about it.

"Ah, well," Penny said now, shoving her glasses back up on her nose. "We've got enough going on with the fancy new resort opening this weekend."

April *hmm*'d politely, dug her debit card from her bag, and tossed it on the counter. Owen whipped it away, then set her latte in front her. She gulped at it greedily, burning her tongue a bit.

"I hear it's to be quite the gaudy affair," Penny said, leaning closer to April and whispering. Loudly. Penny didn't really do quiet.

April nodded as Owen handed back her card and receipt. She knew Cloverwild was a luxury resort and was indeed rumored to be extravagant. April had no idea if it actually was *gaudy*; she hadn't seen it yet, but when a vacation spot's entire purpose was to bring in tourists with a lot of money, it was bound to be pretty high-end.

"It's not gaudy," Owen said. "It's Mia. She's a classy broad."

"Ah, yes," April said, tucking her card away again. "Just what every classy broad wants to be called."

Owen laughed. "I've seen the main lodge," he said, wiping down the counter. "It's gorgeous. Should bring in a lot of good business."

"There's a fine line between gorgeous and gaudy," Penny said, pointing her straw at him before sliding it into her water, and turning to face April again. "Your car outside has a lot of stuff in it. Heading out of town?"

April sighed. No way around it really—sooner or later people would notice there were vacationers in her house and she wasn't frequenting the city square quite as much.

Goddamn small towns.

"Actually, *Penny*," she said, voice probably a bit too saturated with attitude, "I'm headed to Cloverwild myself. Going to teach an art class there this summer."

Penny's brows shot up. "And you're living there? Why in god's name would you do that?"

April gave her a toothless smile.

"Ah, well, maybe you'll meet a nice hot thing while you're there," Penny said, her voice dripping with *meaning*. "It's been, what? Three years?"

April's smile dropped away. "Not you too," she said.

Penny presented her palms in surrender but proceeded to surrender absolutely nothing. "I'm just saying that Elena what's-her-name was always too big for her britches. And Ramona's got her one true love now, living her dream. It's your turn, isn't it?"

She smiled beatifically at April, who refused to show any emotion whatsoever on her face. Absolutely not.

"And on that horrifying note," she said, taking her coffee and tucking her phone into her pocket. She hopped off the stool while Penny tutted, Owen cracking up behind the counter. "Have a lovely day, everyone."

She walked to her car and opened the door, but as she slid inside, the lid from her coffee cup popped off, and half of the heavenly brew spilled down her favorite Sleater-Kinney T-shirt. She fell into her seat, Bianca hissing as April just sat there, letting the warm liquid soak through the cotton to her skin.

"Fucking figures," she said, then started the engine and drove toward Cloverwild and all her bright new opportunities.

OWEN HAD BEEN right—Cloverwild was gorgeous.

The lodge itself was a huge, two-story Craftsman facing the lake, with a large patio area built over the water that contained a firepit and several Adirondack chairs. Cabins dotted the property in the distance, along with a pier and a dock where canoes and kayaks bobbed in the lake. Carrying both Bianca and Bob in their carriers, who were growing quite restless by this point, April walked up the white-and-gray pebbled path to the wrap-around front porch, which was filled with cushioned furniture, rocking chairs, and tiny rustic tables the color of maple syrup. A string of lights circled the porch, already lit and dancing softly in the early afternoon breeze.

She climbed the stairs and set the cat carriers behind a chair, hoping they'd stay hidden and quiet while she checked in with Mia and got her cabin key. She hadn't exactly cleared housing her cats with Mia, but she had no other options at this point.

"Be right back, babies," she said.

Bob mewled pathetically, and Bianca simply glared at her through the slats in the carrier, her ice-blue eyes disdainful.

"Yes, yes, I know, I'm a mess," she said, straightening and catching sight of her warped reflection in the wavy glass set into the large oak door. She pulled her black blazer tighter around her coffee-soaked shirt, hoping it hid most of the stain. Her hair fell just shy of her shoulders, and her most recent color experiment—purple and teal streaks through her natural dark—was starting to grow out a little, giving her locks a faded, iridescent look she loved. Her makeup was on point—winged liner and dark red lips—despite the slight shadows under her eyes.

She blew out a breath, buttoned her blazer, the scent of espresso wafting around her as she did so, then pushed the door open.

Inside the lodge's lobby, it was just as immaculate. Rustic wooden beams crossed the twenty-foot ceilings, squashy couches were arranged by a roaring fire, their buttery brown leather accented with plaid-patterned pillows in navy and hunter green and burgundy for a bit of color. An enormous wagon wheel chandelier cast a warm amber light throughout the room, in addition to the watery glow of a single stained-glass lamp on the oak reception desk by the staircase. It was simple and decadent all at once.

The space was busy, full of preparations for opening day, which would kick off with a party tomorrow evening. People hurried about, carrying luxury sheets and towels to guest rooms upstairs, as well as outside to the larger guest cabins near the lake and the smaller staff cabins around back toward the woods. Others filled rustic shelves with colorful books and knickknacks, carried racks of clear glasses to the bar, straightened paintings on the walls.

She even spotted a two people walking by in pink leotards and leggings, sheer skirts around their waists, hair in tight buns at the napes of their neck. April remembered hearing Cloverwild would have dance instructors à la Patrick Swayze in *Dirty Dancing*, as well as gourmet meals served in a huge dining room complete with a shiny dance floor, waterskiing, guided midnight hikes to Moon Lover's Trail, spa treatments, watercolor classes, and pottery. You name it, Cloverwild was probably offering it.

For the right price.

April spotted Mia behind the front desk, her phone cradled between her ear and shoulder while she tapped way on her iPad. Mia was in her midforties and had brown skin and long dark-and-silver braids. Her family's grocery store—which had started as a stall at the Clover Lake farmer's market back in the 1940s and was now a statewide chain, soon to go national if the rumors were to be believed—had given her the means to invest in prime lakefront real estate and open a resort such as Cloverwild.

"Hey, there," Mia said as April approached the desk, taking her phone off her ear and tossing it—a bit violently, if you asked April, onto the desk. "Good to see you."

"Everything going okay?" April asked as Mia took a slug from the largest coffee cup April had ever seen. It was like a Big Gulp from 7-11.

"Ask me tomorrow," Mia said. "No, wait, ask me next month. Maybe even September. Hell, ask me in five years."

"That good, huh?" April asked. She knew opening a new business was hard as shit—she couldn't imagine getting one of this scale off the ground.

Closing a business, however . . .

April shook her head, ignoring the sudden spike of panic and sadness in her gut.

Mia seesawed her hand in the air. "Big picture is fine. Little tiny details that make me question my existence on earth? That's a different story."

April laughed. Mia was funny. Always had been. She had a dry sense of humor April appreciated, and as one of the first out-and-proud lesbians April ever met, Mia was a bit of an icon in April's mind, a touchstone for all the baby queers in Clover Lake.

"Let me grab your cabin key," Mia said. "Your cabinmate hasn't checked in quite yet."

"No worries," April said. "More time to get settled." She'd known from the jump that she'd have a cabinmate, who was also her assistant teacher for the art class. April was ready for the distraction, and actually excited to plan a fun and unique curriculum for the guests.

"Here you go," Mia said, handing her a gold key dangling from a dark green keychain in the shape of a canoe, along with a single sheet of paper. "That's your itinerary, your cabinmate's number, your class schedule, things like that. There's a map of the property on the back. It's all online too, but some people like a physical copy."

April tucked the key in her pocket, then thanked Mia before heading for the door and her contraband cats, scanning the paper as she went.

Her eyes snagged on a set of letters.

A name.

She froze, slowly turning back toward the desk.

"Hey, Mia?"

"Yeah, hon?" Mia asked, now shuffling through a stack of papers.

"Is this right?" April's heart had sped up—sped up and left its designated place in her body, catapulting around like a pinball.

"Is what right?"

"This name." April blinked at the two words. "My . . ."

Her cabinmate.

Her co-teacher.

"It's all correct, whatever it is," Mia said, who understandably didn't have time for whatever meltdown April was currently experiencing. "Checked it myself this morning. Excuse me." She frowned down at her phone, then hurried off toward the kitchen.

April barely noticed any of that though. Barely heard Mia's answer. She stood in the middle of the room, fingers damp on the paper, her vision blurring as she stared down at the name of the very person who had ruined her entire life three years ago.

ASHLEY HERRING BLAKE is an award-winning author. She loves coffee, cats, melancholy songs, and happy books. She is the author of the adult romance novels *Delilah Green Doesn't Care*, *Astrid Parker Doesn't Fail*, *Iris Kelly Doesn't Date*, and *Make the Season Bright*, the young adult novels *Suffer Love*, *How to Make a Wish*, and *Girl Made of Stars*, and the middle grade novels *Ivy Aberdeen's Letter to the World*, *The Mighty Heart of Sunny St. James*, and *Hazel Bly and the Deep Blue Sea*. She's also a coeditor of the young adult romance anthology *Fools in Love*. She lives on a very tiny island off the coast of Georgia with her family.

VISIT ASHLEY HERRING BLAKE ONLINE

AshleyHerringBlake.com

🅘 AshleyHBlake

🅟 AEHBlake

Ready to find
your next great read?

Let us help.

Visit prh.com/nextread

Penguin
Random
House